A FIRE OF DRIFTWOOD

A
FIRE OF
DRIFTWOOD

A Collection of Short Stories by

D. K. BROSTER

WILLIAM HEINEMANN LTD
LONDON

First Published 1932

*Printed in Great Britain
at the Windmill Press*

"And lo! things swimming here and there,
  scant in the unmeasured seas,
The arms of men, and painted boards,
  and Trojan treasuries."
                              Aeneid i. 118-9.
            (William Morris's translation)

CONTENTS

I

II

I

OUR LADY OF SUCCOUR

OUR LADY OF SUCCOUR

Yes, the gold was only gilt,
    And you never knew it ;
Cracked the cup, the wine half spilt,
    Lees a-tremble through it.
But you thought the ore was true,
    And the draught unshaken:
Doubtless, dreams are best for you,
    Dreamer . . . till you waken!
                Les Illusions Retenues.

In Madame de Seignelay's *Souvenirs de ma Jeunesse* she speaks more than once of a gentleman whom she used to see at her uncle's house in Angers, when she stayed there as a child about the year 1816. This person, a M. de Beaumanoir, made a great impression on the youthful mind of Madame de Seignelay, ardent Royalist as she always was, for he had fought with La Rochejaquelein and Bonchamps in that great Vendée, "dont on n'est jamais arrivé à me conter trop d'histoires," as she confesses.

"He was tall," she says, "but not too tall, had the grand air to perfection, laughed rarely, possessed a charming smile, and limped a little in a way that I found ravishing, for did I not know it to be the result of a wound gained in those combats of heroes and martyrs? M. de Beaumanoir, when I knew him, must have been about eight-and-forty. And I was ten—a child voracious of information, especially on the subject of the Vendée; but I never could arrive at any definite stories of my hero's heroic deeds. Himself I never dared to question, for, though I adored, I feared him, with a delicious tremor which, alas! I have not felt for many a long year.

3

"One day, however, I remember summoning my courage and going up to him where he stood alone by the portentous curtains which used to deck my uncle's salon windows.

"'Monsieur le Vicomte,' I said breathlessly and suddenly, 'is it really true that you actually knew le saint Lescure?'

"M. de Beaumanoir started, and looked down at me (no child of mine has ever worn such hideous frocks as I wore in those days). 'C'est toi donc, petite Vendéenne,' he said, smiling. 'Yes, it is quite true. Do you want to hear about him? He was a good man!'

"'A saint!' I murmured piously.

"M. de Beaumanoir smiled again, and said—I think to himself—'There were saints among the Republicans, too.'

"But at the time that last astounding utterance of my hero's so wrought upon me that all recollection of what he subsequently told me of M. de Lescure was effaced. The idea of righteousness in the ranks of the foe intrigued me to such a point that I sought counsel of my uncle. When I referred the matter to him he first looked puzzled and then began to smile.

"'Et de qui donc t'a-t-il parlé, Charlotte?' he asked. 'D'un saint ou d'une sainte? Of the latter, I'll wager.'

"'I do not understand,' I replied, somewhat offended. Nor did I understand for years, and though I worshipped M. le Vicomte none the less fervently for his startling lapse from orthodoxy, I believe that I never had another private conversation with him. It was not until after my marriage that I heard the story to which he must have been referring that evening. . . ."

4

OUR LADY OF SUCCOUR

Adèle Moustier was going to meet an admirer, and from the way she walked through the barley you would have thought each blade a possible conquest. As wars and their rumours in no way deterred Adèle from campaigns of her own, so did her flighty little head remain undisturbed by the very near presence of battle. Only yesterday morning had all Cezay-la-Fontaine been throbbing with excitement; only yesterday evening had it welcomed Rossignol's two regiments after their victorious skirmish with the Royalists in the scarcely league-distant wood of Champerneau. It was still indeed disturbed and jubilant, and Adèle, as the Maire's daughter, might reasonably have been more conscious than she was of Republican fervour. But she was a little indifferent to martial glory, and disliked noise and all ill sights. So she walked through the field with her nose in the air and the points of her second-best cap standing out at a provoking angle. Cezay-la-Fontaine was a good half-mile behind her, and the diagonal path across the unfenced barley was approaching the high-road, when suddenly she uttered a scream. At her feet, in a trampled patch of the ripe grain, lay the dead body of a Vendéan.

There was no mistaking his identity, for on the embroidered vest which showed beneath his short Breton jacket was sewn the symbol of the Sacred Heart, and a thin white scarf, fringed and torn, was wound about his waist. He lay on his back with his arms spread wide, and he was quite young, and had long bright hair. There shot through Adèle a pang of horror and a simultaneous desire to get away, for as she had kept within doors when the wounded were brought in, and had had no dealings with them since their arrival, this form at her feet was a spectacle of a disturbing novelty. The next moment horror had given place to a sort of indignation.

"In the barley, too!" she thought. "Just where one walks!"

It was precisely at this moment that the Vicomte de Beaumanoir opened his eyes.

Adèle stood still, galvanised by the shock of finding two living points of light in the ghastly face. It is probable that the Vicomte saw but indistinctly whom or what he was addressing when he said, without stirring, in a terrible cracked voice that shook Adèle's little soul to its foundations:

"Water . . . for God's sake get me some water . . ."

"Oh, mon Dieu!" said Adèle to herself. The final unpleasantness had descended upon her, and she must minister to a dying man. "There is none," she faltered, and even as she spoke remembered the stream between the field and the high-road. But she had nothing to bring water in. She must go on quickly, or turn back. Yet the wounded man's eyes held her, half-frightened. It was the most disagreeable position she had ever been in, and at the back of her mind was a consciousness that she might feel even more uncomfortable in the future if she left the petition unanswered. She hesitated on the path, looking vaguely round for escape. There was no one else in sight.

The barley rustled as the wounded Royalist dragged himself up to one elbow.

"If you would only dip your handkerchief into a puddle," he said, with desperate pleading. "I want very little . . . only one cannot die while one is so thirsty . . ."

A shiver went through the girl, and she fled precipitately towards the road.

When she got to the stream, a dozen yards away, a complete revulsion of purpose had taken place in Adèle's soul. She had, on starting for that goal, the firmest intention of crossing it by the footbridge and pursuing her way down the road. Instead, she was suddenly stooping over the water with a piece of a broken bowl in her fingers. Possibly the very sight of that opportune bit of crockery, dropped there by the hand of Fate or a careless village urchin, wrought the change. Even with the dripping bowl in her fingers she hesitated; but there was no one on the high-road: she must return and give the water to the man herself. Her hand shook a little as she stooped over him and put the bowl without a word into one of his. The eagerness with which he drank was horrible to witness, and Adèle averted her eyes, only to meet a worse sight. The Vendéan's left leg, to the top of his high boot, was a scarcely dried welter of blood. The same shuddering resentment surged through Adèle. Why should *she* be forced to encounter these disagreeable things? Anyhow, she could go now.

"Mademoiselle, you are an angel," said the young man, looking up at her. . . . "I cannot thank you."

Now that a little life and expression had come back into his mask of a face, Adèle saw that it was handsome, and dimly realised that it was also high-bred. But the light went out again immediately, and, sinking back, the Vendéan lay still once more, with closed eyes.

"Now I can go," thought Adèle joyfully; and she went.

On the footbridge she turned and looked back. The young Royalist was lying very much as she had first seen him, save that he had flung an arm over his face.

The sun was hot . . . of course he could not move into the shade. She wondered how long he would have to stay there—and indeed how he had got there at all. He had spoken of dying; perhaps he was dying now, or dead. If he had not mentioned that unpleasant possibility, or if she had not promised to meet young Lépine at the mill, or even if it had not been so hot in the barley, she would certainly have stopped a little longer—though, of course, she could have done nothing. Certainly, she told herself, she would have stopped—and walked steadily over the little bridge and down the road.

As it happened, Adèle need not have sketched these shadowy justifications for her conduct, for Charles de Beaumanoir was quite unaware of her departure.

Now Jacques Lépine was not at the trysting-place, and in consequence it was an irate Adèle who came along the high-road some twenty minutes later. The misdemeanour of the swain, conjectures as to its possible cause, and schemes for its punishment occupied her mind to the exclusion of everything else. Could he have heard that the blacksmith's nephew said that he had kissed her? Could . . . But here Adèle, who was profoundly indifferent to Lépine *fils* in himself, and merely outraged at his behaviour, caught sight of the little bridge and remembered the Vendéan. She hesitated, because if he was dead she was certainly not going to pass him. But no; people did not die like that. She went over the bridge. He was still there in the barley, motionless, and she approached him slowly. He was breathing, but his eyes were closed.

"He is very ill," thought Adèle. "I wonder what it is like to die." She looked down in silence at his drawn features, at his disordered hair, as gleaming as her own,

8

at the clenched hand, delicate and sunburnt, lying on his breast. A certain conclusion came to her as she looked, and made her heart leap, Republican though she was.

"He is a *ci-devant*, an *aristo*," she said to herself. "He is not a peasant, for all his dress." It seemed to make a difference, and, kneeling down, she touched the hand lightly with her own, and said, "Shall I get you some more water?"

The young man opened his eyes.

"Keep to the right, men; keep to the right!" he said indistinctly. "There are Blues in the clearing . . . Ah, it is you, Eustacie!" He looked hard at Adèle, and his face changed. "Pardon me—I was dreaming. And you have been here all the time, Mademoiselle? You are too kind . . . too kind."

"I wish——" began Adèle, and halted, for she did not know what she wished.

The Vicomte continued to look at her. "You would be still more kind," he said, "if you would tell the—tell your friends that there is a Blanc in the corn who would be very glad to see them."

Adèle stared, puzzled. "Tell them?" she repeated. "But——"

A rather bitter little smile crept round the corners of the set mouth. "Just so," said the Royalist. "If they can shoot straight I should be very pleased to meet them. In my case"—he glanced at his mangled leg—"one desires to postpone it no longer than can be helped. Will you do it, Mademoiselle, and put the crown on your charity?"

Adèle sprang indignant to her feet. "I! Not for worlds! For what do you take me?" She broke off as a sound caught her ear.

Down the road were coming at a trot a troop of Republican cavalry returning from Champerneau on the other side of the wood, where they had been quartered for the night after pursuing fugitives. And the barley-field was open to a horseman's eye if not to a pedestrian's.

Adèle turned round again. She was rather pale. "They are coming," she exclaimed. "What shall I do?"

"A la bonne heure!" said Charles de Beaumanoir. "You can do nothing, Mademoiselle, but go away as quickly as you can. My best thanks for the water, and your company."

But Adèle still stood there, chained by an indecision which was revealed in her attitude. The quick eye of the officer in command was caught by her pose, and flashed from her to the prone figure in the barley. The riders were halted, and he was off his horse and over the foot-bridge in a moment, drawing a pistol from his sash as he came.

"Let Mademoiselle get away first," observed the Royalist coolly, without moving. Adèle seemed fascinated with terror.

The officer, a young man with a tight-lipped mouth, glanced at him, and replaced the pistol. "Is this your prisoner, citoyenne," he said to the girl, "or your lover?"

"He—I——" began Adèle, between anger and confusion, but the Republican did not wait for an answer to his pleasantry.

"When did you get that?" he demanded curtly, pointing to the Vendéan's injury.

"Last night," said the Vicomte.

"You are an officer?"

"Yes."

"You were with your main body at Champerneau?"

"In advance of it."

"And where did they mean to retire to, in the event of a defeat?"

"I have not the faintest idea," responded M. de Beaumanoir languidly. His interlocutor, seemingly satisfied, abandoned the topic and embarked upon another.

"And your leader was, you said——?"

The Vicomte glanced up sharply at him. "I did not say."

"Well, you can say now, then. It was either Talmont or d'Autichamp."

"You must ask somebody else," said the Vendéan, with a return to his indifferent manner. "I do not intend to tell you."

"That is a pity," responded the officer, with an ugly little smile, "for I intend that you shall." He moved a little nearer to the prostrate man and repeated his question, still smiling. "Come now, who was it?"

"I shall not tell you."

The smile dropped from the Republican's face.

"I can find a way to make you, canaille d'aristocrate," he said through his teeth, and, walking round him, deliberately aimed a kick with his heavily-booted foot at his captive's shattered leg.

A scream broke from the young man. Adèle put her hands over her ears.

"Come, tell me," said the officer. "It's of no use being obstinate—you will have to tell me in the end."

"Never!" gasped the Royalist. "Oh, for God's sake shoot me at once! I swear I will not tell you!"

"We shall see," quoth the other, and he repeated his expedient. The form at his feet quivered and then lay still. Charles de Beaumanoir had fainted; and just as his tormentor, bending quickly over him, arrived at that conclusion, an interruption of another sort occurred.

"Coward! coward! Stop—stop instantly!" cried a girl's voice, and Adèle Moustier, carried out of herself for the first time in her existence, confronted the Republican across the insensible body of his victim with clenched hands and sparkling eyes.

"Eh, citoyenne!" returned the officer lightly. "Quelle mouche te pique? What enthusiasm for a cursed Chouan! Do you know that it becomes you devilishly well, though?"

And Adèle, to whom the most wonderful thing of her life had just happened, turned away with a giggle and a toss of the head.

The officer, after surveying her for a moment, summoned two of his men, and she heard him telling them to take the Chouan and convey him somehow—he did not care how—to the church where their own wounded lay. "The citoyenne will perhaps show you a short cut," he suggested.

"Indeed I shall not," snapped Adèle; and, unwilling to witness any more distressing scenes, she started off homewards at a good pace.

II

Our Lady of Succour, with the Child in her arms, looked down with the same grave pity on her own untended altar and at the figure lying at the foot of the shallow steps before it. Partly on account of the sanctity of the original Madonna at Guingamp, partly because the chapel was so small, it had escaped iconoclastic attention. On either side of the gracious figure still stood the attendant saints: St. Yves, in his notary's dress, and

Ste. Anne, with the child Virgin at her side—saints dear
to Bretons of north and south, of Tréguier and Auray.
But no priest served the altar now, and it was seldom
that anyone was seen in the little chapel saying the Litany
of Our Lady of Succour, as many had once done, with
devotion and faith.

Yet the tender and pitying face had been the first to
greet Charles de Beaumanoir's eyes when, after his deep
swoon, he opened them to find himself lying at the foot
of the altar. The memory of his long night of agony in
the barley-field, whither, without any conscious motive,
he had dragged himself to die, of the thirst that was worse
than the pain, and of the culminating anguish, were
blurred in the merciful unconsciousness in which they
had ended. His brain was too dulled now to be acutely
sensible of suffering, and still less of the presence of
others in the body of the church—from which, indeed,
the chapel was cut off by its position in a line with the
high altar. He was alone in a great silence at the feet of
the Mother of God, and he was not uncontent, gazing
at her with the fixity of eyes only partly conscious of
what they were looking at, until the twilight began to
enshroud her.

When dusk had fallen came a surgeon and his assistant,
and, after some parley, probed his injured limb and set
and dressed it by the light of a couple of lanterns. Before the operation was over the young Royalist had
fainted twice; at its beginning he had contrived to express an opinion that it was not worth the trouble of
doing, and at its end the surgeon was much of the same
advice.

"I would not have done it but for orders," he muttered
as he rose. "Poor devil! Since it is done, could one get

13

some woman of the village to sit up with him to-night?"

"What! With a Chouan!" exclaimed his assistant. "Ma foi! not likely!" And the old surgeon, too busy to waste his time in useless commiseration, gathered up his tools and went.

A little later that evening, happening to meet his Commandant in the street, he was by him borne off to sup at the Maire's, where that officer was quartered. And Adèle, presiding at her father's table, found the talk veering round to the subject of the wounded Royalist prisoner.

"Well, if we took only one," remarked the Commandant with some complacency, "he is at least an officer. By the way, was it not you who captured him, citoyenne? From the description I had from Captain Larive, I think it must have been you."

"My daughter," observed the Maire rather pompously, "though a good Republican as any, could not pass by the distress of an injured foe. The female heart, citizen Commandant, is ever thus constituted."

"And well for us," returned the soldier, "that it is so. A man might envy the Chouan. Citoyenne Adèle, I drink to Beauty's charity!" And he lifted his glass with a bow to Adèle, who simpered becomingly, while the surgeon looked at her and had an idea.

He contrived to draw her aside after the meal.

"Citoyenne," he said abruptly, "could you find it in your heart to do a further act of kindness?"

Adèle, who preferred the Commandant's conversation, stared at him.

"I am sure I don't know," she replied impatiently. "What is it?"

"That poor devil of a Vendéan we picked up in the

barley. He hasn't a soul to look after him, and he needs it badly. I have more than enough of our own men to see to to-night."

"You want me to go and sit up with him—to nurse him?"

M. Guillon nodded. "If you could manage it."

"Thank you!" exclaimed the girl indignantly. "I have something better to do than to——" She stopped, feeling uncomfortable under his gaze. "Is he very ill?" she asked in a softer tone. "What should I have to do?"

He told her. She balanced the idea for a moment in her mind.

"Oh, I couldn't!" she said at last, with a little shudder. "I feel quite faint when I think of that leg of his. . . . Perhaps when he is better . . ."

The surgeon shrugged his shoulders and turned away. "You'll not be wanted then, my girl," he growled. "Confound them! They are all alike!"

And so Charles de Beaumanoir went alone through that night, and the next, and the next. It is true that he did not know it, and, indeed, in the midst of delirium many figures swept by him, and one stayed—a figure that in some way was always the same, though sometimes it wore the face of his mother, dead these many years, and sometimes of his betrothed wife, far away in England; and now it was a peasant girl's; and once there stooped over him, with infinite pity in her eyes, a lady in a faded blue mantle and a tarnished crown.

III

During this period Adèle Moustier made occasional

inquiries as to the progress of the wounded Vendéan, deriving a small but satisfying glow at the heart from her kind action. When one or two of her associates reproached her with her interest in this enemy of the nation, the glow was fanned into a momentary flame. She saw herself the traditional noble and womanly figure tending an injured foe. Penetrating the future, she beheld herself seated by the side of the wounded man, soothing him, talking to him, reading to him—when he was well enough to be soothed, talked to, and read to. This, she gathered, would not be for some time. There was a day when the surgeon, meeting her by chance, told her urgently that it would never be. She did not believe him; but as she sat before her glass that night, brushing out the thick fair hair which gave her so much pleasure, she thought a little of the Royalist and was sorry, though her principal feeling was annoyance that she should be asked to do ridiculous and impossible things in connection with him. However, the next day she had forgotten about him, and, as just at this time Lépine *fils* was being brought into great humiliation and subjection, it was with quite a little shock of surprise that she learnt, a few days later still, that the prisoner was out of danger.

And on that a sudden impulse seized Adèle. Having elicited from her informant, a woman of the village, that the Vendéan was quite conscious, and that his wounded leg was not visible, she presented herself the same afternoon at the church door with a small covered basket on her arm. A Republican soldier with his arm in a sling was smoking on the steps. He removed his pipe and stood aside for her to pass with a deferential air which made her pleasantly conscious of her errand of mercy. But when she questioned him as to the whereabouts of the captive, it was with visible surprise that he told her the brigand was in the *ci-devant* chapel of the *ci-devant* Virgin. Understanding this designation to apply to the chapel of Notre Dame de Bon Secours, Adèle slipped up the south aisle, endeavouring not to see any uncongenial sights. But there were not above a score of wounded remaining, and they were all in the nave, which, save for the presence of the dismantled high altar and the pillars, had the appearance of a rather ill-organised hospital.

The Vicomte de Beaumanoir was lying facing the entrance of the little side-chapel, and Adèle came upon him abruptly. Some charitable person had bestowed upon him a blanket and a coverlet, but his only pillow was a rolled-up military greatcoat, whose dark hue served admirably to enhance the drawn pallor of his features. He looked up full at Adèle, with bright and sunken eyes, but did not seem to know her. After a moment she went in and stood by him, and at that a look of recognition broke on his face.

"You have come . . . again!" he said, in a voice not much above a whisper.

"I am so sorry I have not come before," responded Adèle—and at the moment she spoke the truth. "I . . . could not."

"But you are here now!"

"I have brought you some soup," went on the girl in an embarrassed voice, the gratitude in his eyes at once pleasing and reproaching her. "I am afraid it has got rather cold."

But he could not feed himself, and so, after a little hesitation, she slipped an arm beneath his head and gave him the liquid spoonful by spoonful. "What a horrible pillow!" she remarked as she withdrew her arm. "Is that all you have had?"

"It did very well," said the young man in his faint voice.

"I will bring you another," said Adèle, putting the empty bowl into her basket. "I must go now; my father will be wanting me." (M. le Maire was out for some hours.) "I will come again to-morrow, if I can."

The Royalist said nothing, but his eyes followed her. She felt it, and went out of the church in great spirits.

Next day she brought the pillow in the best pillow-case she had. Was not her *protégé* a *ci-devant?* This time the young man's face lit up with a smile as she appeared.

"Mademoiselle, you are too kind to a foe," he murmured, in a voice perceptibly stronger than that of yesterday. "Mon Dieu, that is good!" He shut his eyes as his head sank back on the cool linen, and Adèle bundled the rejected greatcoat into a corner.

Coming back, she sat down on the altar-steps and looked at him. How different he was from Lépine, from the blacksmith's nephew, even from the young notary at Doué! She wished that she knew who he was; and the simplest plan seemed to be to ask him.

"Would you mind telling me your name?" she said, for her a trifle timidly.

"Beaumanoir," said the young man without opening his eyes. "Charles de Beaumanoir—the Vicomte de Beaumanoir when titles were in fashion."

Adèle's heart gave a little skip. She had been sure of it.

"And now you will tell me yours, Mademoiselle, will you not?" went on the Vendéan, opening his eyes and smiling at her; and she told him. His gaze roamed from her to the Madonna above her.

"There is another name that I should like to know,"

18

he said. "What Virgin is that?"

"Oh, that's Our Lady of Succour!" responded Adèle carelessly. "Nobody pays much heed to her now, though she used to have a great many devotees once."

"I see—out of fashion!"

"Oh, more than that!" retorted Adèle. "Nobody of course believes in any bonne Vierge now—except the Blancs," she added hastily.

"And I am a Blanc," said Charles de Beaumanoir, smiling.

"I forgot," said Adèle, a little confused. And she started from her seat on the steps, for a man was standing in the entrance to the little chapel. It was the old surgeon.

If Adèle was startled, he was astonished. "So you have come at last, citoyenne," he said sardonically. "Well, since you are here, you can help me to dress this knee."

Adèle gave one shuddering look at the roll of fresh dressings which he pulled out of his pocket, and fled past him without a word.

"Never do I go near that chapel again!" she exclaimed, as she arrived, hot with anger and speed, at her father's door. Nevertheless, she woke next morning to a vague feeling of disappointment. She liked going to see her *ci-devant,* and it was a shame that she should be kept away. No doubt he would be expecting her. If she could only get a guarantee against further molestation she would yet go.

"Papa," she said in the course of the morning, "I think you might invite that M. Guillon to supper." And the Maire, a complacent parent, entirely unaware of his daughter's works of mercy, obeyed her suggestion. Adèle succeeded in seeing the old surgeon alone for a moment as he was leaving.

"It is a pity, Monsieur Guillon," she began in her best manner, "that you have prevented my going any more to see that poor young man. I think he . . . looked forward to my visits."

"Very probably," said the old man drily. "And how have I stopped them?"

"I have told you once," responded the girl, with heat, "that I cannot, that I will not, have anything to do with his wound!"

"I thought you had changed your mind, Citoyenne Adèle. I beg your pardon. It shall not be suggested again. Moreover, it does not much matter."

"And why not, pray?" asked Adèle. "Do you want him to die, after all?"

"He will not die of his wound, Mademoiselle," returned M. Guillon.

His tone was so significant that Adèle was frightened. "What on earth do you mean?" she cried.

The old man bent a rather enigmatical glance upon her. "You had not thought of it? Yet you know the law against returned *émigrés*—and he is an *émigré*."

Adèle slowly changed colour. "You mean that he will —that he will——"

"That he will be shot—when he is well enough," returned the other grimly.

"It is not possible to do such a horrible thing!" said the girl in a low voice. "And you—how can you suffer it, after——"

"After doing my best to keep him alive?" He shrugged his shoulders. "I am under orders, Mademoiselle, like the rest of us. And I only heard it yesterday."

He went, and Adèle spent the first sleepless night of her life.

IV

Two days later Charles de Beaumanoir beheld his benefactress slip as before into the chapel. She deposited a basket on the altar-steps, threw him an oddly constrained little word of greeting, and went past him into the corner by the altar. Turning his head languidly, he saw her groping for something behind a piece of faded hanging. As she dropped the curtain and came back she met his gaze and flushed crimson, stood for a moment looking on the floor, turned, and walked slowly to the entrance to the chapel, then came as slowly back. A curious pallor sat on her smooth cheeks as she began to unfasten her basket.

"I have brought you nothing," she began in a low uncertain voice. "It is only a pretext. You must go—you must get away at once. You will go, Monsieur le Vicomte, will you not?"

The Royalist smiled, a little sardonically. "I would do much to oblige you, Mademoiselle, but the difficulties—"

"Oh, must you jest upon it!" cried Adèle, stung by his tone. "You shall go—I will help you. Do you know what they will do to you if you do not get away?"

"Yes, Mademoiselle," said the Vicomte quietly, "I do. But I beg of you not to distress yourself." For Adèle's pretty lip was trembling; for a moment she had quite forgotten how unbecoming were tears—then, steadied by the thought, caught violently at her composure.

"Listen," she said. "There is an old forgotten door out of this chapel, behind the hangings there. Between nine and ten to-night I will come to the door with a man and a cart. If you cannot drag yourself as far as the door I will come in and help you; they cannot see in from the church. Then Joseph will drive you under his load of hay to any point you wish where you will find friends— to St. Etienne, for instance, which is full of brig . . . of Royalists."

"Useless!" said the captive. A momentary flush had however passed over his thin face. "How is a man to account for carting his hay that distance so late in the evening? It would only be to sacrifice another life."

Adèle shook her head eagerly. "No one takes the slightest notice of what Joseph does. If he threw his hay into the pond, no one would be surprised. He is not—he is an idiot. But he will do anything for me, and nobody will stop him. If they did—if you were found even—no harm would come to him. They would not hold him responsible. I will swear it—by her if you wish." She pointed to Our Lady of Succour.

Again the young Royalist's gaze strayed up to the face of the Madonna and back to Adèle's.

"And what of you?" he said.

"I shall not appear in it at all," answered the girl. "Joseph will do what I tell him, and next day he will have forgotten all about it. No one will know anything of me. I shall just go home to bed, and next morning, when it is found out, I shall be more surprised than anybody."

The young man gazed very hard at her, trying to find out if she were indeed speaking the truth. As a matter of fact, she was doing so; but whether the Vicomte would have ended by believing her was to remain in doubt, for, perhaps fortunately for Adèle's scheme, the advent of M. Guillon stopped further protest or argument, and Adèle, whispering, "Be ready at nine!" fled as on a previous occasion.

The hours thereafter were leaden-footed and weighted with a thousand warring emotions, and yet in the end the sound of a turned handle made Charles de Beaumanoir's heart beat like the suddenest of surprises. The hangings moved slightly. In the dim light from the body of the church, supplemented scarcely at all by the ineffectual little lantern set on the altar-steps, a muffled black figure slipped to his side.

Adèle bent over him so low that her drapery touched his face, and with her lips at his ear whispered, "You must try to do with me alone to help you out. Joseph is so clumsy; he would make too much noise. Do not make a sound!"

Silently, and fighting back the anguish every least movement cost him, he got to one knee—helped by her strong arms, to his feet. His head swam with the pain, and fell back for a moment uncertainly on her shoulder. "Courage," she whispered, "it is such a little way"; and together, infinitely slowly, they traversed the few yards that separated them from freedom.

Outside loomed Joseph's cart. The owner, a lanky figure whose face in the darkness was indistinguishable, took hold of the Vendéan on the other side.

"How shall we see to get him into the cart?" asked Adèle. "You have no light, Joseph? There's a lantern in the chapel; I'll get that." She withdrew her support.

When at last the Vicomte was got into the wagon he was far too spent with physical pain to care whether the remainder of his flight accomplished itself or not. Yet as Adèle knelt above him in the cart, and piled the hay hastily over his body, her face a spectral whiteness in the gloom, he groped suddenly for her hand and carried it to his lips. But Adèle bent and kissed him on the mouth. Then, blushing furiously, she scrambled without a word from the cart and ran back to the chapel door.

As the cart moved slowly away she reflected. It was no less than the truth that she ran little risk of detection; had it been otherwise she would not have done what she had done. Furthermore, she knew that even were her complicity discovered she would not pay the penalty. Her father might bluster, but he was not a Roman parent. At the present moment, however, she was faced by an unforeseen difficulty—that of covering, for the next hour, the prisoner's absence. She had unexpectedly learnt that a sergeant made the round of the church at ten o'clock, and the sight of the empty pallet would inevitably lead to a pursuit which, in the morning, would be too late. To prevent premature discovery was almost as much to her interest as to the Vendéan's.

The church clock chiming a quarter to ten above her head sent her thoughts scurrying. Panting with a sudden sense of pursuit, she slid through the door and closed it noiselessly behind her. All was quiet in the church save for the voice of a wounded man down the nave, who was talking in sleep or delirium. Invisible in the gloom of the empty chapel, she stood by the deserted pallet, tore off her cap and thrust it into her pocket, and, swiftly unpinning them, shook down her fair locks, so that her head at least should bear some little resemblance to the fugitive's. Then she lay down on the mattress and drew the rough covering well over her.

Sergeant Michel Bernard was by nature a punctual man, and, moreover, he was anxious to get back to the game of cards in which he had been interrupted. The last stroke of the hour had scarcely died away before

Adèle heard, down the nave, the whine of the inner leather door. Footfalls, which gradually disentangled themselves into those of two men, came up the aisle, pausing for a second—it seemed a year—at the entrance to the chapel, and passing thence round the other chapel at the back of the high altar. Adèle breathed freely again. But in a moment she heard the footsteps stop, hesitate, and return, and in the stillness the sergeant's voice remarking gruffly to his subordinate:

"What the devil has the *ci-devant* done with his light? It was there at half-past eight."

Adèle's heart died within her. She had forgotten the lantern; it was still outside, and the men were evidently coming to see what had become of it. If they looked at her closely they must see in a minute that she was not what she pretended to be. She cowered under the blanket, holding it over her face. The heavy boots stumbled past her.

"*Sacré nom d'un nom!* Where can it have got to?"

"What does it matter?" asked the younger soldier, yawning noisily. "Perhaps the *aristo* prefers the dark."

"Even if he does he can't have eaten the lantern! He could not even have reached it."

"*Dame!* Then it's one of the other *ci-devant's* miracles," suggested his companion, pointing laughingly to the Madonna. "Perhaps she has taken it away to please him."

"It means that someone has been here," said the sergeant, glancing suspiciously round the chapel.

"La petite Moustier, perhaps?"

"Impossible. I saw her leave at dusk, and there is no door open."

The younger man yawned again. "Confound your

25

lanterns, sergeant, and confound this Loire wine—how sleepy it makes a man! Ask the Chouan himself, and have done with it. Here, I'll ask him."

He came, and, stooping over Adèle, shook her lightly by the shoulder.

"Wake up, dog of a Vendéan, and tell us what you have done with your lantern!" Laughter and sleep strove in his voice. "Doesn't he sleep soundly? Wake up, *aristo!* . . . I say, sergeant, supposing he's slipped off the hooks. . . . Just hold your light here a moment, will you?"

The lantern lifted above the supposed sleeper revealed nothing but the top of a fair head. There was, however, a curious tension about the upper folds of the blanket— a phenomenon which unhappily invited scrutiny.

"I wonder why he sleeps like that," observed the loquacious subordinate, and he gave a little tug to the blanket. It remained fixed in its place even more firmly than before.

"Pull it down!" suddenly thundered the sergeant. "Off with it! By God——!"

The oath coincided with Adèle's scream as the covering was wrenched from her clutch.

v

M. de Beaumanoir did not often go to Paris. Possibly he found Restoration Paris not much to his taste. Once in two or three years, however, he would come up from Anjou to visit a relative (being especially dear to the younger generation), to transact an hour or so's business, and to bring back a new silk dress for his housekeeper to

the rather grim and tidy dwelling where years of her excellent precision had something effaced the traces of that
little Eustacie de Soleure who had once ruled it so
happily and so carelessly. That all too brief episode
seemed now as far away as the other which had made it
possible; but it lived ineffaceably, like the other, in the
memory of Madame de Seignelay's hero. It was too
sacred and too poignant to be often looked at. . . . The
other, too, had the salt of pain to keep it alive. For
strange reports had got afloat in the countryside about
the consequences of Adèle's exploit. Some said that her
father had turned her out of doors, others that he had
beaten her within an inch of her life, others that she
had been sent to the prisons of Nantes as a favourer of
aristocrats. A still more dramatic version had it that she
had only escaped shooting, in the place of the man she
had saved, by the intercession of a Republican officer. In
time, and by indirect routes, these rumours came,
strangely intertwined, to the ears of Charles de Beaumanoir, painfully dragging out a long convalescence in the
Bocage. He was wild with self-reproach; but there was
nothing that he could do—nothing except to remember
all his life, not so much that he owed that life itself to a
woman's compassion, as that in his debt to the little
peasant girl of Cezay-la-Fontaine lay those short and
radiant years of his married happiness. And he had
always remembered.

However, when the Vicomte did happen to be in Paris
he would pay a species of state visit to the Opéra, accompanied thereto usually by a niece or two, but going sometimes by himself, and feeling, on such occasions, very
much alone in the midst of a new and somewhat alien
type of society. It was on some such thought as this

that he glanced round the house one evening in the spring of 1824 between the acts of Gluck's "Armida." It was something of a gala night; the latest star was singing, and the effect of so many brilliant toilettes and sparkling orders was quite dazzling to a provincial. Yet, looking up at a box above him, the Vicomte saw with amazement a smiling young face that he knew. It was that of the little Vendéenne to whom he used to tell stories, eight years agone and more, in an old house at Angers. And from her box Madame de Seignelay, the bride of a few months, saw and recognised her old friend, too.

"There is my dear Monsieur de Beaumanoir!" she cried to her husband. "How delightful to see him again! Make him come up, Georges—I positively must speak to him." And, all sparkling with youth and excitement, she signalled to Charles de Beaumanoir with her fan.

The Vicomte came, with his well-remembered little limp, as handsome as ever, but a little greyer and older. The sight of her charming and irregular young face, displaying so plainly its pleasure at seeing him again, warmed his heart as he bent and kissed Madame de Seignelay's hand. And she, as he sat by her, began on the instant to ply him with a hundred questions, contriving between a score of "Don't you remembers?" to interpolate a quantity of vivacious information about her neighbours.

"You say you know nobody, Vicomte? I do not believe it. You must know Monsieur de Chateaubriand by sight; and that is the great Duchesse de Carentan down in the box a little to the left of you. You know she tries to keep a *salon à la Rambouillet* under his present Majesty. Oh, and do you see the stout lady with the

diamonds and the pink satin *à faire frémir,* almost opposite, on the other side of the house? Is she not terrible?"

"You cannot expect an old man to have as good eyes
as you, madame," responded M. de Beaumanoir. "I can
see a quantity of pink satin, it is true, but I can hardly
distinguish features from here. Who is the lady, then,
since she is fortunate enough to interest you?"

Madame de Seignelay laughed. "I don't know who
she was originally—some shopkeeper's daughter, I fancy
—but they say she has already changed her name three
times, so that her natal one is quite securely buried by
now. She is the wife of Brunner—the Brunner, you
know, who made his fortune out of commissariat con-
tracts under the Corsican. Now he has more money than
he knows what to do with; but I daresay he manages
to get rid of a good deal on his wife's diamonds. . . .
But here is the curtain going up; I must not talk any
more."

A little later the brilliant and laughing throng was
emptying itself down the staircases into the *foyer.* Not
the least merry there was the little Vendéenne as she
came down on the arm of her childhood's hero.

"Come home and sup with us, Vicomte," she whispered
as they got to the bottom. "You will not? But I cannot
lose you again so soon.—Ah, there is the pink lady again.
. . . Georges, do try and persuade M. de Beaumanoir to
return with us to supper."

In the crush at the foot of the staircase Madame
Brunner, penned with her spouse into an angle, was
fanning herself with great violence. As she jerked her
head about, a magnificent diamond ornament scintillated
on the hard golden hair above her vulgar, red, not ill-
tempered face, and myriads of points of light shot out

from a similar collar round her fat throat. Her loud voice, the gleam of her jewels, and the overpowering hue of her gown drew the eye in spite of itself, and Charles de Beaumanoir, wedged at a little distance, looked, like the rest.

Suddenly Madame de Seignelay felt the arm on which her hand was resting tremble violently. She had been speaking over her shoulder to her husband, and turned round to her escort in concern.

"Are you ill? What is it?" she asked in a low voice, frightened by the face at which she looked up.

The genuine alarm in her voice steadied M. de Beaumanoir as scarcely anything else could have done.

"It was the heat—for a moment," he replied, wrenching his gaze away and bringing it down to her. "Ah, they are moving in front. Shall we go on too?"

And with the little bride on his arm he made his way out in the wake of Adèle Brunner and her diamonds.

As he put her into her carriage—"Are you recovered?" whispered Madame de Seignelay. "You frightened me; I declare I thought you had seen a ghost!"

The Vicomte smiled a very melancholy little smile. "My dear," he said gently, "perhaps I have . . ."

But it was scarcely a ghost which Fate had shown him in that cruel glimpse; for a ghost is linked with the past, and Charles de Beaumanoir had seen little enough in that prosperous and unlovely vision to connect it with the memory of her whom for more than thirty years he had idealised as Our Lady of Succour.

THE INN OF THE SWORD

THE INN OF THE SWORD*

I

RAMPARTS fence about the fields of Brittany—banks of six feet high, crowned not with a hedge, but with a serried wall of forest trees, impassab'e to an enemy when defenders use it for cover. And on an evening in the early June of 1795, just after the snapping of the uneasy truce of La Mabilais, a score of Chouans stood, scrambled, climbed, and knelt upon a stockade of this description, firing at an unseen foe whose bullets sang through the leaves or thudded into the bank. Bretons all, in loose breeches and gaiters, in the short jackets—black, blue and yellow, or white—each with its double rank of buttons and the Sacred Heart, with long hair and stern harsh features, they gave to the business in hand nothing, indeed, of the mechanical regularity of veteran troops, but all of their sangfroid. One alone, on his knees at the top of the bank, who wore a white scarf round his waist, paused occasionally between firing and reloading and, peering through the tree-trunks, shouted a direction or two; while, a few steps away from the bank, an old man of gigantic stature, kneeling on one knee, wrestled with the lock of his damaged musket. A grim smile was on his face, for a sudden gush of bright chestnut leaves, trickling from aloft, had just shown him how high the slackening Republican fire was becoming. The hot three-quarters of an hour was approaching its end. He ceased for a moment to struggle with his weapon and ran his

* The latter part of this story is based on historical fact.

33

eye along the row of absorbed backs in front of him. The smoke of their own last volley was lifting; would it be answered? . . .

A sharp and venomous discharge split the silence. The old man dropped his musket and sprang to his feet. "Seigneur Dieu! He is hit!"

The young Breton with the white scarf, suddenly carrying both hands quickly to his head, had toppled backwards, and now, slipping heavily from the summit of the bank, rolled over till he lay on his face at its foot.

The old giant had pounced on him almost before the marksmen next their leader had realised his fall.

"Ma Doué! don't stop firing!" he shouted. "It is nothing—a spent bullet. Jean-Marie, you can come—no one else."

And, picking up his young commander, he carried him to a little distance, and laid him down among the broom, his face a tragic mask of tenderness and anxiety.

"Hervé! Hervé! my little one . . . it is not possible. . . . Here, Jean-Marie, give me something to tie up his head."

"It is no good," said the other man in a horror-stricken whisper. "It is the end—he has a bullet through his brain for sure."

"I tell you no," responded his elder angrily, but in a breaking voice. "It is only that there is so much blood. . . ."

And hurriedly, with trembling hands, he tried to staunch the stream pouring from some disastrous source in the dark hair. Meanwhile it spoke many things for the discipline of guerrilla troops devotedly attached to their leader that not a single Chouan had left his post at the hedge to allay his anxiety. The Breton marksmen were firing furiously and revengefully; only now and again would one turn his head over his shoulder and snatch a look at the little group behind him.

"God have mercy on us!" exclaimed the old man at last. "It is impossible to tell. I must get him away. . . . Undo his sash, Jean-Marie, that will serve."

Jean-Marie did as he was bid, and together they tied the silk tightly round the bleeding head, with a handful of moss for a pad.

"Now," said the old man, "go back to your place, Jean-Marie, and see that no one stirs from the bank till the Blues draw off. It is only a question of time. And as for M. Hervé—ask them if they think that l'Invincible can be killed by a mere bullet?"

"You will take him—where?"

"Chez nous. Do not ask me if I can carry him, nephew!" added the old man, with a fierce gleam in his extraordinarily blue eyes. "You will come back when it is all over—or I shall meet you with the saints. Now to your place!" He waved an imperious hand at the bank, and Jean-Marie ran back.

Then Yves le Guerric, murmuring in one breath curses, prayers and little words of love, gathered up his wounded foster-son and leader like a child, and strode off through the broom. He carried in his strong old arms most of his heart, and the brilliant fighter who was the hope of the Royalist cause between Pontivy and Quimperlé—the Comte Hervé de St-Armel, called *l'Invincible*.

II

That evening the cottage had been full of the whirr of

35

the spinning-wheel. A woman had as well work when she is anxious and cannot sleep, though by nine o'clock one must have the luxury of a light. So the room was lit by two smoky rushlights and also, a painter might perhaps have said, by Marie le Guerric's golden head, bent over the embroidery of a man's vest. Opposite to her, on the other side of the open hearth, in front of the *lit clos* which raised its panels to the blackened rafters, sat her grandmother with the wheel. But the wheel had stopped.

"Have you finished, grand'mère?"

"I thought I heard thy grandfather's step," answered the old woman a little tremulously.

Her dead son's child laid down the vest. "I heard nothing," she said, surprised. "How could you hear, grand'mère, with the wheel going and your deaf ear?"

The old woman smiled wisely, still listening, and made no answer.

"I thought I heard firing this afternoon in the direction of Le Daouët," observed the girl, breaking the silence. "It is a week now since my grandfather went away with M. le Comte. Perhaps. . . . Ah! I hear something now!"

The unmistakable step outside was followed by a heavy kick at the door.

"Open, Catherine! It is I—thy husband!"

Madame le Guerric, little and active, ran and pulled the bolt. She gave a cry.

"Yves! what hast thou there?"

"M. le Comte," said her husband succinctly. "Shut the door quickly. And thou, Marie, is the bed ready? . . . No, we cannot see there."

He stumbled forward into the light. Marie had flown

to push back the sliding panel of the *lit clos,* and now stood irresolute, looking at her grandfather, and the slim relaxed body in his arms, with its upturned face streaked by dry red rivulets, and its black hair falling loose from under the stained bandage.

"He is dead!" exclaimed Madame le Guerric, crossing herself. "The saints receive his soul!"'

Yves took no notice, but stood as if unconscious of fatigue, with his motionless burden clasped closely to his breast, and his eyes roving round the little room.

"Put a pillow on the floor in front of the hearth, Marie," he said at last. "I will lay him there for the present. Get some water, Catherine, and bandages—and scissors."

The girl put her arm into the *lit clos,* and pulling out a pillow did as she was bid. Yves laid his foster-son tenderly down in front of the fire, and kneeling beside him settled the languid head on the pillow. Madame le Guerric knelt on the other side and held the bowl of water. Marie stood motionless by the bed. With two women there, it was the old man who tended the hurt. It was his right. He washed away the mask of blood, and with immeasurable carefulness unwound the white and crimson scarf.

"I can't see," he muttered. "Marie, get a candle, and hold it for me. . . . This must be cut off." He put gently aside a lock of stiffened hair; the scissors went through it, and he bent closer. "Blessed St. Yves! The bullet has only glanced off!"

His hands suddenly shook violently. Madame le Guerric uttered praises to the Queen of Heaven, but the girl Marie, holding the candle, had eyes or thought for nothing but the alabaster face at her feet. Her grandfather bent and kissed it.

"My Hervé! My dear son! I knew it could not be. . . . The linen, Catherine!" As his wife folded and cut he sat back on his heels, gazing in a passion of love and relief at the beloved visage. Then, while Madame le Guerric raised the young man's head, he wound the bandage gently round it, and having finished, crossed himself.

"Put back the candle, child," said the old woman. "Go and say thy prayer, and thy grandfather and I will get Monsieur le Comte to bed."

When Marie came back a little later, timidly, to ask if there were anything she could do, Yves and Catherine, conversing in whispers, were sitting on the settle by the fire. The old man had a bowl of soup on his knees, but every moment his eyes strayed to the *lit clos*. When he saw his grand-daughter he beckoned to her.

"Is it not an honour, little one, to have *l'Invincible* under our roof? And hast thou thanked the saints, Marie, who turned aside the bullet?"

"I have thanked Ste Anne and Ste Barbe for Monsieur le Comte's life," answered the young girl gravely.

The old man kissed her. "Go to bed, then, my darling. Thy grandmother and I will watch to-night."

Marie kissed Madame le Guerric and turned to go; but as she went she stooped quickly and picked up something from the floor of beaten earth. It was a long lock of black hair. One end was stiff with dried blood, the other curled loosely over the edge of her palm, as, clutching it tightly, she went out of the room.

III

Jean-Marie came back next morning, with his uncle's musket and the intelligence that the Blues had been forced to draw off with considerable slaughter. His comrades in arms, however, were temporarily disbanded. Never communicative, and abashed perhaps by the presence of his leader—though the latter was still insensible—he had fallen, at the end of his brief recital, to polishing his own English musket, while Yves, sitting by the side of the great bed, appeared sunk in meditation. Through the open door of the *lit clos* could be seen the head and shoulders of l'Invincible, lying as if asleep; only the broad strip of linen round his brow suggested a slumber not entirely natural. And Yves was gazing wistfully at the clear lineaments which bore, even in unconsciousness, something of the disdainful and implacable determination which had gained for their owner his nom de guerre.

"Yes, I hope that the Blues do not know he was hit," remarked Yves at last in a low voice. "It would encourage them too much."

"You are sure that he will recover?" asked his nephew, glancing at the pillow.

"The saints," said Yves solemnly, "did not send us a leader such as he to get knocked on the head as easily as that! . . . And yet he was not always like this. . . . Who should know, if not I, his foster-father? When he was a boy, it was pleasure that he thought of always. Then he grew up to be a man, and wherever he went he left a broken heart behind him."

"One conceives that easily," said Jean-Marie.

D

"N'est-ce pas? But he grew tired of that. . . . It was strange. . . . Listen, and I will tell thee something. One day, before the rebels had pulled down our King's Bastille—which accursed deed thou hast doubtless heard of, Jean-Marie—before all these troubles, M. le Comte was at Versailles, where was a great palace of the King, and the most beautiful gardens in the world. He was there, M. Hervé, with many fine ladies, and young gallants like himself, who did nothing but amuse themselves and make love all day long, and he the most careless and the handsomest of them all. Well, as they were sitting talking and laughing in these gardens a fortune-teller came along, and nothing would satisfy these great ladies and gentlemen but to have their fortunes told. So she told them this and told them that, how this one would be fortunate in love and I know not what, but Mr. Hervé was too indifferent to have his fate told, because in those days nothing seemed worth any trouble. But a lady, I think it was, insisted upon it; so the fortune-teller looked into M. Hervé's palm, and all she said was: 'Beware how you lie at the Inn of the Sword!' "

"And what pray would that mean?" asked Jean-Marie, ceasing his polishing.

"Ah, thou mayst well ask," returned Yves, shaking his long grey locks. "Nobody there could guess, least of all M. Hervé. But they all laughed, and most of all M. Hervé, for he said: 'I am never likely to lie there, my good woman. Do you think my hand looks as though it loved the touch of steel?' And indeed it did not, in those days."

"But," objected Jean-Marie, knitting his brows, "the woman spoke of an inn; she meant to warn M. le Comte not to——"

"Jean-Marie," said his uncle, "thou art little better than an imbecile! As if M. Hervé had thy dull wits! Dost thou not know that fortune-tellers often speak in riddles? It was no inn she meant, but that some day M. Hervé should change his whole life—and that was the strange thing, that she should know it. Tell me, thou who hast fought with him these twelve months, does he not lie every night of his life at the Inn of the Sword?"

Some glimmering of his elder's meaning broke on the slower mind of Jean-Marie, and he nodded silently, thinking of nights under the stars, in the broom and the heather.

"And why has M. le Comte changed?" he demanded after a long pause.

"God willed it," responded Yves simply and with conviction. He turned his head and looked at his foster-son; rose and bent over him a moment, then, sitting down again, drew out his rosary and began to tell his beads absorbedly, while Jean-Marie resumed his interminable polishing.

IV

"Marie!"

"Monsieur le Comte?"

"Bring me my clothes, my child. I am going to get up and go out."

What Yves had told his nephew about his foster-son was true enough. Hervé de Saint-Armel had been an élégant whose chief occupation in life had been doing nothing, and who had shown his individuality only in his graceful and distinguished manner of doing it. The Saint-Armel who had emigrated in 1791 had been a young man of great charm of manner, of rather frail health, polished, nonchalant and disillusioned. But this was not the Saint-Armel who for months had led in a lost cause the Chouans of Hennebont and others whom his brilliant courage and good fortune had attracted to him. The Saint-Armel whom his Bretons called l'Invincible was a very flame of war, an embodiment of its intensest spirit, a fighter whom no odds could turn aside, a leader as reckless of his own person as La Haye St-Hilaire, as fortunate as Aimé du Boisguy, with Cadoudal's hold on his followers and all his power of making himself obeyed. He knew neither hesitation nor regret, and spared his Chouans as little as himself. In that characteristic, perhaps, lay his magnetism for these men of his own blood, capable as they were of an almost fanatical devotion. A word would send any one of them to certain death. And for this leader raised up to it the Royalist cause in the western Morbihan had to thank a woman loved and lost, herself the soul of passionate loyalty, who did not know what she had done, and whose motive hand no one saw. . . .

"Monsieur le Comte," said Marie, appearing at the side of the bed, "you are not well enough to get up!" Her voice strove between timidity and remonstrance.

"Si!" said Saint-Armel, smiling. "It will do me good. Hasten now, child, so that I may take a walk before the sun is too hot."

She went, and beneath the bandage l'Invincible's brow was drawn into a frown. A conversation between Yves and his nephew which he had overheard an hour ago had told him of the peril in which they all lay. The

42

Blues from Pontivy were out in force to search for the leader whose exploits were daily becoming more intolerable. It was said that imperative orders had come from Paris to take him, dead or alive, in the highly reasonable expectation that his personal removal would effect all that encounters with him had failed to bring about. Half-asleep, Hervé had heard this inspiriting news being imparted to Jean-Marie, who had subsequently been sent out on to the hillside to keep watch. Madame le Guerric, too, had been despatched on an errand. The wounded man, who was supposed to be ignorant of the whole affair, knew very well why. If he were found under Yves' roof the consequences for the whole family would be practically the same as for himself. But Yves would never let him leave it in his present condition; he would rather immolate his whole household, if immolation had to be. Therefore Saint-Armel, feigning ignorance, lay still and watched his opportunity; and at last it had come. Yves and his musket had departed a few minutes ago, on some errand. Hervé was no sentimentalist, but there was only one thing to do.

He dragged himself up in the bed, and clasped his swimming head. Under the force of his tenacious will the room steadied itself with surprising quickness. He dropped his hands swiftly as Marie came in and deposited some clothes on a bench.

"There was blood on your coat and your shirt, Monsieur le Comte," she said. "I have got a shirt of my uncle's and his best coat—they are not fit for Monsieur, but——"

Saint-Armel was by no means anxious to make his escape bearing the incriminating signs of conflict. "Excellent," he said cheerfully. "If there was any money in my

43

pockets, give it to me. And you might cut me some bread, Marie."

"But Monsieur Hervé will not attempt to go far?" asked Marie anxiously.

"You are becoming a tyrant now that you are in sole charge," was Saint-Armel's light reply. "By the way, where are Jean-Marie and Yves—did I hear them say that they were going out? And your grandmother, too, is she out?"

The poor girl flushed and then turned pale. "They— my grandfather said—yes, they are out . . . my uncle and my grandfather are on the hill-side . . . in case of any danger. . . ." Unconsciously she looked at him as if imploring him not to press her any further, and it was perfectly clear to Hervé that she knew what was threatening and had been forbidden to tell him.

"I see," he said carelessly. "Well, perhaps I may join them." But it was the last thing that he meant to do.

Marie gone, he struggled out of bed, and, unsteadily enough, dressed himself in Jean-Marie's clothes, took a turn or two about the floor to try his legs, and called for the girl again. She came, looking at him with a vague reproach in her dreamy eyes.

"My pistols, child. Had I a sword when Yves brought me here?"

"No, Monsieur," replied the girl, as she fetched the pistols from the press.

"N'importe. Thank you. Now, shall I take off this bandage?"

"Oh, why, Monsieur le Comte?"

"It is hot," replied Hervé, who did not wish to tell her that he half feared to be recognised by its presence. He put up his hands. "How is it fastened?"

"Oh, don't take it off, Monsieur Hervé!" pleaded Marie. "That is dangerous. See then, I will unfasten it a little and look at the wound, and if it is well enough I will take it off."

"That would be kind," said the young man, with a smile, and straightway sat down on the settle. Marie's fingers fluttered round his brow, but he was not thinking of them. He was engaged in calculations of distances.

"Monsieur Hervé," reported Marie at length, "if I try to take off the linen the wound will bleed again. You must keep it on."

"Very well," said l'Invincible, who rarely wasted words on a hopeless situation. "Thank you, my child. Can you find me a hat of Jean-Marie's, too?"

She ran to a peg and handed him an old one of her uncle's—the ordinary Breton hat with wide brim and pendant ribbons. Saint-Armel put it on.

"That hides the bandage, does it not? Now, if anyone asks you whether I have been here, and you should tell them 'No,' I think you would be absolved for the lie.—Good-bye, Marie." He put out his hand; the thought of thanks had entered neither his mind nor hers.

"Monsieur Hervé," said the girl in a voice of agony, clasping her hands together, "you are going into danger. I will pray for you. But take this medal, too . . . it is Notre Dame du Folgoët. . . ." Unable to say more she put into his outstretched hand a little cheap medal attached to a ribbon. Hervé looked at it a moment and slipped it into his pocket.

"Thank you, Marie," he said gravely. "I will wear it; and I hope that the saints will hear your prayers. Good-bye." He took off his hat, drew her gently to him and kissed her on the cheek—a cold, kind kiss. The next moment he was gone.

v

The Comte de Saint-Armel had walked, at varying rates of progression, for nearly two hours; he had eluded the vigilance of his hosts, who, to be sure, expected nothing less than to see him out of doors, and he had, by circuitous routes, covered a good part of the distance between himself and the hiding-place he had in mind. Many things now warned him that he could not accomplish the impossible; nothing indeed but his indomitable will had carried him so far. In the brilliant, merciless sunshine he now stood at the top of a small eminence, and knew that he could go no further. After all, it was as good a place to stop as any. The gorse bushes which covered the gentle slope were thick, tangled, and in many places of the height of a man; in the middle, round a few stunted firs, there stretched a small clearing. Hervé crossed it. His head ached consumedly; his legs seemed to be made alternately of lead and of paper, and it was with almost a cessation of consciousness that he sank down under the shadow of a large gorse bush. The clearing stretched away on his left, and what instinct still remained to him warned him that it was far safer to lie down, cramped though he might be, in among the bushes rather than on their edge, but he was too spent at the moment to care for safety. He stretched himself out at full length; "I will move in a few moments," he thought . . . and in less than five minutes had sunk into the deep slumber of fatigue and convalescence.

46

The insects hummed over the gorse; the air vibrated with heat; dry pods exploded; a rabbit ran across the opening. Nothing of these did l'Invincible hear, as, tired to death, he lay slackly with outspread arms near the great gorse bush. Nor did he even hear the slight crackle of sticks and rustle of the gorse as two men in the blue and white uniform pressed cautiously through it on the other side of the clearing. They stopped dead like pointers when they saw him, and while one brought his musket to his shoulder and covered the sleeping man, the other turned and signed to his comrades behind. . . .

Hence Saint-Armel came back to waking life to find himself pinned down as he lay, with a grenadier clutching each arm and wrist and an officer standing over him sword in hand.

"Don't move, Chouan!" said the latter grimly, and put his point on Hervé's breast.

The Royalist did not attempt to move, but looked steadily up at his captors and cursed, not fate, but his own choice of a resting-place. But it was too late now for self-recrimination.

"What is your name?"

"I do not understand," replied Hervé in Breton.

"What does he say?" demanded the officer.

"He says he doesn't understand, mon lieutenant," replied one of the soldiers.

"Cursed patois! Ask him then in his own language who he is, and if he knows where l'Invincible is."

To these questions Hervé, still lying helpless, replied that his name was Fleur d'Epine and that he knew nothing of l'Invincible's whereabouts.

"I suppose I shall get nothing out of him," remarked the officer angrily. "The obstinacy of these Bretons is

47

incredible. I dare wager that all the time he knows French as well as I do. Make him get up, Lenormant, and search him. If he makes the least movement to escape shoot him down."

The two soldiers pulled Hervé to his feet, and under the levelled muskets of a couple more he submitted with a fine outward indifference to a systematic search. There was nothing in his pockets except a hunch of bread, half a sheet of assignats for five livres, and Marie's little medal of Notre Dame du Folgoët. The man who had his coat searched the lining without success and threw it angrily down, while the medal passed contemptuously from hand to hand.

"Tie him up," said the lieutenant briefly at the conclusion of the operation, and Saint-Armel's arms were firmly lashed behind him with belts. His great object being to conceal his identity, he thanked Fate that he was not wearing, as his custom was, a fine cambric shirt beneath his peasant's attire, for as he was now stripped to that garment the anomaly would have been patent to the eye. The lieutenant, running his gaze over his figure, studied his impassive face for a moment longer.

"I believe," he said suddenly, "that you know quite well where l'Invincible is. If you tell me you shall go free; if you do not tell me, I shall shoot you at once."

But Hervé was not to be caught thus. Once more he shook his head, and said dully in his patient Breton: "I do not understand."

The pronouncement being translated to him, he returned his old answer that he knew nothing about l'Invincible. An angry flush mounted to the forehead of the officer, and Hervé saw that his threat was not going to be an idle one.

"I can't waste time over this fool," snapped the Republican, "while l'Invincible is probably getting away. Sergeant, draw up six men—over there by the fir-tree will do. Take him over there, Lenormant."

He turned away, and a grenadier, who had evidently been waiting his opportunity, instantly thrust something under the captive's gaze. It was Marie le Guerric's parting gift.

"Where did you get that medal? Answer me!" he demanded, in an almost suffocated voice.

Hervé raised his eyes from that shaking hand to the livid face of a young man about his own age, and shrugged his shoulders.

"Tell me, you——" began the soldier still more violently, when one of the others pushed him roughly aside.

"Shut up, Delorme!—Come along, Chouan!"

The firing-party was already assembled. But as for the Comte de Saint-Armel, he could find nothing better to do at that moment than to survey with a sardonic amusement the situation in which he found himself. He was like to die to save his own life. The position demanded a few moments' reflection. He turned his head and spoke to the man Lenormant.

"What does he say?" asked the officer hopefully.

"He asks that you will allow him five minutes to say his prayers, if you are going to shoot him."

"Oh, he has grasped that fact, has he?" retorted the officer. "Very well; and tell him to look sharp about it. As he is so soon going to join his bonne Vierge and the rest of them, he need not send off a long petition from a distance."

So Hervé was marched over to the fir-tree and there,

his arms still bound behind him, he knelt down on the hot earth and bent his head. But he was not saying his prayers. "If I persist," he was thinking, "I am a dead man in five minutes. If I tell them who I am I get a reprieve of a day or two, most probably, till they can take me to Auray and the guillotine. But if they shoot me now, without knowing who I am, Yves and the rest will go on fighting for some time before they guess what has happened. . . . Shall I tell them?" He had a great distaste for the prospect—absurd enough, since he was only betraying himself. He lifted his head, fantastically undecided—and descried a horseman topping the mound not a hundred yards away. He wore Republican uniform and was followed by two more riders.

The arrival of this individual appeared to cause surprise. The men drew themselves up and saluted as, stout and well set-up, he came riding towards them through the gorse.

"What's this?" he called out as he came within earshot. "Prisoner?"

"Yes, mon commandant," replied the lieutenant respectfully. "I was about to shoot him. He cannot or will not give any information, and I thought——"

"Oh, I have no objection on principle," retorted his superior officer, with a sort of truculent bonhomie. "Only are you sure that you know what you are doing? Stand up, Chouan!" he commanded, urging his horse nearer.

Hervé got to his feet, and, pinioned, defiant, faced the newcomer's increasingly triumphant scrutiny.

"So he will not say where l'Invincible has gone to! Have you thought of asking him where he got the bullet-wound under that bandage? Have you thought of looking at his hands? I do not think that you will find them a peasant's . . ." The stout man swung off his horse with surprising alacrity.

"Untie him," he said curtly, and, as the prisoner's arms fell to his sides, he advanced upon him, holding out his hand.

"You carry your reticence a trifle far, Monsieur l'Invincible," he said, smiling pleasantly. "Or perhaps I should say, Monsieur le Comte de Saint-Armel."

Hervé looked at him for a moment without moving.

"Oh, we have met before," said the commandant. "This is a genuine recognition, not a trap. I had the pleasure of making your acquaintance when I was the prisoner of M. de Silz last year."

Saint-Armel put out his hand. "You come in a good hour, Monsieur le Commandant," he observed gaily. "That is, unless you propose to uphold M. le Lieutenant's summary measures."

"No," returned the other, with meaning, "I must take you to Auray instead. But as I am dealing with a gentleman I will ask for your parole. I have no wish to tie up a wounded man."

But l'Invincible shook his head with a smile. "I prefer material bonds."

"You mean that they are more easily broken?" asked the officer. "I do not think that you will find it so, Monsieur le Comte. I have a carriage and an armed escort waiting for you on the road—you know that we have been hunting for you all day?—and it is kindest to tell you that you are now looking your last on the geographical features which you have utilised with so much success against the Republic."

Hervé bowed. He did not resent the elation which pierced through his captor's speech, but he had no mind to stand longer in the sun than was necessary. "I have small doubt that you are right, Monsieur," he said coolly, and put his hands behind him as a hint that he was ready.

"No, not with those belts, men," interposed the commandant. "Lieutenant, your scarf! That will be less uncomfortable and quite as efficacious, besides possessing a certain symbolism. . . . I am afraid, Monsieur l'Invincible," he went on, as the tricolour sash tightened about Hervé's wrists, "that you must regret our chance interview at M. de Silz's quarters."

A tiny half-contemptuous smile twitched at his captive's mouth.

"I remember regretting at the time that M. de Silz had seen fit to exchange you."

"Why, what would you have done with me, Monsieur de Saint-Armel?"

"Precisely what you are going to do with me," answered Hervé dispassionately.

VI

There still runs a tale in the Baud district concerning the exploit of Yves le Guerric of St. Nicholas and Jean-Marie, his nephew; how they posted themselves with fifteen picked men one night on the Auray road where it runs narrowing through the forest of Camors; how they set upon a body of dragoons which presently came along, the leading horses whereof fell incontinently into a trench which Yves had caused to be dug in the sand and covered over with pine-branches; and how Yves and his men thereupon plucked that famous leader l'Invincible from the closed carriage where he sat fettered in the middle of the escort, opposite a Republican officer with a drawn sword. . . .

It is legend now; it was a fact, and a somewhat bloody one, on that June night of 1795. Out on the narrow road, a quarter of an hour afterwards, a flying moon lit carelessly the scene of the struggle, showing for a moment or two the black bulk of the overturned carriage, with the dead officer lying beside it, in the midst of a huddle of slaughtered horses and men. In the wood it filtered through the pine stems to silver the stern and exultant faces of the Bretons, as they gazed silently at l'Invincible, where he stood and read, by the light of a torch, the letter which Yves had just delivered to him. There was blood on Hervé's clothes, but it was not his own.

"How far is the château de Kermelven from here?" he asked suddenly, folding up the letter.

"About nine miles north-east of Locminé," replied his foster-father, devouring him with his eyes. "Are we to go there now, Monsieur Hervé?"

"This is to warn me to be there the day after to-morrow to meet two ladies bearing an important communication from the Regent. I shall want sufficient men to prevent a surprise."

"You shall have them, Monsieur Hervé," said Yves. "There is plenty of time." He hesitated a moment, fumbling in his pocket. "I hope you will pardon me, Monsieur le Comte," he continued in an apologetic tone, "—and do not stay to read it now—but here is another letter that I promised to give you. It is from my grand-daughter. The poor child is very unhappy. It seems that the little medal which she gave you at parting, when it was taken from you by the Blues, was passed round until it came into the hands of a young man of Pontivy in the battalion, Jean Delorme, who once courted my grand-daughter, and he recognised it as hers. The little one says he has told her that he intends to kill you—and she says it is her fault for giving you the medal. . . . You will pardon the poor child, will you not, for troubling you?"

Saint-Armel took the letter, a little amused. "A good many people have sworn to kill me, Yves," he said carelessly, putting it in his pocket, "—among others the unfortunate gentleman now lying in the road. But I have you to thank that he did not succeed, have I not?" He gave the old man a little smile, and turning away began issuing rapid orders in Breton.

It was not until later that night, as he lay among his followers in the heart of the forest, that Saint-Armel bethought him of the letter, and raising himself on his elbow he struck a light and read it.

Monsieur le Comte,

My grandfather will have told you of the misfortune which has befallen, and how Jean Delorme knew the little medal which I so foolishly pressed Monsieur le Comte to accept. But there is a worse thing, which I have not told my grandfather; and I pray Monsieur le Comte to have pity on a poor girl, and to forget it. But it must be told that he may beware of Jean Delorme. When the soldiers came to look for Monsieur le Comte after he had left our cottage, they found in my room a lock of hair that had been cut from his head when my grandfather dressed his wound, and Jean Delorme came to know of this too, and he thought that Monsieur le

THE INN OF THE SWORD

Comte had given it to me. . . . I cannot sleep for think-
ing of what I have done. . . .

The lines of l'Invincible's face softened for a moment.
"Poor child!" he said, musing. That furious young
grenadier, then, at his capture, must have been Jean
Delorme. He put away the pitiful little missive, and fell
to studying a map of the road to Kermelven.

VII

The little towers of the château de Kermelven, when
they came in sight two days later, showed dark against
a flaming sunset sky. As Saint-Armel rode slowly at the
head of his men—two hundred strong—up the overgrown avenue, he was surprised to find how quickly
Nature resumes her sway over the deserted outposts of
man. The château had been uninhabited but a few years,
yet its surrounding trees seemed already nothing but the
outermost waves of the great neighbouring forest sea, the
sweep of drive before the façade was green with weeds,
and grass pushed triumphant fingers between the stones
of the perron. The house itself, a pleasant-looking build-
ing of no great antiquity, had suffered less than its surroundings, though much of the glass in its shuttered
windows was broken, and the stone escutcheon over the
entrance had been defaced. To Saint-Armel's knowledge the château had more than once served as a convenient secret rendezvous, its position and its deserted
state alike favouring the choice, but he had never seen
it before, and could only hope that the fair Royalists
whom it harboured were not too uncomfortably lodged.

55

The sex of the chosen messengers caused him little surprise, and it was as much in deference to the source of their orders as to the ladies themselves that he had abandoned his Breton dress for the close-fitting uniform of green and black which marked the Royalist and the émigré.

Since his scouts had already searched the vicinity of the château, and he had made his dispositions, Hervé, when he dismounted at the foot of the steps, had but a few orders to give. He went up unaccompanied to the barred door. At the top of the perron, however, he turned and watched the Bretons filing silently off to right and left. Jean-Marie only stood like a faithful dog at the bottom of the steps, and the young man smiled to himself, for he knew that Yves in his suspicious soul was still half fearful of a trap. But he preferred to enter alone, and tapped unhesitatingly on the great door with his sword-hilt.

A grille slid instantly back.

"The counter-sign?" said a man's voice.

"Saint Louis," replied l'Invincible, and the door swung open.

At the foot of the dusty staircase which swept up from the unfurnished hall stood a lady no longer young, but with very bright eyes under her plentiful grey hair. A glance showed Hervé that she was a woman of the great world, and as he went forward, a slim and gallant figure, his bearing took on insensibly more of the courtier than of the Chouan leader. The lady smiled as he bent his handsome head over her hand.

"So you are l'Invincible, the never beaten," she said gaily. "I protest I am honoured to meet you, Monsieur. I am Clarise de Rocquigny, very much at your service."

Saint-Armel bowed low to her ceremonious curtsey.

"I think I once had the honour of meeting you in Paris, Marquise," he said, "but I am ashamed to say that I cannot remember where.—Shall we talk by the fire?"

"I have a worse confession to make," observed Madame de Rocquigny as he led her towards the great fireplace, where a somewhat smoky fire of green wood had been lit to dispel the damp. "I—we—have never heard of you but by your nom de guerre."

"I assure you that arrogant name was none of my choosing," said its owner, smiling. "My real name is Hervé de Saint-Armel."

Madame de Rocquigny gave a little start. A strange expression came over her face as, seating herself in the chair which Hervé brought for her, she allowed herself a full minute's pause ere she began:

"Before we have our little conversation, Monsieur de Saint-Armel, I must make Madame de Bellegarde's apologies. She was so tired that I——"

"Bellegarde!" exclaimed Hervé. "Bellegarde, did you say? . . . I interrupt you, Madame—pardon me!" He was very pale.

But Madame de Rocquigny did not say that, ever since she had heard his real name, she had expected that interruption. She resumed smoothly, wondering, nevertheless, from the look of him whether he heard what she was saying: "Yes, I persuaded Madame de Bellegarde to take a little repose. She will do herself the honour of receiving you later, and she will put into your hands the Regent's commission, while I give you his orders—a division of responsibility, for caution's sake."

L'Invincible sat down beside her; his full attention was hers now, she could see that, and together they plunged

into the discussion of plans relating to Chouan co-
operation with the Royalist expedition even then fitting
out at Portsmouh. But Mme. de Rocquigny, armed
though she was with instructions from Verona, from
the Comte de Provence, the Regent, found that she had
less to teach than to learn.

"I understand why you are l'Invincible," she said at
the end, with her fine smile. "And now, shall we seek
Madame de Bellegarde in the room over there, where we
hope to entertain you at supper?—By the way, Comte,
do not mention her husband to her—you are indeed
scarce likely to have cause. . . ."

Hervé looked at her. "Guillotined?" he asked after a
moment.

"Yes," replied the Marquise grimly; "but not as a
Royalist. He turned Jacobin. She will carry that scar
always. But come!" She swept across the hall, opened a
door, said: "Ma chère, I bring M. l'Invincible," slipped
out again and closed the door behind her.

Here, too, a fire was burning. A lady rose from a
great chair before it—rose, and came no further. Hervé
stood equally motionless by the door, uttering a name,
but under his breath. . . .

"You!" said Madame de Bellegarde. "You l'Invincible!
Oh dear saints, it is not possible!" As white as paper,
she put her hand to her breast.

Still Hervé gazed at her without a word and she at
him; then he went quickly forward, and seizing both
her hands in his dropped on one knee and pressed them
to his lips. She swayed back against the high chair, her
eyes closed. "Hervé!" she said faintly, "I didn't know . . .
I can't realise . . ."

He sprang up and put her gently into the chair. Her

58

beautiful proud head rested like a broken flower against the carved back.

"You, Hervé . . . you!"

L'Invincible knelt down beside her once again. "And why not! why not!" There was flame in his voice and in his eyes.

"Oh, I am proud . . . proud!" she whispered. He put her hand to his lips as he knelt there. Suddenly she leant forward.

"Kiss me!" she said like a queen, and l'Invincible, as pale as the dead, kissed her on the mouth.

VIII

Half an hour later they were still sitting before the fire. The Regent's commission was in Hervé's breast, and now they had reverted to earlier themes, and talked, with a dreamy and contented abandonment, of days before she had married, and he had changed. The air of long-forgotten gardens in the sunshine, of nights of palace floors and violins closed round the couple who had once known nothing else, and now drew a breath so different. To meet thus, to talk thus, had about it some impalpable suggestion of a reunion in the shades, so dim and faded were all those memories, and yet holding something of an unregretted sweetness. Armande de Bellegarde's voice—one of those rare voices whose lightest utterances are happiness to hear—fell silent at last on a remembrance. Instead she looked at Hervé's fine and resolute profile where he sat at her feet, with gaze half-stern, half-smiling, bent on the fire. How he had changed! Had hers been indeed the hand that forged, unknowing, this blade of keenest temper?

"Do you remember," she asked suddenly, "that afternoon at Versailles, and the old fortune-teller who warned you to beware of—what was it—of lying at the Inn of the Sword?"

L'Invincible brought back to her face a gaze almost dreamy.

"Very well," he said. "It was you who caused the prophecy. But the sign has never come my way."

"Nor would you care much, I imagine——" she began, smiling . . . and stopped abruptly.

"What is it?" asked Hervé, astonished.

"Look!" she said, and pointed to the hearth, where on the old-fashioned hooded chimney a many-quartered coat-of-arms, half defaced, showed as crest a mailed hand brandishing a sword.

Hervé's eyes followed her finger. "The device of the Kermelven," he said coolly. "Armande, you are not superstitious?"

She had turned very pale. "No . . . yes . . . I am frightened."

"You!" exclaimed Saint-Armel, and there was real amazement in his tone. She shivered. "You were not going to spend the night here, Hervé?"

"Where am I to go to then?" he asked, laughing.

"Anywhere, so long as you do not sleep under that sign!" she said earnestly. "Sleep under the stars, but not under the sword. I do not care if you think me foolish. Hervé, I implore it of you!"

He got to his feet, quite grave, and stood looking down at her, his eagle glance a little softened. He said nothing, but her eyes answered his, and in another moment she lay on his breast, against the white scarf and the Sacred

Heart, forgetful of the past and future, and even of the
trick of fate which had shown her soul to him.

IX

The candles on the supper-table were not needed, for
it was still light. But, as Madame de Rocquigny said
when she ordered them to be placed there, they gave a
more festive air to a very modest feast. The little company was gay enough; as gay as though the shadow of
past misfortunes and of still more tragic possibilities
were not over each of them. Madame de Rocquigny
played hostess at the head of the scantily spread table,
much too large for the four who sat around it. One of
Saint-Armel's lieutenants, M. de Lage, a gentleman of
the Morbihan who had not emigrated, made up the
party; his fellow-subordinate was on duty outside.

The Bretons who had served the meal had been dis-
missed, and Hervé, yielding to Madame de Rocquigny's
request, was relating by what means he had regained the
proscribed soil of France. Madame de Bellegarde,
abandoned to an absorbed interest, listened with her
to the tale of the perilous landing from a Jersey lugger
almost under the rifles of the patrol at St. Brieuc.

"I assure you that there was nothing remarkable about
it, as far as I was concerned," asseverated Saint-Armel as
he finished. "Those men of the Prince de Bouillon's—
the agents of the correspondence, Chateaubriand, Prigent,
Daguin, Péronne and the rest, are the heroes, not the
émigrés whom they land."

"Well, that is as it may be," returned the Marquise.
"At any rate, we will prepare to drink your health, Mon-

sieur l'Invincible. The late owner left some very excellent wine in his cellar. Do you know that one of your Chouans found this in a half-empty bin?"

"Yes, and brought out a dozen bottles on the sly to the bivouac," finished M. de Lage.

Madame de Rocquigny lifted her hands in mock horror. "Lucky men! But I suppose that there will be a certain number of incapables in your force to-night, for—without offence—I understand that drunkenness is a vice to which Bretons are something prone."

"Not my Bretons, Madame," said Hervé quietly. "Those bottles are back in the bin; and their unauthorised abstraction has been paid for."

A light seemed to break on his subordinate. "Ah, was it for that you ordered——" he began, but so swift and meaning a frown appeared on his leader's brow that he left his sentence unfinished.

"And where are you going to sleep to-night, Monsieur de Saint-Armel?" asked Madame de Rocquigny, slipping into the just momentary pause with the ease of a woman of the world for whom indiscreet questions have lost their savour. "May we offer you a room in the west wing, which is said to be haunted, but where the roof is entire, or——"

Armande de Bellegarde interposed on the instant. "M. de Saint-Armel will not trust our hospitality," she said quickly. "He is ungallant enough to prefer the society of his Chouans à la belle étoile. Am I not right, Monsieur?"

L'Invincible bent his head, a half-amused, half-tender smile showing at the corner of his mouth. "If you will not think me churlish, ladies.—May I give you some more wine, Marquise?"

Armande's eyes, full of a mute gratitude, had not met

his, nor indeed had his fingers closed on the decanter, before a sharp discharge of musketry made the cracked windows rattle. M. de Lage sprang to his feet, Madame de Rocquigny pushed back her chair, but Hervé, unmoved, filled her empty glass.

"Yes, go, de Lage," he said, looking up and nodding. "I will follow you. That was our fire, Mesdames, not the Blues'. There is no force within twenty miles sufficiently strong to account for us; though it is possible that they have driven in my outposts. You will pardon if I go and see?"

He rose, caught up his sheathed sword where it leant against the panelling, made them a smiling little salute with it, and was gone. A thundering fusillade burst out from the direction of the wood as, flinging away his scabbard, he ran bare-headed down the steps.

"My dear," said Madame de Rocquigny, "I think you may be proud of each other."

x

Twenty minutes later it was all over, and Hervé came up the avenue in the midst of his men, giving a word of praise to one, of enquiry to another, and with so much of unusual and but half-contained exultation in his manner, that the words rippled from mouth to mouth: "L'Invincible is pleased with us!" That would have been reward enough for the bloodiest combat; it was more than enough for a momentary brush with an enemy whom they had so easily beaten off.

When they reached the house Saint-Armel made his way to the front, and, running up the steps, lifted his hand. In the other he still carried the remains of his sword, which a Republican bullet had shivered.

"My children, you have done very well. But remember that the night is not yet over. Monsieur le Charron, send the wounded up to the château. Mes gars, I am pleased with you.—Dismiss!"

He saluted them with a smile, and stood there, as he had stood some hours earlier, watching them filing off. When the last man had disappeared he stood there still. The approach of night was filling the air with impalpable incense; a thin slip of a moon, almost lightless, hung timidly over the dark mass of the forest. Down at the foot of the steps old Yves stood motionless, leaning on his musket, and at a little distance de Lage was giving low-voiced orders to a Chouan. The candle-light streamed out from the dining-room, and threw up Madame de Rocquigny's figure against the window. From the distance the hoot of an owl, that sound almost sacred to the ear of a Chouan, brought a smile to the face of Yves, and, turning his head, he looked up at the figure of his young leader on the steps. Hervé, who understood perfectly what was in his mind, nodded to him, and, lifting the hilt of his broken sword as if in salute to the distant bird, turned to go in. But his eyes, as he moved, were caught by his scabbard, lying where he had thrown it on the steps, and he stooped to pick it up.

Even as he bent a bullet came whizzing over his head and smacked into the woodwork of the half-open door behind him.

Saint-Armel had leapt down in an instant from his exposed position. "Somewhere in the shrubbery on the other side!" he shouted coolly to Yves, whose musket was already at his shoulder. "Lend me your sword, de Lage!" But de Lage and the Chouan had already begun to run towards the bushes, rendered by the deceptive dusk a fit hiding-place for any straggler, and, pulling a pistol from his belt, Hervé followed them. The calm of a moment ago was transformed into a palpitating tension. Yet there was nothing to be seen or heard. The great overgrown laurels round the drive were thick, shadowy and mocking; but it was in them, somewhere, that death was lurking. De Lage was hacking at them desperately and rather aimlessly, the Chouan had plunged into their fastnesses, and Hervé, pistol in hand, was giving him directions. All three were on one side of the drive.

"For God's sake come away!" shouted Yves. "Come away, Monsieur Hervé; it's you he wants!" Saint-Armel's disdainful little laugh was all the answer he got ere, frantic with apprehension, and careless whether he killed the Chouan or no, the old man fired at a venture into the laurels, and, lowering his musket, ran forward.

A man in the uniform of a grenadier instantly slipped out of the bushes on the other side of the drive, in the shade of a large arbor vitæ, and, dropping on one knee, took deliberate aim. . . . Yves, the only one who could see the assassin, was the fraction of a second too late.

"He's the other side!" he yelled, and fired.

The two shots rang out simultaneously, and as Jean Delorme sank forward in a huddled heap, Hervé threw out his arms, spun half round, and fell on the weed-grown gravel, shot through the heart. In an instant Yves had caught him to his breast. L'Invincible, opening his eyes, looked up at him with a faint and fleeting smile, and the old man thought to catch the word "Dieu!" or

"Adieu!" he could not tell which. . . .

And in a few moments the two women in the lighted room saw a tall old Breton standing in the doorway with the tears running down his face, and his foster-son once more inert in his arms. But this time l'Invincible would not wake again.

XI

In the little chapel of the château, with candles at his head and feet, his hands crossed over his broken sword, and two great June roses hiding the wound in his breast, Hervé de Saint-Armel lay under the flag of France. Yves le Guerric, his head fallen forward on the fleur-de-lis, and his hands clasped together over his rosary, was kneeling by him when Armande de Bellegarde came softly in, and, looking long at the dead face, stooped and kissed it.

"Yves," she said gently, "do you know the story of the Inn of the Sword?"

Le Guerric raised his ravaged old countenance, and looked at her across the pall of white and gold.

"Were you the lady?" was all his answer.

"Yes," said Armande, "and this is the Inn of the Sword. The sword is the device of the house."

"I did not know it," said Yves fiercely. "Should he have come here had I known? . . . And it was you that brought him here!" he added, with a hushed and savage vehemence.

Madame de Bellegarde took no notice. "See, Yves," she said, more gently still, "here are two roses, and when they bury him to-morrow we will each take one, because we loved him best, and because we are both glad that he sleeps so well at the Inn of the Sword, under the Lilies. . . . You are not sorry, are you, Yves?"

But Yves, instead of answering the beautiful poignant voice, broke into a storm of sobbing.

ON PAROLE

ON PAROLE

Since you display, my dear Antoine, so flattering an anxiety to hear of my sojourn in the country of our hereditary foes, I shall with all my heart give you a short account of it. But remark that I have nothing of great interest to impart to you, unless it be the story of a little misunderstanding which had like to end for me in consequences of the most unpleasant.

You know, in the first place, the chain of events which caused me to find myself in England:—how, desirous, for different reasons, of quitting France for a time, I procured a congé from the gardes-du-corps, and volunteered to serve under the brave and unfortunate Montcalm in Canada; and how I embarked from Nantes in the corvette *L'Assurance*. You know likewise that I never set eyes upon the waters of the St. Lawrence, since somewhere off the southern coast of Ireland we had the ill-luck to fall in with an English privateer, the *James and Mary,* of Bristol, with whom we fought a running fight of more than four hours, until, having lost his mizenmast and other things upon whose names I am not sailor enough to venture, our captain considered that he had done enough for honour, and struck his colours. This mortifying incident occurred upon the morning of June 15th, 1759.

You may conceive me then, in no very good humour, on the deck of the *James and Mary*—which one was glad to see had suffered almost as much as *L'Assurance*—exchanging a few haughty words with her captain, a kind of a sea-bulldog, whose prisoner I was to consider

myself. I do not know why this mariner should have
found me amusing, since I was striving to bear my misfortune as became a gentleman of France and a La
Roche-Sainte-Fère, though I admit that I was angry.
Ma foi, had I not enough cause, seeing before me a sojourn of God knows how long in that isle of fogs and
perpetual roast beef! Also I had received, early in the
combat, a blow from a falling spar upon my forehead; it
was nothing in itself, but it had given me an enraged
headache.

So my sea bull-dog was demanding that I should give
up my sword—"Just as a matter of form, as it were,
Mounseer," he says, grinning. "I don't reckon you'll do
much harm here with that dandified weapon."

"You are not of gentle blood," says I to him. "I will
only give up my sword to a gentleman." Hence it seemed
probable that I should not give it up to anybody, and I
conceived that I would break it and throw it into the sea.

"Oh, Lord!" said the captain. "What a pity, now, that
none of us ain't good enough!—Bill, ask Mr. Henry to
come aft."

With that a young man came over the deck towards
us. He was more than a little dishevelled and grimy (I
learnt afterwards that he had been serving one of the
guns), but there was no mistaking that he was well born.

"Mr. Henry, sir," says the captain, "this here count or
whatever he is won't give up his pig-sticker to the likes
of us, not being gentry. Perhaps he'll let you take it. . . .
This is Mr. Henry Savile," he says to me, "and seeing as
his father, Sir George Savile, Baronet, Justice of the
Peace, is cousin to the Earl of Windermere, and the
owner of this vessel, perhaps you'll think him enough
of a lord to let him handle that toy of yours!"

ON PAROLE

I did not need the insolent pirate's certificates; I took one look at this M. Henri and unbuckled my sword.

The young man bowed to me. "I count myself honoured," he said, with great civility, and I took the blade which was to have served the Marquis de Montcalm and laid it across his dirty palms.

"Monsieur est blessé?" says he then to me, very courteously, and in a tolerable accent.

I assure you, my friend, that the finding on board this horrible *James and Mary* (what a name!) of one person with the manners of a gentleman and the recognisable possession of the French tongue immediately recovered me my spirits, and I said gaily: "Not the least in the world, Monsieur! I have a slight headache from having drunk too much last night." But since (as I afterwards discovered) there was blood on the handkerchief round my head, M. Henri was able to take my little gasconnade for precisely what it was worth.

"If you will allow me, Captain," he said, "I will take this gentleman to my cabin," and to this the master of the *James and Mary* gave a willing consent, saying (as he thought unheard of me) that he was only too pleased to find someone whom the young spit-fire considered good enough to associate with.

Well, that was the beginning of my friendship with M. Henri, son and heir of Sir Savile, Baronet and Justice of the Peace, and this friendship was the cause of all that followed, and, to begin with, was the reason why I did not languish in some hole of a military prison at Plimout or elsewhere. One enters quickly into a friendship or an enmity, I conceive, on board ship, and, moreover, the *James and Mary*—with her prize, alas!—met with contrary winds, and beat about the Irish Channel for two

days longer than she should have done. All this time
my liking for M. Henri (and I think his for me) increased mightily, and by the time we were entering upon
the river of Bristol (I have forgotten its name) he had
persuaded me to become a prisoner on parole, and begged
me to allow him to take me with him on a visit to his
family in Gloscestshir. (You see how hard I have
worked at English to be able to write correctly so extraordinary a name!)

It was not what I should have chosen. From walls
and bars one can escape; from parole, never. But what
would you? One is young; the blue sky is dear, the offer
of a friend tempting; and one can always take back one's
parole. Enfin, after landing at Bristol and going through
the necessary formalities I soon found myself in a post-
chaise with M. Henri rolling through the province whose
name I have already written.

In time, we passed through a small and neat village,
with an air of prosperity in its little gardens full of all
sorts of flowers, up an avenue of old trees, to the château
of M. Henri's father. This was a sufficiently ugly build-
ing, nearly square, and devoid of ornamentation of any
kind—*vrai emblème du caractère britannique,* said I to
myself.

"I see my father on the steps," says my friend, looking
out of the window, and in effect there I beheld the master
of the house, a personage of a high stature and a ruddy
face, in riding costume, with two dogs at his heels.

He greeted his son with much affection, and me with
more cordiality than I had expected.

"I suppose I ought not to say that I hope your stay
with us will be long, sir," he remarked pleasantly, "but,
long or short, I trust that you will find it agreeable.

Harry, show M. de la Roche . . . Roche. . . ."

"Sainte-Fère," I supplemented.

"La Roche-Sainte-Fère his room—the blue room—and see that he has all he needs. You will find your sisters in the garden."

In spite of this hospitable welcome and of the presence of my friend I felt, as I went upstairs, that I had entered the doors of my prison. It was senseless and ungrateful, I grant you, but I could not help it. When M. Henri had left me and I was awaiting the arrival of my valise, I went and, opening the window, calculated the height from the ground. "Tiens!" said I to myself, "even for a drop it is not excessive, and there is a great deal of ivy if I choose to climb." Then I remembered that even a ladder must tempt me in vain.

As I was drawing in my head after this survey I suddenly caught sight of a man's figure going along a garden-path. A moment later he met a lady, whom he kissed. It was too far off for me to be sure, but I had no doubt that I had witnessed the meeting of my friend with one of his sisters. Since the lady by her figure was young, you perhaps suppose that my spirits were cheered by this sight? Not the least in the world! I drew back into my room more melancholy than before. A vision of Sidonie rose before me—that cruel Sidonie who, as you know, was partly responsible for my leaving France. It occurred to me that she might very well be walking at that moment in her gardens at Colombelles— with an escort. I wished that I had not gone away.

The arrival of my effects interrupted my gloomy meditations, and I fell to making my toilet for supper, for the hour was already advanced. I found my friend's sisters, to whom I was shortly presented, of types very different. Miss Lucie, the younger, was the embodiment of fair-haired and blue-eyed innocence—it must have been she whom I saw from my window—while Miss Henriette was dark and tall. But my heart was not in a condition to permit itself to be attracted by either of them. The blonde Lucie appeared very shy. After supper Miss Henriette, who had fine arms and an indifferent voice, sang to the harp, while Sir George went to sleep and I tried to conceal my yawns. When the ladies had retired M. Henri and I played a party of piquet, with which the evening came to a close. As he lighted me to my room M. Henri expressed a fear that I should find my stay a trifle dull, there being little to do in the country.

I confounded myself in protestations, but, mon Dieu, he was right! The next four days are branded on my memory for ever; especially the evenings. But on the fifth I pulled myself together, and, Miss Henriette having shown herself very willing to receive advances, I made her a few; and in the evening gave her a lesson in the French tongue, sitting on a rustic seat in the garden. This employment, faute de mieux, carried me over two or three days more, and then one fine afternoon I overheard Miss Lucie making her sister a scene—about me, if you please! So for the sake of peace I offered to teach her French, too; but they had their lessons separately.

I suppose that almost a fortnight of this sort of existence had passed over my unhappy head when Sir Georges announced one morning at breakfast that his sister Mrs. Wingfield, with her son and her daughter, had the intention of paying him a visit. "That will give you young people the excuse for some festivities, I've no doubt—a dance or what not," he says. "Monsieur de la

Roche-Sainte-Fère, you shall see some of our neighbouring beauties."

"If I have eyes for them, Monsieur," I reply, glancing
at Mlles Henriette and Lucie, but thinking in my heart
of my fair (and by this time I doubt not) false Sidonie.

Two days later arrives the sister of Sir Georges, a pon-
derous dame with a Roman nose and an exalted opinion
of herself, her daughter Julie (much prettier than her
cousins) and her son M. François. At once we become
more gay, so that I bless the coming of these people,
though Madame Wingfield looks at me always through
her quizzing-glass as though I were some strange animal
and puts to me the most tactless questions, and though
M. son fils gives me a desire to take him to some quiet
spot and give him a little lesson in manners. Not that
he knows not how to conduct himself, but because I can
see that he lacks courtesy by design. However, I trouble
myself about him as little as possible, finding his sister
vastly more sympathetic. She had a very passable figure
for an Englishwoman.

It was indeed from the fair Julie that I first heard the
piece of information which I so much misliked. For she
said to me the third evening, under cover of Mlle
Henriette's performance on the harp—

"Did you know, Monsieur, that there was another
French prisoner of war in the neighbourhood?"

"Ma foi, no," said I. "I doubt he has not so pleasant
a captivity nor such charming gaolers as I."

She blushed, and replied: "I fear not, sir, for he is shut
up in Leasonfield Castle."

"And what is his name, Mademoiselle?"

"I fear I cannot remember it," she said; "stay, it has to
do with a flower . . . Fleuranges, that is it; the Comte

de Fleuranges . . . I think he is a general——"

"Good God!" said I. The Comte de Fleuranges, the hero of Raucoux, my father's friend, my boyhood's idol, a prisoner! It was not possible! But Mlle Julie beckoned to her odious brother to confirm her news.

"Frank," said she, "is it not true that there is a French general a prisoner in Leasonfield Castle?"

"Certainly," says Mr. Wingfield, with great gusto. "Fast by the leg; quite a famous general. . . . Bless my soul, didn't you know, Monsieur de la Roche?" (it was thus he was pleased to miscall me). "He was took last month in Germany. Lend you the *Gazette* if you like. They say his regiment ran away——"

"Your mercenaries would hardly have captured him else," said I like a flash, white with fury. "And let me inform you, Monsieur, that the regiment in question is not French, but Irish, and you need not therefore be surprised——"

If I had not suddenly seen Mlle Julie's frightened face I do not know what might not have happened, but her insolent brother was a gentleman also, and, I know not how, we both contrived to leave the subject.

I slept very ill that night. Every time I woke I pictured M. de Fleuranges, the gallant, the proud, eating his heart out in captivity, no doubt in chains, "fast by the leg," as M. Wingfield had said with such glee. The thought revolted and haunted me.

Next day, amid the preparations for the dance, I made enquiries as to the position of this château. I learnt that it was a bare five miles off. M. Henri could tell me nothing about the prisoner, and I did not like to ask many questions. But that evening I retired early to my room. My mind was made up. It had been impossible to get away from the company during the day—for the house was now very full—and after all, what I had to do was best done in the hours of darkness. So, when I felt sure that the household and guests had all retired I leaned from my window and once more scrutinised the ivy; and a little later you might have beheld me clambering down it in the moonlight; for there was a moon, worse luck to it, half grown but potent.

Well, I shall not weary you with recounting how I walked five miles by her rays, how I lost my way three times, how when she withdrew her light I all but fell into a pond, but I narrate to you merely that I arrived, somewhere in the small hours of the morning, before the stronghold in which was immured the hero of Raucoux.

It was called a castle, but for all that it was only one of these square and ugly edifices like the dwelling of Sir Georges, save that it was larger and had two wings. I had expected something with tourelles, at the least. In the freshness of the summer night I walked warily by the side of a great field wherein cattle were slumbering, and looked at this big box of a place, where every window was like its fellow, and wondered how I should distinguish *his* room from any other. The house looked so damnably blank in front, staring at me with its eyes shut, that I did not venture upon the sweep of gravel, but made my way round it. And then came my stroke of luck! For in a window on the first floor, on the outer side of the right wing, there was a light burning.

I scarcely dared hope that it might be what I pictured, yet I crept cautiously nearer. Then I suddenly found my way blocked by a wall of no great height. It was but a moment's work to clamber over it. I dropped into a kind of formal garden, set with flowers which looked pale in the moonlight, and I saw what I had hoped to see.

The light was that of a single candle, which stood by the open window, and near it, his head on his hand and his eyes fixed no doubt upon some book which he was reading, was M. de Fleuranges himself. A gust of emotion seized me at the sight of that noble and heroic countenance, with the scar on the temple, the glorious wound of Raucoux. (It is true that I could not have seen it at that distance, even had it not been on the other side of his face—for he was in profile—but I knew that it was there.) His iron-grey hair was unpowdered and held back by a ribbon, and he was wearing a flowered dressing-gown. He appeared to be alone and unguarded; why, then, was the window open? . . .

After I had sufficiently mastered my emotion to be able to advance I did so, creeping round by the house, and doing no small damage to the flowers, which in return drenched my silk stockings. M. de Fleuranges never heard my stealthy steps; he was absorbed in his reading, or, perhaps, in thoughts of his country. Once or twice he compressed his lips and shook his head as if he did not like his book.

At last I was arrived under the window, and said very softly:

"Monsieur le Comte!"

He jumped. A French voice coming out of the night must have been the last sound he expected. "Ciel! what was that?" I heard him murmur.

Recognising that he could not see me, I moved a little further out from the house. "A friend," says I.

He was at the window, looking down, in a moment. "God in Heaven! a Frenchman! What brings you here? Who are you?"

"René de la Roche-Sainte-Fère," I replied, knowing that he would remember my name, though he could not be expected to recall the child who used to play with his sword.

The hero of Raucoux smote his forehead. "But why —why are you here at this hour? It is nearly two o'clock. Where did you come from, in God's name, and why?"

"I am come to rescue you, mon général," I said earnestly. "I have only just heard that you were captured. At least, if I could arrange some plan . . ."

"Have you taken leave of your senses?" demanded M. de Fleuranges sternly. "Surely you know that I am a prisoner on parole!"

Of course by this time, my dear friend, you will consider me the last of imbeciles not to have thought of such a thing, but I give you my word of honour that it had never for an instant crossed my mind. It was something in the way in which they had spoken of him that had made me draw a picture so different.

"Well, sir?" continued M. de Fleuranges, and he still sounded extremely severe—"what have you to say?"

"Nothing, Monsieur le Comte," said I very truly, being stunned by this downfall of my hopes, and feeling very foolish and suddenly rather weary.

He took the candle in his hand as if he were going to have a closer look at me, then thought better of it.

"Where have you sprung from, child?" he asked more kindly. "You have not, I imagine, come over from France to rescue me?"

I told him that I was a prisoner in like case with himself.

"Well, you had best get back as quickly as you can, or you will give folks cause to say that you are breaking your parole. How old are you, you foolish boy?"

"Twenty-four," said I. I felt more like four, but his tone was suddenly so adorably kind that I could bear even that sensation for the sound of it.

He smiled down at me. "You have this sort of thing in your blood," he said musingly. "Your father . . . but there! Now go, child, before someone hears us!"

"Monsieur le Comte," said I with passion. "I wish you were in a dungeon instead of tied with this cursed parole. At least give me your hand a moment to kiss!"

M. de Fleuranges smiled, and said, "This interview, my dear René, somewhat resembles a scene in a play by the English poet Shakespeare, which I was reading when you interrupted me—sad stuff, it seems to me, and much below Racine. If you were ten feet high, and my arm six feet long, you should have my hand. As it is——"

He was interrupted by a sudden noise. A little further along the wing a window was thrown violently up, and a night-capped head protruded. "Who is there?" demanded a loud voice. "Speak, or I fire!"

I was tolerably certain that this was an empty threat, and in any case I had no intention of betraying my nationality; nor was I sure that this head could even see me. And at that very moment the blessed moon went behind a cloud. It was my chance, so, without a further look up at M. de Fleuranges' window I made straight and quickly across the small garden. There should have been little to betray me had I not fallen over a large watering-pot, on which, with a yell and a shout of "I see you, rascal!" there came a flash and a report. Where the bullet went I know not. When I was on the top of the wall the nightcap fired again; he must have seen me this time, for he hit the wall quite near me. You may imagine that I did not saunter when I was once on the other side.

Yet, my friend, if you have pictured me winged by a shot, arrested by the watch, unable to return to my room and so discovered, you are wrong. I reached home as it was getting light, very much fatigued, but with no further contretemps, climbed up the ivy, undressed, and crawled with dejection into bed. No, the unpleasant consequences of my expedition came by quite another road, as you shall hear.

I awoke to the morning of the ball, undeniably weary and sleepy, and obliged to conceal it. The house was upside down; Henriette and Lucie were too busy to take their lessons, so I gave Julie one instead.

I pass over the dance, which was well enough. I found the English beauties by no means cruel, and not ill dancers either. In fact, could I have forgotten M. de Fleuranges—and Sidonie—I should have enjoyed myself.

It must have been about three in the morning that M. Henri, his cousin the detestable Wingfield, the three or four gentlemen staying in the house, those guests who still lingered and I found ourselves in the deserted supper-room over a last bowl of punch. The ladies had all gone and Sir Georges had retired. I think we had most of us drunk as much as we should, except M. Henri. I was talking to him at the end of the table when I suddenly heard a name uttered, amid laughter, from the knot of gentleman who were standing further down the table. The name was that of M. de Fleuranges, and it was accompanied by some very disparaging expressions.

"What is this?" I said, going towards the speakers.

They looked round, still laughing. "Something you

had best not hear, Sir," said one less drunk than the others, but a M. Jackson spluttered out, "No, it's too damned good a jest . . . tell the Frenchy . . . It's only that your French general has been caught trying to break his parole—by God, ain't it a jest . . . a general——"

"It's a lie!" I said instantly and fiercely enough; but he was too drunk to pay any heed, and, still laughing, sat down suddenly on the floor.

M. Wingfield, however, looked at me with the most disagreeable smile imaginable. "Indeed," he said, "I share your astonishment, Monsieur, but when a prisoner, however distinguished, is found holding a colloquy from his window at two in the morning with some unknown man who makes off when challenged, what other construction can be put upon his actions?"

"By a mind like yours, Monsieur, no other, I dare say," said I, and struck him across the mouth.

Eh bien, mon ami, you know what a commotion ensues after a little incident of this kind—and I think myself that it would have been more becoming if I had kept my hands off him—but in the end, after much talk, and protestations from M. Henri, who was exceedingly distressed, we arranged to meet next morning. So I slept that night with the consolation that if my folly had put a stain on M. de Fleuranges' honour it would very shortly be wiped away, either in M. Wingfield's blood or in mine; preferably in the former.

It was a beautiful morning—as it always is upon these occasions—and the birds were singing distractingly in that corner of the garden (as far as possible from the house) which our seconds had selected. M. Wingfield and his party were already arrived when I got there; I suspected it of being his first affair (in which case I had

84

much the advantage of him), but he seemed composed enough. I resolved that I would pirk him in some negligible spot—the arm for choice—since I had no wish, in the circumstances, to do him a fatal injury. We saluted and crossed swords.

And now, my dear Gabriel, let me give you a piece of advice which may prove invaluable to you should you ever find yourself in a like situation. Do not, as a matter of course, despise the fence of an Englishman. This Wingfield was not a pretty swordsman, but he was a desperately persistent one. And when, after about two hot minutes, I touched him in the left shoulder I cannot altogether deny that I was relieved.

I dropped my point and sprang back, and our seconds crossed swords between us.

"We will go on, if you please," says M. Wingfield, frowning. " 'Tis not worth the tying up"—for his other second was advancing upon him with a handkerchief.

So we began again. I knew by now that my enemy, though he was not so quick on his feet as I (he was a good five years older) and had none of the refinements of the art, possessed a longer reach, and perhaps a stronger wrist. And from the way in which he now came on I could not flatter myself that he intended merely to run me through the arm; his intentions seemed much more bloodthirsty. So, though I did not think that he would succeed in them, I was minded to put him out of action and have done with it. It was just as I began to look closely for an opportunity of putting this design into practice that there was heard, between the click of the steel, the sound of a heavy person running towards us.

Now M. Wingfield probably knew that it must be his

uncle, and I too guessed as much, but—believing myself to be quicker, if not stronger than he—I had the incredible folly to let my eye wander for an instant from his hand (for I always watch the hand and not the point). And I saw Sir Georges in a really extraordinary costume, running over the wet lawn, with his dressing-gown flapping wildly behind him, holding up his small-clothes with one hand and crying loudly: "Stop! stop!" Moreover, I allowed myself to be for the fraction of a second amused by this sight, and it was my perdition. I do not to this day know how M. Wingfield accomplished it, but all of a sudden there was a horrible hot spasm of pain in my side, and I saw him on the lunge and realised, from the nearness of his hand to my body, that he had succeeded in planting a good six inches of his sword between my ribs.

I was furious! His blade being out again in an instant as he recovered, and I not having loosed hold of my own, I made to attack him, but unaccountably stumbled, and was caught in M. Henri's arms. I remember trying to push him away, and swearing that I would go on; then I had the feeling of a great sickness, the lawn suddenly heaved like a green sea, and Sir Georges, the cause of my misfortune, the rose trees, M. Wingfield's rather startled face and the rest of the world vanished from my sight.

Afterwards I was dimly conscious that I was lying on the ground in someone's arms, that something was being pressed hard against my side (I could not imagine why) and that a voice above me, yet miles away, was saying angrily, "It was your fault, Sir, for running in upon us!" And another voice said, "I fear it was, my boy," and added something about a gallant young fool, and how

86

devilish sorry he should be. . . . Then, to my inexpress-
ible relief the voices faded away and left me in peace . . .

And after this, my dear Antoine, I was very ill, though
to be sure I did not know much about it for some time,
whereby I was doubtless spared ennui. It was, however,
a long and wearisome business; in fact I learnt that M.
Wingfield's blade had come very near to liberating me
from my parole for ever. (Again I make you my recommendation about an Englishman's sword-play; for if I
had been more respectful of it I should never have
ventured to look away for that fatal second.) However, at last I was out of the wood, and able to take
interest again in my surroundings.

And one afternoon, while M. Henri was reading to
me, there came a tap at the door. Being drowsy, I paid
little heed to what then went forward, and was therefore highly amazed when, on opening my eyes, I saw
standing at the foot of the bed, looking very noble and
stately, no less a person than M. de Fleuranges.

"Monsieur le Comte!" I exclaimed, trying to raise myself from my pillows. "Oh, how good——"

"Lie down, child," says he, coming to the side of the
bed, and looking down at me very kindly. "I should
have come earlier, had you been sufficiently recovered.
My boy, how could you give me all this anxiety?"

"Why, mon général," says I, "how could I do anything but fight him?" (He had actually felt anxiety on
my account, then!)

"Some people might have explained, René," said M. le
Comte, sitting down on the bed and taking my hand.

At that I think the tears began to come into my eyes,
for I was still very weak, and I could not bear that he

G

should blame me, even though his tone were so kind and humorous. It was quite enough to have been spitted by an English *hobereau* without that added mortification. M. de Fleuranges saw it and put his other hand over mine.

"Everybody is not so chivalrous a knight, ready to shed his blood for the sake of another's honour—and that other an old man," he said. "That was all I meant, mon petit.—No, I have little love for an over-prudent head on a young man's shoulders . . . and you cannot be accused of that possession!"

"I had rather you thought me a fool than a coward," says I rather hotly.

M. de Fleuranges shook his head, smiling. "Oh, youth, youth! Mort de ma vie, will you eat me too?— No, René, I think that if you were my son, though I might have scolded you, I should not have been so very ill-content with you after all."

And as, overwhelmed, I tried to carry his hand to my lips, he bent forward and kissed me.

THE LAUREL OF THE RACE

THE LAUREL OF THE RACE

"You, who desired no laurel of the race,
But the approval of one absent face;
    For whom has earth no home, no place of rest
    Save in the bosom where you may not lie;
Beggared of all but Love's immortal right,
Still for the sake of one you lost to fight . . ."
            S. R. Lysaght. Poems of the Unknown Way

I

MONSIEUR DE SAINTE-ANNE, when he was a good deal younger, had formed a habit of walking for about half an hour after déjeuner up and down the little walk on the south terrace; and it was a custom which showed no signs of loosing its hold upon him with advancing years. Indeed the household supposed their master to perform a sort of daily meditation on this spot, and during the forty minutes or so of the day when the word went round that M. le chevalier was on the terrace, neither coachman, gardener, groom nor domestic of inferior sex would approach him unless obliged to do so. The convention had no legislative basis, nor was M. de Sainte-Anne ever known to show annoyance when necessity had brought about its infraction. Nevertheless it had, by the year 1791, formed itself into a kind of spiritual railing round the south walk between the hours of half-past twelve and half-past one.

On this terrace of his M. de Sainte-Anne appeared to pace alone. Not even the upholders of the convention thought otherwise. But in reality a lady walked with him there; a lady much younger than himself—for he was forty-six—who wore, winter and summer, the same costume, which did not alter from its fashion of twenty years ago. (An exact copy of her and her dress, unseen too, hung on a worn silver chain round M. de Sainte-Anne's neck.) Only her moods varied; sometimes she was merry, sometimes very sad. But she was always in exactly the spirit best suited to that of M. de Sainte-Anne at the time. For this is an attribute of the invisible companion.

In life Adélaïde de Kermel had never walked on this terrace; she had never even set eyes on the manoir of la Gaubrinière and its sunny garden. But M. de Sainte-Anne had planned all his improvements for her; he had planted a special border of pinks, for which he had no particular liking himself, because she was fond of them, and had but lately crossed the tenacious purposes of old François concerning a rose-bush which she loved and François did not. And yet it was many years ago that M. de Sainte-Anne had known that she would never put her little foot on his carefully-tended gravel; many years, even, since she had closed her eyes on all the gardens of this world. But the last of these circumstances in no way affected M. de Sainte-Anne's promenades on the terrace.

And Gabriel-Honoré de Sainte-Anne was not in the least mad. The idea of considering him even a trifle eccentric had never, during twenty years, suggested itself to the minds of the countryside, where on the contrary he was known and greatly respected for his piety and generosity. His Vendéan tenantry gave him a devotion tinged with reverence and awe, speaking of him as of one whose presence lent lustre to the neighbourhood. "Ce bon M. de Sainte-Anne à la Gaubrinière—on lui

donnerait le bon Dieu sans confession!" A Breton by
origin, M. de Sainte-Anne possessed the devout soul of
his race, touched with a slight strain of mysticism of his
own. To that, perhaps, he owed his kindly and almost
gay melancholy, his invariably even temper, and a
peculiar charm of address. Other circumstances may
have contributed also. He had not always been buried
in Bas-Poitou; and he had greatly loved.

It was of course inevitable that some version of his
story should be current among the peasantry, some of
whom remembered him as a youth at la Gaubrinière in
his father's days. It was a simple tale, of a marriage that
should have been, broken by ambitious parents on the
advent of a nobler suitor. Opinions varied as to the
lady's behaviour; some remembered to have heard that
she was as heart-broken as he; others considered that
she could not have loved M. le chevalier very much, or
she would not have yielded to her father's wish. What
nobody guessed was how much Sainte-Anne loved her
still; how the wound which he had carried for three-
and-twenty years was as unhealed, if not so poignant, as
on the day of its infliction; to what degree it had planted
in him that tenderness and charity which they honoured,
and an occasional gentle vein of irony which as a rule
they did not recognise. The lady who walked with M.
de Sainte-Anne on the terrace had a whole life to answer
for.

The owner of la Gaubrinière, however, did not lead
quite a hermit's existence. A guest or two—usually a
former comrade-in-arms—was occasionally to be found
there, and sometimes M. de Sainte-Anne entertained his
neighbours in state. Either of these occasions raised great
commotion in the mind of Marianne the cook and house-

keeper, and scarcely less ferment in those of François the gardener and Jean-Baptiste the coachman, who also waited at table. These retainers were filled to the point of frenzy with a desire that the resources of the manoir should be seen at their best, conscious that these resources were not what they had been in the days before M. de Sainte-Anne grew poorer. But time and opportunities for such hospitality were, by the year 1791, fast slipping away from M. de Sainte-Anne and his compeers. Most of his neighbours could no longer be entertained, even at rare intervals, for they were no longer there. They had emigrated en masse and almost as a point of honour. Yet M. de Sainte-Anne showed no signs of following their example; and, needless to say, he was far enough from being molested by his own tenants, who would most of them have died for him. So he dwelt on in great peace at la Gaubrinière, though in Paris the monarchy was breathing its last, and Marianne grumbled that she had to bake so much bread for charity, and François complained that M. le chevalier was proving most obstinate about a bit of clipped hedge which he, François, wanted to cut differently, and Jean-Baptiste said that the old black mare was no longer fit to drive: and they were all very contented together.

It was his daisy-bushes which M. de Sainte-Anne was considering this morning, as he paced along with his hands behind his back. Those same bushes were very fine, and had certainly done extremely well this year. François was of opinion that there were too many in the border, for his thoughts, always of an utilitarian trend, were fixed on the well-being of the fruit-trees behind, neatly outspread against the wall. Lower down the garden could be seen the spare figure of the old man in his faded blue jacket; and once, when M. de Sainte-Anne looked that way, he caught a severe and reproachful glance from his retainer. M. de Sainte-Anne affected not to be aware of it, but he none the less moved away from the daisies and continued his walk.

He did not, therefore, see that François' attention was suddenly caught, and in a manner which testified to scandalised feelings, by something at the other end of the terrace, and, as his back was turned, the intruder who was walking along that sacred path had advanced some distance before M. de Sainte-Anne either heard or saw him. At last, however, he faced round sharply, and beheld, coming towards him in the sunlight, a well-dressed young man of about twenty years of age, of a gallant and careless bearing. As the older man turned he took off his hat.

"They told me I should find you in the garden, Monsieur le chevalier," he said easily. "Pardon me for presenting myself unannounced. My name is Philippe de Frontillac."

M. de Sainte-Anne, who had taken a step or two towards the newcomer, stopped as though he had been shot, and turned very white. The young man, apparently rather gratified by the effect he had produced, added, "I am on my way from La Rochelle, where I have been settling some provisions of my father's will, and remembering to have heard your name . . ." He paused as though for words of welcome, but got a question instead.

"Is M. le marquis de Frontillac dead?"

"He died this spring," replied the youth.

Sainte-Anne raised his hat. "God rest his soul!" he said quietly, and then held out a hand which shook a little. "You are very welcome, very welcome indeed. As you have no doubt heard, I knew . . . your parents, before you were born."

He had no idea how much the boy knew, and was not much enlightened when the latter said with the same easy grace, "I was told that you knew my mother when she was young. I do not remember her very well myself, for she died when I was but a child."

"I remember her very well indeed," said M. de Sainte-Anne, and a little smile came suddenly round his grave mouth. He laid his hand on the young man's shoulder. "You will at least take déjeuner with me, will you not? Wait for an instant, if you please, while I give orders and then let us walk a little here."

Part of Sainte-Anne's mind, as he came back to the terrace, was wondering whether the sunny path pleased her son as much as it pleased *her,* and whether he would say so. But Philippe de Frontillac, though he was exchanging glances with the daisy faces, did not comment on them.

By the time that déjeuner was ready Sainte-Anne knew that his guest was an only child, that he had lived most of his time in Paris, where he had received a military education, though he had not entered the army, and that now, in impetuous disgust at the trend of affairs in general, he was contemplating emigration. Of his father he said little; of his mother less. And in the dark-panelled dining-room, which proved an excellent setting for the young marquis's brilliant good looks, Sainte-Anne strove in vain to surprise a tone, a word, a gesture which should recall her. Of outward resemblance there was very little, as the chevalier had already assured himself out in the sunlight. The young man laughed and chatted with ease and good breeding, showing himself very agreeable, vivacious and self-possessed. That his attitude was not entirely free from a certain strain of patronage M. de Sainte-Anne was very well aware, but the fact amused rather than displeased him. It was natural that he should seem to this young Parisian a provincial old fogy—and was it not moreover a true estimate? Yet that the lad showed so little of his mother in any way disappointed him extraordinarily. But then she had died when he was so young! A whimsical idea suddenly seized Sainte-Anne of his own responsibility for what he deplored. He himself had absorbed so much of her attention since that day! He must have been smiling at the idea, for suddenly he heard his guest say laughingly:

"What sum shall I offer you for your thoughts, Monsieur de Sainte-Anne? They seem at least to be agreeable ones!"

"I beg your pardon," exclaimed Sainte-Anne, momentarily disconcerted. "I do not often have the pleasure of a visitor nowadays, and have fallen into bad habits. I was thinking how little you resemble your mother."

"Indeed?" returned the marquis. "Yes, I believe that I am more like my father's family." His tone showed no more than a polite interest in the subject, but he went on reflectively after a moment. "From the portraits that we have of my mother, I imagine she must have been very beautiful as a girl."

He finished his wine, and Sainte-Anne, looking keenly at him, put a hand to his own breast, to the miniature of Adélaïde de Kermel at eighteen. . . . No, he could not show it to him.

"I will ring for coffee," he said, rising. But the young

man, pulling out his watch, made a gesture of dismay.

"You will certainly think me a boor, Monsieur le chevalier," he said hastily, "but the diligence leaves the inn at two, and it is now ten minutes to the hour. I am afraid that I must take my leave at once. You observe that I am a good patriot, and no *ci-devant,* in my methods of travelling!"

"And yet you are going to emigrate!" said Sainte-Anne smiling.

The young man shrugged his shoulders. "I daresay I shall return."

"Come and see me again some day if you do," said his host, as he accompanied him to the door. "You will probably find me still buried in my provincial solitude— which nevertheless has its advantages."

"I can see that quite well," replied Philippe de Frontillac. "You in this part of the world are not likely to have your dwellings burnt over your heads by your peasantry.—Forgive my haste; I must walk quickly. Au revoir, Monsieur le chevalier, and a thousand thanks for your hospitality!"

"Good-bye, my boy—God bless you!" said Sainte-Anne, shaking his hand, and stood watching his alert young figure as he went rapidly down the little avenue. It was not until he had vanished that Sainte-Anne awoke to the fact that Adélaïde's son had been under his roof and that he had let him go without the slightest attempt at intimacy. Adélaïde's son had walked up and down her terrace, and he had conversed with him as with any ordinary stranger.—"Except that I took a farewell of him which he must have thought befitted the part of the *père noble!*" he said to himself with irony.

As he turned with a little sigh to go in it clutched at

him like an unexpected hand that if Philippe was Adélaïde's son he was Frontillac's as well. The remembrance
seemed an interpretation of the last hour.

"God have mercy upon me!" thought he sombrely,
"that after all these years I have not forgiven him, and
now he is dead!"

II

Summer—or rather spring—had come round for the
second time, but the terrace at la Gaubrinière, sunny and
alluring as ever, was deserted. M. de Sainte-Anne walked
there after déjeuner no more. He was far away from
such tranquil enjoyment, caught up at last into the flame
of civil war, marching with a handful of scarcely-armed
peasants in the difficult lanes of Vendée, or bivouacking
under the stars. He had, as he said himself, beaten his
pruning-knife into a sword, and so his daisy bushes when
they flowered would smile and nod at vacancy—unless
indeed the lady of the terrace went there without her
companion.

It had not been easy to leave that loved monotony,
but the final choice had presented itself with the imperative summons of a duty. Not only the villagers of la
Gaubrinière and Sainte-Anne's own few tenants, but
those too on the neighbouring estates of emigrated nobles
had clamoured for him to lead them. There was no one
else, they said—and he knew it to be true—no one with
any knowledge of military matters; no one (and this
they also said though he tried to stop them), no one so
good a Christian or with whom they would so willingly
die for their faith and their King. So, on a mid-March

99

morning of 1793, Sainte-Anne took his leave of the terrace. It was highly improbable that he would see it again.

"Ah, well," he said to himself; "I expect they are better gardeners in Paradise—but I do hope that François will leave the old rose-bush as it is, and not cut it down directly my back is turned."

And he felt, as he looked his last on his garden, that it was foolish to regret leaving it so much when he was to have the chance of gilding a dull life by dying for the fleur-de-lis. Nothing warned him that it was not for the fleur-de-lis that he should die.

And now, in mid-May, the setting sun was red over the little town of Parthenay, the shelter of the débris of the Vendéan army after its first defeat. Fontenay, with its Republican garrison, had repulsed them the day before. Six hundred Vendéans had fallen; the Marquis d'Elbée, the senior leader, was wounded; another was a prisoner. Worst of all was the loss, with the rest of the guns, of that venerated piece of artillery, "Marie-Jeanne," the palladium of the superstitious peasantry, round which eighty of them had been cut to pieces.

Sainte-Anne stood at the window of a house in a by-street, and his thoughts were gloomy enough; so gloomy that a sigh from the other side of the room hardly roused him. On the bed against the wall lay his little aide-de-camp, that fourteen-year-old Chevalier de Mondyon who had escaped from his school in Paris, forged himself a passport, and come to Vendée to fight for the King. The sight of the bandaged head smote Sainte-Anne's heart as he looked over at it, for it was he who had sent the ardent lad where he had got the sabre-blow. He crossed the room and sat down on the side of the narrow bed.

"Can't you sleep a little, my dear boy?" he asked very kindly, laying hold of a hot hand.

"I can't think of anything else!" sighed the boy passionately. "He said—whoever he was—that he would not go —imagine it!—refused to go to them . . . refused, refused! Ah! to think that the army holds such a man! . . . Were they all killed?"

"I don't know," replied Sainte-Anne sadly. His face had darkened. "You must not think of it any more. You will never get well quickly if you do—and I need my aide-de-camp. See, I will make your pillows more comfortable, and pull the curtain over the window."

"I can't sleep!" declared the Chevalier de Mondyon. "Every time I shut my eyes I see his cursed frightened face as he pulled round his horse. Oh, my God, if one were to turn coward oneself . . . one day . . . suddenly! Monsieur de Sainte-Anne, I shall pray every night that I may be killed before I become a coward like that man!" And in his growing half-delirium the boy clasped his hands convulsively over his breast, and began a petition of the sort.

"Child, child! leave your future to God and don't pray about it now! Put your head on my shoulder, there, and I will say a *De Profundis* for the souls of yesterday's slain, and after that you will go to sleep in His keeping, like them." And holding the lad's body in a clasp as tender as a mother's, he began in a low voice to say the 130th Psalm, and either the sound of the sonorous Latin or the strong embrace gradually quieted the little aide-de-camp, and he fell asleep.

Half an hour later Sainte-Anne was still sitting in the same position when the door opened to admit a young officer of the Marquis de Lescure's. Sainte-Anne laid a finger on his lips. The newcomer, who had himself one arm in a sling, cast a look of comprehension on the bed.

"You are wanted at headquarters, Monsieur le chevalier," he whispered. "They have been expecting you these twenty minutes. Did you not receive a message?"

Sainte-Anne shook his head. Then with great care he transferred the drowsy head from his shoulder to the pillow, covered up the boy, and went on tiptoe out of the room. The messenger had vanished, but he walked up the steep Rue de St. Jacques to the house which served the Vendéan chiefs for headquarters, not doubting but that he was summoned to a council of war to discuss the means of retrieving yesterday's disaster.

It was always difficult to get the Vendéan peasant to mount guard, and Sainte-Anne went up the stairs without meeting anybody. At a door on the first landing, however, stood not a sentry, but a gentleman with a drawn sword.

"You are late," he said in a grave voice, saluting Sainte-Anne. "They have begun without you."

Sainte-Anne hesitated. He was not of those who love to make a disturbing entry into a room, and he did not consider his opinion so valuable as to warrant it. "Is there no other door by which I can slip in quietly?" he asked; and, relieved to have one pointed out to him, went through it softly, to find himself hurled into a scene of which he had never dreamed.

The room was low, long and ill-lighted by two small windows at the further end. A long table ran down it, and on one side of this sat most of the officers of the Armée Catholique et Royale. The Marquis de Lescure, grave beyond his years, was in the centre, with the fiery Bernard de Marigny on his right hand, and Cathelineau,

the peasant leader whose modesty and devotion veiled
so much military capacity, on his left. Further down the
table Sainte-Anne caught sight, among others, of Stofflet,
the Lorrain gamekeeper, while, not at the table, but near
the window, his elbow on the sill, and his hand propping
his head, with the light glinting on his fair hair, and the
air of one designedly remote from the proceedings, sat
the twenty-year-old Henri de la Rochejaquelein. About
a score of others sat or stood round the walls; and the
gaze of all alike was directed on the figure of a young
man who sat alone on the other side of the table, with
his head bowed between his hands.

Sainte-Anne stood, motionless with surprise, in a dark
corner near the door by which he had come in. No one
had noticed his entrance. From where he stood he
looked down the length of the table. The sound of
Lescure's voice died away—Sainte-Anne had not caught
what he had been saying—and almost immediately the
tall form of Bernard de Marigny rose in his place. His
handsome face was deeply flushed, and an undercurrent
of the rage to which he was subject ran plain to hear in
his voice.

"As commander of the artillery of this army—or of
what is left of it"—he corrected himself bitterly—"I demand the exemplary punishment of the man who is
responsible—I will not say for the loss of our guns, but
for the fate of those brave men who were doing their
best to regain them." He paused for a second, and
Sainte-Anne could see the frowning face of Stofflet beyond him indicate approbation. "It has been averred
that someone instructed him to remain with his con-
tingent at his post—where he was doing nothing—and
not to assist in the attempt to rescue the artillery! It is

hardly necessary for me to ask Monsieur Cathelineau, in whose division he was, whether he sent such an order!"

Cathelineau shook his head. "But, on the other hand, as I have said, I sent him no orders of any kind," he observed, his peasant's accents contrasting less with the other's than did the ring of pity in his voice.

"Yet the evidence goes to show that the accused did receive orders of some sort—but from whom? M. de la Marsonnière, perhaps, but since he is unfortunately made prisoner, we cannot ask him. The only other possible officer is the Chevalier de Sainte-Anne. Is he not here yet?"

Marigny broke off to look round, and at that moment the prisoner took his hands from his face, and showed Sainte-Anne the scarcely recognisable features of Philippe de Frontillac.

A long, long way off sounded a voice—by the accent it was Stofflet's—suggesting that it was dark enough for candles, for one could not see who was in the room or not; and while somebody reached a couple from the mantelpiece and prepared to light them, Lescure's voice, a little nearer, explained that M. de Sainte-Anne had been summoned, and should have been here half an hour ago. Had there not been such rout and confusion one would have known. . . .

These things Sainte-Anne heard, but saw nothing save that grey and desperate face on the other side of the table. He had not even known that the young Marquis de Frontillac was with the army, much less that it was he who had refused. . . . A candle was lit, and then another. It looked like the face of a dead man—and it was the face of Adélaïde's son! And what, O God, could he possibly do to save him? Christ, Who forgavest Peter the coward, grant of Thy mercy a minute, a minute for thought . . .

The lighting of the candles had produced some sort of stir; in proceedings so informal little ceremony was likely to be observed. Marigny had sat down. Someone had lit more candles in a couple of sconces against the wall; the room sprang into clearer light, and Sainte-Anne's sheltering patch of shadow was gone. An exclamation showed that he had been recognised.

"You are here then, Monsieur de Sainte-Anne?" said the Marquis de Lescure in a tone of surprise.

"I have only just come. I did not get the first message," responded Sainte-Anne mechanically.

"But you hear now why we want you," said Marigny, leaning forward. "You have gathered that we are trying the Marquis de Frontillac for an act of rank cowardice which has contributed to the loss of eighty men, and may prove a scandalous example——"

"You should not call a gentleman a coward until the charge is proved!" came in a boyish and impetuous voice from the window.

Marigny took no notice. "Perhaps M. de Lescure will ask M. de Sainte-Anne whether he did not send an order to the prisoner?" he suggested.

Lescure hesitated for a second. It was evident he felt that to put the question was to doom the accused beyond redemption. He glanced towards Cathelineau for a moment, and his voice came out with a jerk.

"Did you send any orders, Monsieur de Sainte-Anne, to the prisoner during the engagement?"

Sainte-Anne had moved forward to the head of the table, and stood there more like a culprit than a witness or one of the company of judges.

"Yes, Monsieur de Lescure, I did." He had torn his eyes from those others and studied a knot in the wood of the table.

"And what were those orders?"

There was a pause, because Sainte-Anne could not yet see more than one step before him.

"I ordered him," he said at length, "to remain where he was."

The moment's silence which followed his answer exploded into amazed expostulation.

"Impossible!" cried Marigny, banging his fist on the table.

"Do you mean what you are saying, Monsieur de Sainte-Anne?" asked Lescure very coldly. "If this is merely an access of pity——"

"It is extremely misplaced," finished Stofflet.

The opposition steadied Sainte-Anne, and roused the fighting strain in him, a possession long forgotten. He looked up and met the eyes of all the table firmly and almost defiantly.

"I have the honour to tell you, Monsieur le Marquis, that it is perfectly true; and I am prepared to defend my action."

"You will certainly have to do so!" sneered Bernard de Marigny, and the same sentiment circulated audibly among those behind him.

"Gentlemen," cried Lescure sternly, "your tone is not becoming! If Monsieur de Sainte-Anne assures me that he sent this order I must take his word, though I find it hard to do so. But I must ask him a question or two. In the first place, I will ask him by whom he sent such an order?"

"By my aide-de-camp, the Chevalier de Mondyon."

"Is he here?"

"No. He is suffering from a sabre-cut on the head, and almost delirious," answered Sainte-Anne, who never thought to thank God for that fact. "I have only just come from his bedside."

"The Chevalier de Mondyon!" said Marigny reflectively. "Is he not——" He broke off, and for the first time since Sainte-Anne's entrance addressed the prisoner. "What sort of a person brought you M. de Sainte-Anne's order, Monsieur de Frontillac?"

Philippe de Frontillac seemed to hear; he seemed to try to remember. Or was he trying to invent? Sainte-Anne looked at him in an agony. "Tell the truth—tell the truth! You are lost if you give a wrong description!" It appeared to him that he had really said the words aloud.

"He . . . he was quite young—a boy of fifteen or so . . ." But the young man had a pitiable look of terror directly he had spoken, as though he would have taken back his words.

"Thank God!" murmured Sainte-Anne; and this time the words passed his lips, though no one seemed to remark them. "This is quite correct," he said, addressing himself to Lescure. "You may remember the boy; he ran away from Paris to join us."

The Marquis de Lescure nodded, and made a little sign of the hand. He was plainly puzzled; even, it seemed, a little disgusted.

And then, to Sainte-Anne's unspeakable relief, Cathelineau got up, and proposed that the prisoner should be considered acquitted, seeing that his inaction was the result of a definite order.

Lescure looked at the "saint of Anjou" as he sat down, at Philippe, and then at Sainte-Anne, still standing at the end of the table.

"I agree," he said slowly, "that that will be the proper course, and that before asking M. de Sainte-Anne for his reason in——"

A second explosion here broke into his words, the centre of which was Marigny and Stofflet. "The reason!" cried the former, leaping to his feet. "Why in God's name did we not have the *fact* earlier?—why have we had to drag it out of M. de Sainte-Anne, why——"

Lescure caught his arm, said something in an incisive voice, and Marigny, checking himself in mid-career, flung himself down again.

"Shall I give up my sword, Monsieur de Lescure?" asked Sainte-Anne, with his head high, and a hand on his hilt. His face was very white.

"Certainly not, sir," responded Lescure sharply. "We are not here to try a superior officer for an error in judgment, however extraordinary—though we may ask you for the grounds on which you made it. We are trying M. de Frontillac for misconduct. I cannot say that his previous answers accord very well with this somewhat tardy testimony of orders sent by you and received by him, but we must let that pass."

"I do indeed regret," said Sainte-Anne earnestly, "that I was not here earlier. But, as I say, I only received the second summons, and even then I had, on the word of a gentleman, no idea of what was going forward."

Lescure bent his head as though accepting the explanation. Marigny and Stofflet whispered together; Cathelineau was staring with a dreamy expression at the table. Philippe de Frontillac had fallen back in his chair, gripping the seat of it. He looked as the drowned may look, swaying in a dim world miles below the life which once knew them; the proceedings scarcely seemed to hold meaning for him now.

Lescure at last rose in his place. "I put it to the opinion of this court that, in consideration of superior orders received, M. de Frontillac be considered entirely exonerated from the charge of cowardice on which he was arraigned, and that his sword be returned to him."

There were only three dissentients, of whom Marigny was one. Lescure put his hand on Philippe's sword where it lay on the table in front of him. "Monsieur de Frontillac, I have pleasure in declaring you acquitted, and in restoring to you your sword. I am sure," he continued in a gentler voice, "that you will wish to withdraw from a scene whose necessity we all regret." He took up the weapon and held the hilt towards the young man.

A painful contraction passed over Philippe's features as, grasping at the table, he dragged himself to his feet and held out a shaking hand. He took the sword, and then his eyes slowly turned from Lescure to the figure of Sainte-Anne. The dull agony in them brought the sweat to Sainte-Anne's forehead—he was going to *thank* him, and then all his lying would be vain! Probably such was Philippe's intention, but he was fortunately incapable of carrying it out, and the next moment, turning without a word, he had stumbled from the room. With the sound of a clatter outside the door, which told that the recovered blade had slipped from his nerveless fingers, the tension within the room relaxed.

"And now," said Marigny, looking at Lescure, "may we ask for M. de Sainte-Anne's grounds of action?"

"If Monsieur le Président demands them, I am perfectly willing to give them," answered Sainte-Anne, studiously addressing himself to Lescure.

The "saint of Poitou" took a look round the faces present. "I think we should be glad to have them," he replied quietly. "But will you not sit down, Chevalier?"

Sainte-Anne pulled forward a chair from the wall and, sitting down at the end of the table, drew imaginary plans upon it with his finger, and proceeded as best he could to explain his motives for sending an order of which he had in fact sent precisely the opposite. For unless he could produce some reason with a sound of plausibility about it Philippe was not yet safe, and to give his own supposed conduct verisimilitude he must make shift to defend it. His comrades listened fairly quietly, with occasional interruptions, but the tone of the meeting, when he had finished, was not cordial.

"There is no more to say," commented Lescure coldly. "I do not like, as a soldier younger and less experienced than M. de Sainte-Anne, to criticise his judgment; I will only say that it seems to me an unfortunate decision." He got up, and others beyond him rose too and began to move towards the door.

Sainte-Anne remained a moment sitting where he was. He felt suddenly very tired. All at once a hand gripped his wrist where it lay on the table, and looking up he became aware of Cathelineau leaning from his place towards him.

"I never thought to admire . . . a liar, Monsieur le Chevalier!" he whispered. Sainte-Anne had a start of amazement and dismay, but the strong, serene face was alight with comprehension. "I respect your secret," added the peasant in a still lower voice, and turned in-

stantly away. Everybody was filing out, and Sainte-
Anne, hanging back a little, went towards the door with
the last few. As he reached it someone put a hand on
his shoulder from behind, and he turned to find himself confronted by the young and ardent visage of Henri
de la Rochejaquelein.

"Will you do me the honour to shake hands with
me?" he said under his breath. His eyes were sparkling.

"Why?" asked Sainte-Anne stupidly.

La Rochejaquelein's mouth broke into a smile. "Just a
fancy!" he responded lightly, and catching Sainte-Anne's
hand in the press he wrung it and was gone.

But Lescure, the man whose esteem Sainte-Anne most
coveted—junior by twenty years though he was—had
passed him without a word. Well, it was not to be
wondered at . .

At the door yet another hand caught him. It was that
of the officer on guard. "Stay a moment!" he whispered,
and as the others poured down the narrow staircase
he drew Sainte-Anne unresisting across the landing,
opened another door and thrust him through, shutting it
behind him.

A huddled figure in a big chair raised itself as the door
closed. Sainte-Anne's first impulse was to turn and go out
again, but Philippe de Frontillac had got to his feet, and
the action would have been a brutality.

III

A long sunbeam slid suddenly out from a cloud-massed
sky and every bird along the road awoke to song. As a
matter of fact, they had been singing quite as loudly be-

fore its advent, but Sainte-Anne had not noticed them. Now, just where the road from Mortagne to Châtillon approached the wood, narrowing itself to enter the aisles like a stream through a gorge, he reined up his tired horse and took off his hat. The early morning breeze stole from the greenness towards him, and a thousand twitterings blew out on it.

"How the birds sing!" exclaimed the rider to himself and half to the faithful Jean-Baptiste behind.

Jean-Baptiste grunted. To him, after a night's ride, bed would have been more acceptable than birds, but he did not say so, and in a moment Sainte-Anne replaced his hat, and moved at walking pace into the wood.

It was just four days and a half since he had emerged from his trying interview with Philippe to realise, with a pang of utter weariness and dismay, that another, scarcely less exacting, lay immediately before him, for there remained the Chevalier de Mondyon to deal with. . . . That was over now, and the boy, sworn to silence, was nursing a sore heart as well as an injured head at Châtillon, whither the army had retired from Parthenay. Over, too, were the four long days of his comrades' coldness, the puzzled, disillusioned half-aversion of his own men, the unveiled hostility of the rest; and the moment, at the time so much more bitter than he could have imagined, when he learnt that the council of war was called to debate a fresh attack on Fontenay and that he had been carefully left out. Half an hour afterwards he had gone to Cathelineau and asked if he could not give him something to do, and the "saint of Anjou," looking at him with eyes that understood everything, had sent him to Mortagne in place of the messenger he was on the point of despatching thither.

Peace was in the wood, and Sainte-Anne, as he rode slowly between the trees in their new attire, felt ashamed of his sore heart. He would have liked to be unconscious of his sacrifice. It was so natural a thing; it was so easy; the price so small—but there was a price. "Little enough to offer you, my dear," he said to himself, putting his hand to her miniature. "And he still does not know why I did it, poor boy! It is still a secret between you and me. . . ."

In a little while the forest road suddenly split into two, and he became aware that he was not certain which path to follow. He pulled up and called to Jean-Baptiste.

"If Monsieur does not know, I do not," said his retainer resignedly. "It looked so different yesterday. But here are some people coming."

Three or four armed peasants were indeed running down one of the paths towards them. Their haste a little surprised Sainte-Anne, and still more the absolute suddenness with which two more appeared, either from the earth or the undergrowth, at each side of his horse's head.

"This is the way to Châtillon," said one of them. "You are M. de Sainte-Anne?"

Sainte-Anne assented, and the man immediately took hold of his horse's bridle, while his companion performed the same office for Jean-Baptiste. The riders, thus accompanied, moved forward, the little group on the path waiting for them.

"Thank you, my friends," said Sainte-Anne as they came up with the rest. "I am greatly obliged to you."

But the hand did not drop from his bridle; on the contrary, the whole party closed round him. Their attitude was unmistakably hostile, and for the first time Sainte-

Anne, looking down on them in wonder, saw the faces around him alight with something sinister and glad.

"What do you want?" he exclaimed, and involuntarily his hand went towards his holster. But before it could get there it was seized in a grip of steel, and he saw that on the other side he was covered by the muzzle of an old musket.

"We want *you!*" grated the voice of the man who had possession of his wrist, his fingers closing tighter.

Amazement took from Sainte-Anne for the moment even the instinct that makes a man fling off at once, if he can, an alien hold. The men were obviously Royalists, but of a type unfamiliar to him. He touched himself with his free hand on the breast where, like his assailants, he wore the emblem of the Sacred Heart.

"Do you take me for a Blue?" he demanded.

Instead of an answer came a sudden scream from Jean-Baptiste behind him. "For God's sake get away! They mean you harm! They. . . . Ah! Jésus-Maria!"

Startled into action by the abrupt way in which the voice was cut short, Sainte-Anne made a violent attempt to free his right wrist, turning his head at the same instant to see what was befalling his retainer. The peasant who held the levelled musket instantly dropped it from his shoulder and seized it by its long barrel. Sainte-Anne had a vision as he turned of Jean-Baptiste, with a scarf over his face, writhing in the grip of a man mounted on the croup behind him. He himself made a second fierce and unsuccessful struggle to free his wrist, was conscious of an acute pain in the side of his head, the sensation of his horse's mane against his lips and face, and nothing further.

114

The chevalier de Mondyon, half-dressed, with bandaged head, was sitting in a big chair by the window in Sainte-Anne's quarters at Châtillon trying to read when, without warning, the door was flung violently open, and a pale and panting man, in whom he did not at first recognise Jean-Baptiste, burst into the room.

"Where is M. de Lescure?—take me to M. de Lescure!" he gasped. "There is not a moment to lose—they are murdering him!"

"Him! Whom?" cried the boy, amazed and jumping up. "M. de Lescure?"

"M. de Sainte-Anne!" cried Jean-Baptiste. "For God's sake come quickly, or tell me where to find someone who will stop it!"

The chevalier de Mondyon did not wait to be asked twice. Forgetful of his injury he snatched up a coat and hurried down the stairs. As they ran up the street Jean-Baptiste told in gasps his broken tale.

"They caught us in the wood—Charette's men—it is all about that cursed cannon . . . they asked M. de Sainte-Anne if he really gave orders . . . not to rescue it. . . ."

The boy uttered an unintelligible sound.

"And when he said that he did——"

"Oh, my God!" cried his companion sharply.

"—They said that they should shoot him . . . I got away . . . they had not done it then. . . . Is this the house, Monsieur le Chevalier?"

The little group about the door parted as the hurrying figures dashed through them, and responded to the boy's cry of "Where is M. de Lescure?" by pointing the way, and adding that he was engaged.

Engaged he was, and with a young man at sight of

whose features, as both he and the Marquis turned round in surprise, the little aide-de-camp's own face changed from pale to livid.

"It is you that have killed him, you cursed coward!" he cried, stamping his foot in an ecstasy of grief and rage.

"Monsieur de Mondyon, what is this?" asked his commanding officer sharply. "By what right do you break in——"

"Because the peasants are murdering M. de Sainte-Anne!" cried the boy, choking. "He has taken *his* sin on himself. . . . Oh, for God's sake make haste, Monsieur le Marquis! Here is his servant will tell you about it. He says they are M. de Charette's men—though he is miles away at Légé."

Jean-Baptiste told. Almost before his brief and breathless recital was ended Lescure was at the door, issuing rapid orders.

"My horse, and twenty men to follow as soon as possible. . . . Yes, you can come, mon enfant, if you wish it. . . . Is that you, Henri? Did you hear?"

"I did," answered La Rochejaquelein briefly. "I shall come, too. My horse is at the door. You know the spot?"

As they galloped out of Châtillon he said to his cousin: "Did you never guess the truth?"

Lescure shook his head. "But I know it now. Frontillac had just been telling me."

"Ah," said the young man bitterly, "if only he had told you a little sooner!"

They had unfastened Sainte-Anne's hands, and putting into them a rosary had led him apart to the oak at the end of the clearing. A little mechanically he knelt down in the young fern. For a moment or two he could not fix his thoughts; they were nothing but a welter of kaleidoscopic impressions—the faces round the council table, the terrace wall at home, the church at Mortagne where, by God's special mercy, he had gone to confession that morning, scenes from the carnage before Fontenay, a dead lamb he had passed in the road—and the fatal gun itself, as he had once seen it after a victory, its gilded ornaments and armorial bearings half hidden under wreaths of spring flowers. . . . Then the pictures vanished, and he was able to taste the savour of what he was doing.

Alone at the mercy of this detached band of the fierce and fanatical men of Western Vendée, the Maraîchins, who followed, not always too submissively, other and less scrupulous leaders, he had not been long in realising that what he had done, four days ago, for Adélaïde's son, for Adélaïde's sake, was only the prelude to something sharper. When he had seen the temper of his captors, the intense conviction with which they had invited him to swear on the crucifix that he was innocent of the loss of Marie-Jeanne and of the blood shed for her, and their readiness to believe him—so sure were they of tracking down the real culprit—his hesitation had been only momentary. He had a vision of Philippe de Frontillac ambushed in those relentless hands, of Philippe, who must not die like that because he was Adélaïde's gift to the world—and because, four days ago, he had somehow made himself responsible for him. He could not meet her in Paradise and say: "I let your only son die when I might easily have saved him." So he had refused to swear, had finally averred that he did give the order to abandon the guns, and had heard without much emotion the Maraîchin leader's solemn: "Then may God have mercy on your soul!"

And to this, then, his long devotion had led him—to disgrace and a violent death at the hands of his own party. Yet the worst, the disgrace, was already over, for to a man of Sainte-Anne's temper death was a little thing; so small a matter that at the end he prayed to be pardoned if, because his desire was so strongly set towards the other life, he were doing wrong in compassing it by a lie, even to save another. . . . Last of all he took out the miniature and kissed it. It had never left him for twenty-five years, but now he could part from it without regret. One needs no pictures in presence of the original.

He got up from his knees and crossed himself. "I am ready," he said quietly; and the muskets came up one after the other to the level. And to himself he added, lest he should be too well understood: "God pardon you, as I do."

The sound of the volley smote ominously on the ears of the three straining riders, still more than half a mile away. And swiftly as they rode, more swiftly still did the men of the Marais slip away into the heart of the wood, having finished their business.

At first the two cousins thought that Sainte-Anne, though past help, was still breathing, and La Rochejaquelein lifted him gently in his arms while Lescure began the commendatory prayer. But in the middle the little aide-de-camp broke through his sobs into speech. "It is no use, Monsieur le Marquis; he is gone. He was gone before we came. . . ." And as La Rochejaquelein silently and sadly laid Sainte-Anne's head back in the broken fern, the boy seized the hand which still grasped the rosary and covered it with passionate kisses.

None of them observed that they had been followed, and that Philippe de Frontillac, one arm across his face, was leaning with his back to them against the oak tree. A sudden click made La Rochejaquelein look up. In an instant he was on his feet and had seized the young man's wrist.

"Good God!" he exclaimed; "will you make his sacrifice useless? Give it up, I say!"

A brief struggle, and Philippe relinquished the cocked pistol, and then, looking neither at him nor Lescure, and heedless of the little figure crouched by its side, he went towards the body of the man who had died for him. A moment he gazed at the calm face, saw on the riddled breast what the balls had left of a woman's miniature, unrecognisable now by him or any other, and stretching out his hands, said, in a rent voice of awe and entreaty:

"Why did you do it? You knew I was not worth it. . . ."

THE ARISTOCRAT

THE ARISTOCRAT

I

WHEN first Anastase saw it dart swiftly across the grass he thought that it was a white rabbit.

Not indeed that Anastase knew much about rabbits in their natural state. He was a Parisian born and bred, and had not often strayed so far out of the city as on this autumn day of 1789, when he stood peering furtively into the little garden at Neuilly.

Anastase possessed a fine Christian name, but little else. Good looks were certainly not his. He was at that age when the traces of a young and bristly beard may, if their owner please, adorn his chin, and Anastase did so please. His vague mouth was easily moved to a grin, though a spark of ferocity shone sometimes in his stupid little eyes. He wore a soiled red cap, a dirty blouse, a forlorn pair of striped trousers, and sabots which did not match. Turning a piece of grass in his mouth, he shifted from one leg to the other as he watched for the re-appearance of the white rabbit from the clump of verbena and wondered whether he could possibly induce it to come within striking distance of him. For Anastase had a very healthy appetite, and the prospect of a meal appeared remote.

Yet Anastase had a home, and he had a bread-winning mother, whose vocation was that of a fish-wife at the Halles, and who gave him more to eat than she reserved for herself, and cuffed him, for all his nascent beard, when there was nothing for either. This at least kept him warm, and lately he had been more often warmed than fed. But yesterday had his mother sworn violently at him, dealt him several blows with a mop-handle, and finally, embracing him, said that better times were coming. She then gave him her share of the meal that she was preparing, which Anastase took and consumed because he dared not do otherwise. Nor indeed did it enter his head to protest. This insensibility was the effect of living under a despotism.

Anastase's presence at Neuilly was also a result of the same system of government; it had transpired upon enquiry that his vigorous parent, in common with some thousand of her sisters, contemplated a personal interview with her sovereigns at Versailles.

"What! ask the Austrian for bread?" Anastase had said contemptuously.

His mother fixed him with a fierce eye. Like many of her class she was, or had been, a royalist at heart. "Never let me hear you use that name again!" she screamed, aiming at him a blow which he was lucky enough to dodge. "You shall not see her then, *misérable!*"

And she kept her word. When the yelling horde of starving women started for Versailles on the morning of October the fifth, Anastase was not among the rabble which accompanied them. To see the pikes and not to be allowed to carry one—to hear the *Ca ira* and not to be permitted to swell it—was ever parental authority stretched so far, to receive so incredible an obedience? Mère Frochot was possibly the best obeyed individual in all France that day.

"Mayn't I go out at all, then?" asked Anastase, almost whimpering.

"Yes," said the tyrant, "you may. You may go anywhere you like, except the way we go. But if you set so much as a toe on the Sèvres road—well, you'll not want to set one anywhere else for a long time! Be sure I shall know of it."

And the great gaunt woman strode away to the Place de la Grève. For all her championship of royalty, she had a rusty sabre at her hip.

Anastase sulked for two hours. Then he lounged about by the quays. Everyone who was not a part of it was talking of the march to Versailles. This annoyed him. Finally he thought that he, too, would go out of Paris, and shortly found himself, with no design at all, looking enviously at this green garden in Neuilly.

And as he looked, and speculated upon the rabbit tribe, and the fortunes of the rich, he heard a voice proceeding from the direction of the house. "Hermine! Hermine!" it called. *"Viens, ma petite! Viens, Hermine! viens pour ton déjeuner!"*

And at this sound the white animal emerged from the tuft of verbena and began to trot with moderate haste towards the house. It was then that Anastase saw his mistake, for the so-called rabbit had a long bushy tail, which at that moment it was carrying stiffly erect, after the fashion of a banner. It was a beautiful white cat.

To Anastase the idea of mistaking a cat for a rabbit appeared, for some reason, supremely ludicrous. Forgetting that he was trespassing, he gave vent to a loud laugh. This caused the piece of grass to fall out of his mouth, and when he straightened himself after picking it up, he dropped it again from surprise. Where she had come from was a mystery, but there, a few paces away from him, stood a very young girl in a white dress. She had the cat in her arms. Anastase had never seen any-

one so fair, so white, so beautiful. She looked at him
with dilated eyes.

"What are you doing here?" she asked, quite gently,
but with the faintest air of command.

"*Dame!*" said Anastase sulkily. "How you frightened
me! I am doing no harm."

The child—she looked about fourteen—glanced at his
lanky ragged figure, and up at his unprepossessing
features.

"Would you please to go, then?"

But Anastase seemed unable to take his eyes off her.
He shifted from one foot to the other, and a vague smile
came over his face. The cat's mistress looked more
puzzled than alarmed. She scanned him again, very
seriously, and added: "Unless there is anything that you
want?"

And at that a strange daring came over Anastase.
Usually he shared the profound hatred and somewhat
nervous contempt with which his neighbours regarded
an aristocrat, but in face of this aristocrat—for of course
she was one—he found his theories sit unaccountably
loose. Perhaps it was because she was so small.

"I should like—to touch your cat, Mamzelle. I—I have
never seen one like her before."

For one instant the little lady hesitated, clasping her
treasure closer. Then she came a trifle nearer.

"You may stroke her," she said graciously.

And Anastase's large dirty hand rested for a second on
the white fur. He drew it gently along, smiling his wide
and rather inane smile. But Hermine did not smile. On
the contrary, her tail began to sway ominously under her
mistress's arm. Never had so bourgeois a touch pro-
faned her coat. And as Anastase, almost in an ecstasy,

prepared to pass his hand a second time along that expanse of snow, Hermine struggled, and turning, buried her pearly little teeth, sharp as needles, in the objectionable member. As her unfortunate admirer hastily withdrew it she leapt from the encircling arms and fled swiftly into a bush.

The child gave a cry of horror. Perhaps she expected some retaliatory measures on the part of the victim. But the youth was looking at his bleeding thumb with an air of pleased curiosity.

"*Tiens!* what small teeth!" was his remark.

"It is bleeding! Oh, I am so sorry. Never, never has she done such a thing!"

Anastase sucked his hand. "I thought it was a rabbit," he murmured rather inconsequently.

"If Monsieur will allow me to tie it up," said the child, with the phrase and the tone she would have used to one of her own rank; to such a height had Anastase's misfortune exalted him.

But the hero was too shy for this privilege. The sight of the proffered scrap of cambric alarmed him, and he thrust his hand deep into his trouser pocket.

"It's nothing, Mamzelle. I was bitten by a dog once," he said proudly. "Look, your cat is coming out!"

The outraged mistress turned round. Underneath the lowest laurel leaves a pair of brilliant eyes watched her.

"Ah, little serpent!" she cried, stooping. "Ah, graceless little viper! Come here that I may scold thee. Come here and beg Monsieur's pardon!"

But at this exordium Hermine retreated into the inner fastnesses of the laurel and was no more seen.

"No déjeuner for thee, then," said her mistress, with determination. Anastase wished the meal might be

passed on to him, and as if the little lady had surprised
this desire on his face she said quickly and rather timidly:

"Would you like something, too—some refreshment?"

Anastase unhesitatingly admitted that he would. But
when the girl told him to follow her to the house he
hung back. This aristocrat and her marvellous cat might
be charming, but in her château was probably a dungeon
like those which the demolition of the Bastille had dis-
closed only this summer. It was much better for a good
patriot to remain without, and put some bread and meat
in his pocket to eat on the road. Suppressing his reasons,
Anastase intimated his preference for this course, and
while the white lady departed to comply he lay down
and tried fruitlessly to lure Hermine from the laurel
bush. It did not strike him how trustingly he was being
treated by her owner. By drawing his finger along the
dead leaves beneath the bush he succeeded in gaining
a scratch from a flashing white paw.

"She has scratched me!" he announced, with pride, as
Mademoiselle came back over the lawn. But his grin was
so purely the grin of delight that this time the vixen's
proprietress did not apologise. She watched Anastase
stuffing the bread and meat into his pocket.

"With this," said the latter, suddenly becoming talka-
tive, "and with what my mother brings back from
Versailles, we shall do, Mamzelle."

"Versailles!" repeated the child in surprise; "why is
your mother at Versailles?"

"She has gone to see the King and the Aus——the
Queen," responded Anastase importantly.

Mademoiselle looked still more puzzled. "Your
mother—is she then——"

"My mother belongs to the Halles, Mamzelle. She

has gone to ask the King for bread. I saw them go—
thousands of them, and men, too. Oh! the fine sight!"

Mademoiselle had turned very pale.

"Thousands of them!" she repeated. "Then there will
be fighting——"

"Fighting?" said Anastase, who had begun to move
off. "Why should there be fighting? My mother loves
the King and Queen."

"It means some disaster!" said the child, wringing her
hands. "Please go! please go! I must send to see. There
will be fighting with the *gardes du corps*. Oh, Victor,
Victor!"

"My mother loves the King and Queen," reiterated
Anastase, repeating the fact lately impressed on him. "She
will protect the *gardes du corps*. Good-bye, Mamzelle."

But the promise of this protection, which seemed to
Anastase so potent, could not have carried much conviction to the heart of his benefactress, for as he slouched
out of the gate he turned, and saw that she had sunk
down on the damp grass by the laurel bush with her
hands before her face. He was sorry for the distress of
this aristocrat, though he did not grasp its cause, and he
stood a moment meditating. Just then the white cat
emerged from the laurel in pursuit of a dead leaf.
Anastase watched her gambols for a minute longer with
an admiring smile, and then, considerably cheered, set
forth on the road back to Paris, munching as he went.

II

Outside the guard-house at the Montmartre barrier
on a warm night of June a group of persons of more or

less unprepossessing appearance were lounging and talking. It was not exactly their business, since the municipal
guard was there for the purpose, but it was a congenial
employment, this stopping of all out-going travellers and
demanding their passports. In this task a good patriot
might both show his zeal and enjoy some fun, for the
last traveller had been a *ci-devant* attempting to escape
with a forged pass. That was more than an hour ago,
and he was now safely on his way back under arrest,
having played his last stake, and lost.

Little but flight, indeed, remained to the royalists by
the middle of the year of grace 1792, and it was quite
worth while to spend an hour or so at the barrier and
see them trying to get through. Sometimes, too, there
were pickings to be had; this last *aristo*, for instance, had
been relieved, when he was stopped, of several small
objects worth possessing. One of these now shone, beneath the light from the *réverbère,* in the hands of a
youth who could scarcely believe his good luck, for it
was a gold snuff-box, heavily chased, with some glittering stone set in the lid. It seemed to the present owner
so dazzling a fortune that he forgot, as he looked at it,
how he had laughed when it was taken from its past
possessor, and how the *ci-devant,* with his white face,
had laughed, too. A little later an informal drawing of
lots, consequent upon a quarrel, had bestowed the spoil
on Anastase Frochot.

It was very welcome, for the two years and eight
months which had passed over Anastase's untidy head
since he watched a white cat at Neuilly had not im-
proved his fortunes. True, he was bigger and stronger,
he could and did carry a pike on occasions with the best,
and he had now no mother to cuff him. But somehow

he missed her blows, and the scanty savings which she had left him had long ago come to an end. He sometimes got odd jobs to do in the Cité, but he was often hungry, and a disposition never very industrious had found still less invitation to industry in times so compact of riot and robbery. So at this moment Anastase, standing apart from his comrades, turned over the little box and wondered how much it would fetch. The occupation showed his face a good deal less vacant and something more brutalised than of yore. His old wide smile had in it now a twist of ferocity and cunning.

"To think that they carry things like this in their pockets!" he was reflecting. *"Sacrébleu!* I wish heaven would send us another."

As if in answer to his prayer the noise of wheels was heard approaching in the soft night. The whole place was on the alert in an instant; the guard turned out, the loungers started forward from the wall. "Another fly come to the web, brothers," shouted a jocular spirit. "Let us see if it be a fat one."

The carriage approached at a steady trot. Anastase thrust his treasure into his pocket.

"Halte!" The command was echoed by half a score of voluntary assistants and they sprang to the horses' heads. But the driver pulled up readily enough.

"Descend, citizens, and show your passports."

The loafers crowded round as the soldiers opened the door of the berline, and there emerged, first, a handsome young man in a long redingote, and then a young girl in a cloak, whom he assisted to alight. She was not veiled, and as the light struck on her pale, frightened little face, Anastase recognised his demoiselle of the white cat.

He had never seen her since that day. Once or twice he had thought of her, but more than once of the wonderful kitten which he had taken for a rabbit, comparing, not to their advantage, the starved tabbies of the Cité with that phenomenon. Directly he saw the lady of Neuilly he knew, of course, that she and her companion were aristocrats escaping. He followed them in.

The young man was showing his passport to the official designated for the purpose.

"The citizen Mosset," read the latter aloud, sitting at his high desk, "*aged* 26; *height,* hum, hum; *occupation,* bookseller; *destination,* Rouen." He broke off and looked at the traveller, who sustained the scrutiny firmly. "The *citoyenne* Mosset, wife of the above, *aged* seventeen; *height*—— your wife is very young, citizen."

"We have only been married a week," responded the young man. He was pale, but perfectly calm, while the girl was trembling visibly, and seemed to be looking furtively, among the rough and scowling faces, for someone who was not there.

"*Corbleu!* it is a honeymoon, then!"

"If the citizen likes to put it so," said the young man, with the glimmer of a smile. "In reality it is a less pleasant journey which we take—that of business. We are hoping to set up a bookshop in Rouen."

"*Tiens!* but he is a good liar, that one!" thought Anastase. "Mademoiselle is fortunate!"

"And your stock-in-trade, where is that, then?" asked the official, with an air of cleverness. "I see no signs of it."

The fugitive aristocrat smiled again, as one who smiles at an ignorant question. "We are going to treat for a business," he explained. "Surely the citizen would not

have us encumber ourselves with a library before we
have a roof to put it under."

"Oh, in that case!" said the commissary satisfied.
"Good luck to you, then, Citizen Mosset. Here is your
passport; it is quite in order." The young man took it
with a steady hand, and began to replace it in his pocket-
book, not noticing the attention with which the loiterer
nearest to her was regarding his companion.

"What has the *citoyenne* got under her cloak?"

The girl shrank back as the owner of the rough voice
seemed about to pull aside her mantle, and the young
man swung round, his eyes on fire. But he had mastered
himself in an instant.

"Show them, *mon amie*," he said gently, and as she
seemed reluctant, or too terrified, to obey, he lifted her
cloak a little way himself. Anastase gazed open-mouthed,
for in Mademoiselle's arms, more beautiful than ever,
was her white cat, half asleep. Stifled cries of admiration
went round the room, and the young man with a smile
dropped the corner of the cloak and offered his arm to
his wife.

"Stop a moment!" cried the same voice. Its owner
advanced to the throne of authority. "Citizen commissary, that fine beast is no bookseller's cat. It is such a
cat as would belong to these *sacrés aristos*."

"That is true," said the commissary reflectively, and he
got down from his stool. "Let me see the animal again."
And again Hermine's repose was disturbed.

The commissary's brow grew dark as he gazed upon
her. And Hermine, thoroughly annoyed, uttered a little
moan of vexation, and, fixing him with her sea-green
eyes, began to swish her tail. She did not in the least
realise that two lives were hanging upon it while she

thus drew attention to its size.

"It is true," repeated the commissary. "None but *ci-devants* could have a cat with such a tail, with such fur, and of such a colour. Your passport again, if you please, Citizen Mosset."

But ere the sinister turn of affairs produced by Hermine's presence became any darker the door opened. A very tall man in the uniform of the National Guards came in.

"Ah, bonsoir, citoyen," he said genially to the commissary. "Bonsoir, Mosset; bonsoir, ma cousine. Off to Rouen, I suppose?"

The little lady of Neuilly, with her cloak thrown back and Hermine tightly clasped in her arms, turned to him with a look of unspeakable relief. The commissary seemed staggered.

"Citizen," he said respectfully, for this was one whose patriotism could not for a moment be doubted, "the passport is correct, it is true, but since this cat——"

"What cat?"

"This cat which the *citoyenne* does not deny to be hers, and which could belong to no one but a *ci-devant*——"

The newcomer interrupted with a laugh. "And which does still belong to one, I'll wager," he said. "Come, has my cousin been so untruthful as to pretend that it is hers? You must know that she has a passion for stray cats, and this one, I suppose, has taken her fancy. But all the cats in the world can't make my pretty little cousin other than a good patriot."

"What my wife's cousin says is perfectly true," put in the young man. "I was going to explain, had you given me time. My wife found this fine cat about a week ago

134

wandering about, and took it in. Pray permit her to take it with her, for she is becoming much attached to it."

"Everything with you happened a week ago," returned the commissary gruffly and suspiciously. "You were married a week ago, you found the cat a week ago, and I should like to know whether a week ago you had not quite a different name, and that with a title in front of it?"

Applause of a savage nature greeted this thrust. Three people there knew how near it went home, and Anastase guessed, for it was suddenly revealed to him that this must be the unknown "Victor" for whose safety Mademoiselle had been so anxious on a certain October day. The National Guard frowned.

"Since I tell you that the *citoyenne* is my cousin," he said, with dignity, "and that I have known this young man, whom she has just married, for several years, I think there can be no question of titles, citizen commissary. You will be taking me for a duke in disguise next. We waste time in trifles. You yourself say that the passport is in order. *Eh bien!* if you still need to be convinced, I am sure that my cousin will readily give up this aristocratic cat to prove her *civisme.*"

He bent over the girl smiling, but his eyes were very anxious. And the eyes of the little bride—for such she really was—swam in imploring tears.

"I *couldn't!*" she breathed desperately.

"Mademoiselle—Madame—you *must!* Every minute that you stay here——"

"I had rather die than part with Hermine!"

"*Soit!*" said her former servant, in a voice audible to her alone. "But will you set M. le Comte's life, too, against a cat's?"

She gave no answer to the question, but she glanced in agony round the circle of hostile faces. Already they were closing in on them—already a hand was laid on her husband's shoulder, and he was looking at her sombrely. She saw that they were all waiting for her, and she knew suddenly that she had more need of courage than ever she would have in her life again—no, not if she were to go to the scaffold.

"Certainly, the cat is not mine," she said in a clear little voice with scarcely a tremble in it. "My cousin is right. I ought not to keep her. I—I will leave her here. To whom shall I give her?" All the faces swam before her, so that she could not distinguish one to whom she would be less unwilling to commit Hermine than to the rest.

"Give her to me," said a hurried voice in her ear. "I remember you at Neuilly—no, devil take me if I say a word of it; but your cat bit me—I'd like to have her—I don't mind if she does bite—give her quickly, and go!"

She turned, looked Anastase in the face for an instant —perhaps recognised him, and then thrust Hermine convulsively into his arms.

Five minutes later the berline was rattling along outside the barrier, and she was sobbing her heart out on her husband's breast. And the tall National Guard, standing looking after them, wiped his forehead and muttered:

"It was well I came as I promised. *Je m'en doutais. Ce damné chat!* I knew he would make trouble!"

Which was polite neither to Hermine's sex nor to her character in general.

III

And thus began Anastase's life with Mademoiselle Hermine.

To be quite truthful, it did not begin over-well. When Hermine's new owner slipped out from the guard-room he learnt for the first time the extraordinary strength which resides in a cat's lithe little body. Hermine neither bit nor scratched; she kicked. Twice Anastase nearly let her go. At last he put her under his blouse, on which she ceased to struggle so violently and merely uttered little moans similar to those which the commissary's inspection had drawn from her. Never having heard a cat moan in this way before—and indeed it is not usual—Anastase was afraid that he was stifling or choking her. Had he but known, it was moral rather than physical agitation which induced the plaint, and when he loosened his grasp a little the outraged one continued to proffer it no less loudly.

But as he hurried along the walls, too, died away, and Hermine had recourse to a last protest, stiffening herself into a sort of cataleptic rigidity, and thereby filling her bearer with misgivings which he dared not allay by stopping to examine her condition. It was therefore with a thankful heart that, standing at last in the darkness of his dirty little room *au troisième,* he felt his captive leap vigorously from his opened arms. As the light thud was audible on the bare boards he searched hastily for the tinder-box.

Yes, she was superb. Partially obscured from view by the broken rungs of his only chair, whereunder she had retreated, her spotless coat on end with indignation,

Hermine surveyed her ravisher with orbs alight with a fire surpassing anything that ever filled the angriest human eye. The pride and joy in Anastase's heart was crossed with an insidious dismay. Would she always look at him like that? He set down the candle and approached her, calling her name in tones as gentle as his natural roughness of voice would allow. In a flash she was up on the high window-sill, her uplifted tail, which seemed to have grown almost as large as her body, showing against the dirty glass and the gloom of the summer night. Anastase made one step towards her, but only one. It was evident that a less highly born cat would have spat at him; Hermine's visage had all the expression of the act without its sound, and the citizen Frochot came no nearer. He was daunted by her undisguised hostility, and at last, a new idea having occurred to him, he crept out of the room to procure some milk.

When he came back Hermine was still on the window-sill, but her tail was folded majestically round her feet. She now looked more scornful than furious, and emanated a chilling atmosphere of unapproachableness. Anastase set the saucer of milk at a respectful distance and prepared to retire for the night. His toilet being of the simplest, the unfortunate youth lay long on his pile of sacking, the candle burning at his side, ere Mademoiselle Hermine descended from her perch, and walked in a queenly fashion to the broken saucer. The watcher raised himself on to his elbow, full of excitement. Hermine leisurely paced round the receptacle, contemplated the pattern, sniffed at the contents, and was then good enough to put her little nose down to the liquid. Anastase held his breath. The next instant, with a violent shake of her head, she retreated hastily from the saucer, and very markedly sat down with her back to it. The dismayed Anastase fell back upon his couch, racking his brains for the reason of her disgust. The milk, for which he had bartered one of his last *sous* on the next floor, had seemed to him very good; he would have been only too glad of it himself. He could not know that the best milk in the world was insupportable to Hermine unless it were warmed to a certain temperature.

The change of surroundings, which so tries the heart of any cat, was rendered triply offensive to Hermine by the immense descent in comfort and cleanliness—even in the quantity of furniture suitable for repose. Anastase's person clearly bred in her, as at their first meeting, a distaste amounting to horror. Not only did she consider him *canaille,* but she feared him. He could not come within a couple of yards of her but she fled, suspicious as a creature of the woods, forgetting that all her life man had been her humble slave, and reverting to the primitive instincts of her race. For two days she ate nothing—and Anastase very little. He was profoundly dejected.

On the third day, however, Hermine recovered from her phase of fright and primitive instincts, and began slowly to reassume that air grande dame which was peculiarly hers. Her breeding reasserted itself, and, looking now on Anastase as harmless, though excessively objectionable, she condescended to receive from his trembling hand a portion of fish, procured by the sale of the *ci-devant's* snuff-box. There is no doubt that hunger was the real source of this complaisance, but Hermine was at once too clever and too well-bred to let this be seen. She partook of the offering daintily, as one

to whom all food is but a vile necessity. For appearance's
sake, probably, she left the tail end. It was not quite so
fresh as the rest. The elated Anastase ate it himself at
the close of the day.

He did right to be uplifted. Hermine had set a paw
on the path of resignation and tolerance, from which
she never withdrew it. As day followed day she realised
that she was dependent upon this gutter-boy for the food
which, though neither its preparation nor its presenta-
tion was to her taste, was fairly wholesome and abundant.
She may even have been touched, in her rather adaman-
tine little heart, by his really pathetic attempts to pro-
pitiate and to please her. It was little indeed that he
could do; he could not possibly provide the silken
cushions on which she was accustomed to slumber, nor
the Sèvres from which she always ate and drank, nor
the pretty garden where she used to play. The loss of
this latter was perhaps Hermine's most serious depriva-
tion, and the leads outside Anastase's little window
afforded but a sorry compensation. When the youth had
recovered from the twofold horror which seized him the
first time that she had sprung out there—fear lest she
should miss her footing and fear lest she should stray to
another house, both groundless terrors, either action
being impossible—he left the window always open, and
Hermine developed quite a fancy for the gutter, sitting
there in the sun for hours together, meditating or washing herself. She washed at least five hours a day.

It was partly these thorough-going ablutions which
first suggested to Anastase the idea that his room was
not, perhaps, quite clean. It was a thought of staggering
novelty. Waking once in the dark hours of the morning,
he heard, almost with awe, the sound of Hermine's

passionate washing. She lay near him on a chair, and he could not see her, but the rasp of her little tongue over her soft person, and the jiggle of the chair-legs on the uneven floor filled the silent room with the testimony of an almost morbid cleanliness and Anastase with questioning. Why did she wash so much, *la petite aristocrate?* Other animals did not, and certainly not human beings—not, at least, those of his acquaintance. Could it—could it be that she was soiled by living in his room?

Next morning, much disturbed, he looked at Hermine with a gloomy eye. She had been with him a fortnight. Perhaps she was not quite as resplendent as when she came. And the floor? He went downstairs and borrowed a broom, a scrubbing-brush and a pail.

Now of all cats that have ever lived Mademoiselle Hermine was the least endowed with what is known as a mission in life. Few of her race, indeed, are weighted with so inæsthetic a burden. But the fact remains that this aristocratic and self-willed little lady, who was born to be a moment's ornament, who had no morals, no desire for self-improvement, and certainly not a vestige of altruism, took her place as a force making for righteousness in the career of Anastase Frochot. It was not only that the room became cleaner. Anastase had never in his life been possessed of an object on which to lavish his somewhat uncouth affections. He had it now. The afternoon on which Hermine of her own free will first jumped on to his knee was a crisis in his moral history. His love for this white, soft creature, who would often come now when he called her, became thereafter a passion which dragged him home early from the seductive purlieus of the city lest she should be hungry, which kept him there if she was gracious, which even led him to the signal step of an attempt, for her sake, to get regular work.

The time sped on thus till the red Tenth of August. On the evening of that day Hermine, oblivious of the events which were taking place in the Place du Carrousel and elsewhere, was performing her toilet at the open window, when heavy footsteps and voices of an excessive loudness upon the stair caused her to withdraw hastily to the gutter outside. People very rarely came into her proprietor's apartment, but she knew that there were other human beings in the house, of a species recalling those most objectionable persons who had stared at her on the night when her mistress had been torn from her. Two of these, invisible but only too audible, paused now outside the door.

"*Corbleu!* what a day! Who lives here? le petit Frochot?" The handle was tried. "Frochot! Frochot! let us in!" And the owner of the voice began to batter thunderously upon the door.

"Stop that noise, Rameau, you fool!" said another voice. "Frochot is not home yet. I saw him when I left stripping a Swiss in the Cour Royale. *Dieu!* how well we have fought! Come and have a drink—I could drink the blood of tyrants." The voice uplifted itself; "*Qu'un sang impur abreuve nos sillons!*"——and broke off to greet another comer.

"*Hé*—le petit Frochot! *Nom d'un chien,* but you have done well for yourself, mon enfant! We thought you were back, but you have been paying Capet's lodgings a visit, *hein?*"

"I have been in the palace, yes," said the voice of the citizen Frochot. "*Sangdieu,* you should go to that shop if you want to furnish. Look here!"

"For my part," put in the first voice, "I don't want their fine clothes. Give me their cursed lives, that's all I ask. I like to feel the pike go through a satin coat."

Anastase laughed loudly. "I, too, Citizen Rameau. But it spoils it. Go to the devil, and let me in! I'm tired, I tell you."

The pair of voices protested that their owners would enter too, on which Anastase was heard to commit himself to perdition if they did. He seemed to be pushing them away, for the sounds receded, until at last, with a burst of laughter, came up the stairs the question, "Why does he keep his door so tightly locked?" and the reply, "He's got an *aristo* hiding there!"—a pleasantry obviously too absurd to be worth the trouble of a retort.

When it was comparatively quiet the door was unlocked and Anastase came in—a sinister, wild-eyed figure, transformed by the passion of slaughter and the lust of battle, with a long butcher's knife thrust into his belt, red stains on his rags, and a bandaged hand. He fastened the door and threw down upon the floor from over his shoulder a medley of objects; the uniform coat of a Swiss Guard, an empty scabbard swinging from a belt of white and gold, a figured coverlet of Chinese workmanship, all green and yellow dragons, several pieces of lace, and a portion of tapestry hacked off a chair. Then, disengaging from his pocket a couple of watches, a bonbonnière, and a little timepiece in Dresden china, he put them on the table and looked round for his cat.

"Hermine! Hermine!" he called in a thick voice. Hermine was frightened and made no sign, whereupon Anastase went round the room, uttering curses. "Have they got in after all? Little Hermine, where are you?"

At last he saw her outside the window, and leant out to her. But Hermine backed away from his strange voice and bandaged hand, conscious perhaps of the atmosphere surrounding him. Seeing that she was safe, Anastase did not persist in her capture, but went unsteadily to his pile of sacking and flung himself down upon it. In the court below a fire blazed and triumphant figures danced around it all night long.

Alas for the fleeting nature of both good and bad impressions! As Anastase had shown how skin-deep were the effects of contact with his *aristocrate,* so did Hermine forget or condone the temporary shock of his lapse, and remember the tenth of August only as the epoch of the return of a former luxury. For when the rest of the spoil from the Tuileries had been sold or pawned, the silken coverlet snatched from the bed of a princess still decorated the garret, and thereon Hermine complacently slumbered, while Anastase roamed the streets with the key of his room in his pocket. And neither of them knew that his conduct was beginning to attract attention in the house, thickly peopled as a rabbit warren, where an inmate might be as secure from curiosity as in a desert, but where a chance word might light a flame of suspicion very hard of extinction. That word, though purely in jest, had already been spoken, and it was remembered when Anastase continued to keep his meagre apartment inviolable, admitting no one even when he was there—being firmly persuaded that to see Hermine was to desire her, and knowing how slender was the barrier erected by his neighbours between desire and possession. That some person was already bitten with this longing he was convinced by seeing one evening, on opening his door suddenly, an undistinguishable form rise precipitately from a listening attitude on the threshold and scurry down the stairs.

It was the afternoon of the 25th of August. Paris was astir with the freshly-arrived news of the surrender of Longwy. Anastase, as he came homewards, was not sure what the tidings meant, nor was he quite prepared to believe the prognostication that the Prussians would be at the gates in a fortnight, as they were saying in the streets. In the dirty courtyard of his home they were saying it too, with alarm and asseverations, but when he tried to engage a fellow-lodger on the subject the man muttered something and turned away.

Voices came down to him, as he was half-way up the filthy, creaking staircase, and catching his own name he began to run up. The little landing on to which his door opened was occupied by a group of three people; two men, inmates of the house, stood there as a sort of bodyguard to Madame Clémenceau the concierge, who was looking through the keyhole. Fury seized Anastase, and he came up the remaining stairs with a bound.

"What are you doing, old witch?" he shouted, and, taking her by surprise, thrust her fat person away and got between her and the door. Shaking with rage the old woman tried to throw herself upon him, but one of the men held her back.

"Wait—wait till they come," he whispered loudly.

"Wait till who come?" demanded Anastase wrathfully. "And you, Gros Jean, what are you doing here? Be off, or I will throw you down the stairs!" As he advanced threateningly on the individual named both men retreated.

At that moment Madame Clémenceau, peering over the crazy balustrade, began shrieking: "Come up, citizens, come up! He is here!"

Anastase recoiled again to the door. That the excitement was in some way connected with Hermine he was sure, but in what manner her presence could account for the mob of people now tumbling up the staircase he had no idea. One thought only remained to him—no one should get in to see her. He waited, fierce and uneasy. The persons on the stairs were some of them fellow-lodgers; some he recognised as belonging to his section, and most of them were, like himself, the dregs of Paris. Greatly to his surprise three National Guards in full uniform pushed through the rest, and one of them, shouldering his way on to the landing, demanded with authority to be told why he was sent for and by whom.

"By me," said Madame Clémenceau, with unction. "I denounce the citizen Frochot here. Oh, that I ever took him under my roof! He has a cursed *ci-devant* concealed in his room!"

"You lie!" responded Anastase, with great promptness. "Do you think, you silly old beldam, that I am a friend of *aristos!*" He gave a snort of laughter.

"He has a female *aristo* concealed in his room," went on Madame Clémenceau in a higher key. "She has been there since the tenth. He lets no one in, and he takes food to her when he thinks nobody is looking. But I have watched him, and so have others. Moreover, we have listened at the door, and heard him speaking to her."

Anastase glanced about him and clenched his fists. Escape was impossible—but then he did not want to escape. Surely he could prevent the door from being opened!

"I swear it's all a lie!" he cried passionately. "You

146

know it, you, Lepaux, and you, Rameau." But there was no response.

"I swear to you by the nation that there is no one there, and never has been," continued Anastase in desperation. The sweat began to come out on his forehead, and it was only by an effort that he kept his hands off his accuser. "Is it likely there should be a damned *aristo* in my room —I who killed three Swiss on the tenth and helped to throw *ci-devants* out of the window of Capet's palace?"

"All very well," said the National Guard. "And doubtless the citizen is a good patriot, and the *citoyenne*, in her zeal, has made a mistake. Therefore open the door and let us see inside."

Anastase gave a snarl of rage. "No!" he screamed, with an oath. "You must take my word. My room is my own. There is no one there, I tell you."

"Liar—liar!" yelled Mère Clémenceau. "You know there is—and we will have her out!" A chorus from the landing and the stairs substantiated her.

The suppressed fury of this outburst and the fierce expectant faces turned up to him recalled to Anastase a sudden vision of something which he had witnessed a few days ago in the streets concerning a cat. They might do that to Hermine. No doubt he should have complied with the eminently reasonable request of authority, but then, too, he knew his world. At any rate, he lost his head, and by so doing gave ample colour to the charge against him.

The two nearest men, hurled backwards, brought down Mère Clémenceau in their fall. At once the tumult became indescribable. The first National Guard threw himself on the rebel; Anastase caught him neatly between the eyes. The uttermost rage and a kind of insensate joy possessed him. "I will not open!" he screamed. "Spawn of the devil, go to hell!" The space was so cramped that he really had a momentary advantage.

The whole stairway resounded with cries of: "Kill him! kill him! Break down the door! Bring her out!" The second National Guard, abandoning his musket, prepared to throw himself likewise on the defender of aristocrats, and seeing this, Anastase suddenly remembered his knife. Before either of them could do anything the man's comrade, better inspired, seized his weapon by the barrel and swung it high above his head. The knife glittered uselessly in its owner's hand, and the butt of the musket, breaking down the arm he raised too late, caught Anastase with fearful force on the left temple. He gave vent to an inarticulate cry, and went down like a slaughtered animal. Next moment the door fell inwards, and with cries of *"Mort à l'aristocrate!"* the assailants poured into the citadel.

The sole occupant of the room was a rather sleepy but alarmed white cat, standing with arched, protestant back upon a heap of green and gold embroidery in the middle of the table. But Anastase, with that blood upon his hands which had not availed to save his own, was gone, for the sake of a cat, into a world to which (as is commonly held) they are not admitted.

Half-way down the staircase Hermine, to whom the subjugated Mère Clémenceau was whispering endearments, began very self-containedly to purr.

THE ADMIRAL'S LITTLE LETTY

THE ADMIRAL'S LITTLE LETTY

I

THE June sun was shining dazzlingly on the chalk cliff, and scarcely less dazzlingly upon the flower-beds of the little house, already old in 1812, which crowned it. It poured likewise into the rustic summer-house near the cliff edge, pleased, no doubt, to encounter there two bright objects which it took the opportunity of making brighter still—the scarlet coat of a young officer in his Britannic Majesty's uniform, and the little drooping golden head of the girl who sat beside him on the bench, and whose hands he was holding in his own.

Although he had known the wearer of that high-waisted muslin gown since she was a child—not that the years were many which divided her from that estate —it was only yesterday that Captain Harry Gifford, of the Third Foot, acquired the right to sit in summer-houses with her. It was only yesterday, in this very place, that those still childish lips had murmured a tremulous "Yes" to the question which Rear-Admiral Sinclair Lovel—at present away assisting his country to rule the waves—had duly authorised Captain Gifford to put, but with a recommendation not to frighten "little Letty." "She is very shy, very easily alarmed, my boy." Yes, the Admiral's little Letty, whom Harry Gifford might now fairly count as his own, was all that—she always had been.

And now she was unhappy to boot, for, though Captain Gifford had yesterday, at Miss Caroline Lovel's invitation, removed with his effects from the "Dog and Duck," down in Rayham village—where he was staying on sick leave, the result of a French ball through his leg in March—to Cliff Cottage, where his Letty was paying her annual visit to her aunt, he had this very morning received a summons to his regimental depôt at Canterbury; and the summer-house on the cliff, which twenty-four hours ago had witnessed a proposal, was already the scene of a lovers' parting.

But that parting was not for long, as Harry Gifford kept on assuring his betrothed; he fully expected to be back by supper-time to-morrow, for this barbarous command could not possibly mean, as Laetitia feared, his instant return to his regiment in the Peninsula. That, he declared, was out of the question, with the wound in his leg still unhealed—"fortunately," he added, as a concession to his Laetitia's misgivings. It was indeed the first time that those recurrent splinters of bone had appeared to him in the light of a blessing.

"And you will find plenty to do while I am away, my Letty," he said consolingly; "though, indeed, these little hands of yours don't look as if they could do anything but pick flowers!" And he put a kiss on them.

Laetitia raised her deep, soft, infantine blue eyes. "But I can do a great many things," she protested. "I think that you should release my hands now, if you please, Captain Gifford."

"Surely, sweetheart," exclaimed the young man in dismay, "I am not to be Captain Gifford to you now that I am going to marry you, when I have always been Harry before?"

"I have heard Aunt Caroline say that a betrothed young lady cannot be too circumspect," observed

Laetitia, with a sudden adorable primness. And before Captain Gifford could reply Miss Caroline Lovel herself, all grey curls, grey silk and lace, appeared in the doorway of the summer-house.

"My dears," she said, a little out of breath, "Captain Gifford's chaise is at the gate."

Taking the stout stick which lay against the bench, the wounded hero got, with some difficulty, to his feet. And then, Miss Caroline having discreetly withdrawn, he perceived that this parting was not going to be without its compensations.

"Oh, Harry, Harry," whispered his timid Letty, clinging to him quite oblivious of her last remark, "come back soon—soon!"

Captain Gifford was gone, yet the sun still continued to shine on Rayham. It was, indeed, weather too fine, one would have thought, for Miss Lovel's gardener to retire to bed with lumbago, and for Jane, her servant, to continue, as she did, a prey to violent toothache. Least of all for dear old Jacob Takerson, the most venerable of the village fishermen, to begin suddenly to slip his cable altogether, as the Admiral would have said. Miss Lovel went to see him, and found him resigned and patriarchal. "A scandal to hint that he ever smuggled," she said on her return, with moist eyes. "I cannot think why dear Sinclair should always believe it."

Many of these bright, empty hours Laetitia passed mournfully in the summer-house, sacred to such wonderful memories, there counting off the very minutes until her lover's return. But supper-time and even bed-time on the second day brought no Harry; and then indeed Miss Caroline, usually the more apprehensive of the two, had to combat her niece's fears. No, she was sure that Captain Gifford was not at that moment embarking for Spain, nor did she think that he was lying at death's door in some wayside Kentish inn with a sudden aggravation of his nearly healed wound. But when, at last, sleep came to Laetitia that evening in her room over the porch, the pillow beneath her flushed cheek was as damp as though the roses and jasmine outside had nodded over it on a showery day.

II

Laetitia was roused from sleep by a recurrent, muffled noise, which it took her some time to identify; and when she did so it was with a jump of the heart. Someone was actually knocking on the front door in the porch beneath.

How extraordinary—and how alarming, for it must be quite late, past midnight! Muffled yet regular, the knocks continued. But of course it was Harry, who had returned, even at this unseasonable hour, because he knew that his continued absence would be causing her anxiety.

Yes, but who was to admit him now that he had come? Poor Jane, after her two previous sleepless nights with the toothache, had been sent to bed almost drugged with some legendary posset of Miss Lovel's. If she were asleep it would be inhumanity to wake her; and, if she were not, almost equally inhuman to drag her out of her bed in pain. Miss Caroline could not be expected to show herself to Captain Gifford in undress. It appeared then that, unseemly and unmaidenly though it might be, there was nothing for it but to admit Harry herself.

Laetitia slipped out of bed and, catching up a shawl, leant out among the jasmine which was so amazingly sweet in the night air. "Captain Gifford—Harry!" she called timidly. "I will come down and open the door." But her betrothed, ensconced in the porch below, could no more hear her than she could see him, and the knocking continued. Then the best was to put on some clothes as quickly as possible and go down—poor Harry, with his wounded leg, standing there so long! Letty drew back, lit a candle, and began to pull on her shoes and stockings, in the middle of which operation the knocking came to an end, and she heard Captain Gifford limp out of the porch and go away round the other side of the house.

"Harry, wait!" she cried in distress, tying the ribbon of her sandal round her ankle; but her voice did not carry from the middle of the room, and the halting steps died away in the night. How dreadful—suppose he should go away altogether!

With trembling fingers Laetitia huddled on her dress over her night-gown, stopped not to pin up the two long braids which lay on her shoulders, but seized the candle and crept speedily and rather guiltily down the stairs.

The door of Cliff Cottage opened straight on to the larger of its two parlours, a hall, in fact, which was used as a dining-room. By the time Laetitia reached it the knocking had begun again, and now it sounded less stealthy and more annoyed. Poor, poor Harry—in the circumstances there was hope that he would not be too much shocked at her opening the door in person. She put down the candle on the round mahogany dining table, and, running to the door, drew the bolts, of which she could only just reach the topmost. Nervously she then turned the key. "It is I, Harry; pray do not be surprised!"

It was she, on the contrary, who was surprised at the haste with which her lover entered, almost colliding with her as he limped past. Without apology he made for the nearest chair, and dropped into it as if he could stand no longer. He was not in uniform, as on departure, and was wrapped to the eyes in a cloak.

"At last!" he exclaimed. "I began to think that nobody would ever hear. However"—with an impatient movement he disentangled himself from the cloak—"let us lose no time about the boat. Is your master—your father—getting up, my good girl? If not, see that he does so at once."

Long before the end of this astonishing recommendation, Laetitia Lovel was backed against the table, her clasped hands pressed convulsively against her mouth to prevent herself from crying out, her frightened eyes fixed on the speaker like those of a rabbit on a snake. It wasn't Harry at all—nor anyone remotely resembling him! She had admitted into this unprotected house, at dead of night, a perfectly strange man, who was also, from the way he spoke, that horror's crown of horror, a foreigner!

"Meanwhile," went on the intruder, leaning forward with a frown, and passing both hands gingerly over his right knee, which had something tied round it, "meanwhile, get me something to eat quickly, and a drop of spirits. I have had the misfortune to——" But at this point Miss Lovel, putting her hands over her face, gave vent to an irrepressible sob of anguish, and the speaker looked up in surprise. "*Que diable!* What is the matter with the girl?"

There being no answer save a second sob, he suddenly leant forward and snatched up the bedroom candlestick, the only source of illumination, from its place on the table, and, holding it up, surveyed the little bowed head with its fair, braided hair. Then his glance went beyond her to the faintly gleaming gilt of the frame that surrounded the portrait of Admiral Sinclair Lovel, telescope, frigate, and all. At what could be seen of that mariner he gazed a second with fascinated horror, shot a hasty, bewildered glance round the rest of the room, and pulled himself to his feet. *"Mon Dieu, je me suis donc trompé de maison!"* he said under his breath. *"Imbécile que je suis!"*

At the sound of the French, Laetitia's worst fears were confirmed. A spy—or one of the vanguard of that long-threatened invasion which everyone (except Aunt Caroline) had given up fearing now . . . Dover, Canterbury, no doubt, in French hands . . . and with Canterbury, Harry too! No wonder he had not returned! She raised her terrified face.

"Oh, Sir, we are only women in this house—there are no men—spare us!"

"Spare you!" repeated the Frenchman (if he was one). "Spare *you!* The question is rather whether you will spare—— You say there is no man in the house?"

Oh, she ought never to have told him that; she ought to have pretended . . .

"Then you *can* help me," went on the stranger very quickly. "I see that I made a mistake to come here, but I thought that this was the house of Mr. Takerson—Takerson the fisherman. Tell me, then, how to get to him, and I will go at once."

Oh, joy! But Takerson, that dear old man—and what

could a French spy be wanting with him in any case?—
Takerson could receive no visitors to-night.

"You are unwilling to do even that much for me?"
asked the intruder sharply, seeing her hesitation.

"No—it is not—at least . . . I do not know who you
are, Sir; but Takerson is very ill—dying, they think.
You could not see him if you did go to his cottage."

She had disconcerted him in her turn. His face
changed. "Ill—dying!" he exclaimed. "You are not lying
to me, *hein?* Then I must find someone else—someone
with a sailing-boat. Have you no other *contrebandiers—*
what do you call them—yes, smugglers—here?"

He had come nearer, tall—taller than Harry himself—
menacing, even though he seemed to be supporting himself with a hand on the table. Why had she told him
that Takerson was ill; why did she not now direct him
to one of the other fishermen and be rid of him, which
was what, at this moment, she most desired on earth?
As to smuggling, what had this man to do with any
English smuggler? Something seemed to swell in
Laetitia's breast. Was she, her father's only child, to help
a French spy to get off with his information—for if he
was so anxious to be gone, he could not be one of a
horde of victorious invaders?

Trembling exceedingly, and gripping her hands
together to give herself courage, Laetitia said, "I—I cannot help you to get away. I am . . . an English girl,
and you are——"

She stopped. Would he strike her—perhaps strangle
her?

He did not seem to contemplate it. On the contrary,
he became less menacing, drawing back a trifle, and,
half-sitting, half-leaning on the table, he said quite

gently, "What do you think I am, Mademoiselle? I am only a poor devil of a prisoner of war from Portchester Castle who is trying to get back to France in time to see a dying mother. Will you be so cruel as to stop me now, at the last stage? See, I will show you that I am speaking the truth. Look at these." He put a hand inside his coat, pulled out a packet of worn letters, and spread them on the table, pointing with a long thin finger to the words of the superscription, repeated on one after the other: *"Prisonnier au château de Portchester, près Portsmouth, Angleterre."* Above this was some name which Laetitia, owing to the distance which she kept and the foreign handwriting, was unable to decipher, but she saw that it was prefaced by the word *"Capitaine."*

"You see, Mademoiselle," went on her visitor, looking at her with dark, melancholy eyes, as he replaced the packet in his breast. "And those letters are from my dear mother, whom I shall never see again if you do not help me a little. It was her illness which decided me to escape. But if you inform the authorities I shall be taken back to Portchester, and I shall not complain if you think that is your duty. . . . Only, perhaps you would have the charity to give me first a crust of bread and a drink, for I have had neither to-day. I will stay here quietly."

How could she go out in her night-gown at dead of night and "inform the authorities"? How could she do it even if she were fully dressed and knew whom to inform, while he sat there on the table, so helpless and gentle, with his mother dying, and said he would wait, and only asked for a crust? Laetitia stifled a small sob which was not, this time, born of alarm.

"I will get you something to eat—and then I must

think. Please sit down. I will light these candles."

She applied the bed-room candlestick in turn to the six wax-lights of the two candelabra which stood on the dining-table, and, without looking at her visitor again, but aware that he had obeyed her, and lowered himself into Miss Lovel's high-backed chair, pattered off to the larder in search of food. The acuteness of her dread had subsided, and she no longer felt personally afraid of the invader; but, on the other hand, the situation remained highly unconventional, and she had the warmest desire to get rid of him as soon as possible. Suppose Aunt Caroline were to wake and come down, or suppose Harry were to knock at the door—the real Harry? He would hardly come now, though, for it must be nearly one o'clock. Indeed, she almost wished he would, for then the burden of deciding what she ought to do would be taken from her.

She selected a half-eaten pie and a loaf, and clasping them to her small person, and quite forgetting the need of a plate, came stealthily back into the parlour. The room was now adequately lit, and at the table, in the glow of light, the escaped prisoner—oh, what had happened to him? He had fallen back in the corner of the chair, and with that white, upturned face and those closed eyes he looked like a dead man. Only, unlike a dead man's, his hands were gripping the ends of the arms of the chair.

"Oh, what is it?" came faintly from Miss Lovel's lips as she stood rooted by this sight. He was far more alarming thus than before.

In the ghastly pallor of his face the Frenchman's eyes, opening slowly, made two dark pools. "Have you some brandy?" he feebly asked. *"Je regrette infiniment . . ."*

Laetitia plumped the pie upon the table and scuttled across the room to the high glass-fronted cupboard where the Admiral's best port had been decanted for Harry. With trembling hands, the decanter clinking on the glass, she poured some out, and quakingly bore it over to the table.

"H—here is some wine, Sir. We have no brandy."

The fugitive put out an uncertain hand, several inches away from the glass which she was holding out, as though his sight played him false, and, afraid lest she should have actually to hold the wine to his lips, Laetitia nerved herself to capture the wavering hand and put the bowl of the wineglass between its cold, damp fingers. Her visitor drained the glass, sighed, and sank back in the chair again, the hand with the empty wineglass hanging slack at his side.

"He's going to drop it," thought the agonised Laetitia. "And oh, what can be the matter with him?"

But the Admiral's port was generous, and she had not been niggardly with it. Its recipient was already rousing himself again, passing a hand over his forehead. "A thousand thanks, Mademoiselle," he said, holding out the wineglass with an attempt at a smile. "I apologise if I alarmed you. It has passed now." But he was still very pale.

"You—you are——" faltered Laetitia.

"Oh, I am not ill. When I . . . left Portchester Castle I brought away with me a souvenir, a bullet in the knee, *voilà tout.* At times it pains me, and perhaps because I have walked so much, and have not eaten since yesterday morning——" He shrugged his shoulders.

"A bullet!" stammered Laetitia, the colour going out of her face too. "And nothing to eat since yesterday."

"But I see that you are going to remedy that," said her guest, casting a pregnant glance in the direction of the pie. "And as for the musket-ball, *n'en parlons plus.* No, never mind for a plate, Mademoiselle"—he was jerking rather than pulling his chair nearer to the table as he spoke—"for I shall not need one; and I have a knife in my pocket." He stretched out an arm and secured the dish, while Laetitia, nevertheless, went to the cupboard again. Oh, dear, if he were really going to eat nearly a whole pie, the process could not be very short; and here she still was with him in a toilette far from complete. In the end Aunt Caroline *must* hear a man's voice. He had already got out a clasp-knife, but when she laid a table-knife and fork before him, he exchanged it for those more usual implements, and began without more ado or apology. Yes, he must have been starving; yet, though he ate like a wolf, he ate like a gentlemanly wolf. Not that Miss Lovel stayed to catch more than a glimpse of the first onslaught, since, having got out the decanter and placed it at his elbow, for which, his mouth being full, he thanked her with a look, she immediately retreated to the hearth and stood there with her back to him.

What was going to happen when the meal was done? How should she get rid of him? And he was wounded —it was dreadful to turn him out. Mercifully, she had seen nothing of this wound; first the darkness and now the table hid his legs; but suppose she should—she who had fainted last week when Jane cut her finger.

The pie seemed to have lasted a surprisingly short time after all, for she had reached no decision when the Frenchman was addressing her again: "And now you permit that I drink your health, Mademoiselle?" She

turned and saw that he was holding out his glass towards
her, and could not fail to notice the difference in his
appearance. He was younger than she had thought, not
five-and-thirty, perhaps—though to eighteen that was a
considerable age—and better-looking. "To the kindest—
and fairest—daughter of Britain!" He drained his glass
and set it down. "And now I am ready to face any fate
that you may decide to inflict on me. As already it is
late, I will go and give myself up if you wish—*c'est-à-
dire* if I have not to go too far!" Leaning on its arms,
he got halfway out of the chair, but a spasm of pain
passed over his face, and he sat down again. "I fear that
was a *gasconnade* on my part. I will stay here then, as
your prisoner, until they come for me."

"Oh, no, no!" cried Laetitia; "that is impossible—you
cannot do that!"

He leant back in the chair and looked at her. "It must
be the one or the other, Mademoiselle—since your
patriotism will not assist me to a boat."

Laetitia began to twist her hands. "There *is* no boat! I
mean, no fisherman would take you to France . . . I had
no idea that Takerson . . . Oh, what is to be done?"

The fugitive continued to lean back without moving,
but she realised that his dark eyes, which she felt so
sad, were fixed on her very keenly. What she did not
realise was how experienced they were. "*Eh bien,*" said
their owner after a moment. "It seems to be an *impasse.*
I may not stay; I cannot go. *Que faire,* as you say?"

He *must* go, he *must* go, even if he only went a little
way. She could not return to bed and leave him there!

"Of course, if I had wings like a *goéland*—what is it
you call it—a seagull——"

"Ah!" cried Miss Lovel suddenly, as one struck by an

idea, and he paused. "But I cannot grow them, *chère demoiselle,*" he finished after a moment, with the shadow of a smile.

"No," said Laetitia slowly. "But listen: at the foot of the cliff, below our garden, above highwater mark, there is an old boathouse. No, no, there is no boat in it now, but there used to be one, the *Seamew*—that reminded me. If you could get so far, nobody goes there much . . . and perhaps to-morrow your knee would be better and you could go on to some other place——"

"You do not then intend to give me up?" he asked, lifting his eyebrows.

Laetitia looked at the floor. "I—I would rather not," she said.

Her visitor shut his eyes for an instant. "*Merci . . .*"

"But this is my aunt's house," went on Laetitia; "I do not know what she would do. And I must tell you that —that the gentleman to whom I am betrothed returns to-morrow, and he is an officer—a Captain in the Third Foot, and——"

"And he . . . yes, *parfaitement.*" The fugitive was all alertness now. "We must not meet, that is evident. Can one lock this shed you speak of?"

"No, I do not think that the door will fasten at all. And the path down to it is steep, Sir."

The Frenchman made a wry face. "If I slip let us hope I shall be drowned outright. And you will show me this path, Mademoiselle?"

"I will show you the *top* of the path," corrected Laetitia. "You will really attempt it?"

For answer her visitor pulled himself to his feet. "You have not been a prisoner for three years, Mademoiselle, or you would not ask me! I shall arrive there somehow—

by sliding if need be." He took a shuffling step or two away from the table, drawing his breath rather sharply. "I see a cane there—dare one borrow it?"

"Yes, yes," replied Laetitia in a sudden panic, thinking she heard movements overhead. "Come quickly, and very quietly, or my aunt will hear."

He did manage, somehow, to be quiet in spite of his boots and his lameness; yet it seemed centuries before they were safely outside the door leading into the garden and she had lit the lantern which always hung there, and centuries more before they stood in the soft night air at the head of the steps cut in the faintly glimmering chalk, with the sound of the sea gently thudding below, and Laetitia could give the lantern into the fugitive's own hand.

"There is a handrail all the way," she said, "but you must be careful!"

He shifted the stick on which he had leant, took her hand and carried it to his lips.

"And to-morrow you will come and look for my corpse?" he asked softly.

"To-morrow—oh, I don't know," said Laetitia, hastily withdrawing her hand. "Be quick, because the preventive cutter may be about, and see the light going down the cliff."

"*En vérité*, you think of everything unpleasant, Mademoiselle!" he replied almost mockingly. His next words she hardly heard, so absorbed was she in watching him take the first couple of steps downward. "*Au revoir, petite fleur de nuit!*" His head and shoulders vanished from against that paleness which was the June sea at one in the morning; and, drawing a long breath, Laetitia retreated from the edge. Then she paused and listened;

it was so still that she could hear his uneven footsteps, accompanied by little falls of chalk. Suppose he slipped? But the path was not dangerous; it had often served for her own unadventurous feet; he would not slip. She scurried back and bolted the door behind her.

Thank God, she was rid of him at last! But what a night; what a terrible experience! How could she explain her actions to Harry, to Aunt Caroline? If only she need say nothing about them, for everything had sprung from her unnecessary haste to admit her lover. But it was a cane of Harry's which the Frenchman had taken, Harry's destined port which he had drunk, and to Aunt Caroline he had bequeathed an empty pie-dish.

Yet, if she told them, what would become of him down there in the boat-shed?

III

It was the afternoon of the next day, and the gulls, if no one else, could see a little muslin-clad figure with a basket in her hand going down the cliff path between the white chalk and the blue sea. The gulls, however, could not know that it was not the weight of the basket which made her go so slowly.

Laetitia's heart was quite as heavy as her basket, for she knew herself to be both wicked and unfortunate. She had had the amazing depravity not to tell her aunt a word about the midnight guest, offering instead a lie to account for the disappearance of the pasty; and—perhaps in punishment—the postman had brought her a letter from Harry saying that he had had to go to London and would not be back for three more days.

Meanwhile, there was this dreadful incubus on her hands, this damaged Frenchman in the boathouse down here—unless (oh, if only it might be!) he had somehow removed himself.

The old wooden boathouse to which Laetitia was descending was rather precariously situated on a platform, partly timber, partly stone, built out for its reception under the chalk cliffs, which were, indeed, shored up behind it, but which were always crumbling away. It had existed before Miss Lovel's occupation of Cliff Cottage, and when Laetitia had paid the first of her long visits there eight years ago it had housed a small sailing-boat, the *Seamew,* on board which Miss Caroline, even in dreams, would never have ventured herself. And the Admiral having soon condemned the site of the boat-house as the choice of a lunatic, the *Seamew* was sold, and the shed only used occasionally for the storage of seaweed or wood. Yet, despite the Admiral's prediction, the cliff had not yet fallen upon it, nor had the waves succeeded in destroying its miniature jetty—Fate might, in fact, have been preserving it for the reprehensible use to which the Admiral's daughter was now putting it.

Laetitia rather ludicrously tapped at the unfastened door, and, receiving no answer, pushed it diffidently open, and saw that the Frenchman was lying on some planks and old sails in a corner, evidently asleep. And, although the boat-shed could in no sense be regarded as a gentle-man's bedroom, Miss Lovel was immediately conscious of deep embarrassment. She had never seen a man asleep before, even in a chair . . . Surely it was indelicate to look at this one as he lay stretched on those hard planks, partly covered by his cloak. But her whole behaviour

was of an indelicacy! It was almost more than an indelicacy (if such a thing were possible) to think, as she
found herself doing, that, in spite of fatigue and dis-
order, he was handsome—not, of course, in the same way
as Harry.

She crept forward, put down her basket where he
could reach it, and tiptoed back to the crazy door, where
the sunlight and the breeze, desiring to enter, made the
dim, damp old shed seem ten times more gloomy and
uncomfortable.

"Mademoiselle!" came a voice behind her.

She turned, startled. "Oh, you are awake, Sir?"

"Could one forgive oneself if one slept through the
visit of an angel?" The fugitive was raising himself on
an elbow. "Mademoiselle, *de grâce,* stay a moment—
and forgive me if I do not rise. It takes so long, and
the angel might fly."

The angel remained poised for flight. "I hope your
knee is not worse," she said from the doorway.

Its owner made a grimace, and did not answer. "You
have descended that horrible path—and brought me
that?" He pointed to the basket.

"I could not let you starve down here," murmured
Laetitia, looking troubled.

"And *M. le Capitaine* of Foot—is it possible that he is
equally complaisant?"

"Captain Gifford has not returned yet. Otherwise, I—
could not well have come."

The Frenchman gave a tiny whistle. "Not returned!
I have more than I deserve of good luck! He comes
to-day, though—to-morrow?"

"Not for three days, he writes," replied Laetitia slowly
and almost unwillingly.

"Three days! In three days I can surely find a fisherman who——"

"No, no," said Laetitia quickly; "I am sure you would
not, in this village. Do not delude yourself, Monsieur.
Alas! I think I did very wrong to urge you to come
down here, for if your knee is no better I do not see how
you are going to get away from this shed again, even
supposing that you are not discovered."

A half-mocking expression came over his face. " 'Easy
is the descent to Avernus' indeed," he said lightly,
"though, *parbleu,* it was not so easy! But to retrace one's
steps—*voilà la difficulté*. Do you read Virgil in Kent,
Mademoiselle—no, Cæsar, I suppose? Then it seems I
am fairly a prisoner in your boat-shed, my benefactress.
However, I have three days' grace—a delightful prospect,
if you will come and see me sometimes. And after that
you will either have to leave me to starve—but that process takes a long time, you know—or tell your Captain
that I am here . . . unless he finds out for himself."

Laetitia looked unhappily at the ground and said
nothing.

"However," went on the fugitive pleasantly, subsiding
on to one elbow again and feeling among the sails beneath him, "since we are being so frank—and it is a
quality which I adore, Mademoiselle—I will tell you this,
that I do not intend either to starve or to be taken by
your Captain. I am happily in a position to prevent
either alternative." And in his other hand he held up—
not, indeed, in her direction—a pocket pistol.

At sight of that abhorrent object the angel gave a faint
shriek, and conveyed herself, cowering, into the farthest
corner by the door. "Oh, no, no! Please, please, please
put it away!" Her hands were at her ears.

The prostrate man looked at her, smiling. But even with the smile on it his mouth was grim. "I do not mean to use it without necessity, Mademoiselle, either on myself or . . . another. One has three days, I gather."

Laetitia transferred her hands to her face. She saw Harry, all eager to do his duty, coming in here, where *she* had planted this horrible danger, pictured a shot ringing out, Harry staggering back, and . . . She burst into tears.

"One has three days," repeated the voice in the corner inexorably. She sobbed aloud; the breeze rattled the half-open door impatiently. Oh, that she had never heard that knocking last night!

"Mademoiselle—Mademoiselle *Ange*," said the voice again, and now it was no longer hard, "do not cry, *je vous en prie*. If I could, I would give you this thing to throw into the sea; but I must have some means of preventing myself being taken back to prison alive. I will not shoot your Captain, I promise you—I will choose the other way."

He meant that he would shoot himself! "No—oh, no!" sobbed Laetitia. She seemed always to be uttering that monosyllable. "Something must be done—but I don't know what."

The Frenchman looked at her from his couch very intently, his brows contracting a little. "Perhaps one can think of a plan presently. In the meantime, Mademoiselle, do not weep so. See, I have put the pistol away again; perhaps there will never be any need for me to hold it to my head. For my poor mother's sake, I hope not . . . Tell me, how did you account to your good aunt for there being no pie this morning? Or have you told her the truth?"

The transition was so unexpected that surprise helped Laetitia to self-control. She dried her eyes. "No . . . I . . . decided not to. And for the pie—I am ashamed to say that I hid the dish and said that I thought it must have been stolen in the night—through the larder window. I opened the window myself." She sighed; success in crime had not brought her elation.

"And yet you say that you do not know what can be done! *Mais,* Mademoiselle, you have inspiration—genius! And now all this that your bounty has brought me—for, *ma foi,* do I not see a ham in this basket?"

"I went out to a farm this morning and bought half a ham, so that nothing more should be missed from the larder," said the Admiral's little Letty. "The bread is from the village shop. There is some water in a bottle too."

"You did that—you thought of all that—you carried all that weight for me?" exclaimed Letty's incubus. "Mademoiselle, your goodness confounds me! If you will not come nearer, I must contrive somehow to reach you and kiss your hand for that." And he began to throw the cloak off his legs.

"Oh, don't do that!" said Letty quickly. "Please stay there—I will come."

And as far as the basket on the floor she did come, and knelt down to unpack it.

Back on his elbow again, the Frenchman watched her for a moment. "But it is your hand that I want now, not the ham!" he said whimsically.

So, shyly, she had to stretch it out. The eyes which were so unlike Harry's gave her a look which Harry's—even in the summer-house—had never given her; and she was glad of that, for it made her dizzy. Then their owner bowed his head and put his lips gently and reverently upon her hand.

Half an hour later Laetitia came up the cliff path with an empty basket in her hand, and in her brain a dull wonder at herself and at what she had agreed to do. She scarcely knew who had proposed the bold and elaborate plan, but she did not think it was she. It had seemed to formulate itself as they talked, as she was held there by her pity for the wounded, hunted man, her unwilling admiration for his spirit, by some secret fascination which she had never felt in Harry's presence. Not that the Frenchman attempted to make love to her—she would have fled in a moment if he had; not that she wanted to stay there, seated uncomfortably on an old water-keg out of the *Seamew,* while pale, gentle, animated, and faintly smiling, he somehow wove round her the strands of this plot which she, Laetitia Lovel, was to carry through—the plot to pass *him* off at need as Captain Gifford, returned unexpectedly from London, and to secure a boat to be brought to the miniature jetty outside the boathouse, that he might row himself and her to Session's Cove, the little fishing hamlet about a couple of miles round the headland in the other direction from Rayham. Small as it was, Session's Cove possessed an inn, and that inn, as Laetitia was aware, a chaise; and the innkeeper knew her, though he had fortunately never seen Harry. She was to hire the chaise to drive them both to the little town of Witton, about eight miles from Session's Cove, and there, in Cross Street, she was to drop Captain Casimir de Jouy (she knew his name now), after which the rest of his flight, connected mysteriously with some man who lived there, would be his own affair.

As for her, she would drive straight back to Rayham
. . . and the confession to Aunt Caroline.

Could it really be she who was going to do this—who
was proposing to drive half a score of miles with a
strange man, who had undertaken to make all the delicate and difficult arrangements for his transit, tell lies to
the villagers here and at the Cove, hoodwink her aunt,
and even, if need arose, pass off Captain de Jouy as her
own dear Harry? Surely she had become someone else,
some bold gipsy girl, such as she had occasionally seen
and trembled at—someone certainly with a wicked heart,
who could lie and feign, and use dearest Harry's new
and sweet relationship to her as a cloak for what would,
unexplained, look like the worst kind of faithlessness to
him.

But oh! she was doing it to save Harry, to save them
from each other; to ensure that there should not be a
stranger lying at the foot of the cliff with a bullet
through his heart, sped there by his own hand—but most
of all to save Harry: for how could she really trust the
fugitive to take his own life rather than Harry's?

And the worst of it was that she could not begin to do
anything until to-morrow, and had so long meantime to
think about the risks of the plan, its shameful audacity,
and must yet keep her preoccupation from her aunt.
Fortunately, Miss Lovel was not observant. Any pensive-
ness she put down to a very natural cause, and said com-
fortingly that evening, as they sat at their needlework
together, that perhaps Captain Gifford would return to-
morrow after all, and that indeed, after the pie being
stolen in that dreadful way last night, she should be glad
to think it.

Laetitia put down the fine seam she was sewing. "I

do not expect him," she said in a hurried and almost alarmed voice.

Struck by the tone, Miss Caroline looked at her niece over her spectacles. "You are not feeling offended with him, Letty, I hope?" she asked, a little anxiously. "It is not his fault, my dear, that his duties detain him. A soldier——"

"Oh, yes, yes, Aunt; I know that," cried Letty, bending her head quickly over her recovered sewing. "Of course, I am not so foolish as to be offended."

For the tenth time she thought, why not tell Aunt Caroline the whole story? But how would that improve matters now? Miss Lovel could not get the fugitive away—*would* not, probably—and would certainly not approve of the present scheme for removing him. And she would tell Harry about him directly he came back, or, more probably, tell the village constable to-morrow morning—or even to-night, perhaps, if only from timidity at the idea of an armed Frenchman being anywhere on the premises. Had not the French Invasion been Aunt Caroline's nightmare for years?

No, there was no help anywhere; she must continue in this terrible deceit, and pray, pray with all her might that Harry did not return before the Frenchman was gone.

IV

"Bring a small rowing-boat round to the old landing-place for you and the Captain this afternoon at half-past four, Miss?" repeated Peter Church doubtfully, setting down the creel of fish which he was carrying up Rayham beach. "And leave it there, and goo back by cliffs? But, askin' pardon for the liberty, can the Cap'n manage a boat wi' that there game leg of his'n?"

"Of course he can, Church," replied Laetitia with dignity. "You will do as I say, please. One of us will be down at the landing-place when you come."

"Very good, Miss Letty," said Peter Church, pulling his forelock. "I'll be round there, and bring that there little boat o' mine, the *Saucy Sal,* 'cos she's light. Didn't know as the Cap'n had come back, Miss."

"He returned rather late last night," explained Laetitia, and walked up from the strand, its whitewashed cottages and nets, with a hot face and a beating heart. Lying to a fisherman—and unable to ask him not to repeat her lie.

But, provided that he did not repeat it at Cliff Cottage, it was all to the good that the village should believe Harry to be back there. Oh, how dreadful it was!

"And how are you going to occupy yourself this after-noon, my love?" inquired Miss Caroline at their three o'clock dinner, which Laetitia was finding it so hard to swallow.

"I thought of visiting old Betty," replied her niece, with her eyes on her plate. Old Betty, once in Miss Lovel's service, was now ending her days in a farm on the other side of Rayham. "I have not been to see her for a long time."

"Very kind of you, my dear; but be sure not to stay late," counselled Miss Lovel, "for since that wicked theft from the larder I am convinced that there is a most desperate character in the neighbourhood."

The lie—another lie—was necessary to account for her absence, but it made Laetitia's departure in the opposite direction very difficult to accomplish unseen. So it was nearly twenty minutes past four when, bonneted and cloaked, she hurried in a panic down the cliff path, thankful that the old gardener had not yet returned to work. Church's little boat was already rounding the headland from the village. If she were not there he might take a fancy to seek for her in the boathouse, and then . . . She herself had meant to go in there first, but there was not time now.

She ran down to the little jetty and stood there, the wind fluttering the hem of her light dress, apprehensively watching Peter Church's leisurely approach. He was facing the bows as he paddled the *Saucy Sal,* and she could see a kind of submerged amusement on his features.

"The Cap'n not here yet, Miss?" he inquired as he came alongside. "Then I'd better stay in the boat till he do come."

"No," said Letty, with unwonted decision. "Please get out and tie up, and do not wait."

"Very well, Miss," said the fisherman obediently, and he scrambled out, made fast the painter to a ring, and then, to Laetitia's horror, began to direct his steps towards the boathouse. She darted after him and caught him by the arm.

"Where are you going, Church—what do you want?"

He stopped in surprise. "One of them old sails to hang over her side as a fender, Miss; there's a little backwash from the cliffs and her paint's new."

"There are no sails in there," declared Laetitia desperately, still clutching his jerseyed arm. "There's nothing of the sort in there now. Never mind the boat's paint;

I—Captain Gifford—will make that good. Please don't wait!"

She was aware that her extreme anxiety to be rid of him was astonishing Peter Church, but she was beyond caring for that. Muttering something about having seen the sails there last month, he nevertheless prepared to obey. "Shall I tell the Cap'n as I goes up through, Miss?" he asked.

"No," answered Laetitia, faced by this fresh peril. "I meant to have said . . . please do not go through our garden at all—take the other path. You see, Miss Lovel does not know about this—this row we are taking—she is always a little nervous of the water. You understand?"

It could not be said that Peter Church actually winked, but a species of seismic disturbance took place on his bronzed and wrinkled countenance. "Bless you, Miss Letty, I understands. No one up there shan't see nothing of me. A pleasant time to you both, Miss. I wouldn't go too far out if I was the Captain."

"No, we do not intend to," said Letty, at last speaking the truth; and, pulling his forelock, Peter Church started with bent shoulders and heavy foot up the cliff path. Laetitia, looking after him, let three long minutes elapse before she went to the boathouse door and knocked. There was no answer. She pushed it open and stepped into the twilight within. Nobody! Could it be possible that he was gone already?

She uttered his name to put the seal on her relief.

"*Me voici*," replied a muffled voice, and her new-born hopes fell dead as M. de Jouy threw back the old sail which he had pulled over himself and whose existence she had just denied.

"I thought your good mariner might have a fancy to

enter," he explained gaily. "So I withdrew beneath this, hoping that he would not tread upon me. He is gone, and the boat is there?"

"Yes," said Letty, trying to keep her disappointment out of her voice; upon which the Frenchman observed, *"Vogue la galère, alors,"* and began to struggle up.

He seemed in high spirits, which did not desert him during the process of embarkation, though it was evident that it cost him considerable difficulty, if not pain. But once he was seated on a thwart, his leg, with its roughly bandaged knee, stretched out stiffly before him—just as Harry sat—he took up the oars as one not unaccustomed to handle them, and pulled the boat's head round in the direction of Session's Cove. Laetitia's most unwilling adventure was in full swing.

Despite the sun, and the cloak on her shoulders, she felt the cold of nervousness as she sat there at the tiller and looked less at the unknown man who was rowing her (whom she now saw for the first time by the full light of day) than at the white cliffs near whose feet they were passing. If only this voyage could have taken place at twilight, when the world was not so brightly illuminated! But the necessity of preserving some appearance of plausibility had forbidden that alleviation. Save in daylight the real Harry would not have taken her driving, nor would she have gone to visit old Betty. If only she *were* sitting with old Betty now!

"You must not look too pensive, Mademoiselle," said Casimir de Jouy at last, smiling and resting for a moment on his oars. "Remember who is supposed to have the privilege of accompanying you at this moment."

"But there is no one up there to see what I look like," responded Laetitia, glancing upwards at the cliffs. "And

. . . I cannot look happy when I am not."

"Are you not a little happy?" he asked, half-wistfully. "When one does so good and courageous an action. . . ." She shook her head mutely, and looked away over the shining water.

"My debt is all the greater then," said the fugitive humbly, and went on with his rowing.

The sea was so smooth and the *Saucy Sal* so light that Session's Cove came in sight sooner than Laetitia had anticipated. Although it now consisted of no more than half-a-dozen fishermen's cottages, tradition said that the place had once been as large as Rayham, and its decaying inn was supposed to date from those more spacious days. And here, Laetitia knew, she would be faced by the most difficult part of the whole business; because, once disembarked, she must leave the supposed Captain Gifford on the beach and go herself to engage the chaise. Even if he could have walked as far as the inn, it was not desirable to subject M. de Jouy's appearance and accent to scrutiny—perhaps, indeed, it was fortunate that the real Captain Gifford's lameness made it natural for his counterfeit to remain by the boat until the chaise came down to the beach to pick him up.

The little beach in question was quite deserted when they got there, half to Letty's relief—though how, this being the case, they were to land she did not know. There was no jetty of any kind. But her companion, rowing hard, drove the *Saucy Sal* shoreward in shallow water till her nose grounded in the sand.

"Stay where you are, Mademoiselle," he commanded. "You shall not get your feet wet, I promise you." And, almost before she knew what he was about, he had struggled over the side into the shallow, glittering wavelets, and was trying to pull the boat still further up. But he could not stir it.

"Oh, stop, stop!" cried Letty. "You will hurt yourself, Sir!"

"Can you jump from here, then? If not, I will lift you."

Choosing the lesser of two evils, Laetitia accepted his two hands, and sprang or was swung clear of the envious white line on the sand.

"You have not wetted your feet—no?" inquired her cavalier, limping out through the water himself.

Laetitia did not answer, for at that moment she descried a boy of about sixteen running towards them over the beach. If she could despatch him to the inn for a chaise it would be better than going herself; and, with a half-word to that effect to M. de Jouy, she started to meet the runner.

His senses quickened by the sight of a shilling, the youth proved agreeable and reasonably intelligent. Yes, he would tell the landlord that Miss Laetitia Lovel, of Rayham, and her betrothed, Captain Gifford, who had rowed round from Rayham, wished to drive at once to Witton on a matter of business which Captain Gifford had suddenly remembered when in the boat. All possible haste must be made, and, Captain Gifford being wounded in the leg, the chaise must come down to the beach for him. The messenger ran off, having promised, in addition, to return with assistance to pull the *Saucy Sal* above high-water mark; and the couple stood alone on the shore again, their backs to the sea, the fugitive leaning heavily on his stick, and Laetitia with her eyes fixed on a trail of seaweed at her feet, and very conscious amid her anxiety, that Captain de Jouy's eyes were fixed

on her. And she was going to drive eight miles alone
with him, and he a Frenchman!

But she reflected that he would not dare to behave un-
becomingly, for he must know that she would scream,
and then all would be over for him. After a moment she
stole a look at him under her bonnet, and was half-
relieved, half-repentant. Even if he happened to be looking at her, he was not thinking of her; his thoughts, it
was plain, were much further away.

All at once his gaze became alert again.

"I see our magic coach approaching, Mademoiselle the
fairy godmother," he said cheerfully, and, indeed, an
ancient, swaying vehicle, drawn by a rawboned horse,
had now appeared at the top of the beach, and he instantly began to hobble in that direction.

When at last pedestrians and conveyance met, and
"Captain Gifford" had been assisted in by the sympathetic driver, it did not seem too unnatural that Miss
Lovel and not her betrothed should give the necessary
directions. At any rate, their charioteer showed no surprise, and the musty old chaise, which smelt of straw
and stables, began to reel over the sand towards the road,
while Letty leant back in her corner, shaking too much
from the effects of agitation to realise at once that M. de
Jouy was silently but fervently kissing her hand.

Before she could withdraw it he had relinquished it.

"Did I not say that you were a fairy?" he murmured.
"When has a poor devil of a soldier been so blest before—
for Cendrillon was a girl?"

"Cendrillon—is that Cinderella?" queried Laetitia somewhat nervously, the warmth in his voice a little alarming her.

"But yes, I suppose so—Cendrillon with her little slipper which she loses at the ball. Mademoiselle, promise me that you will not lose your slipper at Witton. But I forget, you are the fairy, not Cendrillon."

"You have such children's tales in France, Sir?"

"Many such, Mademoiselle. Shall I tell you some, to pass the time? No, you do not care for fairy stories now, I am sure. I will tell you some true ones instead."

Anything rather than that he should put kisses of so disturbing a nature on her hand; so Letty listened willingly enough when he began to tell her of people and cities strange to her, of Germany, of the South, describing Spain as Harry certainly had never described it— casting over her, in short, something of that spell which had enmeshed her in the boathouse. Then, though bewildered by it, she had faintly known it to be dangerous; but now . . . it did not matter, because they were to part so soon. And after that she would never see him again.

"Monsieur de Jouy," she said suddenly, as he paused for a moment, "this man who is to help you, who lives in Cross Street?"

"Yes?" he asked. And Spain, its oleanders, its hard blue sky, all vanished, and they were trundling along a Kentish road again, and he in peril.

"Will he know who you are—be prepared for you? I mean . . . you are so lame . . . If you were suspected, it would be difficult for you."

"My good fairy need not be so alarmed," said Casimir de Jouy, with a little smile. "This man and I have met before."

"Oh, at Portchester? But how did he get to you in prison?"

"It was before I went to Portchester," said the Frenchman rather shortly. "What was I speaking of just now?— Madrid, I think. I was going to tell you——"

But Laetitia did not follow him back to Spain; she exclaimed instead, in some surprise, "Then you have not been all these three years at Portchester? I am glad of that. Where were you before that?" And, as her companion did not immediately answer, she said, blushing, "I beg your pardon, Sir; I have no right to ask you questions."

"*Au contraire,* you have every right. Before I was sent to Portchester, I was at Ashford."

"At Ashford! But there is no prison there," said Laetitia, puzzled.

"I was not in prison."

"But how, then . . . for Ashford is not a parole town, is it?"

"No. I had special parole allowed me."

"And then it was withdrawn, and you were sent to prison? What a shame! No wonder you escaped from Portchester."

"You do not condemn that, then?" he asked, looking at her.

"No indeed!" said Laetitia. "But tell me why your parole was taken away."

But that M. de Jouy seemed reluctant to do; he looked out of the window. "If you cannot guess why, do not ask, Mademoiselle," he said, after a moment.

And at that a light dawned on the girl at his side. "Oh!" she said, in tones of indignation. "I *can* guess— and I can guess why you hesitate to tell me. Your case is like one of which my father once told me. You had someone who wished you ill—some enemy in England, who used influence against you. That was it, was it not, Monsieur de Jouy?" Her heart swelled; it was generous of him to wish to keep silence before her on an Englishman's misdoing.

But Casimir de Jouy had turned his head again, and was looking at the innocent face and shining eyes with a strange expression which slowly darkened. "An enemy —*eh bien*, yes, if you put it so. I had an enemy—the enemy that most men have. No, I do not mean the Devil"—his tone was very bitter—"I mean oneself. I was sent to Portchester Castle because I tried to escape from Ashford—in other words, because I broke my parole."

"You . . . broke your parole!" said Letty, in a horrified voice. "Oh, no, I cannot believe that! There was some mistake.—They *said* you had broken it."

"There was no mistake at all," he answered doggedly, but he stared straight in front of him. "I broke my parole by trying to escape . . . I did escape, but I was recaptured. You are shocked, I see, Mademoiselle; but you do not know what it is to be a prisoner in a strange land, eating your heart out to get back to your own, and to those whom you love. And one is none the less a prisoner because one may march freely up and down the street— and be jeered at! There comes a time when a force that has been growing in you says that *no* obstacle shall stand in the way—when you *must* get back, *coûte que coûte*. I had come to that stage. I staked everything on that throw—my honour too—and lost. I don't mean to lose this time!"

Letty had shrunk back as far as possible into her own

corner of the chaise. So he only counted his word of honour as an obstacle; she, too, had been just an obstacle, until he twisted her to his will. If there had been any faintest flavour of romantic achievement in this business which had been forced upon her, it had vanished now.

And in the ensuing silence he said harshly, "What a fool I was to tell you that! I forgot that you are a sailor's daughter and a soldier's fiancée." He laid his hand on the door. "Let me get out here, on the road, and do you turn back, Mademoiselle."·

"No," said the Admiral's little Letty, biting her lip to keep back those curious tears, half of anger, half of something else. "I do not—at least, I hope not—break *my* word!"

The trot of the slow horse and the rumble of the wheels were all she heard when she had delivered this thrust, the boldest thing she had ever said in her life. Her heart beat furiously as the words escaped her, but the man at her side folded his arms on his breast and bowed his head and said nothing; only once he sighed, and for half a mile no further word was exchanged between them.

In that silence Laetitia gradually became aware of a faint clacking sound in the distance; told herself at first that it was not horses' hoofs, then that if it were it did not necessarily mean pursuit, and at last was constrained to ask her silent companion whether he could hear anything.

"I have heard hoofs behind for some time," he answered, without moving. But his nearer hand, she saw, was tightly clenched, and the other—was it clutching something hidden in his breast? Terror seized her, lending her an unwonted imperiousness.

"If we are stopped, promise me that you will not use that pistol!"

At that he turned his face, and Letty saw its anxiety and its recklessness. It renewed her urgency. "Promise! Promise! You said there was no danger, or I would not have come with you. Promise not to fire!"

"And let myself be recaptured for the second time! You ask a good deal, Mademoiselle!"

"I will not have an Englishman shot!" said Letty hysterically. "Promise, or I shall open the door and jump out."

"I do not see how that would help your Englishman," observed her companion dryly. "You may remark also, Mademoiselle, that I show no signs of wishing to fire at anybody—not even at myself." And he added mockingly: "I understand. You think I would not do the last in any case? Perhaps you are right. *Eh bien,* I engage not to fire the pistol. You may even take charge of it if you wish."

"No, no," said the girl, shrinking away.

"I thought you might not believe a mere promise now," he explained.

Laetitia did not answer, but turned away her head that he should not see the two large tears which were slowly forming and which would roll down. Casimir de Jouy looked at her oddly with his brilliant, melancholy eyes, out of which the sardonic expression had faded. "I could *make* you believe it," he said, more to himself than to her. "But I will not. I have been too unkind to you already, little preserver. . . . Now they are about to overtake us."

With a hand which was not quite steady he let down the nearer window, and there floated in clearly the steady

186

clop-clop behind, drawing momentarily more close.

"But these are not pursuers!" he exclaimed, suddenly flashing a lightning glance round on Laetitia. And he fell back in his corner with a long breath as there drew abreast and passed, one after the other, two men who, to judge from their appearance, might have been farmers. They had plainly no more interest in the chaise than that evoked by its shabby state and leisurely progress, and one of them, as he went by, was heard to shout jovially to the driver that he thought it was about to lose a wheel.

Five minutes had not passed before it was obvious that this prophecy was well founded. The chaise stopped, the driver descended, made an examination, and, appearing at the window—Laetitia's, by good fortune—announced that if they went slowly and carefully, they might, he thought, reach the "Bull" on the outskirts of Witton, but would certainly get no further. Had not the gentleman been so lame, he would not have suggested attempting even that goal. Letty agreed that there was nothing else to be done; at the "Bull" the wheel might be repaired or a fresh chaise hired.

This meant, however, that M. de Jouy must get out before they arrived at the inn; it would be most rash of him to show his face there. But M. de Jouy, as they resumed their vacillating way, said dryly that he should certainly accompany Mademoiselle Lovel as far as the "Bull"; that he was not going to leave her planted alone in Witton in difficulties. Had the chaise been in a condition to turn round and drive straight back to Rayham, as originally planned, it would have been different. And nothing Laetitia said would shake him; so in the end they lurched on in silence, and before long came to the outskirts of Witton, and their parting was not far off.

The sooner the better, said Laetitia's heart to her; not
that she feared any enchantment now. Harry, dear
Harry, might not be able to talk with such a silver
tongue, but it was still more impossible to imagine him
breaking his word of honour.

VI

"And what are your wishes, sir?" enquired the host of
the "Bull," ushering into his hostelry the young lady and
the limping gentleman whom a chaise on the point of
breaking down had just deposited at his door. They had
no baggage, yet he added: "Were you thinking of
making a stay here, or going further?" He looked at the
gentleman, but it was the lady who answered.

"Neither," said she hastily. "Captain Gifford and I
have come here on business, and will shortly return.
Please go and see if the wheel can be mended."

"Captain Gifford" had meanwhile strolled uncon-
cernedly across to the window. Directly the door closed
behind the landlord, Laetitia hurried to his side. The
window looked on to an apparently deserted yard.

"Now there is nothing to stay for, Monsieur de Jouy,"
she said in fevered tones. "You see, I can easily order a
fresh chaise from the landlord, if the wheel cannot be
mended quickly. I am quite safe here, and I have money.
Go, for heaven's sake, while you can!"

Casimir de Jouy looked down at her, seemingly undecided; but she noticed a tiny pulse beating quick in
his temple.

"Do you know your way from here to this man's
house in Cross Street?" she asked. "If you were to get

188

out of this window into the yard—no, there is another door in this corner of the room."

"Much wiser to go openly by the front of the inn," said the Frenchman in a low tone.

"Go any way," urged Letty, "as long as you go quickly —before the landlord comes in again—while they are repairing the wheel. Oh, I implore you not to wait!"

Her distress, her sincerity, and the good sense of what she said were so evident that it would have been both folly and unkindness to delay. And even Laetitia's inexperience could see that the man beside her, for all his outward composure, was wrought up to no ordinary pitch. "Go, for your mother's sake!" she begged. To her surprise, a flush swept across his face, and for a second he dropped his hawk's eyes. But the next moment they were looking at her inscrutably and he was paler than before.

"I will go. I know you would not take the thanks of a dishonoured man, but, if I could, I would kneel to you."

He put the end of her cloak to his lips, and catching up his hat from the table, limped to the door. There he turned. "Adieu, little flower of the night. God give you a safe journey back to your garden!" The door shut behind him.

It was over, the culminating tension and anxiety. But where was the immeasurable relief that Letty had promised herself? Her eyes were full of tears. Yet who was she to judge him? Had she not been cruel? She sat down on the window-seat. Now he was through the entry, perhaps; now doubtless starting to hobble down the street.

Presently there was a knock and the landlord came in again.

"The driver of the chaise, Madam, hopes to have it re-

paired in another half-hour. Will you and the gentleman—Captain Gifford, I think you said—be pleased to
wait so long? I believe the Captain has gone into the
town."

After all, how simple! "Yes, we will wait until the
chaise is ready." (No need to say yet that "the Captain"
would not return in it.) "Let me know directly the wheel
is mended."

So he had got unsuspected out of the "Bull," at any
rate. How soon would he be clear of Witton, and in
what manner?

If only he had not broken his parole—or if only he had
not told her of it. . . .

Dear heavens, this was never he, back again! There
was a hurried, limping step approaching the door. What
madness! The door opened as she rose to protest; there
was a glimpse of scarlet, the door was violently shut, and
inside it, stiff as a ramrod, and with a face like a sheet,
stood—Harry!

Laetitia remained incapable of movement. It was like
the end of the world to her—a thing that could not
happen. And yet all the time something was whispering: "You might have expected this!"

"Where is he?" demanded Harry—but was this Harry,
who looked at her like that?

She tried to say "Who?" but the word would not come.

"Where is the man with whom you have run off—the
man masquerading under my name?"

"He has gone. Harry, Harry dearest, I was not running away with him—indeed I was not!"

Captain Gifford gave a sort of laugh. "Do you take me
for the village idiot? Sit down, Laetitia. Who is the man
—and where is he?"

"I cannot tell you, Harry . . . but I was not running away with him. Take me back to Aunt Caroline."

"He has deserted you already, then? But I daresay you can find another in a day or two—you did not waste much time in picking up this one. But of course you did not expect me back so soon!"

His words were like hail, like knives. "Harry, Harry, you *must* believe me! I will explain some day."

Harry advanced till only the table stood between them. "You will not have the chance, Miss Lovel! And, indeed, how can you 'explain' a plot such as you and your lover had concocted? I hurry back to Rayham, find that you have publicly given out that I had already returned, ordered a boat, and—good God, it's enough to send a man crazy! No, don't be frightened. I can keep my hands off a woman, I hope—but the *man* is going to give me satisfaction. Where is he? You don't leave this room until you tell me!"

On the other side of the table Laetitia had sunk down in a huddle, her face in her hands. Was her life to be ruined—for a stranger who was nothing to her? No—no! But she could not betray that stranger yet.

She lifted a small white face in which her eyes looked like drowned periwinkles. "I will tell you about him to-morrow, Harry."

"You will tell me now—or not at all. You will never have the chance again!"

Then she *must* tell him!

"He was . . . an escaped French prisoner . . . who came to the house by mistake the other night . . . and partly because I was sorry for him . . . and partly because he frightened me . . . I agreed to help him to get away . . . as far as this. Then I was coming back . . .

but the wheel of the chaise——"

"I saw it at the door. But for that mishap you would be through Witton now, you and your—— A French prisoner, bah! That is an ingenious cloak—which of you invented it?"

Oh, God, he wasn't going to believe her now that she had told him the truth! What more could she do? "Harry," she said in an agony, "I know I did wrong in helping him—but not to you."

"Not to me, when the scoundrel took my name (which you must have given him), even caricatured my limp!" burst out Captain Gifford, as if this were the supreme outrage.

"He is not a scoundrel—and it wasn't a caricature," said Laetitia, trying to keep back the sobs which threatened to choke her. "It was real—he has a bullet in his knee. Perhaps if it had not been for that limp when first he came—oh, Harry, you *must* believe me! You can punish me in any other way—but you must believe me!"

"My God, I only wish I could!" said poor Harry. "But it is too much to expect me to swallow! You, my little Letty, as timid as a bird, do such a thing for a man who was nothing to you! No, it's not credible!"

"Pardon me," said a voice from the corner by the window, and a door closed gently. Someone with a halting step came forward through the dusk. "I am afraid that you do not know much about women, Captain Gifford. . . . There is no need for your sword, Sir—I am unarmed . . . and your prisoner at discretion."

For a moment Casimir de Jouy held his arms wide, while Harry, his sword half out of the scabbard, stared at him petrified. Then, with Letty's cry of "Why have you come back, Monsieur de Jouy—why have you come back?" in his ears, he slammed home the weapon, hobbled up to the intruder, seized him by the wrist, and glared at him. The Frenchman met his eyes unmoved, and Laetitia Lovel burst into tears.

"If this is not part of the plot——" began Harry at last.

"Hardly, Sir, since I am giving up my chance of liberty to set your fears at rest," responded the other dryly.

"Will you swear that you did not come back for quite another reason?"

"To see Mademoiselle? Miss Lovel despises me, Captain Gifford, for having broken my parole; I assure you she does not wish to see me again. It is you I have come to see. As I turned the corner of the street just now I saw an officer galloping towards the inn. I feared—just what has happened, and so I came back a little while ago into the yard here. The window is open. I apologise that I listened; but I was not anxious to come in if I could avoid it. But—I could not. Will you take my surrender as a pledge that Mademoiselle speaks the truth absolutely—that I am merely an escaping prisoner whom she helped because she was afraid of him?"

He was as cool as if he were not throwing away what he had sacrificed so much to win. And Harry Gifford, who for a brief space had been a prisoner himself in Portugal, was dumb for a moment.

"You must be mad," he said uncomfortably. "You realise what I—what my duty is?"

"*Mais naturellement.* In the meantime, I am sure that, as a fellow-sufferer, you will excuse me if I sit down?" And the Frenchman did so, and leant his brow on his hand at the table. He had not even glanced at Laetitia.

Harry Gifford looked at him again, limped to the door

193

by which the fugitive had entered from the yard, and locked it, rang the bell violently, and went over to Laetitia, a little porcelain figure of tragedy.

"Letty," he said, in a low, shaken tone, "perhaps some day you will be able to forgive me for the things I have just said to you. I was mad, darling, with . . . with the shock. . . . But for the moment I have my duty to do, and this is no place for you, dear. You must withdraw. The landlady will look after you, and then we will go back to Rayham together." He scrawled a note in his pocket-book, tore out the leaf, and when the landlord answered the summons, held it out to him. "Send this up to the barracks at once, and tell your wife to come and look after this lady."

"I *must* speak to him," said Letty, in an almost extinguished voice as the door closed again. "He has given up too much. Oh, I wish he had not done it!" Her mouth was trembling like a child's.

"Yes, speak to him," said Harry gently, and turned away.

Letty went blindly to the table. Casimir de Jouy tried to get to his feet, and could not. *"Excusez-moi,"* he said. The light had gone out of his eyes, and he looked years older. Letty held out her hands; the tears were running down her face.

"Oh, no—no; I don't despise you!" she said brokenly. "I think you are——" She could not get it out. "But why have you done it? And your mother in France—your poor mother . . ."

He had been going to take her hands, but at that he stopped. "Never grieve for her, Mademoiselle," he said in a dead voice; "she went to God ten years ago. Yes"— as Letty made an involuntary movement—"I lied to you,

194

to gain your compassion—which you see now how little I deserve. I was desperate—that is my excuse. But even liberty can be bought too dearly, and you"—his voice sank till it was almost inaudible—"you were like to pay too heavy a price for mine, little flower. That is why I came back. *On n'a pas tout à fait oublié son devoir.* Adieu, and forget the distress I have caused you." And he took the hands which, unable to speak, Letty was holding out again, and rested his throbbing forehead an instant on them. Then he kissed and thrust them away from him, and Harry Gifford drew her towards the opening door.

"I suppose you will want to search me?" said Casimir de Jouy a moment later, looking up into Harry Gifford's troubled face as he stood by him. "Must I stand up?" He was startlingly pale.

"No," answered Captain Gifford. "If you will turn out your pockets it will suffice. But look here"—he broke off abruptly—"what is this about a bullet in your leg? You . . . I am going to get you some cognac." And without waiting for an answer he went to the door and shouted for brandy.

The Frenchman propped his chin in his fists and stared into vacancy. But when Harry Gifford came back to him he was turning out his pockets as desired, and finished before he took the glass.

"*Merci,*" he said quietly. "If you have no objection, Captain Gifford, I will drink to your happiness, for the wrong I have done you is only in appearance." And, as Harry did not stay him, he drained the glass to him. "As I say, I forced Mademoiselle (who was most unwilling) into helping me—partly by working on her compassion, but chiefly by threats of shooting you or myself. But I never threatened *her* . . . I hope you believe that?"

"Yes," said Harry, "I do." A pause, and he said, looking past his captive, "It was deuced fine of you to come back. . . . I am sorry, 'pon honour, that I can't let you go again. Perhaps an exchange——"

"You forget," said the other. "A man who has broken his parole is never exchanged."

Harry Gifford bit his lip. "At any rate," he said awkwardly, after a second's silence, "I'll see to it that you get proper medical attention. Hallo, what's this?" He grabbed at the little pistol on the table. "I thought you said you were unarmed?"

Casimir de Jouy leant back in his chair, his hands in his empty pockets. "So I was. The pistol, as you can see for yourself, is not loaded—never has been. May I ask you, as a favour, not to tell Miss Lovel that?" The brief, tired smile held something of real amusement. "I had no ammunition, *voyez-vous*. I wish the sentries at Portchester had been in like case."

After all, it was getting dark when Laetitia drove back to Rayham with Harry—the real Harry. But they had a fast chaise and pair. Before ever they entered it Captain Gifford had made his *amende* and had been forgiven by one whose only thought was to be forgiven herself. Happily, the dire peril which had threatened their love in the inn parlour had led, not to recrimination, but to gratitude for a great danger averted; and so for most of the drive they were both rather silent—silent and thankful.

Indeed, they were nearly at Rayham when Laetitia, her hand still fast in her lover's, said, with a sudden sigh:

"Oh, Harry, there ought not to be wars. At least, there

ought not to be prisoners."

"But you would not have every prisoner killed, dearest?" returned the matter-of-fact Harry. "That would be worse, surely."

"Yes, of course. . . . Harry, he did frighten me dreadfully at first with that horrible pistol, because he threatened to shoot you—or himself."

"Yes, dear; he told me so."

"But in the chaise I got him to promise that even if we were stopped he would not fire it. That was good and noble of him, Harry."

"Yes, darling," agreed Harry, with a transient smile.

"Oh, Harry," said Laetitia, holding his hand tighter, "I'll never have any secrets from you again! Not that I should have kept this a secret if you had been here."

"Then we must never be parted, must we, sweetheart?"

"No, never, because I am so foolish and easily frightened."

"Are you?" asked Captain Harry Gifford. The Admiral's little Letty—and his—had come back; but had he and the Admiral been all her life a little mistaken about her? "It seems to me that you——but never mind! You were driven into it, I know, and it is all over now, and we will not think of it any more—nor of how cruel I was to you, my blessing."

"Dearest Harry!" murmured Laetitia.

But for the man who had used her for his own ends, and yet had thrown away, on her account, what he had so desperately craved and so nearly attained, it was not over—it was beginning again. Letty's eyes filled, she put her head against the edge of Harry's epaulette, and, for the seventh time since his departure, dissolved into tears.

197

"My poor darling," said Harry remorsefully, his recent brutality looming larger than ever, "my poor little Letty! Did I frighten you so? Forgive me, forgive me!"

But that was not why Letty was crying.

II

ALL SOULS' DAY

ALL SOULS' DAY

THE old priest was out when we called at the *presbytère*, but we were told by his housekeeper that he would soon be back, and were invited to wait in the parlour. We had come there, Horsfield and I, because when our friend Travers was working at the history of the Morvan, he had said that the Curé of Chatin-en-Brénil had been extremely kind to him, and was very pleased to see visitors, especially English visitors, in his quiet corner of that green Burgundian land with its astonishing memorials of the Middle Ages, those little walled towns and the great abbey church which is one of the glories of France. So Horsfield and I, who were doing a walking tour from Sens to Dijon by way of Auxerre, had settled to call upon the old man as we passed through Chatin-en-Brénil.

Nor were we sorry to rest awhile in that dark and very cool parlour, hung with a few bad sacred prints and having straight-backed chairs arranged with precision below them. After a little, however, Horsfield got up, drawn as he always is by the presence of a bookcase, and went to the small row of shelves on the wall by the window.

"Our Curé has one or two good bindings here," he remarked. "In fact, if this isn't a seventeenth-century English tooling I'll eat my hat!" Moved by the holy enthusiasm of the bibliophile he stretched up a hand, plucked forth a book, surveyed and opened it. "Look!" he cried triumphantly, and spread it open on the table in the middle of the room.

It was a Dutch-printed Latin copy of *The Imitation of Christ,* of the year 1620, and though I know little of bindings I saw the significance of the faded inscription on the fly-leaf. *Mildmay Fane*—presumably the name of the original owner—was written high up in the right-hand corner; and then lower down, and evidently at a different time, *hunc librum ad L.R.E. de V. dedit anno MDCXXXI in memoriam misericordiæ non obliviscendæ;* and lower down again, *Ora pro anima N.C.*

"That's interesting!" I exclaimed—"given by an Englishman to a Frenchman in 1631! I wonder what it is doing here, and who N.C. was?"

But as I spoke the door opened, and the Curé hurried in, full of gentle apologies for keeping us waiting, of pleasure at making our acquaintance, and of enquiries after the well-being of Travers, "cet aimable écrivain si passionné pour l'histoire et les antiquités de notre beau pays du Morvan." He was himself the most charming old man possible, to whom it was easy to utter our rather shamefaced excuses for having made free with his book-case—for the à Kempis was lying open on the table—and our avowals of curiosity regarding its original possessor.

"Ah, there you have a great treasure," he said, smiling, taking the *Imitation* with a certain reverence into his fragile old hands. "It has been a kind of heirloom in my family since it was given to an ancestor of mine.—Messieurs, a bargain: if you will stay and take *déjeuner* with an old man to whom it is a pleasure to meet an Englishman, I will tell you the story of your countryman and of the inscription in his book."

We were only too pleased to stay, and though I fancied the housekeeper was not so pleased, and that I heard vociferations from the kitchen, we had an excellent little *déjeuner*. The old priest was so charming a mixture of shrewdness and naïveté, of humility and knowledge of the world, that his conversation was wholly delightful. After the meal we went into the little walled garden, and sat under a pear-tree, where our coffee was brought out to us, after we had assisted the Curé to hunt a fowl out of his bed of seedling wallflowers. "I think the blessed St. Francis must have omitted to preach to the *basse-cour*," he said ruefully, as we came back. "For my part I often feel most unchristian to my sister the hen."

When we had finished our coffee he drew the book out of the pocket of his cassock. "I must warn you that this is a story for the fireside in winter, and not for all this"—he waved his hand to include the little green garden, the warm and fragrant air, the stocks and wall-flowers, flagging a trifle in the sun, and the drowsy cooing from an unseen dovecot—"but it does not matter.

"This book, then, was given to a member of my family by its owner, Mr. Fane, an English gentleman of great gifts both of mind and body, a very noble person—*une âme d'élite,* as we say—whose good qualities were like to suffer ruin through a disaster which befell him in early manhood. This calamity, brought about through no fault of his own, plunged him into circumstances which were leading him in a direction very different from the path wherein he had early set his steps, and to which, by the mercy of God, he afterwards returned, through what strange agency you shall hear.

"About the end of the year 1629 Mr. Fane, then a little more than thirty years of age, was visiting Paris on his return from a foreign tour, when he had the misfortune to incur the enmity of a certain Chevalier de Crussol, a man of notoriously evil life. They had met but a few times when a violent quarrel took place between them, in which Mr. Fane, so far as human judgment goes, had undoubted right upon his side. As a result of this disagreement Mr. Fane held himself in readiness to receive a challenge from the Chevalier. The expected cartel was never sent, but M. de Crussol took other means to avenge himself. As the Englishman was returning alone at night from a ball he was set upon by the Chevalier and several of his lackeys, who, after a brief struggle, left him for dead in the street.

"The door at which Mr. Fane fell, with half a score of wounds upon him, was that of the house which Carl' Egidio, the Grand Duke of Parenza, was making his residence during a private sojourn in Paris. By the Grand Duke's domestics, then, Mr. Fane was found in the early morning, and, being carried within, was there cared for during the space of two or three months. For many weeks of this time his life was despaired of, and he was unable to give any account of himself. However, the Grand Duke, seeing that he had to do with a gentleman of condition, whose appearance, moreover, had from the first attracted him, spared nothing of his hospitality and care. It so chanced that Mr. Fane had despatched his servant to England before he entered Paris, and that none of his acquaintance in the city was aware of his presence there, nor, in consequence, of the disaster which had befallen him. There was no person therefore to make enquiries concerning him, nor to reveal his identity, which he, lying for weeks unconscious, was equally unable to disclose. The result of this general ignorance, when he returned at last to sense and life, was not long in reaching Mr. Fane's ears. His friends, in England and

France alike, believed him dead, slipt out of life by some
such door, perhaps, as that through which he had so
nearly passed; and in England the lady whom he had
hopes of winning was married to another.

"Mr. Fane now fell into a great despair and blackness
of soul. So much did he feel the faithlessness of her
whom a few short months' silence could so alienate, that
the idea of a return to England was abhorrent to him.
Nor to his disordered mind did it appear to signify that
he had, after all, escaped the sword of his enemy. He
persuaded himself that his friends had forgotten him,
and when the Grand Duke, who had conceived a violent
attachment for his company, implored him to return with
him to Italy, Mr. Fane consented with a sort of indifferent pleasure, saying bitterly that a dead man had
no right to come to life again. He accordingly left Paris
in the train of the Grand Duke.

"Dead he was, in another and a more real sense—not,
indeed, so dead as the majority of those with whom he
now consorted, but with scarcely a trace remaining of
that interior life which had once been to him the only
existence worthy of the name. Carl' Egidio, a prince of
cultured vices, called him saint and recluse, and strove
to draw him more intimately into the circle of his own
pleasures, but that Mr. Fane was of a different fashion
from most of the grand-ducal associates did not, after
all, confer on him any real title to those names. Yet the
pleasures of the court held little savour for him, and
sometimes, on his knees with the others at the sumptuous
masses which they all attended (for Carl' Egidio was extremely orthodox), faint and bitter memories of better
days broke into his soul. And the shy little Grand
Duchess Maria Maddalena, the poor little bride who re-

gretted her convent, talked to him at times on themes
which had once been more than a name to him; and
these conversations, he could not but know it, were
almost all she had to prevent their becoming names to
her also. It was for her sake that he suffered the mention
of things once dear, now inexpressibly alien to him, and
perhaps a little for her sake too that he kept himself
clean of the grosser forms of vice.

"But these could not fail, in time, to close upon him.
The ladies of the court were none too difficult, and he
had every gift to commend him to a woman. Before the
winter was come Donna Flavia Ranuccini, a married
kinswoman of the Duke's, had lured him along a
perilous path of intimacy to a disastrous end. He did
not love her, but she had wrested from him as much as
he had in those days to give to any woman; and to an
intimacy of such a kind, at that time and in such
surroundings, there could be but one conclusion. Mr.
Fane was only fulfilling, alas! what his world expected
of a gentleman of fashion, when after a year's residence
in Parenza he made preparations for becoming Donna
Flavia's acknowledged lover.

"It was ten o'clock on the second evening in November.
October, so lately fled, had carried off few leaves from
the trees in the Duke's beautiful gardens, into which
Mr. Fane sat looking from a window-seat of his apartment in the palace. A half-moon, sometimes obscured by
light fingers of cloud, shone on the statues among the
trees, the dryads and fauns, and the Silenus in the middle
of the nearest plot, and through the open casement came
now and then the shiver of the leaves. Half lying on the
deep seat the Englishman propped his chin on his hand
and looked out. Something in the tall cypresses reminded

208

him of a graveyard, and the white and silent statues of monuments—or ghosts. Ghosts might well walk in the palace gardens, the ghosts of those who had played out their lives there, on the lawns and terraces in summer, or in winter in the apartments on the other side, now alight with revelry from which he had withdrawn himself—for what? Donna Flavia's letter was in his pocket —in a few years she, too, would be a ghost of the garden —and he? But he was already dead, and had a right to walk already. And then he remembered—what indeed he had forgotten merely for an hour or two—that it was All Souls' Day.

"Even as he remembered it the heavy window-curtain swayed slowly out from its place, as a curtain by an open window will do either with a gust of wind or with the opening of a door. But the wind was nothing save an occasional light shudder in the garden, and the door at the end of the long dimly-lit room had in truth been opened, for, turning his head on the instant, Mr. Fane heard it softly closed. Looking down the room he discerned the figure of a man coming towards him, and with some vexation wondered who entered unannounced at such an hour. But as the intruder came nearer he started from the window with his hand on his sword. It was the Chevalier de Crussol.

"He was dressed, as always, with some elaboration, in rich and pale satins, with his dark lovelocks falling over Venice point, a jewel in his ear, and a medal, or an order, on a broad ribbon about his neck. Bare-headed, with his left hand, sparkling with rings, resting lightly on his sword-hilt, he came slowly down the room towards his foe, and his short velvet cloak swung from his shoulder as he walked. But when he was within a couple of yards from Mr. Fane he suddenly halted, and stood looking at him with an air of extraordinary seriousness. Mr. Fane's last recollection of him was very different, and of the wild passions and vindictive triumph which had then been imprinted on his countenance there was now no trace, nor indeed of any other emotion. All expression seemed to have been wiped, as with a sponge, from his face, which yet bore everything by which a man may recognise one whom he has loved, or hated.

" 'What do you want here?' asked Mr. Fane, finding his voice at last under his amazement.

"The Chevalier made no answer, nor moved, but continued to look at him with eyes of a strange flickering greyness.

" 'Speak, in God's name!' cried Fane. 'What are you here for? Are you mad?' And indeed there could scarcely be any other explanation of his audacity.

" 'Do you not know,' said the Chevalier in a low tone, speaking French, 'that it is the *jour des morts?*'

"The sound of his voice carried Mr. Fane back in an instant to the dark street in Paris, the torches, and the swords. 'I know it,' he returned in the same tongue. 'And you have, perhaps, a fancy to join them?'

"His visitor paid no heed, but continuing to look at Mr. Fane with the same indescribable calm, said gravely: 'I am come to warn you of peril.'

" 'Another assassination!' exclaimed the Englishman bitterly.

" 'Rather self-murder,' replied the Chevalier, with not the faintest sign of blenching at the taunt.

"His composure, but still more the reference to his own private affairs, was too much for Mr. Fane. 'Now, by Him that made me,' he began, springing towards him. The Chevalier retreated a step and put up a hand to stay him; but Mr. Fane never touched him. In after-years, I believe, he could never satisfactorily account for the reason of sudden enlightenment; the figure, even in the subdued light, was so distinct, so real, with all the visible attributes of breathing humanity about it. But on his closer advance he knew.

"He recoiled very slowly, crossing himself almost mechanically, and the dead murderer and his living victim stood looking at each other across the riven veil. There was no fear in Mr. Fane's heart, but awe certainly, and a great wonder. Why had the creature come—to ask his forgiveness? No, for as the thought shot through his mind (he forgetting for the moment what had already passed between them) the apparition answered it. 'I am beyond the reach of human pardon, Mr. Fane; but I entreat you, by Him you named just now, not to do this thing.'

"The strange dead eyes were full upon him, passionless and yet compelling. Fane was shaken, but to be brought to book by one whom he could not but know to be infinitely worse than himself touched his sore and haughty soul too sharply. The human passion swept away with it the sense (which one might have supposed overpowering) that he was speaking to no living man. 'Enough,' he said shortly, and added: 'You find yourself, surely, on a strange errand, Monsieur de Crussol!'

"'The messenger,' returned his visitor almost inaudibly, 'is not accounted of.—And you will not listen, nor stay your steps before it be too late?'

"Mr. Fane, without replying in words, made a gesture of negation, and a clock in some recess of the room struck the quarter. It was the hour at which he had ordered

211

his chair to await him. The figure of his visitant stood between him and the door through which he must pass to gain the courtyard, not that door at the end of the room by which the Chevalier had entered, but a *porte de dégagement* on the left of the window. He looked towards it impatiently, in a way that would have been plain to an earthly guest.

"'Mr. Fane,' said the figure, holding up his hand, while for the first time a trace of emotion thrilled in his low and even voice, 'Mr. Fane, I will call another to stay you. You shall not dare to pass that door.'

"And with that he turned on his heel, as naturally as a living man might turn. On the wall, not far from the door, there hung a beautifully carved crucifix of ivory and silver, Carl' Egidio's gift to his favourite. Before Fane had time to interpose, the spirit of his enemy had it in his left hand, and in his right, the light glinting dully upon it, a little dagger which he drew from his breast. Now he was at the door, and put the crucifix high up against the central panel, and, holding it thus, drove the stiletto through the ring deep into the wood. Then he half turned, looked round at Fane, and—was gone.

"Mildmay Fane wiped the sweat from his forehead. The room was empty, just as it had been a few minutes ago, save for the white Christ hanging over against him, nailed to the wood by an assassin's dagger. The sense of having dealt with the unseen was a thousandfold more potent now than when he had spoken with the phantom. Great God, what did it mean?—and yet he knew.

"Then he told himself that he was dreaming. But the crucifix upon the door—was it real, or was it not? He went slowly up to it, not daring to touch it. Yes, surely, it was as real as sight could prove it, and the little dagger, with the ruby in the hilt—the dagger which he knew, which had once had his own blood upon it—was fast in the panel. He put out his hand and drew it back again. 'I will leave the Christ there until I return, and if it be there still I shall know that I am not dreaming. I am not afraid of ghosts,' he thought to himself. But he stood for a moment looking fixedly at the Figure so strangely suspended in his path.

"The clock struck the half-hour, and he turned away to get his cloak from the window-seat. When he had his back to the barred door he thought with a smile of his visitor's defiance, 'You shall not dare to pass that door!' He put the cloak about him and walked steadily to it again.

"Ah, God! how the Christ looked at him, under the thorn-crowned brows! And as Mildmay Fane stood with his hand upon the handle, in the act to turn the latch, he suddenly drew back trembling. Not knowing why, but as one dreaming, he put out his hand instead to the Chevalier's poignard. His fingers encountered nothing but the panel of the door, but the crucifix, as though its support were removed, slipped instantly down the polished wood. He caught it as it fell, and, as his fingers closed on the symbol which an incredible act of divine mercy had placed to bar his way, the temptation dropped dead in his breast like a shot bird, and with an over-mastering sense of awe and gratitude he sank upon his knees with the crucifix pressed to his lips.

"A week later he had left Parenza for ever. Of all the Grand Duke's gifts he carried away with him but one, and left nothing behind of permanency but his memory to the little Grand Duchess.

"So you see, my children," said the old priest, smiling

213

upon us, "that even if on All Souls' Day you met the ghost of one who had been your enemy—though I hope that neither of you has such a thing—you would not need to think he came to do you harm."

"But, Father," said I, infinitely touched by the sweetness of his tone, "why should it have been his enemy that was sent to Mr. Fane? Do you think it was in expiation of his crime?"

The priest shook his head. "That is not for me to say. Let us hope so. I think that when Mr. Fane prayed before the altar for the repose of the Chevalier's soul, as he did to the end of his life—as he here asked his friend to pray"—he lifted the book—"that must have been a hope with him . . . when he prayed also (as I am sure he did) that he himself, to whom so great a mercy had been given —*misericordia non obliviscenda*—might not be found wanting in the day of the Lord."

THE CRIB

P

THE CRIB

I

Miss Bellamy hesitated a moment before entering. It seemed to her so odd to go into a church in the middle of the morning, when no "service" was proceeding. But it was extremely cold and windy outside, and the noise of the London streets always tired and bewildered her. She had still more than an hour to get through before her momentous interview with Miss Culling, at present the arbitress of her destiny—for upon Miss Culling's considering or not considering her a fit candidate for the post of third-form mistress in the High School over which she reigned, depended more than Miss Bellamy quite liked to face.

"At any rate," she thought, "it will be warm, and I shall have it to myself," and so pushed open the door of St. Perpetua's.

Had Miss Bellamy been more versed in the ways of what she would have called "Ritualistic" churches she might have known that solitude is rarely to be found in them. For they are not empty between services. Moreover, this was Christmas Eve. St. Perpetua's was, however, warm; a faddist might even have called it stuffy. A faint smell of incense greeted Miss Bellamy's disapproving nostrils, and there were, to her surprise, quite a number of people in the church. Most, but not all, were on their knees. To its congregation St. Perpetua's was a home; but home life has its disadvantages, and to-day, even as most houses were being decked, somewhat to their disorganisation, with holly and mistletoe, so here the last touches were being put to the adornment of this house, a proceeding which involved a certain amount of disturbance. But the effect pleased Miss Bellamy, save that one decoration—if decoration it were to be called—distinctly shocked her. This was the Crib, with its figures, half life-size, of the Child in the straw, and those who adored, down even to ox and ass, or at least the heads of them, looking in from behind.

"The Virgin Mary, too!" thought Miss Bellamy indignantly. "This is a very Roman church!" And she passed swiftly by, to sink into a chair, and be alone with her anxiety.

Miss Bellamy hardly ever went to church, not that she was irreligious, but because there never seemed to be time. On Sundays she was always tired, and besides, it was the only day that she could attend to the repair of her all-but-shabby wardrobe, and give a little quiet companionship to her invalid mother. But she began to think, as she sat there in St. Perpetua's, her hands nervously grasping her worn purse-bag, that people no doubt came to this place to pray for things they wanted—were doing it now, perhaps—and perhaps they sometimes got them. Surely if God understood how terribly important it was for her to get this post, of which she had heard in so unexpected a fashion, and for which she was going to be interviewed on so unusual a day. . . . And suddenly she found herself on her knees, praying as she had not prayed for years.

It was not, however, for long. The scraping sound of chairs being moved on the tiled floor did not disturb her, nor the subdued intercourse of the decorators, nor the coming and going of people, nor even the fact that something unpleasant was being done to the pedal notes of the organ. It was a loud whispered conversation behind her which shattered her prayer, a conversation conducted in male voices, and concerned with the Crib.

"I am so glad that we have been able to get a more appropriate figure of the Holy Child," said one voice. "It is preposterous to be obliged to use, as we generally do, the image of an infant of about two years of age, instead of one even approximately like a new-born baby. At any rate, this doesn't look more than a few months old. I had it specially cast, you know."

Miss Bellamy glanced round and saw two priests in cassocks, both young, and rather alike, save that he who had spoken wore his biretta—not that she knew its name—more on the back of his head than the other, and seemed to be invested with the greater authority.

"About the positions, now, Woodward," went on this latter, stepping back, and viewing the Crib with a critical eye. "Somehow the composition doesn't seem to me to be quite right. I believe St. Joseph has got out of place. Now last year we had him—where exactly was it we had him? If we were to move that shepherd a trifle. No, it is the Blessed Mother herself that is wrong. One can't visualise her kneeling just there."

A pause, while he shifted the figure.

"If you ask me," said he addressed as Woodward, "I think—though I don't know much about babies—that if I had been Our Lady I wouldn't have let the Child a moment out of my arms, especially if He had to lie on straw like that! I always fancy I should like a Crib where she holds Him, not worships Him, newborn as He is, from a distance."

"Then you would lose the full idea of adoration."

"Not a bit!" returned the younger man stoutly. "Mothers don't need to set their babies on the floor to adore them. They can accomplish that quite as well with them in their laps. My married sister . . ."

"The cases are hardly similar," observed the elder priest dryly. "Also you know quite well that you are using the word 'adore' with a different connotation. What a bother! I've fetched down this bit of back-cloth. Give me the hammer and a couple of tacks, there's a good fellow."

Knocking followed, and then the younger man said reflectively, looking at the Christ-child: "I suppose it's not irreverent to imagine that Our Lord was just as much trouble as any other baby. They seem to like that stage so much—mothers, I mean—the stage when their children are quite tiny and can't do anything for themselves, and must, one would think, be a horrible nuisance. My sister used to lament no end when my nephew passed out of it, and said she would give worlds to have him back again—like *that,* you know. I can't help thinking that Our Lady must still sometimes—no, that would shock you!"

He had at least succeeded in shocking Miss Bellamy, to whom it did not seem quite decent to regard the Virgin as a real person, who, nineteen hundred years ago, had had feelings like any other woman. The theme, however, was not pursued, but when, a moment or two afterwards, she heard the authoritative young man, now displeased with the type of palm tree depicted on the canvas back-cloth, launch into the impressions of Bethlehem which he had gathered on his recent visit to Palestine, she began to wish that he had remained there, and, instead of moving further away, she got up and left the church.

II

At four o'clock that afternoon Miss Bellamy again pushed open the door of St. Perpetua's—but a very different Miss Bellamy from the morning's. The dreaded interview was over, and she had got her post—too old, too unmodern as she had thought herself—and she had even been offered a salary beyond her hopes. Because this fortune, which still seemed too good to be true, had carried her far from her usual self, and because she felt full of gratitude, she had come back to St. Perpetua's, where she had prayed in the morning, though for so short a time.

It was rather dark inside the church now, but here and there a light had been turned up. From the far end of one of the aisles came a low murmur, but that, and its conjunction with the glimmer of a surplice, held no significance for the little teacher, who was, besides, too much overwhelmed with her own happiness to see much that was external to her. She did, however, notice—for she had to pass her—that between the two great candles now alight on either side of the Crib was kneeling a woman with a shawl over her head. She herself went on up the church, and threw herself on her knees, her eyes wet. What did this success of hers not mean for her old mother, her struggling widowed sister, even for herself! She did not know whether to weep or sing. . . .

After a while footsteps went down the church, and in another moment a cassocked figure passed her where she knelt. It was the senior curate, he of the tilted biretta, who had just disposed of his last penitent, and was hoping that he should have time to snatch a cup of tea before Evensong. And for that reason he trusted that the shabby-genteel little woman, now the only worshipper but one left in St. Perpetua's, was not waiting to make her confession—a quite groundless apprehension. But the slight hesitation with which he passed her caused in Miss Bellamy, who knew nothing of the coming Evensong, an equally groundless fear that he wanted to shut up the church, and supposing therefore that she must go, she got up reluctantly from her knees and followed him, at a little distance, down the aisle.

And thus she was witness of a thing as strange to her as it was to the senior curate. For as they went down the aisle they both saw the woman kneeling before the Crib lean over the faldstool and put out a hand towards the little plaster baby. The priest in front of Miss Bellamy hesitated; then he went quickly forward.

"I am afraid that you mustn't touch the figures," he said gently.

The woman drew back her hand at once, but did not move from her knees.

"Some poor, half-crazed creature who has lost her child, probably," thought Miss Bellamy, with a pang of pity. "I expect the clergyman thinks so, too. I suppose he will turn her out, especially if he is going to lock up."

But if such were the senior curate's intentions he thought better of it, and all he did was to say: "Haven't you been here rather a long time? There are others who may want to say a prayer before the Crib." He half glanced round at Miss Bellamy, who had no such purpose.

THE CRIB

The kneeling woman seemed not to hear. Her hands were now lightly clasped in front of her on the fald-stool; her face was hidden by the folds that fell round it, but she seemed to be gazing straight and absorbedly at the Child. It was impossible to know whether she were old or young, even whether she were or were not "a lady," a point about which Miss Bellamy was something particular. It was true that she had a shawl over her head like a poor woman; or was it a mantilla, in which, so Miss Bellamy had heard, ladies were accustomed to worship abroad, in Roman Catholic countries? At any rate, it was very graceful, and completely baffling.

As she neither moved nor spoke, the priest gave her a last puzzled, compassionate glance, then, lifting his biretta, bowed to the Crib and went out.

This surprised Miss Bellamy a good deal; had he, perhaps, thought *her* responsible for this poor woman? Since, however, he was evidently not going to lock up the church, she herself need not leave it yet, and so she sat down in the nearest row of chairs and returned to the contemplation of her good fortune. To think that she would at last be able to give her mother one of those nice quilted dressing-gowns of Japanese silk; she would get her a fairly expensive one, as it would probably wear longer and thus be cheaper in the end. Then that really stylish coat and skirt in New Oxford Street; or would it be better to go on with her present costume and purchase instead a small neck-fur? A fur gave such a finish, besides being warm; and those known as coney-seal or seal-coney. . . .

Miss Bellamy pulled herself up. It was not for such reflections as these that she had come into a church. If she must think of such unsuitable things within its walls

223

she had better go. She rose, ashamed; but, having extricated herself from the row of chairs, stopped dead.

The worshipper at the Crib, whose presence she had temporarily forgotten, was kneeling now between the lighted candles with both arms passionately outstretched, and there was that in the attitude which pierced the little teacher, unimaginative as she was, with an instant feeling of being in the presence of something that she could not fathom—something great and even sacred. *Was* she a mother who had lost her child? The pose suggested neither grief nor madness. And, just as Miss Bellamy was wondering whether she could tiptoe gently past without being observed, the woman rose from the faldstool altogether.

"She is going to take up the Child!" thought Miss Bellamy, with a leap of the pulses. And with that she remembered the conversation overheard this morning, and illumination seemed to come to her. This was a mother —a little unbalanced, no doubt—who yearned to see her baby as it had been when it was small, and the plaster image, bearing perhaps some chance likeness, had been the nearest fulfilment of her desire. And though Miss Bellamy was not conscious of a thwarted motherhood in her own barren life, though she held that people nowadays made far too much fuss about babies, there was in her heart some chord that responded, almost with pain, to the beautiful movement with which the veiled woman stooped, put out her arms and gathered up the Christ-child into them from the straw, and stood there, her head bowed to the cold cheek as though it were alive and breathing, and there were no one else in the world but it and she.

"It might really be her own!" thought Miss Bellamy.

224

Her eyes began suddenly to fill with tears, and she sought hurriedly in her bag for her handkerchief.

It was at that moment that the woman turned round, the little plaster baby in her arms, and, at last, Miss Bellamy saw her fully. . . .

The candles, the dark church, swam together in a golden haze.

"Oh, do You feel like that in heaven?" she gasped, and, falling on her knees, hid her face.

.   .   .   .

The senior curate, coming back into St. Perpetua's rather early before Evensong, was much perturbed to find, in an otherwise empty church, the shabby little woman in brown whom he had previously seen there, huddled together, with her face hidden, in the aisle not very far from the Crib. Her attitude was odd, suggesting that she had fainted while on her knees, but the most singular thing, which did not occur to him till afterwards, was that she was not in front of the Crib, but at right angles to it. At present his desire was to revive, if necessary to remove her, and procuring a glass of water he hastened towards her, relieved to find, when he bent over her, that she was quite conscious, though dazed.

"Let me help you to a chair," he suggested kindly. "I'm afraid you have had a shock or something. Hadn't you better sit down? Perhaps a little water——"

With his assistance the little brown woman did regain her feet, but she would not sit down, and refused the water. She was very pale.

"That—that woman," she began, and stopped.

"Yes? Did she frighten you? She is gone now. But won't you——"

"Do you know who she is?"

"No, I had never seen her before, to my knowledge; I did not see her face even then. But she is not here now; you were alone when I found you. I hope she didn't annoy you?"

Miss Bellamy continued to look at him in a way which certainly carried out his theory of shock. "But I— I saw her face!" she said in a shaking voice. Then she suddenly acceded to his previous request and sat down on the nearest chair. "I saw her face!" she repeated, and to the priest's dismay hid her own in her new, cheap gloves.

"Please tell me if there is anything I can do?" he asked anxiously.

She did not answer for quite a long time; then she spoke without lifting her head. "Could I speak to that young man who was here this morning with you?"

"Father Woodward, do you mean? Yes, certainly. He'll be in the church in a moment. You see we're just going to have the First Evensong of Christmas Day. I daresay he's in the sacristy now; I'll see."

.   .   .   .

As Miss Bellamy told her experience to the younger priest in the strictest confidence, it was never subjected to the clarifying processes of public analysis and discussion, and the magic formulæ of "subjective hallucination," "subliminal uprush," "suggestion," and the like were never pronounced over it to resolve it into its (doubtless) component elements. On the contrary, Christopher Woodward's face was very wistful as he glanced down the church towards the Crib in the intervals of Evensong, and, after the service was over,

226

he went to the Crib and kissed the spot where she had stood who was, to his thinking, without shadow of question what the little high-school mistress had taken her for.

He was no doubt a most credulous young man.

THE BOOK OF HOURS

THE BOOK OF HOURS

I

M. le Cure, stooped over his lettuces, had from the rear
something of the look of an elephant gone faintly green—
for though he did possess a less ancient cassock he
certainly never wore it when gardening. But if you were
going home from your work, and paused a moment to
glance over the low wall of the *presbytère* and to exchange salutations, you had, of course (being in front of
him), a more ordinary and human impression. M. le
Curé, his face rather red from bending down, would
straighten himself, and his blue eyes, the eyes of genera-
tions of fishermen, would twinkle a greeting at you. Or
he might possibly observe, without the twinkle, that he
had been unable to identify you at Mass last Sunday, or
ask if it were true that at Père Mathieu's cabaret. . . .
But in that case you had probably hurried past without
exposing yourself to untimely questions.

If, however, you had a guiltless conscience, or if its
burdens were those which you were fairly certain could
not have come to M. le Curé's ears, you might converse
a little over the limestone wall. After a few words on
the weather, the crops, the plenty or scarcity of the
sardine catch, you would say: "Eh bien, Monsieur le
Curé, and what has St. Caël done for us this week?"

And M. le Curé, rubbing the end of his nose with an
earthy forefinger, would reply, "He has sent us seven
francs" (or three-fifty, or ten, as the case might be). "We
advance—by God's grace we advance. . . . Hervé, my

son, have you ever found a real remedy for slugs?"

"Never, mon père," you replied fiercely. And you perhaps added, "If St. Caël——"

M. le Curé would shake his head with decision. "He is not to be troubled about a little thing like that!" "As soon ask St. Michael!" his tone implied. And of course it was not for you to bandy words with his Reverence on the relative importance of the saints, though you remembered that Madelon Le Meur, over this very wall, had once upheld that as Our Lady was so fond of lilies she might well be applied to in the matter of garden pests.

The fact was, you were tempted to think, as you trudged homewards, that St. Caël was much more approachable in your young days, before the Curé had exalted him so high above his peers. Your mother used to invoke him for her chilblains. For St. Caël, though doubtless of world-wide fame, was the special patron and property of Roscaël, since it was his birthplace, and it was not as if M. le Curé owned or had discovered that bright-pictured Book of Hours of his. You knew that it had been kept at the *presbytère* for many hundreds, perhaps thousands of years. True, it was M. le Curé's idea to suggest to those persons who came to examine the relic that they should contribute to the fund for re-roofing the church, and it was owing to M. le Curé's exertions that Roscaël was going once more to celebrate the lapsed Pardon of the saint, to whom, as all the village knew, he had a special devotion. So perhaps, after all, M. Rivoallain had a right to preserve St. Caël from unsuitable petitions.

*   *   *   *   *

In the dark room, oppressively shiny and tidy, which

served him both for dining-room and study, M. le Curé was finishing the sermon which he meant to deliver next Sunday—the great day of the Pardon—on the patron saint of Roscaël.

For five years M. Rivoallain had been living and working for this event, when the holy fisherman would once more behold his festival celebrated as befitted his fame and sanctity. It would only be a small affair, not comparable, naturally, with that of Ste. Anne de la Palue or of Folgoët, but neighbouring villages as well as his own would have the opportunity of doing honour to the saint of Roscaël—a chance that had not been within their reach since the middle of the seventeenth century, when for some unknown reason the biennial Pardon had ceased.

As saints go in Brittany, St. Caël was a modern of the moderns, for he died in 1352, whereas most of the lights of Armorican hagiology came over from Wales, Cornwall or Ireland in the sixth century (often in a stone boat or other unlikely bark). St. Caël was not of an age to compete with St. Tugean (who in Irish is Eoghain, and patron against hydrophobia) nor with Ste. Avoye (whose Cornish name is St. Ewe, and whose boat you may see in her chapel), nor with Ste. Triphène (who is invoked against troublesome husbands), nor with St. Winwaloe, nor with the great St. Gildas. Caël himself had venerated these his fore-runners. Yet, to keep him company in the younger ranks, he had St. Yves, the great lawyer saint whom all North Brittany reverences, for St. Yves was still living when St. Caël, a little fisherboy, was running barefooted over the seaweed.

The Curé's pen was abominably bad, and not noticeably the pen of a ready writer. As a matter of fact, he never wrote out his sermons, but next Sunday was an occasion.

"In this, mes chers frères," he painfully inscribed on the speckly, hairy paper which he had torn out of an old account book, "in this we distinctly see a likeness to the blessed St. Peter himself. It is recorded of St. Caël that he caught in one day no less than . . ."

But the miracles of St. Caël were so deeply engraven on the hearts of his devotees that he did not need to commit them to writing. He gladly made a series of little dots on the paper, and, pushing up his yellow-tinted glasses, passed on to his peroration.

"How deeply, mes chers frères, should we not venerate the inestimably precious relic which we possess of this great saint! You have all seen, you will all see again to-day, the Book of Hours of St. Caël, preserved by the piety of our forefathers. Consider how often his holy fingers have turned these leaves, how these beautiful pictures have gladdened his eyes . . ."

M. Rivoallain rather fancied that at this point he would raise aloft the precious thing, whether he spoke his little discourse from the altar steps or from the pulpit. He desired that all the pilgrims, especially those from a distance, should at least have a sight of it, but these dear souls—their fingers were not always over-clean . . .

While he was considering this point he laid down his pen, and taking off his spectacles stared at the vivid scarlet geranium in a pot on the magenta tablecloth. This combination of tints in no wise discomposed the old priest; he merely thought, "There are colours as beautiful and bright as these in the book; if I were to hold it open in my hand, they could surely all see them? And if I did, what picture should I select?"

His mind's eye beheld a sea of eager faces looking up at him, and, glad always of an excuse for getting out the Book of Hours, he drew a key from the recesses of his cassock, went to a side-table, unlocked the home-made wooden case which sheltered the relic and brought the manuscript to the place. Not very large, and bound in a green tooled morocco binding of a much later date, it opened at the illumination for Terce, where two astonished shepherds, looking awkwardly up to heaven, beheld a blue, vaporous cloud of angels singing out of a very solid book. If you risked a crick in your neck you could ascertain that they really *were* reading off "Gloria in excelsis, in terra . . ." and could surmise that "pax" was over the page. The third shepherd, standing on one leg, played a pipe. There were also their sheep, their large dog; in one of the vignettes intertwined with the border another shepherd, dressed in yellow and having a green hood, clasped a bagpipe—a sight always interesting to the Breton, who plays upon its cousin the *biniou*. And at the bottom of the page the pastors of Holy Writ and of Romance had fairly met, for two ladies were making a wreath in a forest, and in the lap of one of them a shepherd, not of Palestine but of Arcadia, lay asleep.

M. Rivoallain fondly considered this scene. Or should it be the martyrdom of St. Stephen, another of his favourites? He turned to it. The proto-martyr, clad in a blue dalmatic with a red collar or amice, knelt with folded hands on the very green grass, while three individuals of great resolution and close proximity hurled stones at him, the most vigorous of all, who wore scarlet hose and a pink jerkin, having a neat basket of these missiles ready to his hand.

Now, were the glories of this scene visible from any

great distance? The Curé rose rather lumberingly from his chair, set the Book of Hours up against the geranium, and, retreating from it as far as he could, stood with his head on one side and his fingers reflectively rubbing his chin.

He was, therefore, in the midst of a very nice exercise of judgment when Mélanie his housekeeper brought him in a visiting-card, and was followed almost immediately by its owner.

M. Rivoallain looked from one to the other in a fluster, for, duly to impress the neat, dapper little gentleman who had doubtless come to demand a sight of the treasure, that relic ought to be extracted with due formality from its case, and not be discovered at large propped up against a flower-pot. . . . All the more so since (as another glance at the card assured him) the newcomer was actually from the Bibliothèque Nationale itself.

"You have come to see the Book of Hours, Monsieur?" he suggested.

"If you please, Monsieur le Curé," said the little man, bowing very politely. "Ah, I observe that you have it there. No doubt you often avail yourself of the pleasure of looking at it."

M. Rivoallain, bringing forward a chair, explained why the treasure was out of its case.

"Yes," said M. Leroy (for such his card proclaimed him), "they told me at Trévennec, where I am staying, of the Pardon—in fact that was how I heard of the existence of the MS. I might, otherwise, not have had the privilege of examining it. Ah, this is fine work!"

He sat down, affable and competent, fixed a pair of pince-nez on his nose, and began to turn over the pages with quick, careful fingers, while M. Rivoallain, over-joyed at the attention of an expert, hovered near him.

M. Leroy began at the beginning, and looked at St. John, seated on his neat islet writing his Gospel, his eagle by his side holding the pencase in its beak; passed rapidly over St. Luke, sitting on a wooden throne covered by a sort of blanket, very bright indeed, of scarlet with blue stripes, sharpening his quill to the same end, his ox, adorned with pale blue wings, quiescent beside him; and over St. Mark, in a grand pinkish marble chair, armed with a writing board, his lion standing on its hind legs. St. Matthew was missing. He looked at the picture of the Virgin, in a blue robe, spinning, while an attendant angel in scarlet and green carried something resembling a tankard in his hand, and in the border another held out a pot of daisies in flower—just as in the next picture an angel offered the Child cherries from a basket.

M. Leroy passed more rapidly over the Hours proper, with their typical scenes of Annunciation and Visitation or Flight into Egypt, and paused over the saints at the end, in their stiff and naïve attitudes. There was St. Paul, Damascus-bound, on his great stumbling white horse; St. Andrew looking rather ruefully at his cross; St. Denys in cope and mitre stretching his neck to the blow of the axe; St. Nicholas and the three salted children, St. Mary Magdalen, neat and self-satisfied in the wilderness, with a jar of ointment and a palm, and St. Catherine of Alexandria surveying the destruction of the wheel of torment by a red arm, holding a hammer, which emerged from the heavens.

And he examined the fanciful little grotesques of the margins, the blue-booted bear blowing on a horn, the running greyhound with a snail on its back, the lame, crutch-supported creatures, half men, half animals, the mermaid combing her hair, the harpy wearing a mitre, the hundred and one joyous inventions. He examined, too, the fadeless peacocks, the brilliant jays and woodpeckers, the butterflies that dwelt in the foliated borders, and ran his eye, no doubt, over the prayers in the soft tongue of old France, that addressed with so chivalrous a quaintness the "fair Sire God" and the "sweet Lady of mercy."

At last he finished.

"Very pretty, very pleasing indeed," said he. "Admirable workmanship! Thank you, Monsieur le Curé, for your kindness. You have a treasure. I wonder to whom it really belonged."

"But—to St. Caël!" said the Curé, astonished.

The little man shook his head. "Pas possible. For when did he die, your St. Caël?"

"In 1352," stammered M. Rivoallain. "But I assure you, Monsieur, it is so—this Horaire has always——"

"Yes, yes, a very natural tradition, no doubt," replied M. Leroy, smiling indulgently. "But as this illumination was done early in the fifteenth century, and your good saint departed this life in the middle of the fourteenth, you will admit that it could hardly have belonged to him!"

"But, Monsieur, saving your presence, we *know* it belonged to St. Caël! It has been handed down to us for hundreds of years." Yet M. Rivoallain was shaking, and his ruddy face had fallen in.

"Mon cher Curé," said the official of the Bibliothèque Nationale, "I admit that these diapered backgrounds do partake more of the character of the fourteenth than of the fifteenth century, but that is a natural survival, since

238

this MS. is early fifteenth. A little way back I noticed the date; I never thought that you were not aware of it. Where is it?" He turned back and pointed to the page where the scribe had written *Factum et completum est anno quo pugnatum est apud Azincurtum.*

"Agincourt," said M. Leroy. "You know the year of that—1415."

"I—I—yes, I seem to have heard it. But——"

"You want proof?" asked the visitor. "Any history —any schoolbook." He looked round at the scanty library. "The very thing!" And springing up he had plucked forth an old volume of Michelet and turned to the table of contents at the end. "You see?"

"But—might there not have been two battles of Agincourt?" suggested the Curé miserably.

"God forbid!" ejaculated M. Leroy. "But indeed I thought you knew, Monsieur le Curé, and that all this was just a pious fraud to keep alive the memory of St. Caël. I am not saying a word against the existence of the saint, only, you know, a poor fisherman could never have possessed a book like this, that took years to illuminate! Probably it was done for some great family in the neighbourhood—though I did not observe any arms in the borders—and found its way here somehow, perhaps in the seventeenth century, for the binding is of that date. Then the legend grew up around it. There is no reason why it should not continue to flourish."

Out of a stricken face the old blue eyes were looking at M. Leroy as if he were the Evil One. He got up, a little shaken from his competence and affability, but still smiling.

"Now, Monsieur le Curé, do not run away with the idea that I am a Freemason or worse! I am really, I

hope, a tolerable Catholic. This—this unfortunate discovery has no bearing whatever on the existence of St.
Caël. Paste a slip of paper over those fatal words—
though, on consideration, as nobody but myself ever
appears to have read them, it is scarcely necessary. That
is why the date has never come to light—the pious souls
who have examined the MS. from an interest in St. Caël
had not sufficient learning to read the Latin, or sufficient
acquaintance with illuminated work to make them suspicious. On the other hand, those who may have observed the date had not sufficient interest in the saint to
inquire when he died. That jumps to the eye, I think."

No doubt it did, but M. Rivoallain was in no condition to appreciate the logic of the explanation. His
elbows were on the magenta tablecloth, his gnarled hands
clasped over his face. M. Leroy put a sympathetic hand
on his shoulder.

"Come, come, do not be so distressed! Surely you see
that this has no sort of real bearing on the story of St.
Caël."

"If I tell them that this book was never St. Caël's,"
interrupted the Curé in a shaking, almost passionate
voice, "they will think, these poor sheep of mine, that
there was never a St. Caël at all, that he had no existence,
and we here . . . I cannot describe to you, Monsieur,
what he is to us . . ."

"Well, do not tell them then!" repeated M. Leroy, in-
tent on consolation. "Do as I say—paste a slip of paper
over the words! If they think the Book of Hours a relic
of their saint, then a relic of their saint it is to them!
Voyons, Monsieur le Curé, for your poor or the church,
or what you will, and a thousand thanks! I regret, really
I regret, that I mentioned the date."

But neither M. Leroy's pragmatism nor the ten-franc piece which he left on the table was of any avail. His host was too broken even to see him from the room, and the door was hardly shut before the tears were running down his nose. One indeed dropped on to the green morocco, and even in his overwhelming grief the Curé was conscious of this calamity and hastily drew forth his coloured handkerchief to mop it up. Then he thought, "What does it matter? The book was never St. Caël's!" and the waves met over his head again. He had known nothing like this since his mother died a quarter of a century ago.

When Mélanie shortly afterwards came in to lay the cloth he got up, took the Book of Hours and put it in its case, keeping his back turned the while. Mélanie was full of the visitor and chattered till she had everything ready.

"I expect there will be more people than ever come to see our book after the Pardon," was her final remark as she left the room.

The Pardon! He had forgotten the Pardon. He sat staring at his omelette. How could there be a Pardon now? How could he hold up in the church the book whose pages St. Caël's fingers had never turned, go through all that scene which he had pictured with such pleasure? Then his rather slow brain, dazed by the recent shock though it was, took a revolution swifter than ordinary. Of course, this did not affect the Pardon! St. Caël was St. Caël, even if the Book of Hours . . . even if all his own heart had gone out of it. He need only omit the holding up of the MS., the references to it in his sermon.

But he had spoken of his intention to many people, and

it had penetrated even to other parishes. What would be thought if he did not carry it out? And what, too, in the future, if he refused to show the Book of Hours to visitors, or told them that it was not the saint's after all?

M. Rivoallain tried to eat some omelette, but it choked him. He was beginning to see the choice that lay before him—the choice between burdening his own conscience or shaking the faith of his flock. For he knew it to be not a mere fancy but a plain fact, that the belief of the parish of St. Caël was so bound up with St. Caël's book (to which, indeed, some had gone so far as to assign miraculous properties) that if he took away the book he took away St. Caël also. And that was a prospect too horrible to be contemplated.

He had only five days in which to decide, and there was no one to whom he could go for advice, save perhaps the Bishop, and Monseigneur was just recovering from the effects of an operation. Besides, he felt that he could not bear that anybody should know . . .

At last he left his déjeuner and went across to the church. Over his altar the old plaster statue of St. Caël, net in hand, fish at his feet, gazed stonily across at the opposite wall. The Curé knelt down.

"I will do it," he murmured after a time. "God forgive me if it is very wrong! Blessed Caël, intercede for me!" And he looked up earnestly at the image, with a glimmering hope of the saint's giving him some sign that, despite the undoubted date of Agincourt and the repute of the Bibliothèque Nationale, the Book of Hours had really been his after all. But he seemed to see nothing save *Factum et completum est anno quo pugnatum est apud Azincurtum*, and the page at the end of Michelet's *History of France*.

II

"Waal!" ejaculated Mr. Silas M. Silsbee, "if this don't lick creation! How in thunder did they prodooce them colours. And look at the cunnin' little critters around the edges! Who'd this belong to, did you say, Abby?"

"It belonged to St. Caël, who died in 1352," replied M. Rivoallain dully, looking at the Transatlantic visitors without interest. The two years which had passed over his magenta tablecloth had nothing assuaged its brilliancy, but there was no geranium now in the middle. Nor was there any evidence of a twinkle in M. Rivoallain's eyes.

"Holy snakes!" exclaimed Mr. Silsbee. "Why, Christopher C. hadn't even begun to think of putting out over the Brine-jug then! Wasn't even born, I reckon. St. Caël—that's the pious individooal you have some great doin' for here, nope?"

This question being translated by Mr. Silsbee's friend, the Curé replied that the Pardon was indeed drawing near for the second time.

"See here," proceeded the American, continuing his investigations, "what's under this slip of paper? It don't seem part of the original proposition."

"Our forefathers," said the Curé in the tone of one repeating a lesson, "had an idea of humour which is not ours. The jest was considered a little too broad, and it was thought better to do as you see."

"Seein' it all appears to be Latin in the regions roundabout," observed Mr. Silsbee's friend, "I can't see there was much call for the censor. Who was this St. Caël, anyway?"

243

"St. Caël is supposed—I mean to say he was . . ." began M. Rivoallain and forthwith launched into the usual account of the saint, at the end of which Mr. Silsbee, looking covetously at the MS., remarked:

"Waal, he had a dandy picture-book! Not for sale, I reckon?"

M. Rivoallain shook his head.

"I kin give you a pretty long price, Abby? I guess what I'd shell out would just about build you a new church right away, heating apparatus and all!"

"It is not for sale," repeated the old man, his look wandering away as if he had no interest in a question to which there could be but one answer.

Mr. Silsbee seemed disappointed. "Not much of the patent safe about this contraption you keep it in," was his next observation, as he watched the priest lock up the treasure in its wooden case. "Everybody plum honest about here, I suppose?"

"Nobody would wish to steal so holy a relic," said M. Rivoallain.

"That old Abby," remarked Mr. Silsbee to his friend as they got into his car outside the *presbytère,* "don't take any more stock in his defunct medicine-man than what you and I do, Jackson. Seemed kind of tired when he did the talkee-talkee about him.

"I guess he was sick," returned his friend. "Looked sort of haunted. Why, ain't you made a mistake, or are you calculating to go back to Trévennec after all?" For the car was turning in the direction of the little town which they had just left.

"Yes, sir," said Mr. Silsbee with a chuckle. "I guess I'm goin' to spend another night at that old flea-reservation, the 'Tête-Noire.' And I might—I only allow I *might*

—put out to-night in the automobile for another toor round this Roscaël place. Sort of see it by moonlight, you know. It's gotten quite a hold on me . . . And if I did the trick I'd likely boost straight up and board the *Lorraine* 'stead of waiting for the next boat. It might be wiser. See?"

"Silas!" replied his friend admiringly, "I reckon I'll live to see you in Sing-Sing yet!"

*   *   *   *   *

Long after the American's car had driven off, the Curé remained sitting in his dining-room, his hands hanging between his knees, his eyes fixed, seeing nothing. Two years ago he would have been in his garden, attending to his vegetables; the June sunshine invited him at this moment to that once-pleasant labour. But he went out very little now, save when duty called him to the church, or to his parishioners—who, only too aware of the change in him, speculated on its cause, but never came near the truth. A few of the elder inhabitants seriously held that he was bewitched. For, as Mr. Silsbee's friend had said, he looked haunted. And haunted he was, not by the lie told two years ago at the Pardon and repeated, Heaven knew how many times since, but by the very Nemesis which he had striven to avert from his people. M. le Curé of Roscaël, the devotee of the fisherman, the promoter of his highly successful festival, no longer believed in his patron saint.

A mind which has never known a doubt has its own insecurity. And doubt had invaded M. Rivoallain's soul as the sea sidles in over the flat shores round Mont St. Michel. First one landmark had gone, then another. All his life he had believed that the Book of Hours belonged

245

to St. Caël. He would as soon have doubted that the Blessed Virgin gave St. Dominic the rosary. But if one thing which he had so implicitly believed could be false, so could others. Perhaps St. Caël, as well as his book, was only a legend. In vain he told himself that the date of the Book of Hours disproved nothing. The process which, by a sudden flash of insight, he had foreseen as inevitably working in the minds of his flock took place in his own, for, after all, he was bone of their bone and in no wise different from them. And when St. Caël had begun to fade it was but natural that the elder saints also lost little by little their niches in his mind, and that a mist increasingly shrouded the figures once so real to him, to whose protection and intercession he had used to run with so childlike a faith.

And meanwhile devotion to St. Caël increased, and more visitors came, and the church roof was repaired, and the biennial Pardon was coming nearer. Once again he would hold up the Book of Hours and say the words which he knew to be false, about a man in whom he did not believe. But the lie itself troubled him little; so many things seemed lies now. The day would come when he did not believe anything at all, when he would be a materialist like the chemist in Trévennec; and then he might as well be dead. How was he, already, any better than these curious visitors (whom he took to be a variety of English)? In fact he was worse, for they, probably, had never had teaching about the saints, and could not be expected to believe in St. Caël or anybody else. No, he must do what he had now for some time been contemplating—go to the Bishop and ask to be relieved of his cure.

And with that resolution firmly fixed he went dejectedly to bed and dreamed a dream.

He was walking along the shore past the lighthouse, and it was getting dusk. The waves were coming in strongly, with a rhythmical plash of sound, and at their edge, pulling in a net, was a solitary fisherman. The Curé saw, when he got up to him, that he was not one of his flock, and that he was wearing a very elaborate old Breton costume, such as may be seen in the Museum at Quimper, but hardly anywhere else in these degenerate days. This man, alone and unaided as he was, was accomplishing this usually heavy task with celerity and little apparent effort, but M. Rivcallain instinctively offered to help him.

The moment that he laid hold of the dripping meshes the net ceased to come in. "Oh, pardon, mon ami," said the Curé in his dream. "I fear that I am hindering, not helping you. But—have you any hope of finding anything in the net?"

"Yes," said the strange fisherman in a Breton which M. Rivoallain had some difficulty in understanding, "I am hoping to find a book which I left in these parts a great many years ago." And he went on pulling at the net, which, now that the Curé had removed his hands, was swishing through the water as if it were running in of its own volition.

While M. Rivoallain was puzzling over this curious reply the end of the coil came suddenly in, and there, in the thin foam of the waves, gleaming with a green phosphorescence, lay, not a fish, but a book which the Curé knew as well as his own breviary. He gave a cry. "But you cannot have that! It is ours!"

Then the fisherman turned his face for the first time on him, and M. Rivoallain knew him and fell trembling to his knees on the wet sand.

"And do you think, my son, that you are worthy to keep it?" asked St. Caël sorrowfully. "No, it is time that I took it back. . . ."

The halo round his head grew enormous and blinding, and he increased hugely in stature. He might have been the lighthouse itself. . . . The Curé had time for this feverish comparison and woke with a cry.

Although it was June there was the sound of storm without, and the noise of the waves was still in his ears, a sort of throbbing. He was exceedingly frightened. Prayers to St. Caël came pouring from his heart—even from his lips. He did not find him a shadow now . . . The dawn found him shuddering and praying; yet he was nearly late for his Mass. He should have said it at St. Caël's own shrine, but felt that he dared not, and the faithful already in position were considerably surprised to see him making his way to the Lady altar. Still more would they have been astonished had they known that he was trusting in the Mother of Mercies to protect him against his and their patron saint.

It was not till M. Rivoallain was on his way back from the church that an idea visited him which was half hope, half fear. He had rather feel St. Caël's wrath than his non-existence. If St. Caël had really taken away his book then the book he had taken was really his. His displeasure would at least prove his being. Did he wish to see the side-table empty of its burden? He dared not look at it for some time, but when at length he ventured to let his eyes stray in that direction and saw the case in its accustomed spot, his hope was patent to him and he knew corresponding and bitter disappointment. Of course, it was only a dream. . . .

He spent the morning in drafting a letter to the Bishop. Later in the day the remembrance forced itself upon him that the piece of paper fastened over the date needed attention. He had not yet found a paste that would keep it long on the smooth vellum, and the next time he had to show the book to visitors it might have curled up and betrayed its secret. So, with a heavy sigh, he went over to the side-table, took out his key, and opened the case. There was nothing there.

In his expensive Manhattan drawing-room Mr. Silsbee shows with pride his unique early fifteenth-century French *Book of Hours*. He calls it a missal, assigns it variously to "those old times before the Reformation," or to the days of Charlemagne, and says that he bought it at a sale in a "shatto." But in a more confidential mood he may relate, besides his trouble in smuggling it through the Customs, the nefarious but quite simple way in which he removed it, one dark night, from the house of the old priest who didn't seem to value it. And he holds himself morally justified because the old man wouldn't sell it, and because none of the doors were locked, and any ordinary key fitted the case—which he left behind to delay discovery.

But his real justification—if it be one—is quite other, and he does not know of it. He may indeed guess at the black consternation which long reigned in Roscaël, but he has no idea of the miracle he helped to work, and that his shameless larceny is the cause why M. le Curé once more ties up his lettuces of an evening and is ready to chat over the wall—though, of course, one chief topic of conversation is no longer available.

FATE THE EAVESDROPPER

FATE THE EAVESDROPPER

"I wonder," said Marten, switching on the electric light, "whether I shall catch the 8.40 to-morrow?"

Agnew shut the door of the fencing-room. "Will it matter if you don't?" he enquired.

"Will it matter if I don't?" repeated Marten, with much scorn, facing round upon him. "You know I can't get up to town until three if I miss it!"

"Well?"

"Agnew, you are insulting! At nine o'clock to-morrow there will probably be laid upon the table in my chambers a brief in the case which is to make my reputation! And then you suggest that it doesn't matter if I miss the early train!"

The other smiled as he came forward in his neat fencing jacket—a smile that lit up his dark and rather ugly countenance in a manner as unexpected as it was pleasant.

"Divine optimism!" he exclaimed. "Then why spend your last hours in this employment if, as I gather, you haven't finished packing?"

"Packing be hanged!" responded his friend. "I have made up my mind for a last bout with you." He walked across the room to where the row of foils depended hilt downwards from the rack. "Besides," he went on as he looked for his own, "it isn't only packing. I promised——"

"I know what you are going to say," broke in Agnew.

"Yes, we always follow the same programme, don't we?" observed Marten, who, with his back turned, was examining the interior of his fencing glove with some interest. "I go round to say good-bye, and she says she hopes I shall soon be home again, and I say I hope so, too—and that's all." He turned round at the conclusion of this brief speech and his expression was not cheerful.

Agnew put one arm on the narrow shelf above the disused fireplace. "Will it be—all—this time?" he asked quietly, without looking at his companion.

"Oh! You mean shall I . . . ? No, not again—just yet." Marten's tone was gloomy. "I leave that for you, my boy," he went on. "Lucky dog, you never have to say good-bye in the sense that I do."

"Because I so seldom say good day," returned his friend, with a sigh. "Lucky? I don't believe that, living here always, I see half as much of her as you do when you come home." He rested his head on one hand, and with the fingers of the other began to trace patterns on the dusty green paint of the mantelpiece.

Marten sat down on the bench against the wall, immediately under the row of foils. "Yes," he said reflectively, tapping his feet with his weapon, "we are both deuced unlucky. I suppose it's the knowledge of our common misfortune which keeps us from quarrelling."

Agnew raised his eyes from his uncleanly occupation and smiled. "I should have thought that knowledge wasn't needed."

"No more it is, thank Heaven. But you know we aren't doing the proper thing; we aren't doing what's expected of us."

"Surely you don't seriously mean——" began Agnew, surprised.

"I do though," asseverated Marten, rising and laying down his foil. "It never seems to occur to people that two men can be—well, in the situation we are in with regard to *her,* and remain on speaking terms with each other, much less let it make no difference. And when you go about with the glowering visage which you sometimes present to the world"—he laid his hand on Agnew's shoulder—"you give them wherewithal to draw false conclusions of the deepest dye. I am positive that in certain misguided circles here we are looked upon as deadly enemies—or, at least, as two men who ought to be deadly enemies."

The deadly enemy gave a short chuckle.

"In fact, those circles would expect me to inform you, with the proper intonation, that 'a time will come!' And now I come to think of it," pursued Marten, "the proper thing would be to take the buttons off—supposing it were possible to do such a thing nowadays." He caught up his foil by the point. "Just that away," he went on, swinging it to and fro with the button between his thumb and finger, "just that away, and what a difference! We should at least feel that we were playing our parts properly."

"Do you think she'd take the survivor?" asked the elder man, half amused, half grave.

"To be quite candid, I'm pretty sure she wouldn't," replied Marten, drawing on his glove. "Still, alas! we are not sufficiently romantic to put it to the test.—But, I say, Agnew, do stir yourself a bit! We shall be here all evening at this rate!" And he took down his mask.

Agnew moved slowly from the fireplace and walked to get his foil.

"No secret villainy, now!" called out his friend, who had taken up a place in the middle of the long, bare room. "My button's on all right—see that yours is!"

255

"Absit omen!" said Agnew to himself. "Do shut up, Marten—that's a beastly uncanny thing to say! Don't you know that Fate sometimes listens at the door."

"What! And deigns to take suggestions for catastrophes from our poor remarks! A very neat idea; I salute in you the Ibsen of the future. At the same time I should be grateful if you would postpone your tragic meditations and hurry up." He slipped on his mask with real or pretended impatience.

Agnew came forward. He was examining the button of his foil, for though that tiny flattened tip at the end of a modern foil cannot come off, since it is one with the blade, if its covering wears through it may cause a tear or even a scratch. As he looked up he caught Marten's glance, derisive even through the close black wire of the mask, and smiled in a rather shamefaced fashion.

"Idiot!" was his friend's comment. "Your Fate is no fencer if she fancies she can make a button drop off!"

"One never knows," retorted Agnew, putting on his own mask, and they fell on guard.

The foils clicked and flickered in the strong light as the conflict went to and fro, with thuds of the fighters' soft-soled shoes and now and then an exclamation. Marten, the better fencer of the two, and seldom touched, never in their frequent bouts found Agnew an easy opponent, for he had endurance and pertinacity, and when he did get home there was usually no doubt about the hit. At the end of five minutes or so the combatants stopped as though by mutual agreement, and took off their masks, both somewhat out of breath.

"By George, you've no light hand, old chap," remarked Marten, laughing, as he rubbed the top of his right arm.

"I'm awfully sorry," returned his assailant penitently. "It was very clumsy of me to hit you there."

"Oh, don't apologise. You're fearfully difficult to keep out, you know. Have you kept count of the hits?"

"Three against me and two against you."

"Sure? I thought you got me three times?"

"No, I didn't. But I bet you I touch you three times in the next five minutes!"

"Not if I can help it," retorted Marten; "but come on then!" And they began again.

Scarcely a minute had elapsed before Agnew, after parrying an attack in sixte, disengaged and got in a neat riposte. "One!" he exclaimed as Marten recovered. They both laughed, and stood an instant with dropped points until Agnew suddenly took the offensive with considerable vigour, whereupon there ensued an encounter which a *maître d'armes* might have considered a trifle too much of a scrimmage. It terminated only as Agnew drove his point home with force fair and square on his opponent's breast. "Two!" he called out triumphantly.

But, even as he shouted, he wondered why the supple blade should shorten instead of bending—why he should feel none of the familiar springy resistance; the foil was scarcely curved and yet. . . . He recovered as quickly as he could, but the end of the foil seemed caught. Was Marten playing a trick, holding it . . . for he had put up his left hand to mark the hit . . . was Marten . . . ?

"Marten, Marten, what is it?" he cried in a sudden agony of horror and fear. For Marten's foil had clattered to the floor, and he himself, with his chin thrown up, was reeling backwards, his right hand out, clutching at the empty air. Then, with a sound like a sob, he swayed sideways, dropped heavily to the floor, struggled up on one

257

elbow and sank back again. Next instant Agnew's eyes fell on the end of his own foil, which he was still holding. "My God!" he said under his breath, and flinging it down with a gesture of the extremest repulsion, snatched off his mask and was on his knees beside Marten.

"Frank, for Heaven's sake. . . ." He lifted off his friend's mask.

"Touché!" gasped Marten. "You've got . . . me this time . . . old man!"

"Oh, my God!" said Agnew again. "Here, let me see. . . ." And he began with shaking hands to undo the buttons of the fencing-jacket.

"It can't . . . be much," said Marten jerkily. But his face, under the sweat of combat, was of a queer pallor. Agnew's fingers, clumsy with haste, struggled with the innumerable buttons up the left side of the jacket, which seemed as if they would never unfasten; his eyes all the while held by the stain surrounding that tiny square hole on the breast. But, though the white surface showed it up so horribly, it did not seem to be spreading.

"Don't be in such a . . . blue funk!" went on Marten, with an attempt at laughter; and added, much more faintly: "Fate . . . you were right. . . ."

Agnew gave a short choking laugh. He had forgotten their conversation. "Yes," he returned, with another spasm of merriment, "the cursed thing has broken, some way above the button.—That was the downstairs door; someone's come in!"

"What?" exclaimed Marten, rousing himself. "Look here, they mustn't find me like this . . . help me up!"

"No, no! You can't stand!" Agnew was now at the shoulder-buttons. "Stop there and I'll send him for a doctor."

"Nonsense—there's nothing much wrong—only the shock. I'll drive home and no one will know . . . otherwise people might say . . . not an accident. Give me a hand!" And, setting his teeth, he scrambled painfully to his feet and stood uncertainly with Agnew's arms round him.

The footsteps, which had paused on the landing below, could now be heard briskly mounting the last flight of stairs.

"You can't stand," reiterated Agnew in despair. "It's madness, and what *does* it matter?"

But Marten paid no heed. "I'll—sit in the corner there . . . switch off that light . . . he won't see. You send him off sharp."

It was sorely against Agnew's better judgment, but there was no time to argue. Together they got to the bench in the recess by the gas-stove. Marten sank down on it with his back to the door; and Agnew had scarcely withdrawn his hand from the switch before the door opened and revealed the smiling face of M. Leblanc, the club fencing-master, in overcoat and bowler. Hardly knowing what he did, Agnew took a few steps towards him.

"Ah, bonjour, messieurs!" said the Frenchman gaily. "Vous faites donc assaut?"

"Yes," answered Agnew, and tried to add something else, but his tongue was dry against his palate.

"Bon!" The little twinkling eyes went round the room. "Mais M. Marten, qu'est-ce qu'il a?"

"Marten? Nothing. He's . . . resting."

But, even with the light above him extinguished, the attitude of that figure was surely . . . not usual; and evidently M. Leblanc thought so, for he said—but casually, and with a twirl of his little moustache, "Tiens! il a l'air d'être bien fatigué!"

"I'm all right," said Marten hastily, in a queer, breathless voice and without turning his head or moving.

And then Agnew to his own amazement found himself laughing, laughing quite loud, for the Frenchman had remarked that he was a tiring opponent. But he stopped when M. Leblanc went on: "Voulez-vous que je reste pour vous rectifier?"

"No," stammered Agnew. "No—not this evening."

"No, no," joined in Marten, turning his head a little this time. "Besides," he added, half to himself, "we have fin . . . finished."

Agnew shivered. If Leblanc did not go he must tell him. However, the little fencing-master *was* going; he had only looked in to see who was using the *salle,* he announced, and started for the door. But as he turned to bestow a parting glance on Agnew, standing like a statue in the middle of the room, his quick eye saw the foil lying on the floor. Agnew sprang forward, but it was too late; the Frenchman had picked it up.

"A qui ce fleuret?" he asked, holding it up. "On ne doit pas le laisser traîner par——" He stopped with an audible catch of the breath, for his eye had run along the blade to the smeared and broken point.

Agnew was speechless; he formed his lips to say: "It broke," but no sound came. The two men stared at each other, the same apprehension looking from the eyes of each. Yet Agnew knew all the same that Marten had heard, had turned his head, was rising stumblingly from his seat. And in another moment, having steadied himself by one hand against the wall, he had come straight, and even quickly, into the glare of the electric light, and stood there with it beating down on his fair, crisp hair and ashy face, one arm across his body.

"I assure you, Monsieur Leblanc," he said slowly, "that it was a pure . . . a pure. . . ." He stopped as though seeking the word, put his hand to his throat, lurched suddenly towards them, and, slipping through the little fencing-master's outstretched arms, fell in a heap at Agnew's feet.

THE PROMISED LAND

5

THE PROMISED LAND

In the church of San Domenico at Siena, on a certain fine spring day not long ago, two ladies and a young man were studying and appraising, not for the first time, the great "Swoon of Saint Catherine" there. The young man, who looked like a budding don, spoke as one to whom all pictorial art is as an open page, and the ladies held their own on almost equal terms. None of them carried guide-books of any kind, since all were specimens of the truly cultivated traveller.

Two other people were presently heard to enter the empty church. At the sound of steps the cultured looked round apprehensively, lest that horror of horrors, the voluble and loud-speaking guide, should be one of them, and they themselves should be assailed by his detestable English and his still more detestable flow of information. This indeed they were spared, though something almost as repugnant befell them.

The newcomers were two middle-aged ladies in dust-cloaks and mushroom hats, the one large and stout, the other small and thin, and before ever they reached the famous fresco the greater was reading aloud to the less out of a betraying red volume.

"This is by Sodoma, and double-starred, Ellen. Baedeker says——"

Shuddering violently, the cultured trio instinctively retreated, and before much of what Baedeker said had polluted their ears, they were outside San Domenico altogether, leaving Saint Catherine to the elderly Philistines. The young man took off his pince-nez with a judicial air.

"What good purpose can possibly be served," he remarked, "by the visit to Italy of such travellers as those, one's mind fails even approximately to conceive. What can Siena mean to them—Siena of all places, with her delicate, evasive charm, Siena who sits within the walls which have grown too vast for her . . . and smiles? I sometimes see a resemblance in this wonderful town," he finished, "to La Gioconda."

His companions gave this rare thought their attention and criticism. Then they all went for the fourth time to the Baptistery. It was while they were looking at the Knight of Malta that the younger of the two ladies suddenly said, "I remember now, Cecilia, where I have seen those two old Baedekerites before. They are at our hotel."

"Oh, are they the old things sitting at that table in the corner? I thought last night that the stout one looked intelligent in a rough-and-ready sort of way. She must have dragged the smaller with her against her will, I should say—*she* didn't look as though she were enjoying Siena much. Did you notice them, Ralph?"

"No, why should I?" asked the young man. "But I *shall* notice them henceforward, in order to avoid them. 'Double-starred by Baedeker!' Oh, ye gods!"

In due time "the two old Baedekerites" also emerged into the sunshine, and the larger put that invaluable companion into a small corn-coloured satchel adorned with red and green wools.

"Now, Ellen," she said cheerfully, "I think you have seen enough for this morning. We must leave Fontebranda, and all that, till this afternoon, and then we can take our time over Saint Catherine's house."

Ellen said, "Yes, Caroline"; and their sensibly clad feet began to carry the couple away from San Domenico. But had Ralph Shilleto and his cultured ladies known of the dull, despairing revolt beneath the lace-draped hat of the smaller Philistine, whom they surmised to have been "dragged abroad" by the larger, they might possibly have been more interested, for the moment, in her than in the masterpiece which she and her companion had desecrated.

To have the dream of a lifetime fulfilled—and spoilt in the fulfilling; to enter at last the Promised Land, and find it a desert; that was the tragedy which, in her sixty-first year, had befallen meek, unimportant Ellen Wright, and was heavy on her now. At every turn the murdered dream cried aloud to heaven: Fontebranda, name like a lovely and heroic poem . . . but not when her cousin Caroline Murchison uttered it; the tower of the Mangia, that tall lily which could take your soul soaring up with it into the blue . . . but not when Caroline stood beside you reading out its dimensions. The same blight everywhere—over Perugia, with its fierce, beautiful, massacred Baglioni, even over Assisi the holy. In two days Florence would be added to the holocaust, and then the tour in Italy, the lode-star of thirty un-eventful years, would be over, and the two of them would be back in their little house—Caroline's little house—at Lower Waddington, and what remained of wonder in the experience would finally evaporate as Caroline re-tailed it to callers over the teacups.

"You are very silent, Ellen," observed Miss Murchison when they reached their room in the hotel. "A bit tired, aren't you? I should just sit quiet a little before lunch if I were you. I shall go down to the lounge and read the English paper. That book on Saint Catherine is under my knitting over there."

"Yes," said her cousin. Her lips were trembling. She began to pull the pins out of her hat.

"You'd better keep your hat on for lunch, hadn't you?" suggested Caroline, turning at the door. "Or else do your hair again. That hat of yours always presses it down in such an unbecoming way."

"I will put it on again for lunch," agreed Ellen meekly. "But I must take it off now, my head aches."

"It always will if you go out with the wrong glasses, as you did to-day," returned practical Caroline, and she departed, giving the door a cheery bang.

Miss Ellen Wright finished taking off the hat. From habit she went to the mirror, not because she wanted to see herself there, nor even in order to judge whether her cousin's condemnation of the effect of her hat on her coiffure were justified. She took no interest in her own appearance beyond wishing that it should be a tidy one; she knew that she was just a plain, skimpy, dowdy, un-interesting old maid of sixty, tolerated in Lower Wad-dington only because she was, so to speak, a part of the larger, better-off and masterful cousin with whom she lived and had her being. A part of Caroline—yes, that was the trouble . . . and a part which was not allowed to have its own existence, scarcely its own thoughts, and which now had had its life-dream killed by Caroline's insisting on sharing it with her.

The eyes of withered speedwell grew for a moment fierce. Then the light died out of them. Ellen sat down and leant her scantily-covered grey head against the chair, reproaching herself for her ingratitude. Caroline was so kind, so practical, and arranged everything so efficiently.

But oh, if she could only sometimes get away from her! If only her own tiny annuity had permitted of a separate cottage, even though it were in the same village. Well, once "Rosemead" *had* been hers, till she had made that dreadful muddle over an investment, so that in some way still incomprehensible to her there had been nothing left of her money at all. But Caroline, kind Caroline, had somehow bought "Rosemead" from her, and sunk the purchase money on her behalf in this annuity, and, since the little house was then hers, had come to live in it as well. And everybody had said what an excellent arrangement this was for Ellen, and how much better Miss Murchison ran the place.

That was seventeen years ago. And for seventeen years Caroline had continued to be kind and capable and over-bearing; and Ellen always, of course, so grateful to her. And yet . . . she had come to hate Caroline.

Ellen sat up quickly in her chair. How dreadful! Had she really thought that? No, no, no!

But she *had* thought it; at least, she feared so. And if it were true, it was Italy which had shown her the truth, Italy of the clear air and the bright, unclouded skies . . . and naturally, for it was over Italy that the nearest approach to a pull of wills had come in all those seventeen years. Of course, like a much weaker side in a tug-of-war, Ellen had been vanquished, for all her resistance. She had fought hard against Caroline's accompanying her to the Promised Land; yet Caroline had come.

Sitting there in the big upholstered arm-chair, clasping and unclasping her bony, veined hands, Ellen Wright went over the affair for the hundredth time. Long before she and her cousin had lived together, in the days when she herself was a little, timid, inadequately-paid governess, already nearing thirty (and no more able to cope with the unruly ways of children than at eighteen) a visit to Italy had begun to seem to her, though of course unattainable, worth—as people said—selling one's soul for. Each year she had contrived to save a pound or two towards the improbable realisation of such a scheme, but these meagre economies being nearly always swallowed up the next year, she desisted at last, disheartened. But for nearly thirty years she went on reading about Italy, its history and its art, and by the latter some seedling love of beauty in her ordinary little soul was sustained at a higher level than, to look at her, one would ever have suspected. When, about the middle of those years, "that good Miss Murchison" descended upon her like an eagle, and plucked her and her little house out of the abyss, it had not taken Ellen long to discover, on the evidence of photographs, that to her cousin Italy was not an un-attainable dream, for she had once spent a month there. And Caroline on that had found out Ellen's secret, and chaffed her about it.

"Fancy you, Ellen, wanting to go to Italy! I can't see you there, somehow; you'd be frightened of the bullocks and their long horns, for one thing!"

Nourished by the photographs, several of which now hung framed in the drawing-room (but not by Miss Murchison's descriptions), Ellen's dream went on. And then, this last autumn, had come from the skies the most romantic event of her drab existence—the means of its realisation.

About five years earlier there had turned up one afternoon at "Rosemead," a stranger, a young-old man driving a big car, who had asked for Ellen, had told her that he was the son of her elder brother Charlie who had

"gone out to the Colonies" when Ellen was a girl, and
who had, it now appeared, made money in that vague
region. He was dead; Charlie the Second had inherited
his means, had returned to England, and was thinking
of marrying and settling down. With the instinct of the
Colonial he had sought out his only remaining relative
in the old country. By good fortune Caroline was out
when he called, and from the timid, stammering little
spinster who was that "Aunt Nellie" whose ten-year-old
presentment in a tartan dress, and with long sausage
curls, had been familiar to him since his boyhood, and
whose sole completely articulate utterance for some time
was a regret that he had missed Caroline—or that Caroline had missed him—he did contrive, thinking the
photographs on the walls hers, to draw the admission of
her Italian longings.

"Funny!" he said. "I've always had a wish to go there
too. Tell you what, Aunt Nellie, I'll take you there one
of these days. Come for a spin now; my car's Italian, as
it happens."

But no, on the whole Ellen had thought, no, she would
not go for a drive. Caroline might very well return,
and think it strange that she had gone out without telling
her; she might even see her, driving in a large motor-
car with an unknown man. Yet she would dearly have
liked to go, for she had never entered anything more
sumptuous than a taxi.

"Well, I'm real sorry, Aunt Nellie," declared the
visitor. "But remember now, when I've got fixed up with
a house, I'll take you to Italy—sure thing!"

The car bore him away from the gate of "Rosemead"
. . . into complete silence. For four years at least Ellen
waited for that summons to Eldorado, at first expecting it

every day, then once a month or so, then . . . "Of course he didn't mean it," Caroline would declare. "How could you be so silly, Ellen! Master Charlie's off to Italy long ago with someone else—and not with a middle-aged aunt, you may be certain!"

And Miss Murchison, as ever, was right—save about the epoch of Charlie Wright's visit to Italy. For one morning last October, after she had relinquished the smallest glimmer of hope, Ellen had found on her breakfast plate a letter with an Italian stamp.

"That must be from Charlie," observed Caroline, who, after due examination, had put it there. As Ellen's distant cousin she claimed the latter's nephew as well as everything else pertaining to her. "Well, he's taken long enough to write to you, and you see, I told you so—he's gone to Italy without you!" She took off the tea-cosy, while Ellen with shaking fingers opened the letter. "What has he got to say for himself?"

He said, penitently, that he was ashamed to think that Aunt Nellie must believe that he was a chap who didn't keep his promises; that he fully meant to have come to see her again, but that he had not settled in the old country after all—he did not state where he had settled. And now he *was* in Italy, it was true, but on his honeymoon, so that Aunt Nellie would understand that he could not well ask her to join him. But, to make good his offer as best he could, he was sending her a cheque to enable her to go there in the spring for a month or five weeks, and was, with his own and "Belle's" love, her affectionate nephew.

The cheque had fallen from Ellen's hand to the tablecloth, so Caroline saw it at once. But in any case she would have known all about it ere the day was out.

"That's generous of Charlie, I must say—but stupid too," commented Miss Murchison. "There's your egg getting cold, Ellen. For how are you going to find anyone to go with you, paying their own expenses? The money he's sent won't take two people."

"Oh, I'll find someone," said Ellen hastily—all the more hastily because she instantly saw what would happen if she did not succeed. But she *would* succeed, and pay for the "someone" out of the cheque, and go to Italy for a shorter period, rather than have Caroline accompanying her!

She did not sleep a wink that night for excitement, and that was only the first of many wakeful nights caused by her nephew's letter. For of course she could not find anyone to go with her. She had no friends of her own in Lower Waddington now; all who came to the house were Caroline's associates. A ghostlike couple from her girlhood's days were summoned up by letter, but one proved to be crippled with rheumatism, and the other the wife of an underpaid clergyman, who wrote that it was quite impossible to get away, and anyhow it was poor John who needed a holiday, not having had one for eight years. But Ellen could not go with "John" to Italy. And all the time she felt that her cousin was waiting for what she knew must be the outcome of this quest.

Caroline's attitude, too, while she waited, had been so inevitable, like a stream of lava, slow, but bound to get you in the end. It had progressed from the initial: "Of course *I* should be the best person to go with you, having been to Italy before, and knowing all your little ways so well; and if I could afford the money, and could leave the house and the garden and the Boys' Club and the Zenana working party, I really should not mind going again," to the final: "I can't bear for you to be so disappointed, Ellen, and I'll manage it *somehow*. Miss Colson will take the Wednesday evening classes for me, and Ruth Brown cuts out quite well now that I've taught her. I have some money put by. Yes, I'll manage it, and come with you. There now, you needn't worry any more!"

In vain Ellen had said that rather than take Caroline from her many activities in Lower Waddington she would go to Italy alone. Caroline simply laughed in her "breezy" way—how tired Ellen had become of the local ladies who found Miss Murchison "breezy"—and it was plain that she would never be allowed to carry out such an idea . . . no, even though she had thoughts of stealing away to London, by the night train, and so starting. Caroline would only have come after her. She had to give way, to say it was very kind of Caroline; and to let her make all the plans.

And the whole marvellous experience was, as Ellen had known it would be, ruined.

Nor would she ever be able to come again. This journey was, or should have been, the one shining oasis in the sand of a dull life, and instead it had been but a bitter mirage. Everything that Caroline touched lost its charm, its beauty, its freshness. Even the lower church at Assisi, when Caroline explained the Giotto frescoes which Ellen had loved, in reproduction, for years, took on the feeling of some suburban place of worship, and St. Mary of the Angels became a sort of South Kensington Museum, with the Portiuncula, to Ellen a veritable shrine, placed in it for intelligent preservation. . . . And yet what fault could be found with Caroline? She was kind in her masterful way, thoughtful for Ellen's health, bargained with the cab-drivers and the shopkeepers in the way that Italians respect, made the money go as far as possible, arranged everything admirably.

Arranged! Yes, that was it. What would it not be to have a week, even a day, when she, Ellen, could go out by herself and wander as she pleased amid all this beauty, sit down when she liked, go on when she liked, miss some sight, even if it were "starred," because she wanted to linger over one that was not! But the day after to-morrow they would go on to Florence—to Ellen's expectation the crown of all their seeing—and she knew exactly what would happen there. She saw herself being trotted through the cells of San Marco, past those white wonders of frescoes of which she had thought for years, with "Come on, Ellen, you're so slow—here's another!" The idea was intolerable! She would rather not go to Florence at all, so that *that* at least could remain a dream for ever, even though her eyes never rested on its loveliness.

Would it be any good suggesting their leaving out Florence?

Of course it was not. She half proposed it at lunch. "I *said* you were overdoing it!" exclaimed her cousin. "Leave out Florence—you must be mad! Why, there's more to see there than in all the other places put together! But if you feel like that, we can easily take an extra day here in Siena, where it is quieter, so that you can get a good rest before going on."

"No, no—I'm not at all tired," declared Ellen. But she looked very white, and sent away the last two courses untasted.

After that Caroline, of course, insisted on her lying

275

down that afternoon, announcing that she herself would not go out either. They could do Saint Catherine's house on the morrow.

It was easier not to resist, and Ellen very unwillingly climbed on to her half of the double bed in their room. This was the first time they had shared a bedroom. Caroline had insisted on it here, in order to economise for Florence, which she said they would find expensive. The measure had not saved much, and Ellen hated it. She lay there, her dress off, in her petticoat bodice and stout moreen underskirt, very hot, inside the mosquito curtains which, early in the year though it was, had been specially put up at Caroline's request, and Caroline read aloud an extremely gushing book on Florence. But, Ellen summoning up enough courage at last to say that she would like to go to sleep, Miss Murchison obligingly stopped, and, taking up her knitting instead, for she was never without occupation, proceeded with the manufacture of her winter stockings.

The monotonous clicking of her needles might have soothed a really sleepy person, but to Ellen, who was not sleepy, the sound was like the crossing and recrossing of hot wires inside her head.

"Won't you go out, Caroline?" she ventured at last. "My head does ache a good deal. I think I will stay here, but I don't want to prevent——"

"Something you've eaten has upset you, I can see," commented Miss Murchison, continuing to knit steadily. "I wonder if it could have been——" and she ran over various dishes to which the crime might be assigned. "Or else you've got a touch of fever. No, I certainly shan't go out and leave you."

After a long time it was evening, and they were going to bed. Kind Caroline had not left her for a moment, just as she would be sure not to leave her in Florence.

Now they were in bed. Caroline blew out the candle, because Ellen must get to sleep, and in the morning she would probably quite have got over her "upset."

But it was Caroline, not Ellen, who went to sleep. Those knitting-needles seemed to go on and on . . . or was it mosquitoes humming, though they said it was too early for them? She was enclosed under the same mosquito-net with Caroline for ever—shut up in a sort of bag with her—being slowly suffocated, because Caroline used up all the air . . . more and more. She *must* breathe! She would make a hole in the net on her side of the bed. In the dark she tried to do this with her hands, but the mesh was much too stout. She pulled the net aside, and, reaching out, felt about until she had her nail scissors, which happened to be by the side of the bed, and with these she clipped a small hole near the pillow. That was better; better, too, than leaving the curtain drawn aside, because Caroline would be sure to say that mosquitoes had got in. They could not get in through this little hole, surely.

There, a mosquito *had* got in! Or at least something— something that buzzed and clicked and all but talked. Indeed, as the hours dragged by, it did talk, repeating sentences out of Baedeker, and saying: "You are upset! you are upset!" It went on all night, hot and clicking, all night till the dawn came, and then it flew down Caroline's open mouth and stopped.

But Caroline snored instead—so it was almost the same thing. The uncertain light showed her bulk beside Ellen in the bed. She snored not loudly but maddeningly, with a kind of choke in the rhythm of it. She is never silent, thought Ellen, never quiet; either she talks or reads aloud or knits or snores . . . and besides, at night she flies about buzzing. I know that now.

And suddenly she pulled aside the mosquito-net and slipped out of bed. Could she never get away from her? And would she insist on their sharing a room in Florence, too?

Florence . . . Firenze . . . Fiorenza . . . Dante's city! To wander there in the dawn alone—to wander even in this spoilt Siena! But if she dressed now and slipped out Caroline would very soon discover her absence and come after her and scold her. There was no escape.

She looked at the face half buried in the pillow, and knew quite certainly at last, and with a certain exultation, that she hated it and its small, blunt, purposeful features welded into that expanse of pale fat. And why did not Caroline, who after all was two years older than herself, wear a collar to her nightdress? Her neck was creased with age. So was Ellen's own, but she kept it covered. "Cover up your neck, Caroline, and shut your mouth—you are not talking now!"

No, but she would soon begin again.

Oddly enough, at that moment the sleeper did stop snoring, and, stirring slightly, brought her lips together. And Ellen, in her long solid night-gown with its uncompromising buttons and durable machine-made embroidery down the front, stood staring at her, amazed. Was it possible that she could make her miserable puny will dominant over Caroline's when the latter was asleep . . . that she could then make her cousin do what *she* liked? In that case . . .

Yes, yes, yes—it might be wicked, but she *did* wish it!

. . . just for this once . . . just for Florence . . . she *did* wish Caroline dead!

But that would not make her die. No, "no fear," as she had heard the milkman at home say. She looked at her sleeping cousin with an air of command which sat strangely on her grey-haired, shrunken little figure. "Caroline, I wish you to be dead, so that I can see Florence by myself . . . dead, dead, dead!"

Caroline moved again, and started to snore afresh. She wasn't dead—wasn't going to be dead!

There was a man, an Italian, who had strangled his mistress with a silk stocking. Ellen had read about it in the newspaper a few days ago. Caroline had no silk stockings, still less Ellen. But here was a woollen stocking, the one which Caroline had been knitting with all that clicking, yesterday afternoon. Not long enough.

But need it be a stocking? Somewhere in a drawer was a certain brown and white artificial silk scarf of Caroline's. . . . No, not in a drawer, for here it was in her hands. . . . Fasten one end to something immovable—the young man had done so, to get a good pull, and a young man was likely to be much stronger than she.

Now the scarf was knotted to the arm of the heavy tapestried arm-chair, which could move no further because it was already against the bed. But she would never get the scarf passed round that creased throat without waking Caroline, especially as the mosquito curtains were rather in the way. "O God," she prayed, "help me, so that I can see Florence by myself. . . . If she is alive again afterwards, I don't mind so much. Only help me now!"

"God does answer prayer," she thought, thirty seconds later. "She must be very fast asleep . . . I hope the scarf won't break. . . . No, God won't let it."

You can pull and pull at an artificial silk scarf. It stretches, but it does not break, even when you have your knee, your whole body straining against the side of the bed for better purchase.

Ralph Shilleto was up early that morning, walking to and fro in the strip of garden before the only just opened hotel. He was meditating an article on Duccio di Buoninsegna, and while he was trying to recall to his memory exactly which panels of that master's great picture were in the National Gallery, one of the swing doors was opened, and the smaller Philistine came forth, in her black lace-covered hat and grey dust-cloak, carrying a corn-coloured bag adorned with bright wools.

Mr. Shilleto reflected idly that it was the first time he had ever seen her without the other, and wondered where she was off to, so early, and alone. And as she emerged from the grove of little yellow iron tables before the door, he was moved to salute her with a *Buon giorno* and a lifted hat. The old lady glanced at him as she went quickly past, but it was evident to Mr. Shilleto that she vaguely took him for some Italian. She inclined her head, and murmured a very British-sounding *Buon giorno* in her turn.

"Jove, I should never have guessed that the old thing's eyes were so blue," he said to himself, and returned to his meditations on early Sienese art.

Siena at this hour of the morning, when the air was

cool and pearly clear, and the ox-carts were lumbering in from the country . . . how like heaven! But the really heavenly flavour of it was this new, ecstatic sense of being alone, and free.

During that vigil . . . and afterwards . . . Ellen had had ample time to make her simple plans for getting off to Florence alone, without exciting surprise. (It had been wonderful to find how clear her brain was, she whom Caroline had always called muddle-headed.) Luckily they had always come downstairs in the morning for their coffee and rolls; these were never brought up to them. Luckily also Ellen knew that after their bedroom had once been rather perfunctorily "done," it was never again entered by any domestic, unless summoned, until next morning. She had therefore merely to say, when she went downstairs later on, that the other signora in number 6 was not very well, and wished to be left undisturbed until she rang, to ensure that no one would enter number 6 before to-morrow morning, and perhaps not even then.

As to getting to Florence, she had abandoned the idea of going with luggage, because she could not carry even their lightest suitcase downstairs unassisted; besides, to go with luggage meant a real departure, and paying the bill. Without luggage they would think nothing of her going out of the hotel alone, even rather early. But, though they would imagine that she was only going for a walk, she would get just enough necessaries for the night into that satchel of Caroline's. They had already taken rooms ahead at a pension in Florence; she would go to that, explaining that the other lady was following next day with the luggage. And as for money, of which Caroline had the charge, she knew where that was.

A FIRE OF DRIFTWOOD

It had only remained, then, after dressing, to wait until the hotel should be opened, and to make herself a cup of tea on the spirit-lamp. Quite calmly she had brewed and drunk this, even eating a couple of biscuits, and putting as many as she could stuff into the already packed satchel. For she had no fear now of Caroline, who had stopped snoring when she told her to, and scarcely a memory of what she had done to ensure this, except that it had been difficult, but that God had helped her, because He knew how important it was for her to see Florence by herself. Besides, not liking the look of her handiwork, she had heaped as much as she could of the mosquito net upon it and hidden it.

And so, having told the waiter downstairs, in her stumbling but recognisable Italian, just what she had planned to tell him, here she was, with Siena looking so smiling and friendly that she was almost tempted to linger in it. Yet, in spite of thoughts of the Mangia, it was wiser to get on to her goal by the Arno.

Taking her ticket at the station bothered her a little, because she had never done so before in Italy, and she had to hurry at the last moment to catch the Florence train, which was just going—a piece of good fortune, however, since she had not known if there would be one. But, once in it, what a marvellous feeling of peace and security! The very landscape was clad at last in just that beauty and brightness which she had pictured for years, and which until this morning of freedom she had not seen upon it.

And at a quarter-past twelve she was standing, like an exile come home, on the Ponte Vecchio at Florence, gazing at the snows far away above Vallombrosa. The wind was cold, but there was no one to say: "Now, Ellen, you'll get a chill!" nor to restrain her from spending as long as she liked over the trays of cheap ornaments in the booths there. Ellen had been fortunate in this, that, on leaving Santa Maria Novella, which, being near the station, had been chosen for her first glimpse into Paradise, she had fallen into the hands of a kindly and competent cab-driver, and, knowing that she had plenty of money, and seeing already that Florence was a great deal larger, and incomparably more noisy than Siena, had agreed to charter him by the hour. And he had not only saved her from being swept off the pavements in the narrower streets by the trams which run so alarmingly close to them, but he had conducted the little mushroom-hatted murderess with a minimum of trouble and fatigue to the Duomo, the Baptistery, and to San Marco. For the prolonged midday siesta, when public buildings close and most sensible people enjoy a meal—but the *vetturino's* fare only ate biscuits out of a bag—he agreed to drive her slowly about that she might see the city, merely stipulating that he should have some short interval for refreshment, and it was during this period that Ellen stood on the Ponte Vecchio and knew that she was indeed in Florence.

Then her driver reappeared and drove her up to San Miniato, and with tears in her eyes Ellen saw below her that unforgettable vista of the whole city with its mellow roofs and domes and towers, round which the very mountains seem to have disposed themselves as best to enhance its beauty. And she could look at this as long as she pleased. For one moment, indeed, a tiny thought whisked its tail, minnow-like, in the troubled pool of her brain: "Caroline would have liked this." But another, larger one flicked instantly past: "How glad I am she is not here!"

After San Miniato, down again, to the warm-hued spaciousness of Santa Croce, and thence, after a considerable time, to the tiny chapel in the Riccardi Palace where the most joyous and lovely of processions wends its way to so gay a Paradise. And now it began to seem that the sight-seeing would shortly have to stop for the day, since it was nearing the closing hour, the *vetturino* hinted that he had had enough of this odyssey, and Ellen herself was feeling exceedingly tired. She would just go to San Lorenzo, since it was near, to see the famous Michael Angelos, and then she would be driven over the river to the Pension Spalding, for she intended to devote to-morrow to the picture galleries, and recent experience had taught her that of all forms of sight-seeing this is the most exhausting.

As she came back into the empty church from the sacristy, Ellen stopped and began to reckon up what she would have to pay the driver, and though she had, she thought, more than enough in her purse for the purpose, this seemed a convenient opportunity to get at the flat holland pocket of Caroline's which she had with her, and bring out another fifty-lire note. This pocket, designed for the safe carrying of money upon a journey, hung under her skirt from a webbing strap round her waist. Seeking a secluded corner, she pulled up her alpaca dress to get at her store.

But there was nothing hanging there. The holland pocket was gone.

As she professed herself, nevertheless, able to pay him what he demanded, the *vetturino* was sorry for the little old English lady when, some quarter of an hour later, she came down the steps to where he was waiting for her, and falteringly told him what had happened. *Dio mio,* what a misfortune! And had the signora searched all over the church and the two sacristies and the Chapel of the Princes? Yes, every guardian whom she could get hold of had been searching . . . and coldly had the great Night and Dawn in Michael Angelo's sacristy looked at this incapable member of their sex whose money had not even been stolen from her, but had been allowed to drop off—if indeed it had ever been put on. But Ellen told herself that she remembered having put the pocket on. She must have fastened the buckle of its strap insecurely. She *was* incompetent, as Caroline had so often told her.

Standing there on the bottom-most step under the still unfinished façade of San Lorenzo, almost crying, while the cabman with terrific zeal moved and banged the dusty cushions of his vehicle, Ellen saw but one course open to her—to take the night train back to England. She had her return ticket—it was sewn into her stays—and enough money, after paying the driver, for incidental expenses; at least she hoped so. Without more money than that, as well as without any luggage, she suddenly felt that she could not face explanations at the Pension Spalding. In her panic and her weariness she longed all at once for the shelter of "Rosemead," where she would not have to give explanations or make arrangements, and where she would not need money.

Golden was the light that swam over the bustling, untidy Borgo San Lorenzo—over all Florence, which she must now leave without a glimpse of its wealth of pictures, its thousand and one yet unvisited treasures. But she had seen the best, and she had seen it with her own eyes, unhampered and unchilled by another presence. She had had one whole day in the Promised Land by herself.

More than one day, surely, it seemed to her during the night, sitting upright, hot, very tired, and sleepless, in the swaying train where room had only been found for her with difficulty. She must have had several days in Florence, she had seen so much. And that was how she had spent the money in the holland pocket, for it was a complete mistake to suppose that she had lost it, as Caroline would be sure to say she had.

And at any rate, she was going back to a "Rosemead" which she would have for a while to herself, as she had had it seventeen years ago, and so very, very often since wished that she could have it again.

The fly from Upper Waddington station deposited Ellen at the gate of "Rosemead" about thirty hours after a stricken chambermaid had rushed shrieking down the corridor of the hotel at Siena, and just about the exact time that the local police were deciding that the murder, the work of some unknown criminal, had been committed *after* the other signora had gone quietly out for an early walk, as witnessed to by an English signor staying at the hotel, as well as by a waiter. This signora had not, it was true, returned, and meanwhile all trace of her had been lost; and they knew of no relatives with whom to communicate. Moreover, national *amour-propre* prompted them to keep the matter as long as possible out of the English newspapers.

But Ellen was not troubling herself over what might be happening in Italy; she was sufficiently taken aback to find "Rosemead" securely shut up and the blinds down. Somehow she had not expected this . . . and were the lowered blinds for Caroline? Nor did she know to whom her cousin had entrusted the key, nor what had been arranged about their little servant. After standing for some time irresolute on the neat garden-path, she remembered Mrs. Biddle, a charwoman of such superior probity and cleanliness that it seemed likely the key of "Rosemead" might have been confided to her keeping; so to Mrs. Biddle she went.

Mrs. Biddle, just washing up her own dinner things, was much surprised when Miss Ellen, "looking fair tired out and above a bit untidy," came to ask her for the key. It "give her quite a turn."

"Back already, Miss!" she exclaimed. "Why, Miss Caroline did say . . . dear, dear, and no fires lit nor nothing . . . nor no beds aired! She'll not be best pleased, but 'ow was I to know, Miss? It wants a full week yet to the time she said as she should come back."

"Miss Murchison has not come back," said Ellen, without a quaver. "She is coming later, as arranged. It does not matter about fires or beds, Mrs. Biddle. If you will just let me have the key I can manage quite well."

"Why, Miss, you don't look fit to do that!" exclaimed the charwoman. "After all this furrin travelling, too! And Mary Price gone home to her family, as Miss Caroline arranged, and only yesterday I hears from 'er as 'er sister has got the diptheery, so she can't come back not if she was wanted ever so."

"I shall not require Mary Price in any case. It will do if she comes back when Miss Murchison arrives," said Ellen, who, besides being very tired, was all impatience to get into and possess "Rosemead" before Caroline came back . . . as she was afraid she would do sooner or later.

A FIRE OF DRIFTWOOD

Still talking, still lamenting, Mrs. Biddle put on her bonnet—which was part of her superiorness—and came with Ellen, insisting on opening the house herself, drawing up the blinds (so, if they had been drawn down for Caroline, thought Ellen, at least the funeral was over), making a fire, fetching milk, bread, butter, and eggs from her own home. Nothing could be got in that afternoon, since it was Thursday, when commerce ceased in Lower Waddington. "Drat that there early closing, I always says; it come far too often!" remarked Mrs. Biddle.

When she had gone Ellen went all over the little house with something of the ecstatic feeling she had first known to its full in Santa Maria Novella. Her own, her own again, to do what she liked with! She sat down in Caroline's favourite chair in the drawing-room, and, after crying a little, partly from fatigue and partly from sheer happiness, fell asleep.

By next day, however, she had discovered that there were certain disadvantages in being at "Rosemead" without Caroline, of which the chief was the lack of ready money. It was not true, as she had told herself in the Italian train, that she should not need any money at home. When she had paid the fly from the station she had in her possession three and eightpence in English currency, four excessively dirty Italian lira notes mended with stamp-paper, and a Belgian franc which had been given her in the restaurant-car for a French one. She perceived that she could not keep house, even for herself alone, on that. Caroline, of course, could have had what Ellen knew was called "credit" anywhere in Lower Waddington, but she herself felt, with her usual sensation of insignificance revived in the familiar surround-

288

ings, that she was not Caroline. Moreover, her cousin always discharged her bills weekly, and indeed Ellen believed that at the butcher's and the grocer's she always paid money down, distrusting their book-keeping. And as Ellen had not for years been permitted to do any household shopping, because she always muddled up the different kinds of sugar and did not, so Caroline declared, know scrag end of neck from leg, she felt it would be too great an ordeal to face shop-people now, especially since this would almost necessarily require explanations of Miss Murchison's absence. There was, however, a supply of tinned provisions in the house, and Mrs. Biddle, without being told to do so, had ordered milk and bread to be sent in daily. She had also shown Ellen how to light the gas-stove in the corner of the kitchen— which Ellen had never done before, and only did now with great apprehension—and the weather was so warm that a sitting-room fire was not necessary.

Even so it was borne in upon Ellen that there might come a day when, unless she could procure some money for herself, she might almost wish Caroline back again. She did not know when the next instalment of her little annuity was due—she never did know. She had no cheque-book as Caroline had, no account at the bank. . . . But while she thus brooded over her financial position, the thought of Aunt Sarah's Bracelet rose suddenly in her mind like a beneficent sun. That would save her, that wide gold fetter or cuff, of unexampled ugliness, adorned with a large though inferior diamond, which Caroline had insisted on depositing at the bank when, some years ago, a nonagenarian aunt had bequeathed it to Ellen. Now the legatee, who had temporarily forgotten the Bracelet's existence, thought with relief of its size and the brilliance of the diamond, and was glad that it had never occurred to her to sell it before now, and go to Italy on the proceeds. (But Caroline would certainly have prevented her.) If she could only nerve herself to go and ask for her property back, she would take the train to Shilton, their market town, the fare being only eighteenpence, and sell it to a jeweller there.

It was while Ellen was picturing, with a good deal of alarm, her visit to the bank, and what she should say to "the banker," that something about a receipt came into her mind, and this bright vision was promptly annihilated. It was Caroline who had taken the Bracelet to the bank, and Caroline to whom the receipt had been made out; she distinctly remembered, now, that Caroline had told her this, adding: "You would only have lost it if it had been made out to you, so if you ever want the thing, you must tell me, and I will go and get it for you." She could not even come at her own property without Caroline!

The tears began to trickle down Ellen's cheeks. How unfair it was! But she *must* have money. Did Caroline wish her to starve, just because she was not here?

It was at this point that Ellen's new idea came to her. Why should Caroline *not* be here—at least, why should *she* not say that Miss Murchison had returned, but was unable to see visitors . . . indisposed . . . keeping her bed, in fact? If she could make people believe that, it would be far better than acknowledging that Caroline had not come back with her, and would lead to much less awkwardness. She wished now that she had adopted this line at first, and given Mrs. Biddle this version. It was not true, she recognised, like the other one, about which the only doubtful point was the actual day of

Caroline's return—for return she would of course, in the end. But this new idea, Ellen now saw, was better. For one thing, she could go into a shop and order anything she wanted to be "sent to Miss Murchison," and they would send it, and it would not matter that she, Ellen, had no money, nor would the shop expect Caroline to pay if she were in bed.

She had an opportunity of practising her new story that very afternoon on a crony of Caroline's who appeared about tea-time, and whom, as Ellen answered the door herself, she found herself obliged to admit, at least as far as the little hall, before she could tell her that she had come in vain. "I heard you were back, Miss Wright," said the visitor effusively, "so I thought that I might venture to look in, and see how you and dear Miss Murchison have enjoyed yourselves."

"I am sorry to say that my cousin is not very well," replied Ellen a shade nervously. "I am afraid that she cannot see anyone at present."

"Dear, dear!" exclaimed the caller. "Have you had the doctor?"

"No, it is nothing serious. A touch of influenza, I expect—Italian influenza," pronounced Ellen, who had heard of the so-called Spanish variety. "And I think I had better not ask you to stay to tea, for it is very catching."

The visitor went. This was certainly the better line to take about Caroline.

Having settled that her cousin was in bed in her own room, Ellen had unwillingly to admit to herself that evening that there was a sort of comfort and stability in the idea. A slight feeling of loneliness which had been growing on her was thereby checked. She would make Caroline some nice hot bread and milk to-night; that would be good for her influenza.

Having made it, she carried it, all steaming, into Caroline's empty bedroom and set it down by the unmade and shrouded bed. Then she went downstairs again, lit the lamp, and resumed her peaceful reading of *A Wanderer in Florence,* which brought back to her so delightfully the many pleasant days she had spent there—alone.

Before she ate her own breakfast next morning Ellen took a cup of tea, an egg and some buttered toast up to Caroline's bedroom, and brought down the cold bread and milk. Its untouched condition troubled her no more than it would have troubled a child who places food before an unresponsive doll. During her own breakfast she began to compile the list of edible and other objects which she intended to order "for Miss Murchison"; it was becoming quite a long one, and perhaps before she took it out with her she would do well to show it to Caroline.

She was just thinking of adding to it, she was not sure why, "new silk scarf (artificial)" when she heard an agitated knocking at the back door. Since it could not be a friend of Caroline's, and was probably only the baker, she went to open it. But it was Mrs. Biddle, who stood there, with her bonnet on one side, and her face all red and pale in patches.

"Oh, Miss," she began at once, " 'ave you seen this in the paper about poor Miss Caroline? Oh, Miss, she won't come 'ome no more! Why ever did you go and leave her alone in them 'eathenish parts . . . poor Miss Caroline, as always says to me, 'Mrs. Biddle,' she says, and if she said it once she's said it a 'undred times, 'Mrs. Biddle, you do turn out a room as it *should* be turned out!' Now I shan't never 'ear 'er say that no more!"

" 'Won't come home no more'—what do you mean, Mrs. Biddle?" demanded Ellen. "She *is* home." But Mrs. Biddle, struggling with hysteria, pointed to a newspaper which she had let fall, and Ellen picked this up from the kitchen floor. It was of the sensational type dear to Mrs. Biddle's class, and on the front page was to be seen in large letters: *Shocking Discovery in Italian Hotel. English Lady found Strangled.*

With a growing sensation of indignation Ellen glanced down the column to the accompaniment of the charwoman's sobs. Caroline's name was there (spelt wrongly) and her own (even more incorrectly though phonetically rendered) and their place of residence. Moreover, it appeared that this Miss "Rait" had been traced to Florence, where she had spent the whole of the day sightseeing. The murder had been committed with a scarf belonging to the deceased lady—

A wave of anger burst over Ellen, and she read no further. How dare Caroline put such things in the papers . . . but it was just like her . . . Caroline safe in bed upstairs eating a good breakfast! And how did Caroline know that she had gone to Florence, and what she had done there?

"Stop crying, Mrs. Biddle!" she said, in a tone almost approaching the imperious, at any rate, so unlike anything which Mrs. Biddle had ever heard from her before that she did cease from her lamentations, and looked at her in astonishment. "Stop crying, and go, and take that wicked, lying paper away with you! I am surprised at your reading and believing such things! Miss Murchison is here in bed with influenza; I have just taken her breakfast up to her."

At this Mrs. Biddle's surprise blossomed into sheer

A FIRE OF DRIFTWOOD

amazement. "But you said, Miss, on Thursday, as 'ow you had left 'er behind!"

"I said that she was coming home later, and she has come. But she is not at all well, and she will be very much annoyed at all this. Please go at once, or she will be calling down to know what the noise is about."

Thoroughly bewildered and half frightened, Mrs. Biddle left.

But when she had gone the anger which had sustained Ellen ebbed from her, and she crawled trembling out of the kitchen, clutching the newspaper, which Mrs. Biddle had left behind after all. She was thinking: "If this dreadful lie is in the newspapers, all the village will read it, and people will be coming here to ask me about it . . . I can't, I won't see them!" And with a feverish determination she locked and bolted both the front and back doors.

She was only too right. Before ten o'clock had struck from the wheezy cuckoo clock in the hall, three ladies of Caroline's acquaintance had tried severally to gain admittance, then a man whom Ellen (peering cautiously from an upper window) imagined might be a reporter. But, as long as she made no sound and did not allow herself to be seen, people might think the house was empty. They would not, surely, break into an empty house, however inquisitive they might be! Caroline in her room was quite quiet. But it was her part to take thought for Caroline now, and she was rather proud of the responsibility involved in the change of rôle, so she wrote on a sheet of notepaper in large letters: *"Please go away, so much knocking and ringing disturbs Miss Murchison!"* and, choosing a moment when no one was in sight, darted out and pinned this to the front door.

294

A little later she had another good idea, and, cutting out the "Shocking Discovery," she wrote on another piece of paper *This is quite untrue!* and, having stuck it to the newspaper cutting with an adhesive luggage label, affixed this also to the door. And from eleven onwards she watched the stream of people who were, she feared at last, attracted rather than kept away by her notices, which now there was no chance of removing—the people who knocked, read the notices aloud and made comments, and then gathered in groups on the path talking. At one time Ellen counted twenty-three persons either inside or outside the gate of "Rosemead." But she saw with glee that they dared not, could not, enter the house.

The end came about three o'clock in the afternoon. Feeling rather tired with all this excitement, her vigil, and the absence of any midday meal, Ellen was dozing in the drawing-room below the Italian photographs, when she was roused by a tremendous ring at the front door, followed by a most purposeful knocking. Startled and indignant, she jumped to her feet and went quickly upstairs to her post of observation. Ere she could get there the summons was repeated, even louder. "Be quiet!" she said angrily under her breath, pulling aside the window-curtain with caution.

Next moment a scream rang through the quiet little house. "Caroline, Caroline, come quickly! There's a police inspector at the door . . . and I don't know what to say to him! Why has he come? Caroline, *you* go down and see him! Caroline, *come!*"

They found her in Miss Murchison's empty bedroom, tugging distractedly at the sheeted-over bed, and crying: "It is mean, *mean,* to pay me out like this! *If you don't come I'll do it again!*"

CLAIRVOYANCE

CLAIRVOYANCE

I

"Yes, it's certainly a lovely place," said Mr. Alfred Pickering, the Australian wool-grower come "home," as he looked out through the open French window of the library of Strode Manor on to the great lawn with the lake in the distance. "Of all the houses I've seen in the last couple of months, this is the only one which in the least bears out the description sent me. I think you house agents have mistaken your job, you know; you ought to go in for writing fiction."

Mr. Simpkins (of Pottinger, Simpkins and Marrow) sniggered. "Oh, come, sir! We have to do our best for our clients."

"Well, you don't seem to have succeeded here," retorted Mr. Pickering, "attractive as the place is. I can't understand its having stood empty all this time. How long did you say it was since Mr. Strode went abroad— five years?"

"Fancy his leaving all the beautiful furniture in the house, too!" commented his wife.

"But it has all been well cared for, as you can see," replied Mr. Simpkins, looking complacently round. "As you say, madam, there's beautiful things in the house— antiques, too. Mr. Strode was a noted collector. But his best china—pots they call Bing, or Ming, or some such comic name—is lent to the Victoria and Albert Museum."

"Those, too, are the sort of things you see in museums," remarked Mr. Pickering, with his eyes upon the fan-shaped arrangement on the only wall where bookcases did not rise too high for such a display, and where the elaborate inlay of an early seventeenth-century German arquebus shouldered the tapering length and complicated hilt of a Spanish rapier or the unfamiliar mechanism of a wheel-lock pistol.

"This is the study, I suppose," said comfortable-looking Mrs. Pickering. "But I am sure that if I tried to read in here, I should always be looking out at that beautiful view."

"Yes, madam," agreed Mr. Simpkins, towering over her in his long, light overcoat; "yes, especially when the famous rhododendrons by the lake are in bloom. And, of course, if the house was occupied the grounds would look more as they used to do—not but what the lawn is mown regularly now. But a property always appears to much better advantage when there is someone in it."

"What I can't understand," reiterated the Australian, "is why in five years there hasn't been someone in it, or why it hasn't been bought, since you say Mr. Strode would prefer to sell."

"Well, sir," responded Mr. Simpkins, with a slight tinge of constraint, "it's not everyone who requires a large place like this, all furnished. Gentlemen who would take a lease of a property of this size usually have their own furniture; still more so those who might wish to purchase it."

"Yes, I suppose that's true. But when a man comes back from the under-side of the globe like me, he's glad to find a home all ready to step into. And I should have thought there might have been other chaps in the same position. Have you had *nobody* after it in five years?"

"Oh, several people, Mr. Pickering, several," the house agent assured him in haste. "But for some of them the Manor was too big, for others too small. There's always a something, as the saying is." He broke off suddenly. "Would you kindly excuse me for a moment, sir? There's the gardener out there wanting to speak to me, I see, before he goes home to his dinner."

"I call it charming," repeated Mr. Pickering, as the agent hurried out into the verandah and vanished. "Don't you think so, too, Polly?"

But plump little Mrs. Pickering did not seem to share his enthusiasm. "If you ask me," she said slowly, "I believe there *is* a 'something' about this place which frightens everyone away, for all it seems so bright and has been so well kept up. Just now, when I was looking out at the lake there . . ." She stopped.

"But it was you, little woman, who said you'd always be looking at it if you lived here!"

"I'm not so sure, now, that I should," responded his wife, drawing her breath in sharply. "And, Alfred, didn't you notice, when we stopped the car at that little farm outside the village and asked the way, just before we met Mr. Simpkins, the girl looked almost scared? I wonder if the Manor is supposed to be haunted?"

Her husband chuckled. "The only objection to haunted houses that I've ever heard of is that you can't get servants to stay in 'em. Otherwise I should be no end pleased to have an ancestor clanking round in chains, even if it wasn't my own ancestor. If there's a Johnny of that sort here, so much the better!"

"Alfred, are you really thinking of buying the place?"

"I'm inclined to, if you're agreeable, old lady. I like it fine. The house may not be as old as these fellows make

301

out, but it's none the worse for that, and the grounds only want a little attention—almost a park, they are, too. I should like to buy it lock, stock and barrel, furniture, books and curios—including those queer old guns (if they *are* guns) and swords and things there." He surveyed the trophy of weapons for a moment. "I could put my two bushmen's spears in with them. . . . Hullo, why has this sheath got no sword in it? Japanese work, by the look of it, like that figure in armour over there near you."

Mrs. Pickering was now by the door, looking down at something. "I don't think this cheap rug is worth buying!" she observed critically. "An absolutely shoddy thing—on a valuable carpet like this, too!" She stooped, turned back the rug in question, and became quite silent.

At that moment the lank form of Mr. Simpkins reappeared at the French window, and him Mr. Pickering, still examining the display of weapons, addressed over his shoulder. "I say, isn't there a sword or something missing from here?"

But the house agent did not answer because at the same instant Mrs. Pickering also said, in a voice so queer that her husband immediately turned round: "I see now why this rug was put here. But . . . what made that stain?"

Mr. Pickering came over to view the place. The representative of Pottinger, Simpkins and Marrow followed, more slowly. Colour had sprung into his cadaverous cheeks. "Well, madam, it's hard for me to answer that question, isn't it?" he asked, in a manner attempting the semi-jovial. "Not having lived in the house, you see. . . . Oh, something spilt, I should say, by one of the caretakers we've had here; and, after trying to get the mark out, the woman's gone and bought that cheap rug and put it down to cover the damage. But the carpet could easily be turned round, in which case that side of it would be——"

"Yes, of course it could!" broke in Mr. Pickering cheerfully. His Polly really looked quite strange and upset. "What's come to you, my girl? Accidents will happen!"

"I want to know what the accident was!" repeated his wife, with an odd, pale persistence most unlike her.

"My dear, how can Mr. Simpkins possibly tell us? It's unfortunate there should be a stain, but I can't see that it's of any importance how it came there."

"Allow me, madam," quoth Mr. Simpkins, stooping and replacing the rug. "I will instruct the present caretaker to have a try to get the mark out. I suggest that you come out into the garden now, sir, and have a look at this side of the house. . . . Madam, I am afraid you are feeling indisposed; shall I fetch you some water?"

"My dear Polly, what's got you?" exclaimed her husband in alarm, putting his arm round her plump contours. "Here, I believe I have my flask with me; yes." And with one hand he pulled it out. "Sit down there, dear, on the sofa, and have a drop of this, perhaps with a little water, if Mr. Simpkins will kindly fetch some."

"No!" said Mrs. Pickering, shuddering violently. "No, I won't sit down in this room. Take me out of it quickly —no, no, *no*, Alfred, not through that window—that's worse, much worse! And for God's sake don't have anything to do with the house! Something dreadful has happened in this room."

And as her husband, thoroughly frightened (for she was not by nature an hysterical or fanciful woman), hurried her through the door, she burst into tears.

"Most unfortunate," said Mr. Simpkins about an hour and a half later to his partner in their office in the little county town. "Blanked unfortunate! He was all for taking it, perhaps even for buying it, the Colonial."

"I hope you didn't call him that, Simmie," replied Mr. Marrow, who in shape resembled his name-sake of the vegetable kingdom. "Dominions they are nowadays, Australians."

Mr. Simpkins took no notice. "Yes, I believe he would have bought it if that blessed wife of his hadn't gone off into hysterics in the library. Perhaps I oughtn't to have taken them in there; but if I had made any difficulty about it that would have seemed odd, too."

"What made her go into hysterics?"

"She had moved the rug. It's true that it is in an unusual place for a rug to be. But God alone knows what put the suspicion into her head, because the mark don't look like *that* now—not to my thinking. Funny thing was that at the same moment—the very same moment, mind you—the chap himself saw that the sword was missing; said something about it, too, but I took no notice. (The sheath ought not to be on the wall at all.) And then in a minute or two he had to take her out of the room, fairly howling. Queer creatures, women, damned queer!"

Mr. Marrow, about to light a cigarette, paused. "I think, considering what you and me know about the library of the Manor, we may say that they are. And now it almost looks as if it was a case with this Mrs. Pickering, too, of—what do they call it?—the thing that caused all the trouble five years ago."

"You surely don't mean that she is what they said at the inquest that poor girl was?"

"No, no; I mean the business that started it—clair . . . what the devil is it called?—clairvoyance."

"Oh, that! But if this Mrs. Pickering had had clair-voyance she would have seen——"

"What it's a good thing for her that she didn't see," finished Mr. Marrow, achieving the lighting of his cigarette. "But, damn it all, we've lost yet another possible tenant. I suppose they must have heard something, in spite of all the trouble we took that they shouldn't speak to anyone in the village and get wind of it like the last people did."

"I don't think it was that. And yet when he had soothed her down and got her into the car—for she said she must go straight back to London—he asked me right out, there in the drive: 'Has there been a murder or a suicide taken place in that room? Now tell me the truth, as man to man.'"

"And what did you say, as man to man?"

"I told him the truth, of course. I said: 'No, no murder or suicide took place in that room, I give you my word.' So he asks: 'What did take place there, then?' looking a bit as if he had caught the horrors from his wife, though he didn't seem at all that sort. (No more did she, to do her justice.) I says: 'My dear sir, the house being Queen Anne, lots of things that we know nothing about must have happened in that library.' 'Queen Anne!' says he. 'Queen Victoria, more like! But something very unpleasant took place there, and at a guess five years ago. I shall not take the house. Send in your bill for any expenses you may have been put to over this visit.' Then he got into his car and slammed the door; and that was the last I saw of them. All the woman's fault, like the . . . the affair in the library."

"That's a bit hard," observed Mr. Marrow judicially. "It wasn't really the poor girl's fault; if anybody's, it was Strode's—at least, he was responsible. You may remember that if the medical evidence hadn't been so positive that it was impossible to hypnotise a person into doing a thing like that, he might have been sent for trial.—Did these Pickerings find out that he left the very day after the inquest; just walked out of the house and has never been near it since, in all these years?"

"Not from me, you bet. . . . Well, there's nothing to be done but to go on with that advertisement, *'To Americans and others,'* because it seems pretty hopeless to get anybody else—unless the place could be given another name. No one in England is likely to have forgotten the 'Strode Manor tragedy.'"

"We might head the ad. with this, which I saw used the other day, and by a London firm, I fancy: *'Situate amid inconceivable rurality.'* Not true of the Manor, exactly, but that's no matter. It's a taking expression, that's the main thing."

Mr. Simpkins did not reply. His eyes had a rapt, glassy look; an idea was being born.

"I believe," he said at last, "that if we could hook an American we should do better *not* to keep the story quiet, but to boost it to him for all it was worth. Wouldn't a hundred per cent. Yank be likely to find it full of 'pep'?"

"Simmie," exclaimed Mr. Marrow, "you've hit it! We might even get more for the place . . . when we find the right oil-king!"

CLAIRVOYANCE

II

The close-shaven lawns were brilliantly green, the great rhododendrons in their full rosy magnificence, when the horror happened, five years before. The villagers said that the bushes had never bloomed so luxuriantly since; but then they never went into the grounds to see. They were afraid of meeting her, the delicate pale girl with *those* hands, or perhaps the little boy. . . .

It was not exactly a party; Edward Strode did not like them. But Persis, his seventeen-year-old daughter, had her friend Cynthia Storrington staying with her, even as Mr. and Mrs. Strode had the elegant Mrs. Fleming stopping with them; and three girls and a couple of youths of Persis' acquaintance had come to tea and tennis. Moreover, Catherine, the youngest child—the two boys in between were away at school—was celebrating her birthday and playing with half a dozen small companions of both sexes, under due supervision from nurses, down by the lake and its red and pink bastions of blossom. But though Mrs. Strode had earlier presided over the tea-table in the drawing-room on the other side of the house, she was now sitting with some embroidery on the sofa in the library, where were also Mrs. Fleming, in a Paris frock of extreme simplicity and expensiveness, smoking a cigarette in a long amber holder, and Edward Strode himself, with his little pointed Elizabethan beard, carefully mending a torn page in a recently acquired manuscript.

"Where ever did you get that charming design, Marian?" suddenly asked the guest, coming to the sofa and stooping over Mrs. Strode with a lazy, boneless grace. "Not from any shop, I am sure."

"No. I adapted it from a *tsuba* of Edward's."

"Mercy on us, what's a *tsuba?*"

"The guard of a Japanese sword," replied Mrs. Strode, stitching away. "He has quite a quantity of them, some with very agreeable designs indeed. I have used the best already. This one is actually from the guard of his precious Sadamune *katana* on the wall there, and, not being detached like the others, was a little more difficult to copy, since I would not let him take it off for me." She held up her work. "Any design on a *tsuba* must fit into its more or less circular shape, you see. These little drooping stems are rice."

"But it is exquisite!" exclaimed Mrs. Fleming. "A miracle of design—and of ingenuity. I should like to see the original. A trifle out of place on a sword-hilt, though, somehow—rice."

Edward Strode looked up. "Some hilts have plum blossoms, bamboos blown by the wind, peonies or twisted water-weeds. I will get the sword down for you with pleasure, Erica; it is one of my proudest treasures. I have not had it long, however. The *tsuba,* as it happens, has been rather a sore point ever since Jenkinson was here a fortnight ago, for he had the impudence to say that he was not sure if it was genuine." He made a wry face.

"But the sword——"

"Oh, the sword is genuine enough, and rare, and very old; a poem in steel—a signed poem, too. It's infernal nonsense about the guard, of course; still, I shall not be quite at ease until a better authority than Jenkinson has seen it."

CLAIRVOYANCE

"But, Edward," protested Mrs. Fleming, "surely *you* are an authority on . . . what do you call the things?"

Edward Strode smiled his infrequent smile. "There are seven hundred different specimens of these guards in the South Kensington Museum alone, for there exist about seventy different schools and sub-schools in the art of *tsuba*-making." He was bringing down the sword, scabbard and all from the wall—a long-sword, a *katana,* slightly curved, with the usual long pommel wrapped round and round in an open pattern with dark silk braid, which allowed the pearly incrustations of the ray-skin mount to show through its interstices. The sheath, of magnolia wood ornamented with strips of cane, was old and shabby; but had it been lavishly decorated one would not have looked at it again when the blade was out—as its owner, almost reverently, drew it out now; so mirror-bright was the steel, so perfect in line, so smooth and flawless its marvellous surface. Indeed, Mrs. Fleming, forgetting her desire to examine the guard, said, with something like a gasp:

"You say this is very old—it can't be!"

"It was forged about six hundred years ago; it is dated. Sadamune, the famous swordsmith who made it, worked in the early part of the fourteenth century."

"In the thirteen hundreds! Edward, it's impossible! It might have been made yesterday! Why, the blade of that slim, pointed sword on the wall there—I happened to be examining it yesterday—which I suppose is not so old, looks far older, for it is all flecked and pitted."

"And yet that rapier is three hundred years the junior of this sword. It is a reputed Toledo blade, too. But, my dear Erica, compared with the work of the great Japanese swordsmiths, even the swords of Damascus and

Toledo are, as a French authority puts it, but the efforts of children. Japanese swords are incomparably the most beautiful that the world has ever produced. Do you know that no European sword has ever possessed an edge like this, because if it had the whole sword would be as brittle as glass (since European swords are of the same hardness all over). But here the body of the blade —the very bright part—is of softer temper to avoid the risk of breakage. I have cut through a floating scarf with this beautiful thing, and I daresay it would go with the same ease through a man's leg, bone and all—I have not tried."

"What is that kind of wavy mistiness along the edge?" asked Mrs. Fleming, bending over the weapon.

"That is the *yakiba,* the tempering, patterned so on purpose. There are thirty-two main designs of *yakiba.*"

"Good heavens!"

"Now I will show you an interesting thing," said her host, well mounted on his subject. "You see where the *yakiba* comes round to the point of the blade—the *boshi* —and takes a different pattern?"

"Yes, if you can call anything so ghostly and indeterminate a pattern. I suppose you will tell me that there are several different classes of that?"

"As a matter of fact, there are. Well, this particular one is characteristic only of the smith who made this sword, Sadamune, the great Masamune's favourite pupil; and the shape represents the upper part of the head of Jizo, the god who looks after children, and who is generally represented as a young and handsome man with a beautiful smile."

Mrs. Fleming laughed. "Alas, I can't make out anything remotely suggesting the head of any man, handsome or ugly. But I do see that the sword is a thing of beauty, cold and deadly perhaps, but exquisite.—Now I must look at the guard."

"You do recognise the sword's beauty?" said Edward Strode eagerly. "I am glad of that. As to its coldness, there is a Japanese poem which says that a drawn sword brings a cool breeze into a house even at midsummer. Swords, you know, were formerly in Japan objects of veneration, almost of worship; the swordsmiths lived a semi-religious life, and the forging of a sword was practically a religious ceremony, requiring a ceremonial costume."

"The forging then," commented the visitor, "was hardly of a piece with that in the *Ring*—I mean when Siegfried, clad in his customary hearth-rug, bangs away at 'Nothung' on Covent Garden stage! So these are your bending rice-stalks, Marian. What workmanship! What metal is the guard made of, Edward?"

"Iron—pierced iron."

"And what are these tiny gold dragons on the hilt, under the binding?"

"Those are the *menuki,* to give a better grip," explained Mr. Strode. "The hilt, of course, is more recent than the blade, the *tsuba* too, even if it is really of the school of Miochin, as it purports to be.—Hallo, Persis, have your visitors gone?"

"Yes, Daddy, but only just," replied his elder daughter, appearing at the French window, and sniffing at the big creamy rose which she had plucked from the verandah. "They said they were too hot for any more tennis, lazy pigs, so we went back to the drawing-room and played the 'willing' game—you know. Oh, and Daddy," she stepped into the room, "such an interesting thing hap-

pened. You know how you blindfold a person and put
your hands on their shoulders, two of you, and 'will'
them to do something or other. Yes," as her father
frowned impatiently, "I know you think it silly, but
listen! Cynthia said she was ready to be 'willed'; so we
blindfolded her and told her to make her mind a blank,
and we settled that she should go to the little table
with the snuff-boxes and vinaigrettes, and pick out the
china snuff-box which has that darling little landscape,
and take it over and put it in a particular place on the
mantelpiece. Well, after we had willed a bit she started
off, slowly, and went to the table with us—it was Joan
and I—and picked out the box from the others all
right——"

"I detest this playing with the fringes of a serious
subject like hypnotism," growled Mr. Strode.

"Yes, I know, darling, but listen! Directly Cynthia
got the snuff-box into her hands she began to feel it all
over in a curious way; then, instead of taking it to the
mantelpiece, she suddenly sat down and held the snuff-
box tight, and began to talk very fast; we could not
make out much of what she was saying, and, in fact, it
hardly sounded like her voice. Presently the tears began
to run down her face, and she seemed so unhappy that
we took the snuff-box away from her, and unbandaged
her eyes; and after a bit she woke up and was just the
same as usual.—Daddy, I shan't stay to be looked at like
that. Smell this, and you'll feel better!" She thrust the
great rose into her father's face, laughed, and sped out
again by the way she had come.

"That's rather a curious thing, Edward," remarked
Mrs. Strode after a moment, laying down her embroidery. "Cynthia could not have known the story of

the last owner of the porcelain snuff-box."

"The girl is apparently a sensitive," replied her husband, sliding the Japanese sword carefully back into its sheath. . . . "She's what is commonly called clairvoyante—though to my thinking clairvoyance can nearly always be explained by thought transference from the mind of some other person present."

"But not in this case," said Mrs. Strode quietly. "Persis knows nothing about that little box."

"Cynthia's tears were justified, then?" enquired Mrs. Fleming.

"The last owner of the porcelain snuff-box was certainly very unhappy," replied Mrs. Strode. "But only Edward and I know that."

"Then the girl is undoubtedly a sensitive!" exclaimed Mrs. Fleming. "It seems to me a gift that should be cultivated; it would be invaluable to a collector, for instance. . . . Why, of course, Edward, here is a splendid chance of getting some light on the problem of your *tsuba!* Have Cynthia in and see what she says!"

"I am afraid I should not attach much weight to it. I am sceptical about clairvoyance, for the reason I have mentioned."

"Yet you admit that the girl must be a sensitive. Test her!"

"Another time," said Mr. Strode. "Have you finished looking at the *tsuba,* Erica?"

"But Cynthia is leaving to-morrow, Edward," his wife reminded him, as she selected a fresh thread of silk. "By the morning train, in fact, directly after breakfast."

"So you see that there is no time like the present," urged Mrs. Fleming with a laugh. "You could try her on something else first. Robert" (she was referring to

313

her husband) "would be so pleased, poor jealous darling, to hear that your Mino da Fiesole Virgin and Child, for instance, was only 'of the school.'"

"I don't imagine," said Edward Strode dryly, "that, however jealous Fleming is, he would be satisfied with such an ascription on the authority of an ignorant girl of seventeen. But the manifestation is interesting, none the less."

"Then for heaven's sake let us go and see it!" cried Mrs. Fleming. "Perhaps Cynthia is even now describing the past occupants of those William and Mary chairs in the drawing-room!"

"You forget, there is only Persis with her now," re-marked Mrs. Strode. "The game is over."

"And in any case, I should not have joined in that childishness," observed her husband. "If I made such an experiment at all it would be quietly in here. But of course it is arrant nonsense to imagine that the child could tell one anything of value on a disputed point—anything about the maker of this *tsuba,* for instance."

"One Japanese looking much like another Japanese, even to a clairvoyante," suggested Mrs. Fleming. "On the other hand, suppose the *tsuba* was turned out in Birmingham—don't look so outraged, Edward, I'm sure it wasn't. But do have Cynthia in and see what happens! Marian, do make him!"

Mrs. Strode put down her work. "I will go and ask her to come in here if you are so set on it, Erica. Shall I, Edward?"

Half reluctantly, her husband nodded, and she left the room.

"This should be most interesting," said Mrs. Fleming, laying aside her cigarette-holder. Taking up a strip of

CLAIRVOYANCE

old brocade from the back of the sofa, she spread its
faded silver gilt and roses over the whole length of the
sheathed *katana,* still upon the table, leaving only the
guard exposed. "You know how to start her off, Edward
—since it seems that *is* the method to start her? I have
played at it, too. . . . But I was forgetting," she added
on a different note, "I was quite forgetting that you
know something of hypnotism, as of most things; so she
ought to respond very readily if you 'will' her to see a
Japanese of the proper period working at those charming ears of rice!"

The door opened.

"Here's Cynthia, ready to oblige," announced Persis.
"What can she do for you, Daddy?"

Her father fingered his little pointed beard. "My
dear," said Mrs. Fleming, coming forward, "it is really
I who want you to—oh no, I must not tell you exactly
what. But we hear that you were so clever about . . .
something in the drawing-room."

"Was I?" asked Cynthia Storrington, opening wider
her innocent, dreamy-looking eyes. She was a girl for
whom the word "ethereal" might have been especially
minted, a tall slip of a girl with ash-blond hair and very
delicate features, wearing a green dress the colour of an
early beech-leaf.

Mrs. Strode reappeared. "There is something on the
table here, Cynthia, that my husband wants to make an
experiment about, if you will help him."

"But how can I?" asked the girl. She glanced shyly
at Mr. Strode. "Oh no, I'd rather not, I think. It was
only a game, you know, just now in the drawing-room."

"And *I* don't consider it any more than a game,
Cynthia," said her host quickly. "And if you would

315

really rather not——"

"Oh, Cynthia, do!" pleaded Mrs. Fleming.

"Cynthia, don't be a goat!" admonished Persis more bluntly and perhaps more efficaciously. And she added in an audible whisper, as she went nearer to her friend: "You can make up what you jolly well please!"

"But I don't make up!" protested Cynthia, wrinkling her white forehead. "I don't know what I say!"

"Or do, either? Didn't you know you were crying?"

Cynthia turned crimson. "Don't torment her, Persis!" said that damsel's mother. "My dear Cynthia, take no notice of her, or of anybody else; go back to the drawing-room!"

But Edward Strode had his eyes fixed upon the girl. Perhaps it was the first time that he had ever been quite aware of her particular quality, though it was not her first visit to the Manor. And Cynthia, supersensitive as she evidently was, seemed to be conscious of something unusual in his gaze. She looked at him, then away. "I will try if you like, Mr. Strode."

"Thank you," said he briefly; and Mrs. Fleming added: "That is very sporting of you, Cynthia." Then Persis produced a silk handkerchief of her elder brother's which had evidently served the same purpose previously, and tied it over the dreamy eyes.

"Who is going to do it?" she asked, knotting the ends. "You and I, Daddy?"

"No, not you, because you do not know what the problem is. Mrs. Fleming, who does, will assist in this . . . game of Blind Man's Buff." It was plain that he was ill at ease, ashamed, almost, at taking part, to please his old friend, in what he considered a childish performance.

The two laid their hands lightly on the girl's slim shoulders, and for a few minutes there was complete silence in the room itself. But from without floated in the cries and laughter of the children chasing each other about the rhododendrons, away by the lake, and the sleepy, liquid notes of distant wood-pigeons. Cynthia in her leaf-green frock had stood at first like an image; then, all at once, but still with an automaton-like stiffness, she, and the couple with her, began to move towards the library table. Mrs. Strode and Persis watched them. A little pressure easily directs a blindfolded and susceptible young thing, thought Mrs. Strode sceptically; she had resumed her seat on the sofa and her embroidery.

As she made this reflection there came a knock at the door—for Mr. Strode's sanctuary was never entered without permission. Persis darted out.

She returned. "Bother!" she said in a low voice to her mother. "It's Major Whittingham, come about a licence or something. He wants to see Daddy most particularly, Morton says, and can't wait. He wouldn't keep him more than a couple of minutes. He's in the drawing-room."

Edward Strode heard. "Then I am afraid I must go to him. We had, however, hardly begun." He removed his hands. "My dear Cynthia, a thousand apologies! If you can spare the time to stay here we can resume when I return; I shall not be long."

"Shall I take off the handkerchief?" asked the disappointed Mrs. Fleming as their host left the room; and without waiting for an answer she untied it. "There, sit down, Cynthia; I don't expect Mr. Strode will be more than a few minutes."

Still as if she were in one piece Cynthia obeyed, seating herself in the chair drawn up to the table; and almost immediately one long slender hand began to search over the table's surface. The other she had put up to her eyes. It occurred to Mrs. Fleming that the girl was further "gone" than she had thought, and that perhaps it was not altogether good to have called her back so abruptly.

"I know," said Cynthia suddenly, in a slightly unusual voice, "what you want me to touch. It is here somewhere." She brought down her other hand, and that, too, began to pass over the nearer portion of the table, sweeping about like a blind person's. Together they reached, one the shrouded and sheathed blade, the other the shrouded pommel of the Japanese sword.

"Cynthia, what are you keeping your eyes shut for?" asked Mrs. Strode sharply, leaning forward from the sofa. "Open them, child!"

But Cynthia's eyes were still shut when her left hand clutched the sword through the strip of brocade; still shut when with a couple of imperious gestures she first flung off the strip and then, somewhat to the consternation of the two ladies, drew off the sheath of the *katana* and threw that, too, upon the floor. The long, keen blade gleamed naked on the library table.

"You'll cut yourself," remonstrated Mrs. Fleming almost nervously. "And it isn't the blade that we want to know about.—Whatever is the girl playing at?"

For while the fingers of Cynthia's right hand were clutching the braided ray-skin of the pommel, the fingers of the left felt along the blade, leaving little patches on the unsullied steel.

"You'll catch it for doing that!" muttered Persis, who knew that no ungloved hand must ever touch that sacred surface.

318

"Sadamune made it," said Cynthia in a hoarse whisper. "He never made a better blade. My great-great-grandfather carried it in a sheath of inlaid iron; my grandfather had a scabbard of gold lacquer made for it, and I——"

She broke off and opened her eyes. They had changed colour and character alike; bright and fierce, they were staring out of the window in front of her, and her mouth, the young, fresh mouth of seventeen, was set in a thin, cruel line.

Mrs. Strode was already off the sofa. "Cynthia," she said in a tone of authority, "put down that sword at once!"

Cynthia had not in truth taken it up; it still lay on the table, though the pommel was in her grip. But instead of obeying she laughed, and broke into a run of meaningless syllables, in which the word *wakizashi* kept recurring. Mrs. Strode, if no one else, recognised the Japanese name for the lesser sword which always accompanied the *katana* in a *daimio's* sash.

"Persis," said Mrs. Fleming breathlessly, "go for your father quickly! She—this must be stopped!"

"Oh, Cynthia, don't be a goat!" adjured Persis, for the second and last time; and with the words laid a rather timid hand on her friend's shoulder from behind.

And at that Cynthia jumped up, brandishing the *katana* as though it were of straw, her eyes, which were not her eyes any more, blazing with an unholy rapture, and the strange language still hissing from her altered mouth.

"Daddy, Daddy!" screamed Persis, hurling herself through the doorway, "Daddy, come at once ... *Daddy!*"

"She's gone crazy," said Mrs. Strode quickly. "We

319

must get the sword away from her! Catch her arm, Erica!"

"*I* shall make a sheath for it of my enemies!" sang Cynthia, reverting all at once to English. She had backed to the edge of the open French window, dragging with her Mrs. Fleming, who, unable to get hold of her right arm, had seized the left. On the threshold Cynthia flung her off, and as she stumbled brought down that flashing miracle of sharpness. It did not need a man's arm behind it. Catching Mrs. Fleming between neck and shoulder, going with joy through the soft blue Doucet gown and the chalcedony necklace which matched it, the incomparable edge sliced through the artery and half the neck. Mrs. Fleming fell outside in the verandah, screaming; and there, in a very short time, died.

For one instant Mrs. Strode had retreated towards the sofa. She might, if she had been very quick, have got unharmed from the room—for she had forgotten the children at the far end of the lawn—but she was by nature a brave woman. Catching up in a bunch the heavy bear-skin rug at her feet she came on again, intending to throw it over that terrible young figure by the window, now whirling the long *katana* about in all directions and chanting unintelligibilities at the top of its voice. "Edward will be here in a moment," Marian Strode was telling herself, "Edward and no doubt Major Whittingham, too. If I can just get this over her head . . . or over the sword even . . . O God, if only Erica were not screaming like that! . . ."

But bear-skins were nothing to the Sadamune blade. It flashed once; hair, pelt and mounting parted like butter, and the head of Jizo bit deep into the top of Mrs. Strode's left arm. She dropped the rug, and this time made a rush for the door. The sword instantly pursued her. But she was saved by the figure in Japanese armour standing in the corner, for even as she sank down, almost against the door-panels, she heard Cynthia striking madly at the grinning mask under the helmet, and the steel clattering on the lacquered body-plates. That, too, ceased, as she went into darkness. . . . Two minutes more, and her husband, bursting in, had caught her up in his arms, while out under the pale roses of the verandah Major Whittingham, as pale as they, was just realising that it was of no avail to linger over what lay there. And where was the girl?

Cynthia was gone—to worse. The children by the rhododendrons, thinking it a game, had run to meet her. But Jizo, the protector of children, killed only one outright, and he a rather uninteresting little boy. The rhododendrons saved the rest, even the maimed. She could not easily get in among those flowering fastnesses, or did not trouble to attempt it, slashing at their heads of bloom instead. So the Sadamune blade was stained with green as well before consciousness of what she had done came to the girl . . . if it ever came. She may have jumped from the diving-board still in the full frenzy of whatever centuries-old blood lust the touch of the sword had communicated to her, or she may have awakened. One of the children's nurses, herself injured, was the only witness of the end. The young Death gave a cry which might have been either a laugh or a shriek, then, holding the wet *katana* high above her head, jumped straight off the spring-board into the lake. The nurse, before she herself fainted among the rhododendron stems, saw that she went down like a stone.

When the slayer was found she might have been

Ophelia. There were no stains on the green dress and her hands were empty and clean. The poem in steel lies quiet at the bottom of the lake, with its lovely lustre tarnished and water-weeds growing through the tracery of the disputed *tsuba*. Perhaps when the right oil-king is found to take Strode Manor he will have it retrieved, for it is very valuable.

THE WINDOW

THE WINDOW

I

"We absolutely must see the inside of that jolly old house some time," said Romilly, not only almost daily to himself, but nearly as often to Charles and Meakin, who were staying with him, fishing and sketching, in the little Norman inn. Yet when Charles replied, "All right, old chap, we will," and Meakin said, "Why on earth, then, don't you get hold of the key or something?" Romilly invariably replied that there was plenty of time yet. And so there was, only each day a little less of it, until at last there was none—none, that is to say, in which they, plurally, could enter the house, because Charles had gone back, groaning, to London, and Meakin, with the sister who had come over to join him, had proceeded south to Tours. So Romilly was left alone to finish, if he so willed, the sketches which he was rather fond of leaving unfinished, and to weave and unweave verses round the theme provided for the week by the Saturday *Westminster Gazette*.

But the house, of course, was still there—long, grey, blind-eyed, unnaturally deserted in a tangle of garden and of rank grass. Romilly passed it yet again on his return from seeing off Meakin, for it stood a matter of three or four kilometres away from the hamlet, and once more he uttered under his breath his parrot-cry about the necessity of entrance, adding to it a not un-merited condemnation of himself as a "slacker."

At the "Coq d'Or" that night he asked the patron

to whom he ought to apply for leave to visit the house.

"What, the old Manoir de Boisrobert!" exclaimed M. Bonnet. "Surely Monsieur does not think of going to see that?"

"Why not?" asked Romilly.

"*Mais*—because there is nothing to see!"

"*Entendu.* I did not expect to find it a museum. I want to see inside it all the same."

"But—but——" began the good Bonnet, seeking for words to express the emptiness of the manoir, and finding instead a simple illustration. "Inside," he said, holding out the palm of one hand and tapping it with the forefinger of the other, "inside it is all bare as this. Perhaps even a little falling to pieces—I do not know. No one goes in there."

"Then I shall be the first," retorted the young Englishman. "Where can I get hold of the key?"

The patron did not think there was a key.

"But, hang it all!" exclaimed Romilly, "the house, which is pretty big, must belong to somebody! There's an escutcheon on the gateposts."

Thus pressed, M. Bonnet admitted that he believed it belonged to the State. He had always heard that the old family whose property it once was had been dispossessed in the Revolution.

"Come now, that is quite romantic," observed Romilly cheerfully. "I shall take steps to get in to-morrow somehow, even if I have to climb through a window."

But Romilly had procrastinated too long.

He came in to déjeuner at noon next day to find two newcomers seated at the one long table on which, according to the custom of the "Coq d'Or," meals were indiscriminately served. They were a young good-looking Frenchman—obviously a gentleman—and his wife . . . or sister? The long table stood close to the wall, and as the wall was hung with the votive offerings of those amateur artists who at one time or another had stayed at the "Coq d'Or," Romilly, who sat facing it, was perpetually confronted by a little thing of his own for which he confessed a partiality, a painstaking rendering by Meakin of the ornate church at Caudebec, and Charles's humorous Vorticist picture of which no man had ever been able to guess the subject. This was not surprising, since Charles himself did not know, having painted it for fun. Ninette, the large elderly chambermaid, came as near as anyone to describing it when she said, with a shudder, that it was what things looked like when she had a bad migraine.

And that nightmare of Charles's devising was directly over the dark head and slender neck of the beautiful French girl. She had no colour in her face, but the clearest, most transparent complexion, and when he looked at her Romilly conceived that he should never admire a vermeil cheek again. He longed to see her without a hat. Oh, wholly adorable!

Her name seemed to be Gabrielle—a lovely name. But what was her relation to the young Frenchman who forestalled her every want, and at whom she smiled so enchantingly out of those long, dark, mysterious eyes? He was much fairer than she, which seemed to point to the disastrous conclusion that he was *not* her brother. Unfortunately, a pot of flowers on the table prevented Romilly from seeing her rings. It was not the first time that he had suddenly lost his heart, for he had some natural facility in the exercise, and it was calculated by ribald friends, such as Charles, that since he came down from Oxford three years ago he had fallen in love thirteen times. Certainly he was in a perfect fever by the end of déjeuner, and rushed off to interview M. Bonnet.

"They who came *en automobile?*" asked the landlord. "It is M. Gaston de Précy and his sister."

"*Not* monsieur and madame, then!" exclaimed Romilly with relief.

M. Bonnet smiled. "Monsieur thinks they would make a fine pair?"

"Not at all!" replied Romilly fervently. "A detestable thought!"

"There is something else which will interest Monsieur," proceeded M. Bonnet, rubbing his hands. "It is really a most strange coincidence. They are of the family who once owned the Manoir de Boisrobert, and they have come over to see it. It appears that they have bought it back—I am not quite sure from whom."

"Better and better!" cried the enthusiast. "What a setting for that beautiful creature!"

Indeed, M. de Précy and his sister had vanished immediately after déjeuner, presumably in the direction of the manoir. Happy young man, to have such a companion! Romilly forthwith began to picture himself wandering through the deserted rooms side by side, if not actually hand in hand, with the exquisite descendant of the no doubt exquisite ladies who had lived and loved at Boisrobert. As, however, he had yet to make that descendant's acquaintance, this consummation appeared improbable.

Nor did he make it at dinner that night, though he had the satisfaction of seeing her without her hat, and of feeling at rest on the question of her relationship to the young Frenchman.

It was next morning, about half-past ten, when the newspaper came in, that Romilly first awoke to the fact that everyone was looking very grave. For the shadow of approaching war had been stretching further with every sun that set, and he was perhaps the only person in the inn whom it had not yet touched with its feverish and icy fingers. M. Bonnet in particular was plunged in woe, because in the event of mobilisation he would lose Ernest, who did everything at the "Coq d'Or" except cook. Romilly, remaining at the inn against the return of his divinity, who had gone off very early with her brother to Boisrobert, tried to reassure the patron. "It is impossible that there should be a great war nowadays," he asserted, having read Norman Angell. "It is opposed to all modern interests."

"*Pour ça, vous allez voir, Monsieur!*" was the patron's lugubrious reply. "And look, for instance, at this telegram which has just come for M. de Précy. I would send it to the château after him did I not fear it might miss him. It is undoubtedly bad news, for I have discovered that his father the Comte is a retired general, and he would hear sooner than we. . . . Our beautiful country will be invaded, and I shall lose Ernest! That God may punish that wicked old man, the Emperor of Austria!"

Romilly was disposed to echo this hope, if Hapsburg machinations were going to be the cause of the untimely departure of Mlle de Précy. The telegram looked like it, and it therefore more than ever behoved him to obtain speech with her while yet he could.

It seemed caddish, however, to hang about in the entrance to witness the reception of the telegram, so, when he heard the car approaching, Romilly withdrew into the garden, or rather kitchen-garden, and, ensconcing himself in the arbour among the raspberry canes, tried to occupy himself with a book. And presently the brother and sister came out there too, and walked up and down the plot of grass near the gooseberries, talking earnestly in low tones. Mlle de Précy had her handkerchief in her hand, and dabbed her eyes with it once or twice, but that was all. Then Gaston de Précy hurried away, but she remained a moment at the far end of the plot, her back to the observer, twisting her handkerchief in her fingers. Now was Romilly's chance, if he could only find some excuse for addressing her. And on the path by which M. de Précy had retreated there lay, by good fortune, what would serve his purpose—the opened telegram. Romilly slipped hastily out of his retreat, secured it, and advanced over the grass.

"A thousand pardons, Mademoiselle, but I think that monsieur votre frère has just dropped this," said he in his best French, raising his hat and holding out the little pale-blue scrap of paper.

Mlle. de Précy turned with a start, looking so much surprised that for one awful moment Romilly, with recollections of French novels in his mind, thought that he had put his foot in it, and was handing to his innocent sister some not innocent evidence of M. de Précy's possible amusements. Then she relieved him by smiling and holding out her hand for the missive. "Thank you very much, Monsieur," she said, in the voice that was of a piece with the rest of her. "This is, alas! a telegram that we should be very glad not only to have dropped, but never to have received. My brother must return to Paris at once—it is war."

"It *is* coming, then?" observed Romilly in a tone of suitable solemnity, thinking in reality only of her approaching departure. "Is M. de Précy in the army?"

"Not more than every Frenchman, Monsieur. When he is mobilised he is a *sous-officier* in the 153rd of the line. And my father believes that mobilisation will take place on Sunday."

"So soon!" murmured Romilly.

"So soon!" echoed she, sighing, and began to move towards the inn. Romilly accompanied her, intoxicated to be treading the same plantains. But suddenly she stopped, and, looking at him very directly—she was nearly as tall as he—said, "And if there is war, will England fight?"

Romilly had not had time to weigh that contingency. But with those eyes upon him there could be but one answer. "Mademoiselle, how can you ask such a question?" he replied reproachfully. "What of the Entente?" And then he found himself, with almost appalling suddenness, the prey of a startling resolution. "Why, if there is war, I shall become a soldier myself, and fight side by side with the soldiers of France. And every Englishman, I am sure, will do the same."

For the wholesale conscription of himself and his countrymen Romilly was more than rewarded by the smile which it won. "Monsieur, you are indeed *un preux chevalier,*" said Gabrielle de Précy, and along with that token of her approval she gave him her slim white hand with the marquise ring on the forefinger. And Romilly, his head turning, kissed it as naturally as a Frenchman would have done, and with certainly no less fervour. His own most eager wish at this moment was for instant bloody war—to be involved in some violent personal conflict (so she were witness of it)—to save her brother's life, perhaps, at the risk of his own. . . .

Her voice interrupted these romantic visions. "You speak French very well, Monsieur."

The commonplace compliment took on a new value from her lips. "I believe I may claim some French blood, Mademoiselle," replied the young man, and for the first time rejoiced in that heritage. "My great-grandmother was French, though, as I naturally never saw her," he added, with a smile, "I cannot exactly say that I learnt your beautiful tongue at her knee."

But they were at the inn now, and Gaston de Précy, suddenly reappearing with a leather case of some kind in his hand, cut short the inquiry which Mlle. de Précy was beginning about this ancestress, and confirmed Romilly's worst fears.

"Gabrielle, have you told your maid to pack at once? I beg your pardon—I did not see that you were engaged."

"I was just coming in to tell her, *mon ami,*" replied his sister. "Let me first present you to—to an English gentleman who is going to fight on the side of France."

The young Frenchman shook hands heartily with the three-minutes old volunteer, said a few graceful words, and carried off his sister, with apologies, to make her preparations.

So, although Romilly was able to see the last of them as their Vinot glided away through the dust half an hour later, that interview in the kitchen-garden of the "Coq d'Or" was the nearest he got to wandering hand in hand with Gabrielle de Précy anywhere.

THE WINDOW

II

Romilly's one-time desire had come to pass. There was, quite undoubtedly, war of the kind he had specified, and he himself was fighting side by side with the French—or, to be more accurate, living side by side with them in Rouen. And of this he was already tired.

He got his commission in the spring of 1915, and went out in July. And now, in mid-August, he still abode with his battalion in the City of the Maid, that haunt of tourists, now unimaginably changed, which surged with soldiers of both nations and with nurses— one kind, covered with brass buttons, looking like a female fire-brigade; which gave you tea in the big oak-furnished tea-rooms, just like home, but with better cakes; where the standards of the Allies hung in the Cathedral; and where the familiar red and blue of the French uniform was gradually giving place to the new *bleu d'horizon,* even as the picturesque attire of the Zouave regiments had become a particularly ugly mustard shade of khaki. And Romilly, "fed up" with these impressions, wished with all his heart that he was a despatch-rider, like Meakin and some other Oxford contemporaries.

He had not forgotten Gabrielle de Précy, but he *had* forgotten that what had first moved him to resolve on volunteering was a wild desire to please her, an impulse which had soon been swamped under more serious motives for the same act. One day he saw an officer who looked like Gaston de Précy turn into the old curiosity shop by the "Grosse Horloge," where a burly English N.C.O. was visible choosing a medal of Jeanne d'Arc

333

as a brooch for "the wife," and he had followed the officer in before he remembered that M. de Précy was only a *sous-off*. But as he came out it occurred to Romilly that he was no very great distance away from the old manoir. What if he were now, by means of a motor-bicycle, to pay it that oft-deferred visit? Perhaps by this time Mademoiselle de Précy was living in it! Why had that glorious possibility not struck him before?

Three days later, having snatched at the first available opportunity of a few hours' leave, he was tearing noisily away from Rouen on a borrowed motor-bicycle, with a sketching-block and a box of water-colours behind him, and in his heart a hope that he would not need to use either. Still, they made a good reason for going to Bois-robert.

Alas! when he dismounted after thirty-five minutes' furious riding, at the high old rusty gates, he knew that he had been too sanguine. The place was no more inhabited than it had been a year ago. The only difference was that he could now enter the garden, because the gates were no longer chained together and padlocked. So he wheeled the motor-cycle dejectedly through, wishing that he had not come. Still, as he had come he might as well see the house, if he could force an entrance—for, obviously, any key would be in the possession of the Précys, and it was not worth while trying to find it in the village. He would go there afterwards, and have a chat with M. Bonnet.

He leant the motor-cycle against the curving flight of discoloured steps which led up to the main entrance, and picked his way through the tangle of weeds to the back of the house, where there might be a better prospect of entry. And at the back, after due search, he discovered a little painted door which looked promising, and which, indeed, after some vigorous shoving, fulfilled its promise and admitted him. The woodwork seemed swollen with damp, and that fact had apparently prevented the door from being properly closed and fastened; but it must have been for years in that precarious condition, for several long tendrils of ivy were plastered like hinges across its surface.

That rather melancholy little portal seemed to Romilly to strike the keynote of the whole place, such an impression did it give of age-long desertion and neglect. There was the smell of dry-rot in the dark passages at the back to which the door had given him entrance, and he hurried towards the front of the house and finally came, to the right of the entrance-hall, on a room which did not feel in the least sad or damp. It had a delightful carved mantelpiece, all scrolls and Cupids, two long windows looking towards the gates, and, opposite the door, a large square one through which could be seen the tangle of garden shrubs backed by one or two straggly cedars. The sun was pouring through this window, and thereby contributing not a little to the effect of life and warmth in the room, the charming proportions of which moved all the artist in Romilly. What he had had in his mind was a sketch of the exterior of the house—if he made a sketch at all. But now he knew that what he wanted to draw was this room. It had so much atmosphere that he could imagine its furniture and fittings, and over the hearth should be the portrait of Gabrielle de Précy, as one of her own ancestresses—unless, indeed, he tried to put her into the room itself. How entrancing she would have looked in a hoop and panniers! He got out his materials and set to work.

Was it the idea of painting in Gabrielle, he wondered, which made him begin to feel, after about half an hour's feverish work, that the room really *was* peopled, and by a considerable number of persons? It was almost as if he were painting without permission in an inhabited house, and as if the inmates, naturally enough, resented his presence. Try as Romilly would, the feeling grew, until at last he fancied that the persons in the room— who could exist only in his own imagination—were regarding him with a steadily increasing hostility.

At last he stopped work; it was too uncomfortable. "What rot!" he thought, fidgeting with his brush, and looking almost defiantly at the great square window which faced him. For it was round that window that the hostility seemed to be concentrated, almost as if there were a group of people there, staring at him accusingly. "This room has too *much* atmosphere!" he said to himself, trying to laugh, and resumed his painting. But the conviction of some invisible enmity became at last so insistent that, for the first time in his life, Romilly felt in his breast a spasm of real, naked fear.

"This is too dashed silly!" he exclaimed, springing to his feet; and with the words it dawned on him what was, perhaps, the origin of his state of mind. The room had been getting hotter and hotter as the sun sank; a little fresh air was what he needed; and, relieved at the idea, he went to open one of the long windows on his left hand. But a brief struggle with the long bolt-like fastenings common on windows of the sort convinced him that this was impossible. They were rusted immovably into their sheaths, and the handle would turn

336

neither way. The only hope of fresh air was the other, the big sash window, the one through which the sun was streaming, the one where those people . . . He would certainly prefer not to open that window, nor even to approach it.

He walked across to it, however, with more apparent unconcern than he was feeling. The catch was stiff, but eventually slipped aside; and with some difficulty, for it was large and most abnormally heavy, Romilly raised the bottom sash, pushing it up almost as high as it would go. Then it occurred to him that it would be a good thing to pull down the upper a little also, and he laid hold of this in the only way possible, by putting up his hands outside. This upper sash was very obstinate, and so, bending his arms, and throwing as much weight upon them as possible, Romilly tugged resolutely at its framework.

All at once, with the suddenness of a thunderbolt, something gave way, or rather, some irresistible force wrenched away his hands from their grip on the upper window-frame, and in a second he was brought violently to his knees, receiving at the same moment a stunning blow across his forehead and the bridge of his nose. He had only time to realise that both his arms, just above the elbows, were held immovably in a grip which was causing them excruciating pain, ere he lost consciousness.

Romilly came back, however, very quickly, to the knowledge of what had happened. The lower sash of the window, its old, rotten cords having presumably given way, had come smashing down and pinned him to the sill by his arms; it was its sudden fall which had dragged him to his knees and brought his head into contact with its central rib of frame-work, and with the glass also. The blood dripping from his right eyebrow and mingling with the broken splinters on the grey paint of the woodwork testified to that. It took Romilly a few seconds to realise it all, for the blow had somewhat stupefied him. Then, armed with a vivid sense of resentment, he set about releasing himself. . . .

At the end of four terrible minutes he was still kneeling there, dripping with the sweat both of physical and of mental anguish. He rather fancied that one of his arms was broken, but the pain of the struggle to get them out from under the fallen sash had not deterred him from putting every ounce of strength into the effort. It was useless. The heavy window had him fast; hampered by his position, he could not so much as stir it.

Romilly leant his bruised and bleeding forehead a moment against the glass, and gave a laugh. Here was he, a second-lieutenant in the Fourth Fellshires, in his new khaki, kneeling like a suppliant at the window of an empty room in an empty house, his imprisoned arms outstretched, unable to wipe away the blood from his face, unable to do anything save wait in this ridiculous and constrained attitude till someone came to release him from his pillory. And when would someone come?

It flashed on him suddenly that the French called this kind of window, so much less usual with them than in England, a "guillotine" window. Very funny that! A further reminiscence came from some French Revolution novel, how the women who knitted round the scaffold, like—who was it?—Madame Defarge in *A Tale of Two Cities,* would humorously refer to the guillotine, on the other hand, as the "national window." Again very funny! Before his mind's eye wavered a moment the well-known poster of Martin Harvey as Sydney Carton on the steps of the scaffold. But neither he nor anybody else ever put his *arms* under the falling knife; it stood to reason that they couldn't, because their arms were tied behind them.

A suspicion that he was talking, or rather thinking, nonsense made Romilly shift his position—to the very slight degree that he could shift it. Better not to think of guillotines, because, after all, this was only a window. . . . "Magic windows, opening on the foam"—no, how stupid, of course Keats wrote "casements." He began involuntarily to suit the lines to his own case:

> *"Magic casement, opening on the green*
> *Of perilous woods* (since 'gardens' did
> not scan) *in faery lands forlorn"*—

And, by Jove, they *were* forlorn! Did anybody ever come here now, since the war had, presumably, stopped whatever plans the Précys might have made for the future of the place? Oh, if only he had gone for the key, which would at least have made known to somebody in the village his intention of getting into the accursed house! If only he had not kept it so dark in camp where he was going! He had borrowed Field's motor-cycle, it was true, but he knew that Field had not the remotest idea of its destination.

Unless someone came, then, he would be found here, months hence—a skeleton, perhaps. (How long did it take to become a skeleton?) Not the skeleton in the cupboard, the skeleton in the window—yes, literally, in it, as a fly is in a web, or a mouse in a trap, or a wild creature in a snare. There was a stoat in a gin, once, at home, which . . . Never, never again should a trap be set round Greystoke! He would probably have a long argument with the pater about that, though—if he ever saw him again to argue with.

And the pater mightn't know the truth for years, if ever. Would the Colonel have the decency, after the regiment had gone to the front, to write to the pater and pretend that his son was "missing"? He *would* be missing. Or would it be desertion, when he never turned up again at Rouen, with Field's motor-bicycle?

Outside the window, a little dimmed by the dusty glass, he saw his own hands emerging from the cuffs with the single star. The pain in his bruised and lacerated arms was less now, so long as he kept quiet, but from the elbows down he seemed to be losing feeling in them. They would turn black in time, he supposed. That meant mortification, gangrene. In hospital, limbs like that were cut off. "If thy hand offend thee, cut it off." Good God! if only he could! How did it go on—something about its being better to enter into life maimed, than having two hands to be cast into hell, into the fire that should never be quenched . . . Sunday morning at home, with the Rector reading the lessons . . .

Another few minutes of torture supervened here, as Romilly entered on a second and fiercer struggle to release himself. It only served to confirm the hopelessness of his position, and left him more exhausted than before.

And then he wondered why he had never thought of shouting. The window was already broken, but if necessary he might be able to enlarge the hole by the agency which had created it, his own head. He managed, however, to get his lips to the star-shaped gap in the glass and shout long and desperately, *"Au secours! au secours!"* . . . His own voice died lamentably away in the empty garden, and nothing but the wood-pigeons answered him. He *was* to stay here for ever, then—to die here, pinned to the window-sill in a position which, because he could not change it, was on the way to becoming unbearable. Not in those trenches which he had never seen, not by a German bullet, not for England, nor —foolish dream!—for Gabrielle, but in an empty house, to no purpose, and alone . . .

Romilly strangled a sob, and his head went down on his stiffening shoulder.

Once years ago, so it seemed—he had fancied that there were people in this hateful, sunny room, gathered round this very window. And though he had thought of them as in some way hostile to him, he would have been glad of them now; they would at least have been company in this utter desolation, even if they had exulted in some shadowy fashion over his plight. But the room was empty beyond all thought, and would be empty to-morrow. And first there was the long night to get through. When the sun next streamed through this horrible window, to-morrow evening, how would it be with him then, and how many more sunsets would he have to look at, kneeling here? Please God, not many!

That same sun, indeed, now low, seemed to be beating into his brain, till all inside his head was the colour of blood, and his thoughts, no longer under complete control, began once more to circle round the idea of the guillotine and its fruits. For out there in the garden, against the orange sky, which showed through the forlorn cedar boughs, was suspended a head, a fiery head—

the sun itself, Romilly told himself, against which he
had no protection save to close his eyes. But he saw the
head all the same through shut lids. . . . The head kept
changing, too. Sometimes it was a man's, sometimes a
woman's; once it was an old woman's, with dabbled
grey locks; once a young man's, having something of
Gaston de Précy's look. And once, great God! was it not
hers, Gabrielle's?—the wonderful black hair all dull,
the delicate little mouth hanging open, a trickle of blood
oozing from one nostril, the eyes . . . Horrible, horrible!
. . . Black hair again, round a face which revealed that
shrivelled Indian head in the Pitt-Rivers Museum at
Oxford, that dreadful tiny head no bigger than a doll's,
which once had been a living man's. . . . Romilly's heart
seemed to be stopping; his ears buzzed; the light
through his closed lids turned from red to black, from
black to red. The thought visited him that he was dying.
But death, he knew, would not come for days yet. . . .
Night—a broken night—descended upon him.

III

What was this strange room, small and bare, and who
was this stout, slightly moustached lady all in white
sitting by him? Why was he in bed? . . . What on
earth had happened to his arms? . . . Had it all been
true, then?

But his guardian (whom he discovered to be French)
would answer no questions, and indeed Romilly soon
ceased to ask them—he felt so overpowering a drowsi-
ness. At any rate, whether the business with the window
were nightmare or reality, he was alive.

The deep sleep into which he then fell so refreshed him that five hours or so later the Dame de la Croix Rouge, as she fed him with some very welcome bouillon, announced to him that the doctor had authorised his receiving a visitor, if he wished it, who would answer his recent questions better than she could. And, Romilly intimating his readiness to receive any number of visitors, she vanished, and after a while there entered in her stead a young man in the misty horizon-blue uniform, wearing one of the new trench helmets painted blue to match, with the abbreviated gold stripe of a sergeant on his lower arm, and the *croix de guerre* on his breast— Gaston de Précy.

He saluted with a smile, looking very soldierly and handsome, then advanced, holding out his hand. *"Bonjour, Monsieur!* All goes well this afternoon, they tell me. Ah, I forget, you cannot shake hands yet."

"For heaven's sake, sit down," cried the invalid, "and tell me where I am, and how I got here!"

M. de Précy obeyed him. *"Mon lieutenant,* you are in the French auxiliary hospital at Lerville, and you are here because my sister Gabrielle had so violent a fancy for turning the old Manoir de Boisrobert into just such another, that she carried off my father and a distinguished military surgeon of our acquaintance to view it for that purpose. And as I happened to be *en permission* from the front, I went also. M. le Major's time being precious, we motored over there from Rouen early this morning—fortunately—and found you trapped in the window."

"I was there all night, then?" observed Romilly faintly.

"Parbleu!" said Gaston de Précy with interest. "We wondered how long—my father and I thought you were

343

dead at first; you gave us a fine fright. It took all our united strength to get the window up. I assure you, it made a moving spectacle—a pity that you could not see it."

"Why?" asked the chief actor. "I had seen enough."

"I, the *poilu,*" went on M. de Précy dramatically, "kneel on the floor supporting you, *jeune officier anglais,* insensible, with blood down your face. Over you bends M. le Major, slitting up the sleeves of your *vareuse* to see what damage the infernal window has done to your arms—by the way, I am relieved to hear that they will not be permanently injured. Standing near is my father, looking anxious—and he looks also rather chic, my father, in his general's uniform of the old style, *un peu plus gai que celui-ci, vous savez.* To complete the picture, there is Gabrielle, ready to assist M. le Major, for she is Croix Rouge, *brevetée.* We must have looked like a cinema company rehearsing something pathetic and patriotic about the Allies." Gaston laughed, pushing back the helmet that became him so well, but Romilly was conscious that he now made light of the scene, just because he had, at the time, known another emotion.

"And then?" he asked. (So *she* had been there!)

"Then we put you into the car, where you took up a great deal of room, and brought you here, where Gabrielle is nursing. It was the nearest hospital."

The colour rushed over Romilly's face. "She is here, then, your sister?"

The young aristocrat of a sergeant smiled, a rather mischievous smile, and twisted his little moustache. "Yes, but I wished to see you first, *mon cher lieutenant,* since this is my only chance of doing so. I return *là-bas* to-night—to those dear trenches."

The Englishman began to murmur apologies, and to thank him for his visit. (*First*—did that mean that she was coming too?)

"Oh, I came partly from curiosity," said Gaston de Précy airily. "There is something I want to ask you—no, not what you were doing at the manoir, for that was quite explained by your paint-box, your sketch. What I should like to know—if you will pardon the question—is why you opened that window?" And again Romilly fancied that he detected under his visitor's light tone a note of anxiety.

"Because the room was so hot," he replied.

The young Frenchman made a gesture. "Ah, you English! Always the fresh air! See what comes of it! But, seriously, *mon ami,* that window has a history—of the most unpleasant."

Their eyes met. Things were beginning to come back to Romilly—the dimmed horrors too of that broken night. Gaston de Précy was not smiling now.

"Has the story," asked Romilly at last, "anything to do with—with heads—decapitated heads?"

"Everything in the world," replied the young sergeant gravely. "Shall I tell it to you—yes? . . . In the year 1793, then, there were living in the Manoir de Boisrobert my great-great-grandfather, the Comte de Précy, then an old man, his wife, his eldest son and daughter, two other daughters a good deal younger, and his eldest son's boys, of nineteen and twelve respectively; and (I think) four servants. None of the family had emigrated, but the second son, François, had gone to fight for the Vendéans. One night, soon after the Vendéan defeat at Cholet, he came home a fugitive and wounded, with a price on his head. They concealed him for some time in various hiding-places in and around the manoir—you can see some of them still—aware, of course, that if he were found it would probably mean the scaffold for all of them. But the servants were proved, and the only other person who knew that he was hidden there was a friend of his in whom he had confided during his flight up to Normandy—a man called St. Varent. *Pardon,* did you say something?"

"Nothing," answered Romilly hoarsely. "Go on!"

"*Eh bien,* one evening at sunset, when the family were assembled in the room that you know, a frightened servant rushed in to say that the house was almost surrounded—the Republican soldiers were upon them. François de Précy slipped out into the garden, where there was an underground hiding-place. A few minutes later the Revolutionary authorities were in the room, questioning and threatening. The Comte de Précy and the rest denied all knowledge of the fugitive, asserting that the whole family were present. You can imagine the scene, with its anguishes. It was cut short by the crash of glass, and through the window—*that* window—was flung the bleeding head of François de Précy, splashing the dresses of his young sisters as it rolled to his mother's feet."

Romilly gave an exclamation of horror.

"Dramatic, was it not?" remarked Gaston de Précy grimly. "The soldiers had killed him in the garden, and hacked his head off then and there. I forgot to say that it was his friend, St. Varent, who had betrayed his whereabouts—some past rivalry over a woman, I believe. His vengeance ought to have satisfied him, for every soul in that house, except the boy of twelve—my great-grandfather—went to the guillotine because of his

346

treachery—because of that head thrown through the window."

There was silence. Romilly, looking extremely pale, was lying with his own bandaged head turned away.

"So you see, it has memories, that window," finished the latest of the Précys. "And you seem, *mon cher,* to have awakened them. But I am at a loss to conceive why you, an Englishman——"

"Monsieur de Précy," interrupted Romilly in a queer voice, "you will hate me, but I must tell you. I never heard this story before, not a whisper of it, but it is clear to me now why I got caught in that window, and why I saw—those heads. My great-grandmother was French. I know nothing of her but her name—but that name was St. Varent."

"*Bon Dieu!*" exclaimed Gaston, staring. And he added, after a moment, "It must have been his daughter. There was a daughter, I believe, and there is a legend that she fled to England. You have written a postscript of the most unexpected to our family story!"

Romilly, biting his lip, tried miserably to summon up what he knew of his great-grandmother. But, as he had said, it amounted to nothing. There might have been two families of the same name, he supposed. If not, then in his veins ran the blood which had betrayed Gabrielle's. What had happened seemed to prove it beyond any doubt.

"There was good reason, after all, for the behaviour of the window," said Gabrielle's brother musingly. "Yet, who would have thought that a *house* could cherish vengeance for more than a hundred and twenty years!"

"I feel," said the wretched Romilly, "that I can never

look . . . any of your family . . . in the face again.”

“That scruple is unnecessary,” said Gaston earnestly. “Have you not expiated in your own person, Monsieur Romilly, a crime in which you had no share? Those ghosts should be laid henceforward; there is your blood now on the window-sill. It is not the window’s fault that you got away alive. But I wish I had not told you the story. You need not mention your ancestry to—any other member of my family,” he added, with the glimmer of a smile.

“But I told Mlle. de Précy, the day I first met you, that I had French blood in my veins. It seems to me,” said Romilly, “that I have it on my hands!”

“You can wash it out, then, in the blood of the Boche,” retorted the young soldier instantly. “Believe me, *I* bear you no ill-will, and I know how to hold my tongue. Someone is knocking—another of my family, no doubt.”

It was. In the doorway, more divine than ever, to Romilly’s thinking, in the white dress and the white veil which, nun-like, showed not a glimpse of her glorious hair, stood Gabrielle de Précy.

“Madame la Directrice permits me to visit you, Monsieur, for one minute,” she said, looking at Romilly with a smile in her eyes. “I must make, must I not, Gaston, the apologies of our poor old house for using you so ill?”

“Monsieur le lieutenant and I have settled all that, my sister,” replied Gaston quickly. And he held up a momentary finger of warning at the Englishman.

“Perhaps I shall tell her when we are married,” said Romilly later to himself.

FINIS